THE
BRASS
VERDICT

THE BRASS VERDICT

A NOVEL

MICHAEL CONNELLY

LITTLE, BROWN AND COMPANY
New York   Boston   London

Little, Brown and Company
Hachette Book Group
237 Park Avenue, New York, NY 10017
Visit our Web site at www.HachetteBookGroup.com

First Edition: October 2008

Little, Brown and Company is a division of Hachette Book Group, Inc.
The Little, Brown name and logo are trademarks of Hachette Book Group, Inc.

Library of Congress Cataloging-in-Publication Data
Connelly, Michael.
    The brass verdict : a novel / Michael Connelly. — 1st ed.
      p. cm.
    ISBN-10: 0-316-16629-4
    ISBN-13: 978-0-316-16629-4
    1. Lawyers — California — Los Angeles — Fiction. 2. Bosch, Harry (Fictitious character) — Fiction. 3. Police — California — Los Angeles — Fiction. 4. Los Angeles (Calif.) — Fiction. 5. Lawyers — Crimes against — Fiction. 6. Murder — Investigation — Fiction. I. Title.
    PS3553.O51165B73 2008
    813'.54 — dc22   2008019374

10   9   8   7   6   5   4   3   2   1

RRD-IN

Printed in the United States of America

*In memory of Terry Hansen
and Frank Morgan*

PART ONE

— Rope a Dope

1992

One

Everybody lies.

Cops lie. Lawyers lie. Witnesses lie. The victims lie.

A trial is a contest of lies. And everybody in the courtroom knows this. The judge knows this. Even the jury knows this. They come into the building knowing they will be lied to. They take their seats in the box and agree to be lied to.

The trick if you are sitting at the defense table is to be patient. To wait. Not for just any lie. But for the one you can grab on to and forge like hot iron into a sharpened blade. You then use that blade to rip the case open and spill its guts out on the floor.

That's my job, to forge the blade. To sharpen it. To use it without mercy or conscience. To be the truth in a place where everybody lies.

Two

I was in the fourth day of trial in Department 109 in the downtown Criminal Courts Building when I got the lie that became the blade that ripped the case open. My client, Barnett Woodson, was riding two murder charges all the way to the steel-gray room in San Quentin where they serve you Jesus juice direct through the arm.

Woodson, a twenty-seven-year-old drug dealer from Compton, was accused of robbing and killing two college students from Westwood. They had wanted to buy cocaine from him. He decided instead to take their money and kill them both with a sawed-off shotgun. Or so the prosecution said. It was a black-on-white crime and that made things bad enough for Woodson—especially coming just four months after the riots that had torn the city apart. But what made his situation even worse was that the killer had attempted to hide the crime by weighing down the two bodies and dropping them into the Hollywood Reservoir. They stayed down for four days before popping to the surface like apples in a barrel. Rotten apples. The idea of dead bodies moldering in the reservoir that was a primary source of the city's drinking water caused a collective twist in the community's guts. When Woodson was linked by phone records to the dead men and arrested, the public outrage directed toward him was almost palpable. The District Attorney's Office promptly announced it would seek the death penalty.

The case against Woodson, however, wasn't all that palpable. It was constructed largely of circumstantial evidence — the phone records — and the testimony of witnesses who were criminals themselves. And state's witness Ronald Torrance sat front and center in this group. He claimed that Woodson confessed the killings to him.

Torrance had been housed on the same floor of the Men's Central Jail as Woodson. Both men were kept in a high-power module that contained sixteen single-prisoner cells on two tiers that opened onto a dayroom. At the time, all sixteen prisoners in the module were black, following the routine but questionable jail procedure of "segregating for safety," which entailed dividing prisoners according to race and gang affiliation to avoid confrontations and violence. Torrance was awaiting trial on robbery and aggravated assault charges stemming from his involvement in looting during the riots. High-power detainees had six a.m. to six p.m. access to the dayroom, where they ate and played cards at tables and otherwise interacted under the watchful eyes of guards in an overhead glass booth. According to Torrance, it was at one of these tables that my client had confessed to killing the two Westside boys.

The prosecution went out of its way to make Torrance presentable and believable to the jury, which had only three black members. He was given a shave, his hair was taken out of cornrows and trimmed short and he was dressed in a pale blue suit with no tie when he arrived in court on the fourth day of Woodson's trial. In direct testimony elicited by Jerry Vincent, the prosecutor, Torrance described the conversation he allegedly had with Woodson one morning at one of the picnic tables. Woodson not only confessed to the killings, he said, but furnished Torrance with many of the telling details of the murders. The point made clear to the jury was that these were details that only the true killer would know.

During the testimony, Vincent kept Torrance on a tight leash with long questions designed to elicit short answers. The questions were overloaded to the point of being leading but I didn't bother objecting, even when Judge Companioni looked at me with raised eyebrows, practically begging me to jump in. But I didn't object, because I wanted the counterpoint. I wanted the jury to see what the prosecution was doing. When it was my turn, I was going to let Torrance run with his answers while I hung back and waited for the blade.

Vincent finished his direct at eleven a.m. and the judge asked me if I wanted to take an early lunch before I began my cross. I told him no, I didn't need or want a break. I said it like I was disgusted and couldn't wait another hour to get at the man on the stand. I stood up and took a big, thick file and a legal pad with me to the lectern.

"Mr. Torrance, my name is Michael Haller. I work for the Public Defenders Office and represent Barnett Woodson. Have we met before?"

"No, sir."

"I didn't think so. But you and the defendant, Mr. Woodson, you two go back a long way, correct?"

Torrance gave an "aw, shucks" smile. But I had done the due diligence on him and I knew exactly who I was dealing with. He was thirty-two years old and had spent a third of his life in jails and prisons. His schooling had ended in the fourth grade when he stopped going to school and no parent seemed to notice or care. Under the state's three-strike law, he was facing the lifetime achievement award if convicted of charges he robbed and pistol-whipped the female manager of a coin laundry. The crime had been committed during three days of rioting and looting that ripped through the city after the not-guilty verdicts were announced in the trial of four police officers accused of the excessive beating of Rodney King, a black motorist pulled over for driving erratically. In short, Torrance had good reason to help the state take down Barnett Woodson.

"Well, we go back a few months is all," Torrance said. "To high-power."

"Did you say 'higher power'?" I asked, playing dumb. "Are you talking about a church or some sort of religious connection?"

"No, high-power module. In county."

"So you're talking about jail, correct?"

"That's right."

"So you're telling me that you didn't know Barnett Woodson before that?"

I asked the question with surprise in my voice.

"No, sir. We met for the first time in the jail."

I made a note on the legal pad as if this were an important concession.

"So then, let's do the math, Mr. Torrance. Barnett Woodson was transferred into the high-power module where you were already residing on the fifth of September earlier this year. Do you remember that?"

"Yeah, I remember him coming in, yeah."

"And why were you there in high-power?"

Vincent stood and objected, saying I was covering ground he had already trod in direct testimony. I argued that I was looking for a fuller explanation of Torrance's incarceration, and Judge Companioni allowed me the leeway. He told Torrance to answer the question.

"Like I said, I got a count of assault and one of robbery."

"And these alleged crimes took place during the riots, is that correct?"

With the anti-police climate permeating the city's minority communities since even before the riots, I had fought during jury selection to get as many blacks and browns on the panel as I could. But here was a chance to work on the five white jurors the prosecution had been able to get by me. I wanted them to know that the man the prosecution was hanging so much of its case on was one of those responsible for the images they saw on their television sets back in May.

"Yeah, I was out there like everybody else," Torrance answered. "Cops get away with too much in this town, you ask me."

I nodded like I agreed.

"And your response to the injustice of the verdicts in the Rodney King beating case was to go out and rob a sixty-two-year-old woman and knock her unconscious with a steel trash can? Is that correct, sir?"

Torrance looked over at the prosecution table and then past Vincent to his own lawyer, sitting in the first row of the gallery. Whether or not they had earlier rehearsed a response to this question, his legal team couldn't help Torrance now. He was on his own.

"I didn't do that," he finally said.

"You're innocent of the crime you are charged with?"

"That's right."

"What about looting? You committed no crimes during the riots?"

After a pause and another glance at his attorney, Torrance said, "I take the fifth on that."

As expected. I then took Torrance through a series of questions designed so that he had no choice but to incriminate himself or refuse to answer under the protections of the Fifth Amendment. Finally, after he took the nickel six times, the judge grew weary of the point being made over and over and prodded me back to the case at hand. I reluctantly complied.

"All right, enough about you, Mr. Torrance," I said. "Let's get back to you and Mr. Woodson. You knew the details of this double-murder case before you even met Mr. Woodson in lockup?"

"No, sir."

"Are you sure? It got a lot of attention."

"I been in jail, man."

"They don't have television or newspapers in jail?"

"I don't read no papers and the module's TV been broke since I got there. We made a fuss and they said they'd fix it but they ain't fixed shit."

The judge admonished Torrance to check his language and the witness apologized. I moved on.

"According to the jail's records, Mr. Woodson arrived in the high-power module on the fifth of September and, according to the state's discovery material, you contacted the prosecution on October second to report his alleged confession. Does that sound right to you?"

"Yeah, that sounds right."

"Well, not to me, Mr. Torrance. You are telling this jury that a man accused of a double murder and facing the possible death penalty confessed to a man he had known for less than four weeks?"

Torrance shrugged before answering.

"That's what happened."

"So you say. What will you get from the prosecution if Mr. Woodson is convicted of these crimes?"

"I don't know. Nobody has promised me nothing."

"With your prior record and the charges you currently face, you are looking at more than fifteen years in prison if you're convicted, correct?"

"I don't know about any of that."

"You don't?"

"No, sir. I let my lawyer handle all that."

"He hasn't told you that if you don't do something about this, you might go to prison for a long, long time?"

"He hasn't told me none of that."

"I see. What have you asked the prosecutor for in exchange for your testimony?"

"Nothing. I don't want nothing."

"So then, you are testifying here because you believe it is your duty as a citizen, is that correct?"

The sarcasm in my voice was unmistakable.

"That's right," Torrance responded indignantly.

I held the thick file up over the lectern so he could see it.

"Do you recognize this file, Mr. Torrance?"

"No. Not that I recall, I don't."

"You sure you don't remember seeing it in Mr. Woodson's cell?"

"Never been in his cell."

"Are you sure that you didn't sneak in there and look through his discovery file while Mr. Woodson was in the dayroom or in the shower or maybe in court sometime?"

"No, I did not."

"My client had many of the investigative documents relating to his prosecution in his cell. These contained several of the details you testified to this morning. You don't think that is suspicious?"

Torrance shook his head.

"No. All I know is that he sat there at the table and told me what he'd done. He was feeling poorly about it and opened up to me. It ain't my fault people open up to me."

I nodded as if sympathetic to the burden Torrance carried as a man others confided in — especially when it came to double murders.

"Of course not, Mr. Torrance. Now, can you tell the jury exactly what he said to you? And don't use the shorthand you used when Mr. Vincent was asking the questions. I want to hear exactly what my client told you. Give us his words, please."

Torrance paused as if to probe his memory and compose his thoughts.

"Well," he finally said, "we were sittin' there, the both of us by ourselves, and he just started talkin' about feelin' bad about what he'd done. I asked him, 'What'd you do?' and he told me about that night he killed the two fellas and how he felt pretty rough about it."

The truth is short. Lies are long. I wanted to get Torrance talking in long form, something Vincent had successfully avoided. Jailhouse snitches have something in common with all con men and professional liars. They seek to hide the con in misdirection and banter. They wrap cotton around their lies. But in all of that fluff you often find the key to revealing the big lie.

Vincent objected again, saying the witness had already answered the questions I was asking and I was simply badgering him at this point.

"Your Honor," I responded, "this witness is putting a confession in my client's mouth. As far as the defense is concerned, this is the case right here. The court would be remiss if it did not allow me to fully explore the content and context of such damaging testimony."

Judge Companioni was nodding in agreement before I finished the last sentence. He overruled Vincent's objection and told me to proceed. I turned my attention back to the witness and spoke with impatience in my voice.

"Mr. Torrance, you are still summarizing. You claim Mr. Woodson confessed to the murders. So then, tell the jury what he said to you. What were the *exact* words he said to you when he confessed to this crime?"

Torrance nodded as if he were just then realizing what I was asking for.

"The first thing he said to me was 'Man, I feel bad.' And I said, 'For what, my brother?' He said he kept thinking about those two guys. I didn't know what he was talking about 'cause, like I said, I hadn't heard nothin' about the case, you know? So I said, 'What two guys?' and he said, 'The two niggers I dumped in the reservoir.' I asked what it was all about and he told me about blasting them both with a shorty and wrappin' them up in chicken wire and such. He said, 'I made one bad mistake' and I asked him what it was. He said, 'I shoulda taken a knife and opened up their bellies so they wouldn't end up floatin' to the top the way they did.' And that was what he told me."

In my peripheral vision I had seen Vincent flinch in the middle of Torrance's long answer. And I knew why. I carefully moved in with the blade.

"Did Mr. Woodson use that word? He called the victims 'niggers'?"

"Yeah, he said that."

I hesitated as I worked on the phrasing of the next question. I knew

Vincent was waiting to object if I gave him the opening. I could not ask Torrance to interpret. I couldn't use the word "why" when it came to Woodson's meaning or motivation. That was objectionable.

"Mr. Torrance, in the black community the word 'nigger' could mean different things, could it not?"

"'Spose."

"Is that a yes?"

"Yes."

"The defendant is African-American, correct?"

Torrance laughed.

"Looks like it to me."

"As are you, correct, sir?"

Torrance started to laugh again.

"Since I was born," he said.

The judge tapped his gavel once and looked at me.

"Mr. Haller, is this really necessary?"

"I apologize, Your Honor."

"Please move on."

"Mr. Torrance, when Mr. Woodson used that word, as you say he did, did it shock you?"

Torrance rubbed his chin as he thought about the question. Then he shook his head.

"Not really."

"Why weren't you shocked, Mr. Torrance?"

"I guess it's 'cause I hear it all a' time, man."

"From other black men?"

"That's right. I heard it from white folks, too."

"Well, when fellow black men use that word, like you say Mr. Woodson did, who are they talking about?"

Vincent objected, saying that Torrance could not speak for what other men were talking about. Companioni sustained the objection and I took a moment to rework the path to the answer I wanted.

"Okay, Mr. Torrance," I finally said. "Let's talk only about you, then, okay? Do you use that word on occasion?"

"I think I have."

"All right, and when you have used it, who were you referring to?"

Torrance shrugged.

"Other fellas."

"Other black men?"

"That's right."

"Have you ever on occasion referred to white men as niggers?"

Torrance shook his head.

"No."

"Okay, so then, what did you take the meaning to be when Barnett Woodson described the two men who were dumped in the reservoir as niggers?"

Vincent moved in his seat, going through the body language of making an objection but not verbally following through with it. He must have known it would be useless. I had led Torrance down the path and he was mine.

Torrance answered the question.

"I took it that they were black and he killed 'em both."

Now Vincent's body language changed again. He sank a little bit in his seat because he knew his gamble in putting a jailhouse snitch on the witness stand had just come up snake eyes.

I looked up at Judge Companioni. He knew what was coming as well.

"Your Honor, may I approach the witness?"

"You may," the judge said.

I walked to the witness stand and put the file down in front of Torrance. It was legal size, well worn and faded orange—a color used by county jailers to denote private legal documents that an inmate is authorized to possess.

"Okay, Mr. Torrance, I have placed before you a file in which Mr.

Woodson keeps discovery documents provided to him in jail by his attorneys. I ask you once again if you recognize it."

"I seen a lotta orange files in high-power. It don't mean I seen that one."

"You are saying you never saw Mr. Woodson with his file?"

"I don't rightly remember."

"Mr. Torrance, you were with Mr. Woodson in the same module for thirty-two days. You testified he confided in you and confessed to you. Are you saying you never saw him with that file?"

He didn't answer at first. I had backed him into a no-win corner. I waited. If he continued to claim he had never seen the file, then his claim of a confession from Woodson would be suspect in the eyes of the jury. If he finally conceded that he was familiar with the file, then he opened a big door for me.

"What'm saying is that I seen him with his file but I never looked at what was in it."

Bang. I had him.

"Then, I'll ask you to open the file and inspect it."

The witness followed the instruction and looked from side to side at the open file. I went back to the lectern, checking on Vincent on my way. His eyes were downcast and his face was pale.

"What do you see when you open the file, Mr. Torrance?"

"One side's got photos of two bodies on the ground. They're stapled in there — the photos, I mean. And the other side is a bunch of documents and reports and such."

"Could you read from the first document there on the right side? Just read the first line of the summary."

"No, I can't read."

"You can't read at all?"

"Not really. I didn't get the schooling."

"Can you read any of the words that are next to the boxes that are checked at the top of the summary?"

Torrance looked down at the file and his eyebrows came together in concentration. I knew that his reading skills had been tested during his last stint in prison and were determined to be at the lowest measurable level—below second-grade skills.

"Not really," he said. "I can't read."

I quickly walked over to the defense table and grabbed another file and a Sharpie pen out of my briefcase. I went back to the lectern and quickly printed the word CAUCASIAN on the outside of the file in large block letters. I held the file up so that Torrance, as well as the jury, could see it.

"Mr. Torrance, this is one of the words checked on the summary. Can you read this word?"

Vincent immediately stood but Torrance was already shaking his head and looking thoroughly humiliated. Vincent objected to the demonstration without proper foundation and Companioni sustained. I expected him to. I was just laying the groundwork for my next move with the jury and I was sure most of them had seen the witness shake his head.

"Okay, Mr. Torrance," I said. "Let's move to the other side of the file. Could you describe the bodies in the photos?"

"Um, two men. It looks like they opened up some chicken wire and some tarps and they're laying there. A bunch a police is there investigatin' and takin' pictures."

"What race are the men on the tarps?"

"They're black."

"Have you ever seen those photographs before, Mr. Torrance?"

Vincent stood to object to my question as having previously been asked and answered. But it was like holding up a hand to stop a bullet. The judge sternly told him he could take his seat. It was his way of telling the prosecutor he was going to have to just sit back and take what was coming. You put the liar on the stand, you take the fall with him.

"You may answer the question, Mr. Torrance," I said after Vincent sat down. "Have you ever seen those photographs before?"

"No, sir, not before right now."

"Would you agree that the pictures portray what you described to us earlier? That being the bodies of two slain black men?"

"That's what it looks like. But I ain't seen the picture before, just what he tell me."

"Are you sure?"

"Something like these I wouldn't forget."

"You've told us Mr. Woodson confessed to killing two black men, but he is on trial for killing two white men. Wouldn't you agree that it appears that he didn't confess to you at all?"

"No, he confessed. He told me he killed those two."

I looked up at the judge.

"Your Honor, the defense asks that the file in front of Mr. Torrance be admitted into evidence as defense exhibit one."

Vincent made a lack-of-foundation objection but Companioni overruled.

"It will be admitted and we'll let the jury decide whether Mr. Torrance has or hasn't seen the photographs and contents of the file."

I was on a roll and decided to go all in.

"Thank you," I said. "Your Honor, now might also be a good time for the prosecutor to reacquaint his witness with the penalties for perjury."

It was a dramatic move made for the benefit of the jury. I was expecting I would have to continue with Torrance and eviscerate him with the blade of his own lie. But Vincent stood and asked the judge to recess the trial while he conferred with opposing counsel.

This told me I had just saved Barnett Woodson's life.

"The defense has no objection," I told the judge.

Three

After the jury filed out of the box, I returned to the defense table as the courtroom deputy was moving in to cuff my client and take him back to the courtroom holding cell.

"That guy's a lying sack of shit," Woodson whispered to me. "I didn't kill two black guys. They were white."

My hope was that the deputy hadn't heard that.

"Why don't you shut the fuck up?" I whispered right back. "And next time you see that lying sack of shit in lockup, you ought to shake his hand. Because of his lies the prosecutor's about to come off of the death penalty and float a deal. I'll be back there to tell you about it as soon as I get it."

Woodson shook his head dramatically.

"Yeah, well, maybe I don't want no deal now. They put a goddamn liar on the stand, man. This whole case should go down the toilet. We can win this motherfucker, Haller. Don't take no deal."

I stared at Woodson for a moment. I had just saved his life but he wanted more. He felt entitled because the state hadn't played fair — never mind responsibility for the two kids he had just admitted to killing.

"Don't get greedy, Barnett," I told him. "I'll be back with the news as soon as I get it."

The deputy took him through the steel door that led to the holding cells attached to the courtroom. I watched him go. I had no false conceptions about Barnett Woodson. I had never directly asked him but I knew he had killed those two Westside boys. That wasn't my concern. My job was to test the state's case against him with the best of my skills—that's how the system worked. I had done that and had been given the blade. I would now use it to improve his situation significantly, but Woodson's dream of walking away from those two bodies that had turned black in the water was not in the cards. He might not have understood this but his underpaid and underappreciated public defender certainly did.

After the courtroom cleared, Vincent and I were left looking at each other from our respective tables.

"So," I said.

Vincent shook his head.

"First of all," he said. "I want to make it clear that obviously I didn't know Torrance was lying."

"Sure."

"Why would I sabotage my own case like this?"

I waved off the mea culpa.

"Look, Jerry, don't bother. I told you in pretrial that the guy had copped the discovery my client had in his cell. It's common sense. My guy wouldn't have said shit to your guy, a perfect stranger, and everybody knew it except you."

Vincent emphatically shook his head.

"I did not know it, Haller. He came forward, was vetted by one of our best investigators, and there was no indication of a lie, no matter how improbable it would seem that your client talked to him."

I laughed that off in an unfriendly way.

"Not 'talked' to him, Jerry. *Confessed* to him. A little difference there. So you better check with this prized investigator of yours because he isn't worth the county paycheck."

"Look, he told me the guy couldn't read, so there was no way he could have gotten what he knew out of the discovery. He didn't mention the photos."

"Exactly, and that's why you should find yourself a new investigator. And I'll tell you what, Jerry. I'm usually pretty reasonable about this sort of stuff. I try to go along to get along with the DA's office. But I gave you fair warning about this guy. So after the break, I'm going to gut him right there on the stand and all you're going to be able to do is sit there and watch."

I was in full outrage now, and a lot of it was real.

"It's called 'rope a dope.' But when I'm done with Torrance, he's not the only one who's going to look like a dope. That jury's going to know that you either knew this guy was a liar or you were too dumb to realize it. Either way, you're not coming off too good."

Vincent looked down blankly at the prosecution table and calmly straightened the case files stacked in front of him. He spoke in a quiet voice.

"I don't want you going forward with the cross," he said.

"Fine. Then, cut the denials and the bullshit and give me a dispo I can—"

"I'll drop the death penalty. Twenty-five to life without."

I shook my head without hesitation.

"That's not going to do it. The last thing Woodson said before they took him back was that he was willing to roll the dice. To be exact, he said, 'We can win this motherfucker.' And I think he could be right."

"Then, what do you want, Haller?"

"I'll go fifteen max. I think I can sell that to him."

Vincent emphatically shook his head.

"No way. They'll send me back to filing buy-busts if I give you that for two cold-blooded murders. My best offer is twenty-five with parole. That's it. Under current guidelines he could be out in sixteen, seventeen years. Not bad for what he did, killing two kids like that."

I looked at him, trying to read his face, looking for the tell. I decided I believed it was going to be the best he would do. And he was right, it wasn't a bad deal for what Barnett Woodson had done.

"I don't know," I said. "I think he'll say roll the dice."

Vincent shook his head and looked at me.

"Then, you'll have to sell it to him, Haller. Because I can't go lower and if you continue the cross, then my career in the DA's office is probably finished."

Now I hesitated before responding.

"Wait a minute, what are you saying, Jerry? That I have to clean your mess up for you? I catch you with your pants around your ankles and it's *my* client that has to take it in the ass?"

"I'm saying it's a fair offer to a man who is guilty as sin. More than fair. Go talk to him and work your magic, Mick. Convince him. We both know you're not long for the Public Defenders Office. You might need a favor from me someday when you're out there in the big bad world with no steady paycheck coming in."

I just stared back at him, registering the quid pro quo of the offer. I help him and somewhere down the line he helps me, and Barnett Woodson does an extra couple of years in stir.

"He'll be lucky to last five years in there, let alone twenty," Vincent said. "What's the difference to him? But you and I? We're going places, Mickey. We can help each other here."

I nodded slowly. Vincent was only a few years older than me but was trying to act like some kind of wise old sage.

"The thing is, Jerry, if I did what you suggest, then I'd never be able to look another client in the eye again. I think I'd end up being the dope that got roped."

I stood up and gathered my files. My plan was to go back and tell Barnett Woodson to roll the dice and let me see what I could do.

"I'll see you after the break," I said.

And then I walked away.

PART TWO

— Suitcase City

2007

Four

I t was a little early in the week for Lorna Taylor to be calling and checking on me. Usually she waited until at least Thursday. Never Tuesday. I picked up the phone, thinking it was more than a check-in call.

"Lorna?"

"Mickey, where've you been? I've been calling all morning."

"I went for my run. I just got out of the shower. You okay?"

"I'm fine. Are you?"

"Sure. What is — ?"

"You got a forthwith from Judge Holder. She wants to see you — like an hour ago."

This gave me pause.

"About what?"

"I don't know. All I know is first Michaela called, then the judge herself called. That usually doesn't happen. She wanted to know why you weren't responding."

I knew that Michaela was Michaela Gill, the judge's clerk. And Mary Townes Holder was the chief judge of the Los Angeles Superior Court. The fact that she had called personally didn't make it sound like they were inviting me to the annual justice ball. Mary Townes Holder didn't call lawyers without a good reason.

"What did you tell her?"

"I just said you didn't have court today and you might be out on the golf course."

"I don't play golf, Lorna."

"Look, I couldn't think of anything."

"It's all right, I'll call the judge. Give me the number."

"Mickey, don't call. Just go. The judge wants to *see* you in chambers. She was very clear about that and she wouldn't tell me why. So just go."

"Okay, I'm going. I have to get dressed."

"Mickey?"

"What?"

"How are you really doing?"

I knew her code. I knew what she was asking. She didn't want me appearing in front of a judge if I wasn't ready for it.

"You don't have to worry, Lorna. I'm fine. I'll be fine."

"Okay. Call me and let me know what is going on as soon as you can."

"Don't worry. I will."

I hung up the phone, feeling like I was being bossed around by my wife, not my ex-wife.

Five

As the chief judge of the Los Angeles Superior Court, Judge Mary Townes Holder did most of her work behind closed doors. Her courtroom was used on occasion for emergency hearings on motions but rarely used for trials. Her work was done out of the view of the public. In chambers. Her job largely pertained to the administration of the justice system in Los Angeles County. More than two hundred fifty judgeships and forty courthouses fell under her purview. Every jury summons that went into the mail had her name on it, and every assigned parking space in a courthouse garage had her approval. She assigned judges by both geography and designation of law — criminal, civil, juvenile and family. When judges were newly elected to the bench, it was Judge Holder who decided whether they sat in Beverly Hills or Compton, and whether they heard high-stakes financial cases in civil court or soul-draining divorce cases in family court.

I had dressed quickly in what I considered my lucky suit. It was an Italian import from Corneliani that I used to wear on verdict days. Since I hadn't been in court for a year, or heard a verdict for even longer, I had to take it out of a plastic bag hanging in the back of the closet. After that I sped downtown without delay, thinking that I might be headed toward some sort of verdict on myself. As I drove, my mind raced over the cases and clients I had left behind a year earlier. As far as I knew, nothing had been left open or on the table. But maybe there had been a complaint or the judge had picked up on some courthouse gossip and was running her own inquiry. Regardless, I entered Holder's courtroom with a lot of trepidation. A summons from any judge was usually not good news; a summons from the chief judge was even worse.

The courtroom was dark and the clerk's pod next to the bench was empty. I walked through the gate and was heading toward the door to the back hallway, when it opened and the clerk stepped through it. Michaela Gill was a pleasant-looking woman who reminded me of my third-grade teacher. But she wasn't expecting to find a man approaching the other side of the door when she opened it. She startled and nearly let out a shriek. I quickly identified myself before she could make a run for the panic button on the judge's bench. She caught her breath and then ushered me back without delay.

I walked down the hallway and found the judge alone in her chambers, working at a massive desk made of dark wood. Her black robe was hanging on a hat rack in the corner. She was dressed in a maroon suit with a conservative cut. She was attractive and neat, midfifties with a slim build and brown hair kept in a short, no-nonsense style.

I had never met Judge Holder before but I knew about her. She had put twenty years in as a prosecutor before being appointed to the bench by a conservative governor. She presided over criminal cases, had a few of the big ones, and was known for handing out maximum sentences. Consequently, she had been easily retained by the electorate after her first term. She had been elected chief judge four years later and had held the position ever since.

"Mr. Haller, thank you for coming," she said. "I'm glad your secretary finally found you."

There was an impatient if not imperious tone to her voice.

"She's not actually my secretary, Judge. But she found me. Sorry it took so long."

"Well, you're here. I don't believe we have met before, have we?"

"I don't think so."

"Well, this will betray my age but I actually opposed your father in a trial once. One of his last cases, I believe."

I had to readjust my estimate of her age. She would have to be at least sixty if she had ever been in a courtroom with my father.

"I was actually third chair on a case, just out of USC Law and green as can be. They were trying to give me some trial exposure. It was a murder case and they let me handle one witness. I prepared a week for my examination and your father destroyed the man on cross in ten minutes. We won the case but I never forgot the lesson. Be prepared for anything."

I nodded. Over the years I had met several older lawyers who had Mickey Haller Sr. stories to share. I had very few of my own. Before I could ask the judge about the case on which she'd met him, she pressed on.

"But that's not why I called you here," she said.

"I didn't think so, Judge. It sounded like you have something... kind of urgent?"

"I do. Did you know Jerry Vincent?"

I was immediately thrown by her use of the past tense.

"Jerry? Yes, I know Jerry. What about him?"

"He's dead."

"Dead?"

"Murdered, actually."

"When?"

"Last night. I'm sorry."

My eyes dropped and I looked at the nameplate on her desk. *Honorable M. T. Holder* was carved in script into a two-dimensional wooden display that held a ceremonial gavel and a fountain pen and inkwell.

"How close were you?" she asked.

It was a good question and I didn't really know the answer. I kept my eyes down as I spoke.

"We had cases against each other when he was with the DA and I was at the PD. We both left for private practice around the same time and both of us had one-man shops. Over the years we worked some cases together, a couple of drug trials, and we sort of covered for each other when it was needed. He threw me a case occasionally when it was something he didn't want to handle."

I had had a professional relationship with Jerry Vincent. Every now and then we clicked glasses at Four Green Fields or saw each other at a ball game at Dodger Stadium. But for me to say we were close would have been an exaggeration. I knew little about him outside of the world of law. I had heard about a divorce a while back on the courthouse gossip line but had never even asked him about it. That was personal information and I didn't need to know it.

"You seem to forget, Mr. Haller, but I was with the DA back when Mr. Vincent was a young up-and-comer. But then he lost a big case and his star faded. That was when he left for private practice."

I looked at the judge but said nothing.

"And I seem to recall that you were the defense attorney on that case," she added.

I nodded.

"Barnett Woodson. I got an acquittal on a double murder. He walked out of the courtroom and sarcastically apologized to the media for getting away with murder. He had to rub the DA's face in it and that pretty much ended Jerry's career as a prosecutor."

"Then, why would he ever work with you or throw you cases?"

"Because, Judge, by ending his career as a prosecutor, I started his career as a defense attorney."

I left it at that but it wasn't enough for her.

"And?"

"And a couple of years later he was making about five times what he had made with the DA. He called me up one day and thanked me for showing him the light."

The judge nodded knowingly.

"It came down to money. He wanted the money."

I shrugged like I was uncomfortable answering for a dead man and didn't respond.

"What happened to your client?" the judge asked. "What became of the man who got away with murder?"

"He would've been better off taking a conviction. Woodson got killed in a drive-by about two months after the acquittal."

The judge nodded again, this time as if to say end of story, justice served. I tried to put the focus back on Jerry Vincent.

"I can't believe this about Jerry. Do you know what happened?"

"That's not clear. He was apparently found late last night in his car in the garage at his office. He had been shot to death. I am told that the police are still there at the crime scene and there have been no arrests. All of this comes from a *Times* reporter who called my chambers to make an inquiry about what will happen now with Mr. Vincent's clients — especially Walter Elliot."

I nodded. For the last twelve months I had been in a vacuum but it wasn't so airtight that I hadn't heard about the movie mogul murder case. It was just one in a string of big-time cases Vincent had scored over the years. Despite the Woodson fiasco, his pedigree as a high profile prosecutor had set him up from the start as an upper-echelon criminal defense attorney. He didn't have to go looking for clients; they came looking for him. And usually they were clients who could pay or had something to say, meaning they had at least one of three attributes: They could pay top dollar for legal representation, they were demonstrably innocent of the charges lodged against them, or they were clearly guilty but had public opinion and sentiment on their side. These were clients he could get behind and forthrightly defend no matter what they were accused of. Clients who didn't make him feel greasy at the end of the day.

And Walter Elliot qualified for at least one of those attributes. He was the chairman/owner of Archway Pictures and a very powerful man in Hollywood. He had been charged with murdering his wife and her lover in a fit of rage after discovering them together in a Malibu beach house. The case had all sorts of connections to sex and celebrity and was drawing wide media attention. It had been a publicity machine for Vincent and now it would go up for grabs.

The judge broke through my reverie.

"Are you familiar with RPC two-three-hundred?" she asked.

I involuntarily gave myself away by squinting my eyes at the question.

"Uh...not exactly."

"Let me refresh your memory. It is the section of the California bar's rules of professional conduct referring to the transfer or sale of a law practice. We, of course, are talking about a transfer in this case. Mr. Vincent apparently named you as his second in his standard contract of representation. This allowed you to cover for him when he needed it and included you, if necessary, in the attorney-client relationship. Additionally, I have found that he filed a motion with the court ten years ago that allowed for the transfer of his practice to you should he become incapacitated or deceased. The motion has never been altered or updated, but it's clear what his intentions were."

I just stared at her. I knew about the clause in Vincent's standard contract. I had the same in mine, naming him. But what I realized was that the judge was telling me that I now had Jerry's cases. All of them, Walter Elliot included.

This, of course, did not mean I would keep all of the cases. Each client would be free to move on to another attorney of their choosing once apprised of Vincent's demise. But it meant that I would have the first shot at them.

I started thinking about things. I hadn't had a client in a year and the plan was to start back slow, not with a full caseload like the one I had apparently just inherited.

"However," the judge said, "before you get too excited about this proposition, I must tell you that I would be remiss in my role as chief judge if I did not make every effort to ensure that Mr. Vincent's clients were transferred to a replacement counsel of good standing and competent skill."

Now I understood. She had called me in to explain why I would not be appointed to Vincent's clients. She was going to go against the dead lawyer's wishes and appoint somebody else, most likely one of the high-dollar contributors to her last reelection campaign. Last I had checked, I'd contributed exactly nothing to her coffers over the years.

But then the judge surprised me.

"I've checked with some of the judges," she said, "and I am aware that you have not been practicing law for almost a year. I have found no explanation for this. Before I issue the order appointing you replacement counsel in this matter, I need to be assured that I am not turning Mr. Vincent's clients over to the wrong man."

I nodded in agreement, hoping it would buy me a little time before I had to respond.

"Judge, you're right. I sort of took myself out of the game for a while. But I just started taking steps to get back in."

"Why did you take yourself out?"

She asked it bluntly, her eyes holding mine and looking for anything that would indicate evasion of the truth in my answer. I spoke very carefully.

"Judge, I had a case a couple years ago. The client's name was Louis Roulet. He was —"

"I remember the case, Mr. Haller. You got shot. But, as you say, that was a couple years ago. I seem to remember you practicing law for some time after that. I remember the news stories about you coming back to the job."

"Well," I said, "what happened is I came back too soon. I had been gut shot, Judge, and I should've taken my time. Instead, I hurried back and the next thing I knew I started having pain and the doctors said I had a hernia. So I had an operation for that and there were complications. They did it wrong. There was even more pain and another operation and, well, to make a long story short, it knocked me down for a while. I decided the second time not to come back until I was sure I was ready."

The judge nodded sympathetically. I guessed I had been right to leave out the part about my addiction to pain pills and the stint in rehab.

"Money wasn't an issue," I said. "I had some savings and I also got a settlement from the insurance company. So I took my time coming back. But I'm ready. I was just about to take the back cover of the Yellow Pages."

"Then, I guess inheriting an entire practice is quite convenient, isn't it?" she said.

I didn't know what to say to her question or the smarmy tone in which she said it.

"All I can tell you, Judge, is that I would take good care of Jerry Vincent's clients."

The judge nodded but she didn't look at me as she did so. I knew the tell. She knew something. And it bothered her. Maybe she knew about the rehab.

"According to bar records, you've been disciplined several times," she said.

Here we were again. She was back to throwing the cases to another lawyer. Probably some campaign contributor from Century City who couldn't find his way around a criminal proceeding if his Riviera membership depended on it.

"All of it ancient history, Judge. All of it technicalities. I'm in good standing with the bar. If you called them today, then I'm sure you were told that."

She stared at me for a long moment before dropping her eyes to the document in front of her on the desk.

"Very well, then," she said.

She scribbled a signature on the last page of the document. I felt the flutter of excitement begin to build in my chest.

"Here is an order transferring the practice to you," the judge said. "You might need it when you go to his office. And let me tell you this. I am going to be monitoring you. I want an updated inventory of cases by the beginning of next week. The status of every case on the client list. I want to know which clients will work with you and which will find other representation. After that, I want biweekly status updates on all cases in which you remain counsel. Am I being clear?"

"Perfectly clear, Judge. For how long?"

"What?"

"For how long do you want me to give you biweekly updates?"

She stared at me and her face hardened.

"Until I tell you to stop."

She handed me the order.

"You can go now, Mr. Haller, and if I were you, I would get over there and protect my new clients from any unlawful search and seizure of their files by the police. If you have any problem, you can always call on me. I have put my after-hours number on the order."

"Yes, Your Honor. Thank you."

"Good luck, Mr. Haller."

I stood up and headed out of the room. When I got to the doorway of her chambers I glanced back at her. She had her head down and was working on the next court order.

Out in the courthouse hallway, I read the two-page document the judge had given me, confirming that what had just happened was real.

It was. The document I held appointed me substitute counsel, at least temporarily, on all of Jerry Vincent's cases. It granted me immediate access to the fallen attorney's office, files and bank accounts into which client advances had been deposited.

I pulled out my cell phone and called Lorna Taylor. I asked her to look up the address of Jerry Vincent's office. She gave it to me and I told her to meet me there and to pick up two sandwiches on her way.

"Why?" she asked.

"Because I haven't had lunch."

"No, why are we going to Jerry Vincent's office?"

"Because we're back in business."

Six

I was in my Lincoln driving toward Jerry Vincent's office, when I thought of something and called Lorna Taylor back. When she didn't answer I called her cell and caught her in her car.

"I'm going to need an investigator. How would you feel if I called Cisco?"

There was a hesitation before she answered. Cisco was Dennis Wojciechowski, her significant other as of the past year. I was the one who had introduced them when I used him on a case. Last I heard, they were now living together.

"Well, I have no problem working with Cisco. But I wish you would tell me what this is all about."

Lorna knew Jerry Vincent as a voice on the phone. It was she who would take his calls when he was checking to see if I could stand in on a sentence or babysit a client through an arraignment. I couldn't remember if they had ever met in person. I had wanted to tell her the news in person but things were moving too quickly for that.

"Jerry Vincent is dead."

"What?"

"He was murdered last night and I'm getting first shot at all of his cases. Including Walter Elliot."

She was silent for a long moment before responding.

"My God.... How? He was such a nice man."

"I couldn't remember if you had ever met him."

Lorna worked out of her condo in West Hollywood. All my calls and billing went through her. If there was a brick-and-mortar office for the law firm of Michael Haller and Associates, then her place was it. But there weren't any associates and when I worked, my office was the backseat of my car. This left few occasions for Lorna to meet face-to-face with any of the people I represented or associated with.

"He came to our wedding, don't you remember?"

"That's right. I forgot."

"I can't believe this. What happened?"

"I don't know. Holder said he was shot in the garage at his office. Maybe I'll find out something when I get there."

"Did he have a family?"

"I think he was divorced but I don't know if there were kids or what. I don't think so."

Lorna didn't say anything. We both had our own thoughts occupying us.

"Let me go so I can call Cisco," I finally said. "Do you know what he's doing today?"

"No, he didn't say."

"All right, I'll see."

"What kind of sandwich do you want?"

"Which way you coming?"

"Sunset."

"Stop at Dusty's and get me one of those turkey sandwiches with cranberry sauce. It's been almost a year since I've had one of those."

"You got it."

"And get something for Cisco in case he's hungry."

"All right."

I hung up and looked up the number for Dennis Wojciechowski in the address book I keep in the center console compartment. I had his cell phone. When he answered I heard a mixture of wind and exhaust blast in the phone. He was on his bike and even though I knew his helmet was set up with an earpiece and mike attached to his cell, I had to yell.

"It's Mickey Haller. Pull over."

I waited and heard him cut the engine on his 'sixty-three panhead.

"What's up, Mick?" he asked when it finally got quiet. "Haven't heard from you in a long time."

"You gotta put the baffles back in your pipes, man. Or you'll be deaf before you're forty and then you won't be hearing from anybody."

"I'm already past forty and I hear you just fine. What's going on?"

Wojciechowski was a freelance defense investigator I had used on a few cases. That was how he had met Lorna, collecting his pay. But I had known him for more than ten years before that because of his association with the Road Saints Motorcycle Club, a group for which I served as a de facto house counsel for several years. Dennis never flew RSMC colors but was considered an associate member. The group even bestowed a nickname on him, largely because there was already a Dennis in the membership — known, of course, as Dennis the Menace — and his last name, Wojciechowski, was intolerably difficult to pronounce. Riffing off his dark looks and mustache, they christened him the Cisco Kid. It didn't matter that he was one hundred percent Polish out of the south side of Milwaukee.

Cisco was a big, imposing man but he kept his nose clean while riding with the Saints. He never caught an arrest record and that paid off when he later applied to the state for his private investigator's license. Now, many years later, the long hair was gone and the mustache was trimmed and going gray. But the name Cisco and the penchant for riding classic Harleys built in his hometown had stuck for life.

Cisco was a thorough and thoughtful investigator. And he had another value as well. He was big and strong and could be physically intimidating when necessary. That attribute could be highly useful when tracking down and dealing with people who fluttered around the edges of a criminal case.

"First of all, where are you?" I asked.

"Burbank."

"You on a case?"

"No, just a ride. Why, you got something for me? You taking on a case finally?"

"A lot of cases. And I'm going to need an investigator."

I gave him the address of Vincent's office and told him to meet me there as soon as he could. I knew that Vincent would have used either a stable of investigators or just one in particular, and that there might be a loss of time as Cisco got up to speed on the cases, but all of that was okay with me. I wanted an investigator I could trust and already had a working relationship with. I was also going to need Cisco to immediately start work by running down the locations of my new clients. My experience with criminal defendants is that they are not always found at the addresses they put down on the client info sheet when they first sign up for legal representation.

After closing the phone I realized I had driven right by the building where Vincent's office was located. It was on Broadway near Third Street and there was too much traffic with cars and pedestrians for me to attempt a U-turn. I wasted ten minutes working my way back to it, catching red lights at every corner. By the time I got to the right place, I was so frustrated that I resolved to hire a driver again as soon as possible so that I could concentrate on cases instead of addresses.

Vincent's office was in a six-story structure called simply the Legal Center. Being so close to the main downtown courthouses — both criminal and civil — meant it was a building full of trial lawyers. Just the kind of place most cops and doctors—lawyer haters—probably wished would implode every time there was an earthquake. I saw the opening for the parking garage next door and pulled in.

As I was taking the ticket out of the machine, a uniformed police officer approached my car. He was carrying a clipboard.

"Sir? Do you have business in the building here?"

"That's why I'm parking here."

"Sir, could you state your business?"

"What business is it of yours, Officer?"

"Sir, we are conducting a crime scene investigation in the garage and I need to know your business before I can allow you in."

"My office is in the building," I said. "Will that do?"

It wasn't exactly a lie. I had Judge Holder's court order in my coat pocket. That gave me an office in the building.

The answer seemed to work. The cop asked to see my ID and I could've argued that he had no right to request my identification but decided that there was no need to make a federal case out of it. I pulled my wallet and gave him the ID and he wrote my name and driver's license number down on his clipboard. Then he let me through.

"At the moment there's no parking on the second level," he said. "They haven't cleared the scene."

I waved and headed up the ramp. When I reached the second floor, I saw that it was empty of vehicles except for two patrol cars and a black BMW coupe that was being hauled onto the bed of a truck from the police garage. Jerry Vincent's car, I assumed. Two other uniformed cops were just beginning to pull down the yellow crime scene tape that had been used to cordon off the parking level. One of them signaled for me to keep going. I saw no detectives around but the police weren't giving up the murder scene just yet.

I kept going up and didn't find a space I could fit the Lincoln into until I got to the fifth floor. One more reason I needed to get a driver again.

The office I was looking for was on the second floor at the front of the building. The opaque glass door was closed but not locked. I entered a reception room with an empty sitting area and a nearby counter behind which sat a woman whose eyes were red from crying. She was on the phone but when she saw me, she put it down on the counter without so much as a "hold on" to whomever she was talking to.

"Are you with the police?" she asked.

"No, I'm not," I replied.

"Then, I'm sorry, the office is closed today."

I approached the counter, pulling the court order from Judge Holder out of the inside pocket of my suit coat.

"Not for me," I said as I handed it to her.

She unfolded the document and stared at it but didn't seem to be reading it. I noticed that in one of her hands she clutched a wad of tissues.

"What is this?" she asked.

"That's a court order," I said. "My name is Michael Haller and Judge Holder has appointed me replacement counsel in regard to Jerry Vincent's clients. That means we'll be working together. You can call me Mickey."

She shook her head as if warding off some invisible threat. My name usually didn't carry that sort of power.

"You can't do this. Mr. Vincent wouldn't want this."

I took the court papers out of her hand and refolded them. I started putting the document back into my pocket.

"Actually, I can. The chief judge of Los Angeles Superior Court has directed me to do this. And if you look closely at the contracts of representation that Mr. Vincent had his clients sign, you will find my name already on them, listed as associate counsel. So, what you think Mr. Vincent would have wanted is immaterial at this point because he did in fact file the papers that named me his replacement should he become incapacitated or ... dead."

The woman had a dazed look on her face. Her mascara was heavy and running beneath one eye. It gave her an uneven, almost comical look. For some reason a vision of Liza Minnelli jumped to my mind.

"If you want, you can call Judge Holder's clerk and talk about it with her," I said. "Meantime, I really need to get started here. I know this has been a very difficult day for you. It's been difficult for me—I knew Jerry going back to his days at the DA. So you have my sympathy."

I nodded and looked at her and waited for a response but I still wasn't getting one. I pressed on.

"I'm going to need some things to get started here. First of all, his calendar. I want to put together a list of all the active cases Jerry was handling. Then, I'm going to need you to pull the files for those—"

"It's gone," she said abruptly.

"What's gone?"

"His laptop. The police told me whoever did this took his briefcase out of the car. He kept everything on his laptop."

"You mean his calendar? He didn't keep a hard copy?"

"That's gone, too. They took his portfolio. That was in the briefcase."

Her eyes were staring blankly ahead. I tapped the top of the computer screen on her desk.

"What about this computer?" I asked. "Didn't he back up his calendar anywhere?"

She didn't say anything, so I asked again.

"Did Jerry back up his calendar anywhere else? Is there any way to access it?"

She finally looked up at me and seemed to take pleasure in responding.

"I didn't keep the calendar. He did. He kept it all on his laptop and he kept a hard copy in the old portfolio he carried. But they're both gone. The police made me look everywhere in here but they're gone."

I nodded. The missing calendar was going to be a problem but it wasn't insurmountable.

"What about files? Did he have any in the briefcase?"

"I don't think so. He kept all the files here."

"Okay, good. What we're going to have to do is pull all the active cases and rebuild the calendar from the files. I'll also need to see any ledgers or checkbooks pertaining to the trust and operating accounts."

She looked up at me sharply.

"You're not going to take his money."

"It's not—"

I stopped, took a deep breath and then started again in a calm but direct tone.

"First of all, I apologize. I did this backwards. I don't even know your name. Let's start over. What is your name?"

"Wren."

"Wren? Wren what?"

"Wren Williams."

"Okay, Wren, let me explain something. It's not his money. It's his clients' money and until they say otherwise, his clients are now my clients. Do you understand? Now, I have told you that I am aware of the emotional upheaval of the day and the shock you are experiencing. I'm experiencing some of it myself. But you need to decide right now if you are with me or against me, Wren. Because if you are with me, I need you to get me the things I asked for. And I'm going to need you to work with my case manager when she gets here. If you are against me, then I need you just to go home right now."

She slowly shook her head.

"The detectives told me I had to stay until they were finished."

"What detectives? There were only a couple uniforms left out there when I drove in."

"The detectives in Mr. Vincent's office."

"You let—"

I didn't finish. I stepped around the counter and headed toward two separate doors on the back wall. I picked the one on the left and opened it.

I walked into Jerry Vincent's office. It was large and opulent and empty. I turned in a full circle until I found myself staring into the bugged eyes of a large fish mounted on the wall over a dark wood credenza next to the door I had come through. The fish was a beautiful green with a white underbelly. Its body was arched as if it had frozen solid just at the moment it had jumped out of the water. Its mouth was open so wide I could have put my fist in it.

Mounted on the wall beneath the fish was a brass plate. It said:

IF I'D KEPT MY MOUTH SHUT
I WOULDN'T BE HERE

Words to live by, I thought. Most criminal defendants talk their way into prison. Few talk their way out. The best single piece of advice I have ever given a client is to just keep your mouth shut. Talk to no one about your case, not even your own wife. You keep close counsel with yourself. You take the nickel and you live to fight another day.

The unmistakable sound of a metal drawer being rolled and then banged closed spun me back around. On the other side of the room were two more doors. Both were open about a foot and through one I could see a darkened bathroom. Through the other I could see light.

I approached the lighted room quickly and pushed the door all the way open. It was the file room, a large, windowless walk-in closet with rows of steel filing cabinets going down both sides. A small worktable was set up against the back wall.

There were two men sitting at the worktable. One old, one young. Probably one to teach and one to learn. They had their jackets off and draped over the chairs. I saw their guns and holsters and their badges clipped to their belts.

"What are you doing?" I asked gruffly.

The men looked up from their reading. I saw a stack of files on the table between them. The older detective's eyes momentarily widened in surprise when he saw me.

"LAPD," he said. "And I guess I should ask you the same question."

"Those are my files and you're going to have to put them down right now."

The older man stood up and came toward me. I started pulling the court order from my jacket again.

"My name is—"

"I know who you are," the detective said. "But I still don't know what you're doing here."

I handed him the court order.

"Then, this should explain it. I've been appointed by the chief judge of the superior court as replacement counsel to Jerry Vincent's clients. That means his cases are now my cases. And you have no right to be in here looking through files. That is a clear violation of my clients' right to protection against unlawful search and seizure. These files contain privileged attorney-client communications and information."

The detective didn't bother looking at the paperwork. He quickly flipped through it to the signature and seal on the last page. He didn't seem all that impressed.

"Vincent's been murdered," he said. "The motive could be sitting in one of these files. The identity of the killer could be in one of them. We have to—"

"No, you don't. What you have to do is get out of this file room right now."

The detective didn't move a muscle.

"I consider this part of a crime scene," he said. "It's you who has to leave."

"Read the order, Detective. I'm not going anywhere. Your crime scene is out in the garage, and no judge in L.A. would let you extend it to this office and these files. It's time for you to leave and for me to take care of my clients."

He made no move to read the court order or to vacate the premises.

"If I leave," he said, "I'm going to shut this place down and seal it."

I hated getting into pissing matches with cops but sometimes there was no choice.

"You do that and I'll have it unsealed in an hour. And you'll be standing in front of the chief judge of the superior court explaining how you trampled on the rights of every one of Vincent's clients. You know, depending on how many clients we're talking about, that might be a record — even for the LAPD."

The detective smiled at me like he was mildly amused by my threats. He held up the court order.

"You say this gives you all of these cases?"

"That's right, for now."

"The entire law practice?"

"Yes, but each client will decide whether to stick with me or find someone else."

"Well, I guess that puts you on our list."

"What list?"

"Our suspect list."

"That's ridiculous. Why would I be on it?"

"You just told us why. You inherited all of the victim's clients. That's got to amount to some sort of a financial windfall, doesn't it? He's dead and you get the whole business. Think that's enough motivation for murder? Care to tell us where you were last night between eight and midnight?"

He grinned at me again without any warmth, giving me that cop's practiced smile of judgment. His brown eyes were so dark I couldn't see the line between iris and pupil. Like shark eyes, they didn't seem to carry or reflect any light.

"I'm not even going to begin to explain how ludicrous that is," I said. "But for starters you can check with the judge and you'll find out that I didn't even know I was in line for this."

"So you say. But don't worry, we'll be checking you out completely."

"Good. Now please leave this room or I make the call to the judge."

The detective stepped back to the table and took his jacket off the chair.

He carried it rather than put it on. He picked a file up off the table and brought it toward me. He shoved it into my chest until I took it from him.

"Here's one of your new files back, Counselor. Don't choke on it."

He stepped through the door, and his partner went with him. I followed them out into the office and decided to take a shot at reducing the tension. I had a feeling it wouldn't be the last time I saw them.

"Look, detectives, I'm sorry it's like this. I try to have a good relationship with the police and I am sure we can work something out. But at the moment my obligation is to the clients. I don't even know what I have here. Give me some time to—"

"We don't have time," the older man said. "We lose momentum and we lose the case. Do you understand what you're getting yourself into here, Counselor?"

I looked at him for a moment, trying to understand the meaning behind his question.

"I think so, Detective. I've only been working cases for about eighteen years but—"

"I'm not talking about your experience. I'm talking about what happened in that garage. Whoever killed Vincent was waiting for him out there. They knew where he was and just how to get to him. He was ambushed."

I nodded like I understood.

"If I were you," the detective said, "I'd watch myself with those new clients of yours. Jerry Vincent knew his killer."

"What about when he was a prosecutor? He put people in prison. Maybe one of—"

"We'll check into it. But that was a long time ago. I think the person we're looking for is in those files."

With that, he and his partner started moving toward the door.

"Wait," I said. "You have a card? Give me a card."

The detectives stopped and turned back. The older one pulled a card out of his pocket and gave it to me.

"That's got all my numbers."

"Let me just get the lay of the land here and then I'll call and set something up. There's got to be a way for us to cooperate and still not trample on anybody's rights."

"Whatever you say, you're the lawyer."

I nodded and looked down at the name on the card. Harry Bosch. I was sure I had never met the man before, yet he had started the confrontation by saying he knew who I was.

"Look, Detective Bosch," I said, "Jerry Vincent was a colleague. We weren't that close but we were friends."

"And?"

"And good luck, you know? With the case. I hope you crack it."

Bosch nodded and there was something familiar about the physical gesture. Maybe we did know each other.

He turned to follow his partner out of the office.

"Detective?"

Bosch once more turned back to me.

"Did we ever cross paths on a case before? I think I recognize you."

Bosch smiled glibly and shook his head.

"No," he said. "If we'd been on a case, you'd remember me."

Seven

An hour later I was behind Jerry Vincent's desk with Lorna Taylor and Dennis Wojciechowski sitting across from me. We were eating our sandwiches and about to go over what we had put together from a very preliminary survey of the office and the cases. The food was good but nobody had much of an appetite considering where we were sitting and what had happened to the office's predecessor.

I had sent Wren Williams home early. She had been unable to stop crying or objecting to my taking control of her dead boss's cases. I decided to remove the barricade rather than have to keep walking around it. The last thing she asked before I escorted her through the door was whether I was going to fire her. I told her the jury was still out on that question but that she should report for work as usual the next day.

With Jerry Vincent dead and Wren Williams gone, we'd been left stumbling around in the dark until Lorna figured out the filing system and started pulling the active case files. From calendar notations in each file, she'd been able to start to put together a master calendar — the key component in any trial lawyer's professional life. Once we had worked up a rudimentary calendar, I began to breathe a little easier and we'd broken for lunch and opened the sandwich cartons Lorna had brought from Dusty's.

The calendar was light. A few case hearings here and there but for the most part it was obvious that Vincent was keeping things clear in advance of the Walter Elliot trial, which was scheduled to begin with jury selection in nine days.

"So let's start," I said, my mouth still full with my last bite. "According to the calendar we've pieced together, I've got a sentencing in forty-five minutes. So I was thinking we could have a preliminary discussion now, and then I could leave you two here while I go to court. Then I'll come back and see how much farther we've gotten before Cisco and I go out and start knocking on doors."

They both nodded, their mouths still working on their sandwiches as well. Cisco had cranberry in his mustache but didn't know it.

Lorna was as neat and as beautiful as ever. She was a stunner with blonde hair and eyes that somehow made you think you were the center of the universe when she was looking at you. I never got tired of that. I had kept her on salary the whole year I was out. I could afford it with the insurance settlement and I didn't want to run the risk that she'd be working for another lawyer when it was time for me to come back to work.

"Let's start with the money," I said.

Lorna nodded. As soon as she had gotten the active files together and placed them in front of me, she had moved on to the bank books, perhaps the only thing as important as the case calendar. The bank books would tell us more than just how much money Vincent's firm had in its coffers. They would give us an insight into how he ran his one-man shop.

"All right, good and bad news on the money," she said. "He's got thirty-eight thousand in the operating account and a hundred twenty-nine thousand in the trust account."

I whistled. That was a lot of cash to keep in the trust account. Money taken in from clients goes into the trust account. As work for each client proceeds, the trust account is billed and the money transferred to the operating account. I always want more money in the operating account than in the trust account, because once it's moved into the operating account, the money's mine.

"There's a reason why it's so lopsided," Lorna said, picking up on my surprise. "He just took in a check for a hundred thousand dollars from Walter Elliot. He deposited it Friday."

I nodded and tapped the makeshift calendar I had on the table in front of me. It was drawn on a legal pad. Lorna would have to go out and buy a real calendar when she got the chance. She would also input all of the court appointments on my computer and on an online calendar. Lastly, and as Jerry Vincent had not done, she would back it all up on an off-site data-storage account.

"The Elliot trial is scheduled to start Thursday next week," I said. "He took the hundred up front."

Saying the obvious prompted a sudden realization.

"As soon as we're done here, call the bank," I told Lorna. "See if the check has cleared. If not, try to push it through. As soon as Elliot hears that Vincent's dead, he'll probably try to put a stop-payment on it."

"Got it."

"What else on the money? If a hundred of it's from Elliot, who's the rest for?"

Lorna opened one of the accounting books she had on her lap. Each dollar in a trust fund must be accounted for with regard to which client it is being held for. At any time, an attorney must be able to determine how much of a client's advance has been transferred to the operating fund and used and how much is still on reserve in trust. A hundred thousand of Vincent's trust account was earmarked for the Walter Elliot trial. That left only twenty-nine thousand received for the rest of the active cases. That wasn't a lot, considering the stack of files we had pulled together while going through the filing cabinets looking for live cases.

"That's the bad news," Lorna said. "It looks like there are only five or six other cases with trust deposits. With the rest of the active cases, the money's already been moved into operating or been spent or the clients owe the firm."

I nodded. It wasn't good news. It was beginning to look like Jerry Vincent was running ahead of his cases, meaning he'd been on a treadmill, bringing in new cases to keep money flowing and paying for existing cases. Walter Elliot must have been the get-well client. As soon as his hundred thousand cleared, Vincent would have been able to turn the treadmill off and catch his breath—for a while, at least. But he never got the chance.

"How many clients with payment plans?" I asked.

Lorna once again referred to the records on her lap.

"He's got two on pretrial payments. Both are well behind."

"What are the names?"

It took her a moment to answer as she looked through the records.

"Uh, Samuels is one and Henson is the other. They're both about five thousand behind."

"And that's why we take credit cards and don't put out paper."

I was talking about my own business routine. I had long ago stopped providing credit services. I took nonrefundable cash payments. I also took plastic, but not until Lorna had run the card and gotten purchase approval.

I looked down at the notes I had kept while conducting a quick review of the calendar and the active files. Both Samuels and Henson were on a sub list I had drawn up while reviewing the actives. It was a list of cases I was going to cut loose if I could. This was based on my quick review of the charges and facts of the cases. If there was something I didn't like about a case—for any reason—then it went on the sub list.

"No problem," I said. "We'll cut 'em loose."

Samuels was a manslaughter DUI case and Henson was a felony

grand theft and drug possession. Henson momentarily held my inter-est because Vincent was going to build a defense around the client's addiction to prescription painkillers. He was going to roll sympathy and deflection defenses into one. He would lay out a case in which the doc-tor who overprescribed the drugs to Henson was the one most respon-sible for the consequences of the addiction he created. Patrick Henson, Vincent would argue, was a victim, not a criminal.

I was intimately familiar with this defense because I had employed it repeatedly over the past two years to try to absolve myself of the many infractions I had committed in my roles as father, ex-husband and friend to people in my life. But I put Henson into what I called the dog pile because I knew at heart the defense didn't hold up — at least not for me. And I wasn't ready to go into court with it for him either.

Lorna nodded and made notes about the two cases on a pad of paper.

"So what is the score on that?" she asked. "How many cases are you putting in the dog pile?"

"We came up with thirty-one active cases," I said. "Of those, I'm thinking only seven look like dogs. So that means we've got a lot of cases where there's no money in the till. I'll either have to get new money or they'll go in the dog pile, too."

I wasn't worried about having to go and get money out of the clients. Skill number one in criminal defense is getting the money. I was good at it and Lorna was even better. It was getting paying clients in the first place that was the trick, and we'd just had two dozen of them dropped into our laps.

"You think the judge is just going to let you drop some of these?" she asked.

"Nope. But I'll figure something out on that. Maybe I could claim conflict of interest. The conflict being that I like to be paid for my work and the clients don't like to pay."

No one laughed. No one even cracked a smile. I moved on.

"Anything else on the money?" I asked.

Lorna shook her head.

"That's about it. When you're in court, I'm going to call the bank and get that started. You want us both to be signers on the accounts?"

"Yeah, just like with my accounts."

I hadn't considered the potential difficulty of getting my hands on the money that was in the Vincent accounts. That was what I had Lorna for. She was good on the business end in ways I wasn't. Some days she was so good I wished we had either never gotten married or never gotten divorced.

"See if Wren Williams can sign checks," I said. "If she's on there, take her off. For now I want just you and me on the accounts."

"Will do. You may have to go back to Judge Holder for a court order for the bank."

"That'll be no problem."

My watch said I had ten minutes before I had to get going to court. I turned my attention to Wojciechowski.

"Cisco, whaddaya got?"

I had told him earlier to work his contacts and to monitor the investigation of Vincent's murder as closely as possible. I wanted to know what moves the detectives were making because it appeared from what Bosch had said that the investigation was going to be entwined with the cases I had just inherited.

"Not much," Cisco said. "The detectives haven't even gotten back to Parker Center yet. I called a guy I know in forensics and they're still processing everything. Not a lot of info on what they do have but he told me about something they don't. Vincent was shot at least two times that they could tell at the scene. And there were no shells. The shooter cleaned up."

There was something telling in that. The killer had either used a revolver or had had the presence of mind after killing a man to pick up the bullet casings ejected from his gun.

Cisco continued his report.

"I called another contact in communications and she told me the first call came in at twelve forty-three. They'll narrow down time of death at autopsy."

"Is there a general idea of what happened?"

"It looks like Vincent worked late, which was apparently his routine on Mondays. He worked late every Monday, preparing for the week ahead. When he was finished he packed his briefcase, locked up and left. He goes to the garage, gets in his car and gets popped through the driver's side window. When they found him the car was in park, the ignition on. The window was down. It was in the low sixties last night. He could've put the window down because he liked the chill, or he could've lowered it for somebody coming to the car."

"Somebody he knew."

"That's one possibility."

I thought about this and what Detective Bosch had said.

"Nobody was working in the garage?"

"No, the attendant leaves at six. You have to put your money in the machine after that or use your monthly pass. Vincent had a monthly."

"Cameras?"

"Only cameras are where you drive in and out. They're license plate cameras so if somebody says they lost their ticket they can tell when the car went in, that sort of thing. But from what I hear from my guy in forensics, there was nothing on tape that was useful. The killer didn't drive into the garage. He walked in either through the building or through one of the pedestrian entrances."

"Who found Jerry?"

"The security guard. They got one guard for the building and the garage. He hits the garage a couple times a night and noticed Vincent's car on his second sweep. The lights were on and it was running, so he checked it out. He thought Vincent was sleeping at first, then he saw the blood."

I nodded, thinking about the scenario and how it had gone down. The killer was either incredibly careless and lucky or he knew the garage had no cameras and he would be able to intercept Jerry Vincent there on a Monday night when the space was almost deserted.

"Okay, stay on it. What about Harry Potter?"

"Who?"

"The detective. Not Potter. I mean — "

"Bosch. Harry Bosch. I'm working on that, too. Supposedly he's one of the best. Retired a few years ago and the police chief himself recruited him back. Or so the story goes."

Cisco referred to some notes on a pad.

"Full name is Hieronymus Bosch. He has a total of thirty-three years on the job and you know what that means."

"No, what does it mean?"

"Well, under the LAPD's pension program you max out at thirty years, meaning that you are eligible for retirement with full pension and no matter how long you stay on the job, after thirty years your pension doesn't grow. So it makes no economic sense to stay."

"Unless you're a man on a mission."

Cisco nodded.

"Exactly. Anybody who stays past thirty isn't staying for the money or the job. It's more than a job."

"Wait a second," I said. "You said Hieronymus Bosch? Like the painter?"

The second question confused him.

"I don't know anything about any painter. But that's his name. Rhymes with 'anonymous,' I was told. Weird name, if you ask me."

"No weirder than Wojciechowski — if you ask me."

Cisco was about to defend his name and heritage when Lorna cut in.

"I thought you said you didn't know him, Mickey."

I looked over at her and shook my head.

"I never met him before today but the name…I know the name."

"You mean from the paintings?"

I didn't want to get into a discussion of past history so distant I couldn't be sure about it.

"Never mind," I said. "It's nothing and I've got to get going."

I stood up.

"Cisco, stay on the case and find out what you can about Bosch. I want to know how much I can trust the guy."

"You're not going to let him look at the files, are you?" Lorna asked.

"This wasn't a random crime. There's a killer out there who knew how to get to Jerry Vincent. I'll feel a lot better about things if our man with a mission can figure it out and bring the bad guy in."

I stepped around the desk and headed toward the door.

"I'll be in Judge Champagne's court. I'm taking a bunch of the active files with me to read while I'm waiting."

"I'll walk you out," Lorna said.

I saw her throw a look and nod at Cisco so that he would stay behind. We walked out to the reception area. I knew what Lorna was going to say but I let her say it.

"Mickey, are you sure you're ready for this?"

"Absolutely."

"This wasn't the plan. You were going to come back slowly, remember? Take a couple cases and build from there. Instead, you're taking on an entire practice."

"I'm not practicing."

"Look, be serious."

"I am. And I'm ready. Don't you see that this is better than the plan? The Elliot case not only brings in all that money but it's going to be like having a billboard on top of the CCB that says I'M BACK in big neon letters!"

"Yeah, that's great. And the Elliot case alone is going to put so much pressure on you that..."

She didn't finish but she didn't have to.

"Lorna, I'm done with all of that. I'm fine, I'm over it and I'm ready for this. I thought you'd be happy about this. We've got money coming in for the first time in a year."

"I don't care about that. I want to make sure you are okay."

"I'm more than okay. I'm excited. I feel like in one day I've suddenly got my mojo back. Don't drag me down. Okay?"

She stared at me and I stared back and finally a reluctant smile peeked through her stern expression.

"All right," she said. "Then, go get 'em."

"Don't worry. I will."

Eight

Despite the assurances I had given Lorna, thoughts about all the cases and all the setup work that needed to be done played in my mind as I walked down the hallway to the bridge that linked the office building with the garage. I had forgotten that I had parked on the fifth level and ended up walking up three ramps before I found the Lincoln. I popped the trunk and put the thick stack of files I was carrying into my bag.

The bag was a hybrid I had picked up at a store called Suitcase City while I was plotting my comeback. It was a backpack with straps I could put over my shoulders on the days I was strong. It also had a handle so I could carry it like a briefcase if I wanted. And it had two wheels and a telescoping handle so I could just roll it behind me on the days I was weak.

Lately, the strong days far outnumbered the weak and I probably could have gotten by with the traditional lawyer's leather briefcase. But I liked the bag and was going to keep using it. It had a logo on it — a mountain ridgeline with the words "Suitcase City" printed across it like the Hollywood sign. Above it, skylights swept the horizon, completing the dream image of desire and hope. I think that logo was the real reason

I liked the bag. Because I knew Suitcase City wasn't a store. It was a place. It was Los Angeles.

Los Angeles was the kind of place where everybody was from some-where else and nobody really dropped anchor. It was a transient place. People drawn by the dream, people running from the nightmare. Twelve million people and all of them ready to make a break for it if necessary. Figuratively, literally, metaphorically—any way you want to look at it—everybody in L.A. keeps a bag packed. Just in case.

As I closed the trunk, I was startled to see a man standing between my car and the one parked next to it. The open trunk lid had blocked my view of his approach. He was a stranger to me but I could tell he knew who I was. Bosch's warning about Vincent's killer shot through my mind and the fight-or-flight instinct gripped me.

"Mr. Haller, can I talk to you?"

"Who the hell are you, and what are you doing sneaking around people's cars?"

"I wasn't sneaking around. I saw you and cut between the other cars, that's all. I work for the *Times* and was wondering if I could talk to you about Jerry Vincent."

I shook my head and blew out my breath.

"You scared the shit out of me. Don't you know he got killed in this garage by somebody who came up to his car?"

"Look, I'm sorry. I was just—"

"Forget it. I don't know anything about the case and I have to get to court."

"But you're taking over his cases, aren't you?"

Signaling him out of the way, I moved to the door of my car.

"Who told you that?"

"Our court reporter got a copy of the order from Judge Holder. Why did Mr. Vincent pick you? Were you two good friends or something?"

I opened the door.

"Look, what's your name?"

"Jack McEvoy. I work the police beat."

"Good for you, Jack. But I can't talk about this right now. You want to give me a card, I'll call you when I can talk."

He made no move to give me a card or to indicate he'd understood what I said. He just asked another question.

"Has the judge put a gag order on you?"

"No, she hasn't put out a gag order. I can't talk to you because I don't know anything, okay? When I have something to say, I'll say it."

"Well, could you tell me why you are taking over Vincent's cases?"

"You already know the answer to that. I was appointed by the judge. I have to get to court now."

I ducked into the car but left the door open as I turned the key. McEvoy put his elbow on the roof and leaned in to continue to try to talk me into an interview.

"Look," I said, "I've got to go, so could you stand back so I can close my door and back this tank up?"

"I was hoping we could make a deal," he said quickly.

"Deal? What deal? What are you talking about?"

"You know, information. I've got the police department wired and you've got the courthouse wired. It would be a two-way street. You tell me what you're hearing and I'll tell you what I'm hearing. I have a feeling this is going to be a big case. I need any information I can get."

I turned and looked up at him for a moment.

"But won't the information you'd be giving me just end up in the paper the next day? I could just wait and read it."

"Not all of it will be in there. Some stuff you can't print, even if you know it's true."

He looked at me as though he were passing on a great piece of wisdom.

"I have a feeling you'll be hearing things before I do," I said.

"I'll take my chances. Deal?"

"You got a card?"

This time he took a card out of his pocket and handed it to me. I held it between my fingers and draped my hand over the steering wheel. I held the card up and looked at it again. I figured it wouldn't hurt to get a line on inside information on the case.

"Okay, deal."

I signaled him away again and pulled the door closed, then started the car. He was still there. I lowered the window.

"What?" I asked.

"Just remember, I don't want to see your name in the other papers or on the TV saying stuff I don't have."

"Don't worry. I know how it works."

"Good."

I dropped it into reverse but thought of something and kept my foot on the brake.

"Let me ask you a question. How tight are you with Bosch, the lead investigator on the case?"

"I know him, but nobody's really tight with him. Not even his own partner."

"What's his story?"

"I don't know. I never asked."

"Well, is he any good at it?"

"At clearing cases? Yes, he's very good. I think he's considered one of the best."

I nodded and thought about Bosch. The man on a mission.

"Watch your toes."

I backed the Lincoln out. McEvoy called out to me just as I put the car in drive.

"Hey, Haller, love the plate."

I waved a hand out the window as I drove down the ramp. I tried to remember which of my Lincolns I was driving and what the plate said. I have a fleet of three Town Cars left over from my days when I carried a full case load. But I had been using the cars so infrequently in the last year that I had put all three into a rotation to keep the engines in tune and the dust out of the pipes. Part of my comeback strategy, I guess. The cars were exact duplicates, except for the license plates, and I wasn't sure which one I was driving.

When I got down to the parking attendant's booth and handed in my stub, I saw a small video screen next to the cash register. It showed the view from a camera located a few feet behind my car. It was the camera Cisco had told me about, designed to pick up an angle on the rear bumper and license plate.

On the screen I could see my vanity plate.

IWALKEM

I smirked. I walk 'em, all right. I was heading to court to meet one of Jerry Vincent's clients for the first time. I was going to shake his hand and then walk him right into prison.

Nine

Judge Judith Champagne was on the bench and hearing motions when I walked into her courtroom with five minutes to spare. There were eight other lawyers cooling their heels, waiting their turn. I parked my roller bag against the rail and whispered to the court-room deputy, explaining that I was there to handle the sentencing of Edgar Reese for Jerry Vincent. He told me the judge's motions calendar was running long but Reese would be first out for his sentencing as soon as the motions were cleared. I asked if I could see Reese, and the deputy got up and led me through the steel door behind his desk to the court-side holding cell. There were three prisoners in the cell.

"Edgar Reese?" I said.

A small, powerfully built white man came over to the bars. I saw prison tattoos climbing up his neck and felt relieved. Reese was heading back to a place he already knew. I wasn't going to be holding the hand of a wide-eyed prison virgin. It would make things easier for me.

"My name's Michael Haller. I'm filling in for your attorney today."

I didn't think there was much point in explaining to this guy what had happened to Vincent. It would only make Reese ask me a bunch of questions I didn't have the time or knowledge to answer.

"Where's Jerry?" Reese asked.

"Couldn't make it. You ready to do this?"

"Like I got a choice?"

"Did Jerry go over the sentence when you pled out?"

"Yeah, he told me. Five years in state, out in three if I behave."

It was more like four but I wasn't going to mess with it.

"Okay, well, the judge is finishing some stuff up out there and then they'll bring you out. The prosecutor will read you a bunch of legalese, you answer yes that you understand it, and then the judge will enter the sentence. Fifteen minutes in and out."

"I don't care how long it takes. I ain't got nowhere to go."

I nodded and left him there. I tapped lightly on the metal door so the deputy — bailiffs in L.A. County are sheriffs' deputies — in the courtroom would hear it but hopefully not the judge. He let me out and I sat in the first row of the gallery. I opened up my case and pulled out most of the files, putting them down on the bench next to me.

The top file was the Edgar Reese file. I had already reviewed this one in preparation for the sentencing. Reese was one of Vincent's repeat clients. It was a garden-variety drug case. A seller who used his own product, Reese was set up on a buy-bust by a customer working as a confidential informant. According to the background information in the file, the CI zeroed in on Reese because he held a grudge against him. He had previously bought cocaine from Reese and found it had been hit too hard with baby laxative. This was a frequent mistake made by dealers who were also users. They cut the product too hard, thereby increasing the amount kept for their own personal use but diluting the charge delivered by the powder they sold. It was a bad business practice because it bred enemies. A user trying to work off a charge by cooperating as a CI is more inclined to set up a dealer he doesn't like than a dealer he does. This was the business lesson Edgar Reese would have to think about for the next five years in state prison.

I put the file back in my bag and looked at what was next on the stack. The file on top belonged to Patrick Henson, the painkiller case I had told Lorna I would be dropping. I leaned over to put the file back in the bag, when I suddenly sat back against the bench and held it on my lap. I flapped it against my thigh a couple times as I reconsidered things and then opened it.

Henson was a twenty-four-year-old surfer from Malibu by way of Florida. He was a professional but at the low end of the spectrum, with limited endorsements and winnings from the pro tour. In a competition on Maui, he'd wiped out in a wave that drove him down hard into the lava bottom of Pehei. It crimped his shoulder, and after surgery to scrape it out, the doctor prescribed oxycodone. Eighteen months later Henson was a full-blown addict, chasing pills to chase the pain. He lost his sponsors and was too weak to compete anymore. He finally hit bottom when he stole a diamond necklace from a home in Malibu to which he'd been invited by a female friend. According to the sheriff's report, the necklace belonged to his friend's mother and contained eight diamonds representing her three children and five grandchildren. It was listed on the report as worth $25,000 but Henson hocked it for $400 and went down to Mexico to buy two hundred tabs of oxy over the counter.

Henson was easy to connect to the caper. The diamond necklace was recovered from the pawnshop and the film from the security camera showed him pawning it. Because of the high value of the necklace, he was hit with a full deck, dealing in stolen property and grand theft, along with illegal drug possession. It also didn't help that the lady he stole the necklace from was married to a well-connected doctor who had contributed liberally to the reelection of several members of the county board of supervisors.

When Vincent took Henson on as a client, the surfer made the initial $5,000 advance payment in trade. Vincent took all twelve of his custom-made Trick Henson boards and sold them through his liquidator to collectors and on eBay. Henson was also placed on the $1,000-a-month payment plan but had never made a single payment because he had gone into rehab the day after being bailed out of jail by his mother, who lived back in Melbourne, Florida.

The file said Henson had successfully completed rehab and was working part-time at a surf camp for kids on the beach in Santa Monica. He was barely making enough to live on, let alone pay $1,000 a month to Vincent. His mother, meanwhile, had been tapped out by his bail and the cost of his stay in rehab.

The file was replete with motions to continue and other filings as delay tactics undertaken by Vincent while he waited for Henson to come across with more cash. This was standard practice. Get your money up front, especially when the case is probably a dog. The prosecutor had Henson on tape selling the stolen merchandise. It meant the case was worse than a dog. It was roadkill.

There was a phone number in the file for Henson. One thing every lawyer drilled into nonincarcerated clients was the need to maintain a method of contact. Those facing criminal charges and the likelihood of prison often had unstable home lives. They moved around, sometimes were completely homeless. But a lawyer had to be able to reach them at a moment's notice. The number was listed in the file as Henson's cell, and if it was still good, I could call him right now. The question was, did I want to?

I looked up at the bench. The judge was still in the middle of oral arguments on a bail motion. There were still three other lawyers waiting their turn at other motions and no sign of the prosecutor who was assigned to the Edgar Reese case. I got up and whispered to the deputy again.

"I'm going out into the hallway to make a call. I'll be close."

He nodded.

"If you're not back when it's time, I'll come grab you," he said. "Just make sure you turn that phone off before coming back in. The judge doesn't like cell phones."

He didn't have to tell me that. I already knew firsthand that the judge didn't like cell phones in her court. My lesson was learned when I was making an appearance before her and my phone started playing the *William Tell* Overture — my daughter's ringtone choice, not mine. The judge slapped me with a $100-dollar fine and had taken to referring to me ever since as the Lone Ranger. That last part I didn't mind so much. I sometimes felt like I was the Lone Ranger. I just rode in a black Lincoln Town Car instead of on a white horse.

I left my case and the other files on the bench in the gallery and walked out into the hallway with only the Henson file. I found a reasonably quiet spot in the crowded hallway and called the number. It was answered after two rings.

"This is Trick."

"Patrick Henson?"

"Yeah, who's this?"

"I'm your new lawyer. My name is Mi—"

"Whoa, wait a minute. What happened to my old lawyer? I gave that guy Vincent—"

"He's dead, Patrick. He passed away last night."

"Nooooo."

"Yes, Patrick. I'm sorry about that."

I waited a moment to see if he had anything else to say about it, then started in as perfunctorily as a bureaucrat.

"My name is Michael Haller and I'm taking over Jerry Vincent's cases. I've been reviewing your file here and I see you haven't made a single payment on the schedule Mr. Vincent put you on."

"Ah, man, this is the deal. I've been concentrating on getting right and staying right and I've got no fucking money. Okay? I already gave that guy Vincent all my boards. He counted it as five grand but I know he got more. A couple of those long boards were worth at least a grand apiece. He told me that he got enough to get started but all he's been doing is delaying things. I can't get back to shit until this thing is all over."

"Are you staying right, Patrick? Are you clean?"

"As a fucking whistle, man. Vincent told me it was the only way I'd have a shot at staying out of jail."

I looked up and down the hallway. It was crowded with lawyers and defendants and witnesses and the families of those victimized or accused. It was a football field long and everybody in it was hoping for one thing. A break. For the clouds to open and something to go their way just this one time.

"Jerry was right, Patrick. You have to stay clean."

"I'm doing it."

"You got a job?"

"Man, don't you guys see? No one's going to give a guy like me a job. Nobody's going to hire me. I'm waiting on this case and I might be in jail before it's all over. I mean, I teach water babies part-time on the beach but it don't pay me jack. I'm living out of my damn car, sleeping on a lifeguard stand at Hermosa Beach. This time two years ago? I was in a suite at the Four Seasons in Maui."

"Yeah, I know, life sucks. You still have a driver's license?"

"That's about all I got left."

I made a decision.

"Okay, you know where Jerry Vincent's office is? You ever been there?"

"Yeah, I delivered the boards there. And my fish."

"Your fish?"

"He took a sixty-pound tarpon I caught when I was a kid back in Florida. Said he was going to put it on the wall and pretend like he caught it or something."

"Yeah, well, your fish is still there. Anyway, be at the office at nine sharp tomorrow morning and I'll interview you for a job. If it goes right, then you'll start right away."

"Doing what?"

"Driving me. I'll pay you fifteen bucks an hour to drive and another fifteen toward your fees. How's that?"

There was a moment of silence before Henson responded in an accommodating voice.

"That's good, man. I can be there for that."

"Good. See you then. Just remember something, Patrick. You gotta stay clean. If you're not, I'll know. Believe me, I'll know."

"Don't worry, man. I will never go back to that shit. That shit fucked my life up for good."

"Okay, Patrick, I'll see you tomorrow."

"Hey, man, why are you doing this?"

I hesitated before answering.

"You know, I don't really know."

I closed the phone and made sure to turn it off. I went back into the courtroom wondering if I was doing something good or making the kind of mistake that would catch up and bite me on the ass.

It was perfect timing. The judge finished with the last motion as I came back in. I saw that a deputy district attorney named Don Pierce was sitting at the prosecution table, ready to go with the sentencing. He was an ex-navy guy who kept the crew cut going and was one of the regulars at cocktail hour at Four Green Fields. I quickly packed all the files back into my bag and wheeled it through the gate to the defense table.

"Well," the judge said, "I see the Lone Ranger rides again."

She said it with a smile and I smiled back at her.

"Yes, Your Honor. Nice to see you."

"I haven't seen you in quite a while, Mr. Haller."

Open court was not the place to tell her where I had been. I kept my responses short. I spread my hands as if presenting the new me.

"All I can say is, I'm back now, Judge."

"I'm glad to see that. Now, you are here in place of Mr. Vincent, is that correct?"

It was said in a routine tone. I could tell she did not know about Vincent's demise. I knew I could keep the secret and get through the sentencing with it. But then she would hear the story and wonder why I hadn't brought it up and told her. It was not a good way to keep a judge on your side.

"Unfortunately, Your Honor," I said, "Mr. Vincent passed away last night."

The judge's eyebrows arched in shock. She had been a longtime prosecutor before being a longtime judge. She was wired into the legal community and most likely knew Jerry Vincent well. I had just hit her with a major jolt.

"Oh, my, he was so young!" she exclaimed. "What happened?"

I shook my head like I didn't know.

"It wasn't a natural death, Your Honor. The police are investigating it and I don't really know a lot about it other than that he was found in his car last night at his office. Judge Holder called me in today and appointed me replacement counsel. That's why I am here for Mr. Reese."

The judge looked down and took a moment to get over her shock. I felt bad about being the messenger. I bent down and pulled the Edgar Reese file out of my bag.

"I'm very sorry to hear this," the judge finally said.

I nodded in agreement and waited.

"Very well," the judge said after another long moment. "Let's bring the defendant out."

Jerry Vincent garnered no further delay. Whether the judge had suspicions about Jerry or the life he led, she didn't say. But life would move on in the Criminal Courts Building. The wheels of justice would grind without him.

Ten

The message from Lorna Taylor was short and to the point. I got it the moment I turned my phone on after leaving the courtroom and seeing Edgar Reese get his five years. She told me she had just been in touch with Judge Holder's clerk about obtaining the court order the bank was requiring before putting Lorna's and my names on the Vincent bank accounts. The judge had agreed to draw up the order and I could just walk down the hallway to her chambers to pick it up.

The courtroom was once again dark but the judge's clerk was in her pod next to the bench. She still reminded me of my third-grade teacher.

"Mrs. Gill?" I said. "I'm supposed to pick up an order from the judge."

"Yes, I think she still has it with her in chambers. I'll go check."

"Any chance I could get in there and talk to her for a few minutes, too?"

"Well, she has someone with her at the moment but I will check."

She got up and went down the hallway located behind the clerk's station. At the end was the door to the judge's chambers and I watched her knock once before being summoned to enter. When she opened the door, I could see a man sitting in the same chair I had sat in a few hours earlier. I recognized him as Judge Holder's husband, a personal-injury attorney named Mitch Lester. I recognized him from the photograph on his ad. Back when he was doing criminal defense we had once shared the back of the Yellow Pages, my ad taking the top half and his the bottom. He hadn't worked criminal cases in a long time.

A few minutes later Mrs. Gill came out carrying the court order I needed. I thought this meant I wasn't going to get in to see the judge but Mrs. Gill told me I would be allowed back as soon as the judge finished up with her visitor.

It wasn't enough time to continue my review of the files in my roller bag, so I wandered the courtroom, looking around and thinking about what I was going to say to the judge. At the empty bailiff's desk, I looked down and scanned a calendar sheet from the week before. I knew the names of several of the attorneys who were listed and had been scheduled for emergency hearings and motions. One of them was Jerry Vincent on behalf of Walter Elliot. It had probably been one of Jerry's last appearances in court.

After three minutes I heard a bell tone at the clerk's station and Mrs. Gill said I was free to go back to the judge's chambers.

When I knocked on the door it was Mitch Lester who opened it. He smiled and bid me entrance. We shook hands and he remarked that he had just heard about Jerry Vincent.

"It's a scary world out there," he said.

"It can be," I said.

"If you need any help with anything, let me know."

He left the office and I took his seat in front of the judge's desk.

"What can I do for you, Mr. Haller? You got the order for the bank?"

"Yes, I got the order, Your Honor. Thank you for that. I wanted to update you a little bit and ask a question about something."

She took off a pair of reading glasses and put them down on her blotter.

"Please go ahead, then."

"Well, on the update. Things are going a bit slowly because we started without a calendar. Both Jerry Vincent's laptop computer and his hard-copy calendar were stolen after he was killed. We had to build a new calendar after pulling the active files. We think we have that under control and, in fact, I just came from a sentencing in Judge Champagne's in regard to one of the cases. So we haven't missed anything."

The judge seemed unimpressed by the efforts made by my staff and me.

"How many active cases are we talking about?" she asked.

"Uh, it looks like there are thirty-one active cases — well, thirty now that I handled that sentencing. That case is done."

"Then, I would say you inherited quite a thriving practice. What is the problem?"

"I'm not sure there is a problem, Judge. So far I've had a conversation with only one of the active clients and it looks like I will be continuing as his lawyer."

"Was that Walter Elliot?"

"Uh, no, I have not talked to him yet. I plan to try to do that later today. The person I talked to was involved in something a little less serious. A felony theft, actually."

"Okay."

She was growing impatient so I moved to the point of the meeting.

"What I wanted to ask about was the police. You were right this morning when you warned me about guarding against police intrusion. When I got over to the office after leaving here, I found a couple of detectives going through the files. Jerry's receptionist was there but she hadn't tried to stop them."

The judge's face grew hard.

"Well, I hope you did. Those officers should have known better than to start going through files willy-nilly."

"Yes, Your Honor, they backed off once I got there and objected.

In fact, I threatened to make a complaint to you. That's when they backed off."

She nodded, her face showing pride in the power the mention of her name had.

"Then, why are you here?"

"Well, I'm wondering now whether I should let them back in."

"I don't understand you, Mr. Haller. Let the police back in?"

"The detective in charge of the investigation made a good point. He said the evidence suggests that Jerry Vincent knew his killer and probably even allowed him to get close enough to, you know, shoot him. He said that makes it a good bet that it was one of his own clients. So they were going through the files looking for potential suspects when I walked in on them."

The judge waved one of her hands in a gesture of dismissal.

"Of course they were. And they were trampling on those clients' rights as they were doing it."

"They were in the file room and were looking through old cases. Closed cases."

"Doesn't matter. Open or closed, it still constitutes a violation of the attorney-client privilege."

"I understand that, Judge. But after they were gone, I saw they had left behind a stack of files on the table. These were the files they were either going to take or wanted to look more closely at. I looked them over and there were threats in those files."

"Threats against Mr. Vincent?"

"Yes. They were cases in which his clients weren't happy about the outcome, whether it was the verdict or the disposition or the terms of imprisonment. There were threats, and in each of the cases, he took the threats seriously enough to make a detailed record of exactly what was said and who said it. That was what the detectives were pulling together."

The judge leaned back and clasped her hands, her elbows on the arms of her leather chair. She thought about the situation I had described and then brought her eyes to mine.

"You believe we are inhibiting the investigation by not allowing the police to do their job."

I nodded.

"I was wondering if there was a way to sort of serve both sides," I said. "Limit the harm to the clients but let the police follow the investigation wherever it goes."

The judge considered this in silence again, then sighed.

"I wish my husband had stayed," she finally said. "I value his opinion greatly."

"Well, I had an idea."

"Of course you did. What is it?"

"I was thinking that I could vet the files myself and draw up a list of the people who threatened Jerry. Then I could pass it on to Detective Bosch and give him some of the details of the threats as well. This way, he would have what he needs but he wouldn't have the files themselves. He's happy, I'm happy."

"Bosch is the lead detective?"

"Yes, Harry Bosch. He's with Robbery-Homicide. I can't remember his partner's name."

"You have to understand, Mr. Haller, that even if you just give this man Bosch the names, you are still breaching client confidentiality. You could be disbarred for this."

"Well, I was thinking about that and I believe there's a way out. One of the mechanisms of relief from the client confidentiality bond is in the case of threat to safety. If Jerry Vincent knew a client was coming to kill him last night, he could have called the police and given that client's name to them. There would've been no breach in that."

"Yes, but what you are considering here is completely different."

"It's different, Judge, but not completely. I've been directly told by the lead detective on the case that it is highly likely that the identity of

74

Jerry Vincent's killer is contained in Jerry's own files. Those files are now mine. So that information constitutes a threat to me. When I go out and start meeting these clients, I could shake hands with the killer and not even know it. You add that up any way and I feel I am in some jeopardy here, Judge, and that qualifies for relief."

She nodded her head again and put her glasses back on. She reached over and picked up a glass of water that had been hidden from my view by her desktop computer.

After drinking deeply from the glass she spoke.

"All right, Mr. Haller. I believe that if you vet the files as you have suggested, then you will be acting in an appropriate and acceptable manner. I would like you to file a motion with this court that explains your actions and the feeling of threat you are under. I will sign it and seal it and with any good luck it will be something that never sees the light of day."

"Thank you, Your Honor."

"Anything else?"

"I think that is it."

"Then, have a good day."

"Yes, Your Honor. Thank you."

I got up and headed toward the door but then remembered something and turned back to stand in front of the judge's desk.

"Judge? I forgot something. I saw your calendar from last week out there and noticed that Jerry Vincent came in on the Elliot matter. I haven't thoroughly reviewed the case file yet, but do you mind my asking what the hearing was about?"

The judge had to think for a moment to recall the hearing.

"It was an emergency motion. Mr. Vincent came in because Judge Stanton had revoked bail and ordered Mr. Elliot remanded to custody. I stayed the revocation."

"Why was it revoked?"

"Mr. Elliot had traveled to a film festival in New York without getting permission. It was one of the qualifiers of bail. When Mr. Golantz, the prosecutor, saw a picture of Elliot at the festival in *People* magazine, he asked Judge Stanton to revoke bail. He obviously wasn't happy that bail had been allowed in the first place. Judge Stanton revoked and then Mr. Vincent came to me for an emergency stay of his client's arrest and incarceration. I decided to give Mr. Elliot a second chance and to modify his freedom by making him wear an ankle monitor. But I can assure you that Mr. Elliot will not receive a third chance. Keep that in mind if you should retain him as a client."

"I understand, Judge. Thank you."

I nodded and left the chambers, thanking Mrs. Gill as I walked out through the courtroom.

Harry Bosch's card was still in my pocket. I dug it out while I was going down in the elevator. I had parked in a pay lot by the Kyoto Grand Hotel and had a three-block walk that would take me right by Parker Center. I called Bosch's cell phone as I headed to the courthouse exit.

"This is Bosch."

"It's Mickey Haller."

There was a hesitation. I thought that maybe he didn't recognize my name.

"What can I do for you?" he finally asked.

"How's the investigation going?"

"It's going, but nothing I can talk to you about."

"Then I'll just get to the point. Are you in Parker Center right now?"

"That's right. Why?"

"I'm heading over from the courthouse. Meet me out front by the memorial."

"Look, Haller, I'm busy. Can you just tell me what this is about?"

"Not on the phone, but I think it will be worth your while. If you're not there when I go by, then I'll know you've passed on the opportunity and I won't bother you with it again."

I closed the phone before he could respond. It took me five minutes to get over to Parker Center by foot. The place was in its last years of life, its replacement being built a block over on Spring Street. I saw Bosch standing next to the fountain that was part of the memorial for officers killed in the line of duty. I saw thin white wires leading from his ears to his jacket pocket. I walked up and didn't bother with a handshake or any other greeting. He pulled the earbuds out and shoved them into his pocket.

"Shutting the world out, Detective?"

"Helps me concentrate. Is there a purpose to this meeting?"

"After you left the office today I looked at the files you had stacked on the table. In the file room."

"And?"

"And I understand what you are trying to do. I want to help you but I want you to understand my position."

"I understand you, Counselor. You have to protect those files and the possible killer hiding in them because those are the rules."

I shook my head. This guy didn't want to make it easy for me to help him.

"I'll tell you what, Detective Bosch. Come back by the office at eight o'clock tomorrow morning and I will give you what I can."

I think the offer surprised him. He had no response.

"You'll be there?" I asked.

"What's the catch?" he asked right back.

"No catch. Just don't be late. I've got an interview at nine, and after that I'll probably be on the road for client conferences."

"I'll be there at eight."

"Okay, then."

I was ready to walk away but it looked like he wasn't.

"What is it?"

"I was going to ask you something."

"What?"

"Did Vincent have any federal cases?"

I thought for a moment, going over what I knew of the files. I shook my head.

"We're still reviewing everything but I don't think so. He was like me, liked to stay in state court. It's a numbers game. More cases, more fuck-ups, more holes to slip through. The feds kind of like to stack the deck. They don't like to lose."

I thought he might take the slight personally. But he had moved past it and was putting something in place. He nodded.

"Okay."

"That's it? That's all you wanted to ask?"

"That's it."

I waited for further explanation but none came.

"Okay, Detective."

I clumsily put out my hand. He shook it and appeared to feel just as awkward about it. I decided to ask a question I had been holding back on.

"Hey, there was something I was meaning to ask you, too."

"What's that?"

"It doesn't say it on your card but I heard that your full name is Hieronymus Bosch. Is that true?"

"What about it?"

"I was just wondering, where'd you get a name like that?"

"My mother gave it to me."

"Your mother? Well, what did your father think about it?"

"I never asked him. I have to get back to the investigation now, Counselor. Is there anything else?"

"No, that was it. I was just curious. I'll see you tomorrow at eight."

"I'll be there."

I left him standing there at the memorial and walked away. I headed down the block, thinking the whole time about why he had asked if Jerry Vincent had had any federal cases. When I turned left at the corner, I glanced back and saw Bosch still standing by the fountain. He was watching me. He didn't look away, but I did, and I kept walking.

Eleven

Cisco and Lorna were still at work in Jerry Vincent's office when I got back. I handed the court order for the bank over to Lorna and told her about the two early appointments I had set for the next day.

"I thought you put Patrick Henson into the dog pile," Lorna said.

"I did. But now I moved him back."

She put her eyebrows together the way she did whenever I confounded her — which was a lot. I didn't want to explain things. Moving on, I asked if anything new had developed while I had gone to court.

"A couple things," Lorna said. "First of all, the check from Walter Elliot cleared. If he heard about Jerry it's too late to stop payment."

"Good."

"It gets better. I found the contracts file and took a look at Jerry's deal with Elliot. That hundred thousand deposited Friday for trial was only a partial payment."

She was right. It was getting better.

"How much?" I asked.

"According to the deal," she said, "Vincent took two fifty up front. That was five months ago and it looks like that is all gone. But he was going to get another two fifty for the trial. Nonrefundable. The hundred was only the first part of that. The rest is due on the first day of testimony."

I nodded with satisfaction. Vincent had made a great deal. I had never had a case with that kind of money involved. But I wondered how he had blown through the first $250,000 so quickly. Lorna would have to study the ins and outs of the accounts to get that answer.

"Okay, all of that's real good — if we get Elliot. Otherwise, it doesn't matter. What else do we have?"

Lorna looked disappointed that I didn't want to linger over the money and celebrate her discovery. She had lost sight of the fact that I still had to nail Elliot down. Technically, he was a free agent. I would get the first shot at him but I still had to secure him as a client before I could consider what it would be like to get a $250,000 trial fee.

Lorna answered my question in a monotone.

"We had a series of visitors while you were in court."

"Who?"

"First, one of the investigators Jerry used came by after hearing the news. He took one look at Cisco and almost got into it with him. Then he got smart and backed down."

"Who was it?"

"Bruce Carlin. Jerry hired him to work the Elliot case."

I nodded. Bruce Carlin was a former LAPD bull who had crossed to the dark side and did defense work now. A lot of attorneys used him because of his insider's knowledge of how things worked in the cop shop. I had used him on a case once and thought he was living off an undeserved reputation. I never hired him again.

"Call him back," I said. "Set up a time for him to come back in."

"Why, Mick? You've got Cisco."

"I know I've got Cisco but Carlin was doing work on Elliot and I doubt it's all in the files. You know how it is. If you keep it out of the file, you keep it out of discovery. So bring him in. Cisco can sit down with him and find out what he's got. Pay him for his time—whatever his hourly rate is—and then cut him loose when he's no longer useful. What else? Who else came in?"

"A real loser's parade. Carney Andrews waltzed in, thinking she was going to just pick the Elliot case up off the pile and waltz back out with it. I sent her away empty-handed. I then looked through the P and Os in the operating account and saw she was hired five months ago as associate counsel on Elliot. A month later she was dropped."

I nodded and understood. Vincent had been judge shopping for Elliot. Carney Andrews was an untalented attorney and weasel, but she was married to a superior court judge named Bryce Andrews. He had spent twenty-five years as a prosecutor before being appointed to the bench. In the view of most criminal defense attorneys who worked in the CCB, he had never left the DA's office. He was believed to be one of the toughest judges in the building, one who at times acted in concert with, if not as a direct arm of, the prosecutor's office. This created a cottage industry in which his wife made a very comfortable living by being hired as co-counsel on cases in her husband's court, thereby creating a conflict of interest that would require the reassignment of the cases to other, hopefully more lenient, judges.

It worked like a charm and the best part was that Carney Andrews never really had to practice law. She just had to sign on to a case, make an appearance as co-counsel in court and then wait until it was reassigned from her husband's calendar. She could then collect a substantial fee and move on to the next case.

I didn't have to even look into the Elliot file to see what had happened. I knew. Case assignments were generated by random selection in the chief judge's office. The Elliot case had obviously been initially assigned to Bryce Andrews's court and Vincent didn't like his chances there. For starters, Andrews would never allow bail on a double-murder case, let alone the hard line he would take against the defendant when it got to trial. So Vincent hired the judge's wife as co-counsel and the problem went away. The case was then randomly reassigned to Judge James P. Stanton, whose reputation was completely the opposite of Andrews's. The bottom line was that whatever Vincent had paid Carney, it had been worth it.

"Did you check?" I asked Lorna. "How much did he pay her?"

"She took ten percent of the initial advance."

I whistled. Twenty-five thousand dollars for nothing. That at least explained where some of the first quarter million went.

"Nice work if you can get it," I said.

"But then you'd have to sleep at night with Bryce Andrews," Lorna said. "I'm not sure that would be worth it."

Cisco laughed. I didn't but Lorna did have a point. Bryce Andrews had at least twenty years and almost two hundred pounds on his wife. It wasn't a pretty picture.

"That it on the visitors?" I asked.

"No," Lorna said. "We also had a couple of clients drop by to ask for their files after they heard on the radio about Jerry's death."

"And?"

"We stalled them. I told them that only you could turn over a file and that you would get back to them within twenty-four hours. It looked like they wanted to argue about it but with Cisco here they decided it would be better to wait."

She smiled at Cisco and the big man bowed as if to say "at your service."

Lorna handed me a slip of paper.

"Those are the names. There's contact info, too."

I looked at the names. One was in the dog pile, so I would be happily turning the file over. The other was a public indecency case that I thought I could do something with. The woman was charged when a sheriff's deputy ordered her out of the water on a Malibu beach. She was swimming nude but this was not apparent until the deputy ordered her out of the water. Because the charge was a misdemeanor, the deputy had to witness the crime to make an arrest. But by ordering her out of the water, he created the crime he arrested her for. That wouldn't fly in court. It was a case I knew I could get dismissed.

"I'll go see these two tonight," I said. "In fact, I want to hit the road with all of the cases soon. Starting with a stop at Archway Pictures. I'm going to take Cisco with me, and Lorna, I want you to gather up whatever you need from here and head on home. I don't want you being here by yourself."

She nodded but then said, "Are you sure Cisco should go with you?"

I was surprised she had asked the question in front of him. She was referring to his size and appearance — the tattoos, the earring, the boots, leather vest and so on — the overall menace his appearance projected. Her concern was that he might scare away more clients than he would help lock down.

"Yeah," I said. "He should go. When I want to be subtle he can just wait in the car. Besides I want him driving so I can look at the files."

I looked at Cisco. He nodded and seemed fine with the arrangement. He might look foolish in his bike vest behind the wheel of a Lincoln but he wasn't complaining yet.

"Speaking of the files," I said. "We have nothing in federal court, right?"

Lorna shook her head.

"Not that I know of."

I nodded. It confirmed what I had indicated to Bosch and made me more curious about why he had asked about federal cases. I was beginning to get an idea about it and planned to bring it up when I saw him the next morning.

"Okay," I said. "I guess it's time for me to be a Lincoln lawyer again. Let's hit the road."

Twelve

In the last decade Archway Pictures had grown from a movie industry fringe dweller to a major force. This was because of the one thing that had always ruled Hollywood. Money. As the cost of producing films grew exponentially at the same time the industry focused on the most expensive kinds of films to make, the major studios began increasingly to look for partners to share the cost and risk.

This is where Walter Elliot and Archway Pictures came in. Archway was previously an overrun lot. It was on Melrose Avenue just a few blocks from the behemoth that was Paramount Studios. Archway was built to act as the remora fish does with the great white shark. It would hover near the mouth of the bigger fish and take whatever torn scraps somehow missed being sucked into the giant maw. Archway offered production facilities and soundstages for rent when everything was booked at the big studios. It leased office space to would-be and has-been producers who weren't up to the standards of or didn't have the same deals as on-lot producers. It nurtured independent films, the movies that were less expensive to make but more risky and supposedly less likely to be hits than their studio-bred counterparts.

Walter Elliot and Archway Pictures limped along in this fashion for a decade, until luck and lightning struck twice. In a space of only three years Elliot hit gold with two of the independent films he'd backed by providing soundstages, equipment and production facilities in exchange for a piece of the action. The films went on to defy Hollywood expectations and became huge hits — critically and financially. One even took home the Academy Award as best picture. Walter and his stepchild studio suddenly basked in the glow of huge success. More than one hundred million people heard Walter being personally thanked on the Academy Awards broadcast. And, more important, Archway's worldwide cut from the two films was more than a hundred million dollars apiece.

Walter did a wise thing with that newfound money. He fed it to the sharks, cofinancing a number of productions in which the big studios were looking for risk partners. There were some misses, of course. The business, after all, was Hollywood. But there were enough hits to keep the nest egg growing. Over the next decade Walter Elliot doubled and then tripled his stake and along the way became a player who made regular appearances on the power 100 lists in industry minds and magazines. Elliot had taken Archway from being an address associated with Hollywood pariahs to a place where there was a three-year wait for a windowless office.

All the while, Elliot's personal wealth grew commensurately. Though he had come west twenty-five years before as the rich scion of a Florida phosphate family, that money was nothing like the riches provided by Hollywood. Like many on those power 100 lists, Elliot traded in his wife for a newer model and together they started accumulating houses. First in the canyons, then down in the Beverly Hills flats and then on out to Malibu and up to Santa Barbara. According to the information in the files I had, Walter Elliot and his wife owned seven different homes and two ranches in or around Los Angeles. Never mind how often they used each place. Real estate was a way of keeping score in Hollywood.

All those properties and top 100 lists came in handy when

Elliot was charged with double murder. The studio boss flexed his political and financial muscles and pulled off something rarely accomplished in a murder case. He got bail. With the prosecution objecting all the way, bail was set at $20 million and Elliot quickly ponied it up in real estate. He'd been out of jail and awaiting trial ever since—his brief flirtation with bail revocation the week before notwithstanding.

One of the properties Elliot put up as collateral for bail was the house where the murders took place. It was a waterfront weekender on a secluded cove. On the bail escrow its value was listed at $6 million. It was there that thirty-nine-year-old Mitzi Elliot was murdered along with her lover in a twelve-hundred-square-foot bedroom with a glass wall that looked out on the big blue Pacific.

The discovery file was replete with forensic reports and color copies of the crime scene photographs. The death room was completely white—walls, carpet, furniture and bedding. Two naked bodies were sprawled on the bed and floor. Mitzi Elliot and Johan Rilz. The scene was red on white. Two large bullet holes in the man's chest. Two in the woman's chest and one in her forehead. He by the bedroom door. She on the bed. Red on white. It was not a clean scene. The wounds were large. Though the murder weapon was missing, an accompanying report said that slugs had been identified through ballistic markings as coming from a Smith & Wesson model 29, a .44 magnum revolver. Fired at close quarters, it was overkill.

Walter Elliot had been suspicious about his wife. She had announced her intentions to divorce him and he believed there was another man involved. He told the sheriff's homicide investigators that he had gone to the Malibu beach house because his wife had told him she was going to meet with the interior designer. Elliot thought that was a lie and timed his approach so that he would be able to confront her with a paramour. He loved her and wanted her back. He was willing to fight for her. He had gone to confront, he repeated, not to kill. He didn't own a .44 magnum, he told them. He didn't own any guns.

According to the statement he gave investigators, when Elliot got to Malibu he found his wife and her lover naked and already dead. It turned out that the lover was in fact the interior designer, Johan Rilz, a German national Elliot had always thought was gay.

Elliot left the house and got back in his car. He started to drive away but then thought better of it. He decided to do the right thing. He turned around and pulled back into the driveway. He called 911 and waited out front for the deputies to arrive.

The chronology and details of how the investigation proceeded from that point would be important in mounting a defense. According to the reports in the file, Elliot gave investigators an initial account of his discovery of the two bodies. He was then transported by two detectives to the Malibu substation so he would be out of the way while the investigation of the crime scene proceeded. He was not under arrest at this time. He was placed in an unlocked interview room where he waited three long hours for the two lead detectives to finally clear the crime scene and come to the substation. A videotaped interview was then conducted but, according to the transcript I reviewed, quickly crossed the line into interrogation. At this point Elliot was finally advised of his rights and asked if he wanted to continue to answer questions. Elliot wisely chose to stop talking and to ask for an attorney. It was a decision made better late than never but Elliot would have been better off if he had never said word one to the investigators. He should've just taken the nickel and kept his mouth shut.

While investigators had been working the crime scene and Elliot was cooling his heels in the substation interview room, a homicide investigator working in the sheriff's headquarters in Whittier drew up several search warrants that were faxed to a superior court judge and signed. These allowed investigators to search throughout the beach house and Elliot's car and permitted them to conduct a gunshot residue test on Elliot's hands and clothes to determine if there were gas nitrates and microscopic particles of burned gunpowder on them. After Elliot refused further cooperation, his hands were bagged in plastic at the sub-station and he was transported to Sheriff's Headquarters, where a crim-inalist conducted the GSR test in the crime lab. This consisted of wiping chemically treated disks on Elliot's hands and clothing. When the disks were processed by a lab technician, those that had been wiped on his hands and sleeves tested positive for high levels of gunshot residue.

At that point Elliot was formally arrested on suspicion of murder. With his one phone call he contacted his personal lawyer, who in turn called in Jerry Vincent, whom he had attended law school with. Elliot was eventually transported to the county jail and booked on two counts of murder. The sheriff's investigators then called the department's media office and suggested that a press conference should be set up. They had just bagged a big one.

I closed the file as Cisco stopped the Lincoln in front of Archway Studios. There were a number of picketers walking the sidewalk. They were writers on strike, holding up red-and-white signs that said WE WANT A FAIR SHARE! and WRITERS UNITED! Some signs showed a fist holding a pen. Another said YOUR FAVORITE LINE? A WRITER WROTE IT. Anchored on the sidewalk was a large blow-up figure of a pig smoking a cigar with the word PRODUCER branded on its rear end. The pig and most of the signs were well-worn clichés and I would have thought that with the protesters being writers, they would have come up with some-thing better. But maybe that kind of creativity happened only when they were getting paid.

I had ridden in the backseat for the sake of appearances on this first stop. I was hoping that Elliot might catch a glimpse of me through his office window and take me for an attorney of great means and skill. But the writers saw a Lincoln with a rider in the back and thought I was a producer. As we turned into the studio, they descended on the car with their signs and started chanting, "Greedy Bastard! Greedy Bastard!" Cisco gunned it and plowed through, a few of the hapless scribes dodg-ing the fenders.

"Careful!" I barked. "All I need is to run over an out-of-work writer."

"Don't worry," Cisco replied calmly. "They always scatter."

"Not this time."

When he got up to the guardhouse, Cisco pulled forward enough that my window was even with the door. I checked to make sure none of the writers had followed us onto studio property and then lowered the glass so I could speak to the man who stepped out. His uniform was a beige color with a dark brown tie and matching epaulets. It looked ridiculous.

"Can I help you?"

"I'm Walter Elliot's attorney. I don't have an appointment but I need to see him right away."

"Can I see your driver's license?"

I got it out and handed it through the window.

"I am handling this for Jerry Vincent. That's the name Mr. Elliot's secretary will recognize."

The guard went into the booth and slid the door closed. I didn't know if this was to keep the air-conditioning from escaping or to prevent me from hearing what was said when he picked up the phone. Whatever the reason, he soon slid the door back open and extended the phone to me, his hand covering the mouthpiece.

"Mrs. Albrecht is Mr. Elliot's executive assistant. She wants to speak to you."

I took the phone.

"Hello?"

"Mr. Haller, is it? What is this all about? Mr. Elliot has dealt exclusively with Mr. Vincent on this matter and there is no appointment on his calendar."

This matter. It was a strange way of referring to double charges of murder.

"Mrs. Albrecht, I'd rather not talk about this at the front gate. As you can imagine, it's quite a delicate 'matter,' to use your word. Can I come to the office and see Mr. Elliot?"

I turned in my seat and looked out the back window. There were two cars in the guardhouse queue behind my Lincoln. They must not have been producers. The writers had let them through unmolested.

"I'm afraid that's not good enough, Mr. Haller. Can I place you on hold while I call Mr. Vincent?"

"You won't get through to him."

"He'll take a call from Mr. Elliot, I am sure."

"I am sure he won't, Mrs. Albrecht. Jerry Vincent's dead. That's why I'm here."

I looked at Cisco's reflection in the rearview mirror and shrugged as though to say I had no choice but to hit her with the news. The plan had been to finesse my way through the arch and then be the one to personally tell Elliot his lawyer was dead.

"Excuse me, Mr. Haller. Did you say Mr. Vincent is...dead?"

"That's what I said. And I'm his court-appointed replacement. Can I come in now?"

"Yes, of course."

I handed the phone back and soon the gate opened.

Thirteen

We were assigned to a prime parking space in the executive lot. I told Cisco to wait in the car and went in alone, carrying the two thick files Vincent had put together on the case. One contained discovery materials turned over so far by the prosecution, including the important investigative documents and interview transcripts, and the other contained documents and other work product generated by Vincent during the five months he had handled the case. Between the two files I was able to get a good handle on what the prosecution had and didn't have, and the direction in which the prosecutor wanted to take the trial. There was still work to be done and pieces were missing from the defense's case and strategy. Perhaps those pieces had been carried in Jerry Vincent's head, or in his laptop or on the legal pad in his portfolio, but unless the cops arrested a suspect and recovered the stolen property, whatever was there would be of no help to me.

I followed a sidewalk across a beautifully manicured lawn on the way to Elliot's office. My plan for the meeting was threefold. The first order of business was to secure Elliot as a client. That done, I would ask his approval in delaying the trial to give me time to get up to speed and prepare for it. The last part of the plan would be to see if Elliot had any of the pieces missing from the defense case. Parts two and three obviously didn't matter if I was unsuccessful with part one.

Walter Elliot's office was in Bungalow One on the far reaches of the Archway lot. "Bungalows" sounded small but they were big in Hollywood. A sign of status. It was like having your own private home on the lot. And as in any private home, activities inside could be kept secret.

A Spanish-tiled entranceway led to a step-down living room with a fireplace blowing gas flames on one wall and a mahogany wood bar set up in an opposite corner. I stepped into the middle of the room and looked around and waited. I looked at the painting over the fireplace. It depicted an armored knight on a white steed. The knight had reached up and flipped open the visor on his helmet and his eyes stared out intently. I took a few steps further into the room and realized the eyes had been painted so that they stared at the viewer of the painting from any angle in the room. They followed me.

"Mr. Haller?"

I turned as I recognized the voice from the guardhouse phone. Elliot's gatekeeper, Mrs. Albrecht, had stepped into the room from some unseen entrance. Elegance was the word that came to mind. She was an aging beauty who appeared to take the process in stride. Gray streaked through her un-dyed hair and tiny wrinkles were working their way toward her eyes and mouth, seemingly unchecked by injection or incision. Mrs. Albrecht looked like a woman who liked her own skin. In my experience, this was a rare thing in Hollywood.

"Mr. Elliot will see you now."

I followed her around a corner and down a short hallway to a reception office. She passed an empty desk — hers, I assumed — and pushed open a large door to Walter Elliot's office.

Elliot was an overly tanned man with more gray hair sprouting from his open shirt collar than from the top of his head. He sat behind a large glass worktable. No drawers beneath it and no computer on top of it, though paperwork and scripts were spread across it. It didn't matter that he was facing two counts of murder. He was staying busy. He was working and running Archway the way he always did. Maybe it was on the advice of some Hollywood self-help guru but it wasn't an unusual behavior or philosophy for the accused. Act like you are innocent and you will be perceived as innocent. Finally, you will become innocent.

There was a sitting area to the right but he chose to remain behind the worktable. He had dark, piercing eyes that seemed familiar and then I realized I had just been looking at them — the knight on the steed out in the living room was Elliot.

"Mr. Elliot, this is Mr. Haller," Mrs. Albrecht said.

She signaled me to the chair across the table from Elliot. After I sat down Elliot made a dismissive gesture without looking at Mrs. Albrecht and she left the room without another word. Over the years I had represented and been in the company of a couple dozen killers. The one rule is that there are no rules. They come in all sizes and shapes, rich and poor, humble and arrogant, regretful and cold to the bone. The percentages told me that it was most likely Elliot was a killer. That he had calmly dispatched his wife and her lover and arrogantly thought he could and would get away with it. But there was nothing about him on first meeting that told me one way or the other for sure. And that's the way it always was.

"What happened to my lawyer?" he asked.

"Well, for a detailed explanation I would have to refer you to the police. The shorthand is that somebody killed him last night in his car."

"And where does that leave me? I'm on trial for my life in a week!"

That was a slight exaggeration. Jury selection was scheduled in nine days and the DA's office had not announced that it would seek the death penalty. But it didn't hurt that he was thinking in such terms.

"That's why I'm here, Mr. Elliot. At the moment you are left with me."

"And who are you? I've never heard of you."

"You haven't heard of me because I make it a practice not to be heard of. Celebrity lawyers bring too much attention to their clients. They feed their own celebrity by offering up their clients. I don't operate that way."

He pursed his lips and nodded. I could tell I had just scored a point.

"And you're taking over Vincent's practice?" he asked.

"Let me explain it, Mr. Elliot. Jerry Vincent had a one-man shop. Just like I do. On occasion one of us would need help with a case or need another attorney to fill in here and there. We filled that role for each other. If you look at the contract of representation you signed with him, you will find my name in a paragraph with language that allowed Jerry to discuss your case with me and to include me within the bonds of the attorney-client relationship. In other words, Jerry trusted me with his cases. And now that he is gone, I am prepared to carry on in his stead. Earlier today the chief judge of the superior court issued an order placing me in custody of Jerry's cases. Of course, you ultimately get to choose who represents you at trial. I am very familiar with your case and prepared to continue your legal representation without so much as a hiccup. But, as I said, you must make the choice. I'm only here to tell you your options."

Elliot shook his head.

"I really can't believe this. We were set for trial next week and I'm not pushing it back. I've been waiting five months to clear my name! Do you have any idea what it is like for an innocent man to have to wait and wait and wait for justice? To read all the innuendo and bullshit in the media? To have a prosecutor with his nose up my ass, waiting for me to make the move that gets my bail pulled? Look at this!"

He stretched out a leg and pulled his left pant leg up to reveal the GPS monitor Judge Holder had ordered him to wear.

"I want this over!"

I nodded in a consoling manner and knew that if I told him I wanted to delay his case, I would be looking at a quick dismissal from consideration. I decided I would bring that up in a strategy session after I closed the deal — if I closed the deal.

"I've dealt with many clients wrongly accused," I lied. "The wait for justice can be almost intolerable. But it also makes the vindication all the more meaningful."

Elliot didn't respond and I didn't let the silence last long.

"I spent most of the afternoon reviewing the files and evidence in your case. I'm confident you won't have to delay the trial, Mr. Elliot. I would be more than prepared to proceed. Another attorney, maybe not. But I would be ready."

There it was, my best pitch to him, most of it lies and exaggerations. But I didn't stop there.

"I've studied the trial strategy Mr. Vincent outlined. I wouldn't change it but I believe I can improve on it. And I'd be ready to go next week if need be. I think a delay can always be useful, but it won't be necessary."

Elliot nodded and rubbed a finger across his mouth.

"I would have to think about this," he said. "I need to talk to some people and have you checked out. Just like I had Vincent checked out before I went with him."

I decided to gamble and to try to force Elliot into a quick decision. I didn't want him checking me out and possibly discovering I had disappeared for a year. That would raise too many questions.

"It's a good idea," I said. "Take your time but don't take too much time. The longer you wait to decide, the greater the chance that the judge will find it necessary to push the trial back. I know you don't want that, but in the absence of Mr. Vincent or any attorney of record, the judge is probably already getting nervous and considering it. If you choose me, I will try to get before the judge as soon as possible and tell him we're still good to go."

I stood up and reached into my coat pocket for a card. I put it down on the glass.

"Those are all my numbers. Call anytime."

I hoped he would tell me to sit back down and we'd start planning for trial. But Elliot just reached over and picked up the card. He seemed to be studying it when I left him. Before I reached the door to the office it opened from the outside and Mrs. Albrecht stood there. She smiled warmly.

"I'm sure we will be in touch," she said.

I had a feeling that she'd heard every word that had been spoken between me and her boss.

"Thank you, Mrs. Albrecht," I said. "I certainly hope so."

Fourteen

I found Cisco leaning against the Lincoln, smoking a cigarette.

"That was fast," he said.

I opened the back door in case there were cameras in the parking lot and Elliot was watching me.

"Look at you with the encouraging word."

I got in and he did the same.

"I'm just saying that it seemed kind of quick," he said. "How'd it go?"

"I gave it my best shot. We'll probably know something soon."

"You think he did it?"

"Probably, but it doesn't matter. We've got other things to worry about."

It was hard to go from thinking about a quarter-million-dollar fee to some of the also-rans on Vincent's client list, but that was the job. I opened my bag and pulled out the other active files. It was time to decide where our next stop was going to be.

Cisco backed out of the space and started heading toward the arch.

"Lorna's waiting to hear," he said.

I looked up at him in the mirror.

"What?"

"Lorna called me while you were inside. She really wants to know what happened with Elliot."

"Don't worry, I'll call her. First let me figure out where we're going."

The address of each client—at least the address given upon signing for Vincent's services—was printed neatly on the outside of each file. I quickly checked through the files, looking for addresses in Hollywood. I finally came across the file belonging to the woman charged with indecent exposure. The client who had come to Vincent's office earlier to ask for the return of her file.

"Here we go," I said. "When you get out of here, head down Melrose to La Brea. We've got a client right there. One of the ones who came in today for her file."

"Got it."

"After that stop, I'll ride in the front seat. Don't want you to feel too much like a chauffeur."

"It ain't a bad gig. I think I could get used to it."

I got out my phone.

"Hey, Mick, I gotta tell you something," Cisco said.

I took my thumb off the speed-dial button for Lorna.

"Yeah, what?"

"I just wanted to tell you myself before you heard it somewhere else. Me and Lorna . . . we're gonna get married."

I had figured that they were headed in that direction. Lorna and I had been friends for fifteen years before we were married for one. It had been a rebound marriage for me and as ill-advised as anything I had ever done. We ended it when we realized the mistake and somehow managed to remain close. There was no one I trusted more in the world. We were no longer in love but I still loved her and would always protect her.

"That okay with you, Mick?"

I looked at Cisco in the rearview.

"I'm not part of the equation, Cisco."

"I know but I want to know if it's *okay* with you. Know what I mean?"

I looked out the window and thought a moment before answering. Then I looked back at him in the mirror.

"Yes, it's all right with me. But I'll tell you something, Cisco. She's one of the four most important people in my life. You have maybe seventy-five pounds on me — and granted, all of them in muscle. But if you hurt her, I'm going to find a way to hurt you back. That okay with you?"

He looked away from the mirror to the road ahead. We were in the exit line, moving slowly. The striking writers were massing out on the sidewalk and delaying the people trying to leave the studio.

"Yeah, Mick, I'm okay with that."

We were silent for a while after that as we inched along. Cisco kept glancing at me in the mirror.

"What?" I finally asked.

"Well, I got your daughter. That makes one. And then Lorna. I was wondering who the other two were."

Before I could answer, the electronic version of the *William Tell* Overture started to play in my hand. I looked down at my phone. It said PRIVATE CALLER on the screen. I opened it up.

"Haller."

"Please hold for Walter Elliot," Mrs. Albrecht said.

Not much time went by before I heard the familiar voice.

"Mr. Haller?"

"I'm here. What can I do for you?"

I felt the stirring of anxiety in my gut. He had decided.

"Have you noticed something about my case, Mr. Haller?"

The question caught me off guard.

"How do you mean?"

"One lawyer. I have one lawyer, Mr. Haller. You see, I not only must win this case in court but I must also win it in the court of public opinion."

"I see," I said, though I didn't quite understand the point.

"In the last ten years I've picked a lot of winners. I'm talking about films in which I invested my money. I picked winners because I believe I have an accurate sense of public opinion and taste. I know what people like because I know what they are thinking."

"I'm sure you do, sir."

"And I think that the public believes that the more guilty you are, the more lawyers you need."

He wasn't wrong about that.

"So the first thing I said to Mr. Vincent when I hired him was, no dream team, just you. We had a second lawyer on board early on but that was temporary. She served a purpose and was gone. One lawyer, Mr. Haller. That's how I want it. The best one lawyer I can get."

"I under —"

"I've decided, Mr. Haller. You impressed me when you were in here. I would like to engage your services for trial. You will be my one lawyer."

I had to calm my voice before answering.

"I'm glad to hear that. Call me Mickey."

"And you can call me Walter. But I insist on one condition before we agree to this arrangement."

"What is that?"

"No delay. We go to trial on schedule. I want to hear you say it."

I hesitated. I wanted a delay. But I wanted the case more.

"We won't delay," I said. "We'll be ready to go next Thursday."

"Then, welcome aboard. What do we do next?"

"Well, I'm still on the lot. I could turn around and come back."

"I'm afraid I have meetings until seven and then a screening of our film for the awards season."

I thought that his trial and freedom would have trumped his meetings and movies but I let it go. I would educate Walter Elliot and bring him to reality the next time I saw him.

"Okay, then, for now you give me a fax number and I'll have my assistant send over a contract. It will have the same fee structure as you had with Jerry Vincent."

There was silence and I waited. If he was going to try to knock down the fee, this is when he would do it. But instead he repeated a fax number I could hear Mrs. Albrecht giving him. I wrote it down on the outside of one of the files.

"What's tomorrow look like, Walter?"

"Tomorrow?"

"Yes, if not tonight, then tomorrow. We need to get started. You don't want a delay; I want to be even more prepared than I am now. We need to talk and go over things. There are a few gaps in the defense case and I think you can help me fill them in. I could come back to the studio or meet you anywhere else in the afternoon."

I heard muffled voices as he conferred with Mrs. Albrecht.

"I have a four o'clock open," he finally said. "Here at the bungalow."

"Okay, I'll be there. And cancel whatever you have at five. We're going to need at least a couple hours to start."

Elliot agreed to the two hours and we were about to end the conversation, when I thought of something else.

"Walter, I want to see the crime scene. Can I get into the house in Malibu tomorrow sometime before we meet?"

Again there was a pause.

"When?"

"You tell me what will work."

Again he covered the phone and I heard his muffled conversation with Mrs. Albrecht. Then he came back on the line with me.

"How about eleven? I'll have someone meet you there to let you in."

"That'll work. See you tomorrow, Walter."

I closed the phone and looked at Cisco in the mirror.

"We got him."

Cisco hit the Lincoln's horn in celebration. It was a long blast that made the driver in front of us hold up a fist and send us back the finger. Out in the street the striking writers took the blast as a sign of support from inside the hated studio. I heard a loud cheer go up from the masses.

Fifteen

osch arrived early the next morning. He was alone. His peace offering was the extra cup of coffee he carried and handed over to me. I don't drink coffee anymore—trying to avoid any addiction in my life—but I took it from him anyway, thinking that maybe the smell of caffeine would get me going. It was only 7:45 but I had been in Jerry Vincent's office for more than two hours already.

I led Bosch back into the file room. He looked more tired than I felt and I was pretty sure he was in the same suit he'd been wearing when I saw him the day before.

"Long night?" I asked.

"Oh, yeah."

"Chasing leads or chasing tail?"

It was a question I had once heard one detective ask another in a courthouse hallway. I guess it was a question reserved for brothers of the badge because it didn't go over so well with Bosch. He made some sort of guttural noise and didn't answer.

In the file room I told him to have a seat at the small table. There was a yellow legal tablet on the table, but no files. I took the other seat and put my coffee down.

"So," I said, picking up the legal pad.

"So," Bosch said when I offered nothing else.

"So I met with Judge Holder in chambers yesterday and worked out a plan by which we can give you what you need from the files without actually giving you the files."

Bosch shook his head.

"What's wrong?" I asked.

"You should've told me this yesterday at Parker Center," he said. "I wouldn't have wasted my time."

"I thought you'd appreciate this."

"It's not going to work."

"How do you know that? How can you be sure?"

"How many homicides have you investigated, Haller? And how many have you cleared?"

"All right, point taken. You're the homicide guy. But I am certainly capable of reviewing files and discerning what constituted a legitimate threat to Jerry Vincent. Possibly because of my experience as a criminal defense attorney I could even perceive a threat that you would miss in your capacity as a detective."

"So you say."

"Yeah, I say."

"Look, all I'm pointing out here is the obvious. I'm the detective. I'm the one who should look through the files because I know what I am looking for. No offense, but you are an amateur at this. So I'm in a position here where I have to take what an amateur is giving me and trust that I'm getting everything there is to get from the files. It doesn't work that way. I don't trust the evidence unless I find it myself."

"Again, your point is well taken, Detective, but this is the way it is. This is the only method Judge Holder approved, and I gotta tell you that you're lucky to get this much. She wasn't interested in helping you out at all."

"So you're saying you went to bat for me?"

He said it in a disbelieving, sarcastic tone, as if it were some sort of a mathematical impossibility for a defense attorney to help a police detective.

"That's right," I said defiantly. "I went to bat for you. I told you yesterday, Jerry Vincent was a friend. I'd like to see you take down the person who took him down."

"You're probably worried about your own ass, too."

"I'm not denying that."

"If I were you I would be."

"Look, do you want the list or not?"

I held the legal pad up as if I were teasing a dog with a toy. He reached for it and I pulled it back, immediately regretting the move. I quickly handed it to him. It was an awkward exchange, like shaking hands had been the day before.

"There are eleven names on that list, with a brief summary of the threat each made to Jerry Vincent. We were lucky that Jerry thought it was important to memorialize an account of each threat he received. I've never done that."

Bosch didn't respond. He was reading the first page of the legal pad.

"I prioritized them," I said.

Bosch looked at me and I knew he was ready to step on me again for assuming the role of detective. I raised a hand to stop him.

"Not from the standpoint of your investigation. From the standpoint of being a lawyer. Of putting myself in Jerry Vincent's shoes and looking at these things and determining which ones would concern me the most. Like the first one on that list. James Demarco. The guy goes away on weapons charges and thinks Jerry fucked up the case. A guy like that can get a gun as soon as he gets out."

Bosch nodded and dropped his eyes back to the legal pad. He spoke without looking up from it.

"What else do you have for me?"

"What do you mean?"

He looked at me and waved the pad up and down as if it were as light as a feather and the information on it was equally so.

"I'll run these names and see where these guys are at now. Maybe your gunrunner is out and about and looking for revenge. But these are dead cases. Most likely if these threats were legit, they would've been carried out long ago. Same with any threats he got when he was a prosecutor. So this is just busywork you're giving me, Counselor."

"Busywork? Some of those guys threatened him when they were being led off to prison. Maybe some of them are out. Maybe one just got out and made good on the threat. Maybe they contracted it out from prison. There are a lot of possibilities and they shouldn't be dismissed as just busywork. I don't understand your attitude on this."

Bosch smiled and shook his head. I remembered my father doing the same thing when he was about to tell me as a five-year-old that I had misunderstood something.

"I don't really care what you think about my attitude," he said. "We'll check your leads out. But I'm looking for something a little more current. Something from Vincent's open cases."

"Well, I can't help you there."

"Sure you can. You have all the cases now. I assume you are reviewing them and meeting all your new clients. You're going to come across something or see something or hear something that doesn't fit, that doesn't seem right, that maybe scares you a little bit. That's when you call me."

I stared at him without answering.

"You never know," he said. "It might save you from…"

He shrugged and didn't finish, but the message was clear. He was trying to scare me into cooperating far more than Judge Holder was allowing, or than I felt comfortable with.

"It's one thing sharing threat information from closed cases," I said. "It's another thing entirely to do it with active cases. And besides that, I know you are asking for more than just threats. You think Jerry stumbled across something or had some knowledge that got him killed."

Bosch kept his eyes on me and slowly nodded. I was the first to look away.

"What about it being a two-way street, Detective? What do you know that you aren't telling me? What was in the laptop that was so important? What was in the portfolio?"

"I can't talk to you about an active investigation."

"You could yesterday when you asked about the FBI."

He looked at me and squinted his dark eyes.

"I didn't ask you about the FBI."

"Come on, Detective. You asked if he had any federal cases. Why would you do that unless you have some sort of federal connection? I'm guessing it was the FBI."

Bosch hesitated. I had a feeling I had guessed right and now he was in a corner. My mentioning the bureau would make him think I knew something. Now he would have to give in order to get.

"This time you go first," I prompted.

He nodded.

"Okay, the killer took Jerry Vincent's cell phone—either off his body or it was in his briefcase."

"Okay."

"I got the call records yesterday right before I saw you. On the day he was killed he got three calls from the bureau. Four days before that, there were two. He was talking to somebody over there. Or they were talking to him."

"Who?"

"I can't tell. All outgoing calls from over there register on the main number. All I know is he got calls from the bureau, no names."

"How long were the calls?"

Bosch hesitated, unsure what to divulge. He looked down at the tablet in his hand and I saw him grudgingly decide to share more. He was going to get angry when I had nothing to share back.

"They were all short calls."

"How short?"

"None of them over a minute."

"Then, maybe they were just wrong numbers."

He shook his head.

"That's too many wrong numbers. They wanted something from him."

"Anybody from there check in on the homicide investigation?"

"Not yet."

I thought about this and shrugged.

"Well, maybe they will and then you'll know."

"Yeah, and maybe they won't. It's not their style, if you know what I mean. Now your turn. What do you have that's federal?"

"Nothing. I confirmed that Vincent had no federal cases."

I watched Bosch do a slow burn as he realized I had played him.

"You're telling me you have found no federal connections? Not even a bureau business card in that office?"

"That's right. Nothing."

"There's been a rumor going around about a federal grand jury looking into corruption in the state courts. You know anything about that?"

I shook my head.

"I've been on the shelf for a year."

"Thanks for the help."

"Look, Detective, I don't get this. Why can't you just call over there and ask who was calling your victim? Isn't that how an investigation should proceed?"

Bosch smiled like he was dealing with a child.

"If they want me to know something, they'll come to me. If I call them, they'll just shine me on. If this was part of a corruption probe or they've got something else going, the chances of them talking to a local cop are between slim and none. If they're the ones who got him killed, then make it none."

"How would they get him killed?"

"I told you, they kept calling. They wanted something. They were pressuring him. Maybe someone else knew about it and thought he was a risk."

"That's a lot of conjecture about five calls that don't even add up to five minutes."

Bosch held up the yellow pad.

"No more conjecture than this list."

"What about the laptop?"

"What about it?"

"Is that what this is all about, something in his computer?"

"You tell me."

"How can I tell you when I have no idea what was in it?"

Bosch nodded the point and stood up.

"Have a good day, Counselor."

He walked out, carrying the legal pad at his side. I was left wondering whether he had been warning me or playing me the whole time he had been in the room.

Sixteen

Lorna and Cisco arrived together fifteen minutes after Bosch's departure and we convened in Vincent's office. I took a seat behind the dead lawyer's desk and they sat side by side in front of it. It was another score-keeping session in which we went over cases, what had been accomplished the previous night and what still needed to be done.

With Cisco driving, I had visited eleven of Vincent's clients the night before, signing up eight of them and giving back files to the remaining three. These were the priority cases, potential clients I hoped to keep because they could pay or their cases had garnered some form of merit in my review. They were cases I could win or be challenged by.

So it had not been a bad night. I had even convinced the woman charged with indecent exposure to keep me on as her attorney. And of course, bagging Walter Elliot was the icing on the cake. Lorna reported that she had faxed him a representation contract and it had already been signed and returned. We were in good shape there. I could start chipping away at the hundred thousand in the trust account.

We next set the plan for the day. I told Lorna that I wanted her and Wren — if she showed up — to run down the remaining clients, apprise them of Jerry Vincent's demise and set up appointments for me to discuss the options of legal representation. I also wanted Lorna to continue building the calendar and familiarizing herself with Vincent's files and financial records.

I told Cisco I wanted him to focus his attention on the Elliot case, with particular emphasis on witness maintenance. This meant that he had to take the preliminary defense witness list, which had already been compiled by Jerry Vincent, and prepare subpoenas for the law enforcement officers and other witnesses who might be considered hostile to the defense's cause. For the paid expert witness and others who were willingly going to testify at trial for the defense, he had to make contact and assure them that the trial was moving forward as scheduled, with me replacing Vincent at the helm.

"Got it," Cisco said. "What about the Vincent investigation? You still want me monitoring?"

"Yes, keep tabs on that and let me know what you find out."

"I found out that they spent last night sweating somebody but kicked him loose this morning."

"Who?"

"I don't know yet."

"A suspect?"

"They cut him loose, so whoever it was is cleared. For now."

I nodded as I thought about this. No wonder Bosch looked like he had been up all night.

"What are you going to be doing today?" Lorna asked.

"My priority starting today is Elliot. There are a few things on these other cases that I'll need to pay some attention to but for the most part I'm going to be on Elliot from here on out. We've got jury selection in eight days. Today I want to start at the crime scene."

"I should go with you," Cisco said.

"No, I just want to get a feel for the place. You can get in there with a camera and tape measure later."

"Mick, isn't there any way you can convince Elliot to delay?" Lorna asked. "Doesn't he realize that you need time to study and understand the case?"

"I told him that, but he's not interested. He made it a condition of my hire. I had to agree to go to trial next week or he'd find another lawyer who could. He says he's innocent and doesn't want to wait a single day longer to prove it."

"Do you believe him?"

I shrugged.

"Doesn't matter. He believes it. And he's got this strange confidence in it all turning out his way—like the Monday morning box office. So I either get ready to go to trial at the end of next week or I lose the client."

Just then the door to the office swung open and revealed Wren Williams standing tentatively in the doorway.

"Excuse me," she said.

"Hello, Wren," I said. "Glad you're here. Could you wait out there in reception, and Lorna will be right out to work with you?"

"No problem. You also have one of the clients waiting out here. Patrick Henson. He was already waiting when I came in."

I looked at my watch. It was five of nine. It was a good sign in regard to Patrick Henson.

"Then, send him in."

A young man walked in. Patrick Henson was smaller than I thought he would be, but maybe it was the low center of gravity that made him a good surfer. He had the requisite hardened tan but his hair was cropped short. No earrings, no white shell necklace or shark's tooth. No tattoos that I could see. He wore black cargo pants and what probably passed as his best shirt. It had a collar.

"Patrick, we spoke on the phone yesterday. I'm Mickey Haller and this is my case manager, Lorna Taylor. This big guy is Cisco, my investigator."

He stepped toward the desk and shook our hands. His grip was firm.

"I'm glad you decided to come in. Is that your fish on the wall back there?"

Without moving his feet Henson swiveled at the hips as if on a surfboard and looked at the fish hanging on the wall.

"Yeah, that's Betty."

"You gave a stuffed fish a name?" Lorna asked. "What, was it a pet?"

Henson smiled, more to himself than to us.

"No, I caught it a long time ago. Back in Florida. We hung it by the front door in the place I was sharing in Malibu. My roommates and me, we'd always say, 'Hellooo, Betty' to it when we came home. It was kind of stupid."

He swiveled back and looked at me.

"Speaking of names, do we call you Trick?"

"Nah, that was just the name my agent came up with. I don't have him anymore. You can just call me Patrick."

"Okay, and you told me you had a valid driver's license?"

"Sure do."

He reached into a front pocket and removed a thick nylon wallet. He pulled his license out and handed it to me. I studied it for a moment and then handed it to Cisco. He studied it a little longer and then nodded, giving it his official approval.

"Okay, Patrick, I need a driver," I said. "I provide the car and gas and insurance and you show up here every morning at nine to drive me wherever I need to go. I told you the pay schedule yesterday. You still interested?"

"I'm interested."

"Are you a safe driver?" Lorna asked.

"I've never had an accident." Patrick said.

I nodded my approval. They say an addict is best suited for spotting another addict. I was looking for signs that he was still using. Heavy eyelids, slow speech, avoidance of eye contact. But I didn't pick up on anything.

"When can you start?"

He shrugged.

"I don't have anything...I mean, whenever you want, I guess."

"How about we start right now? Today will be a test-drive. We'll see how you do and we can talk about it at the end of the day."

"Sounds good to me."

"Okay, well, we're going to get out of here and hit the road and I'll explain in the car how I like things to work."

"Cool."

He hooked his thumbs in his pockets and awaited the next move or instruction. He looked like he was about thirty but that was because of what the sun had done to his skin. I knew from the file that he was only twenty-four and still had a lot to learn.

Today the plan was to take him back to school.

Seventeen

We took the 10 out of downtown and headed west toward Malibu. I sat in the back and opened my computer on the fold-down table. While I waited for it to boot up I told Patrick Henson how it all worked.

"Patrick, I haven't had an office since I left the Public Defenders Office twelve years ago. My car is my office. I've got two other Lincolns just like this one. I keep them in rotation. Each one's got a printer, a fax and I've got a wireless card in my computer. Anything I have to do in an office I can do back here while I'm on the road to the next place. There are more than forty courthouses spread across L.A. County. Being mobile is the best way to do business."

"Cool," Patrick said. "I wouldn't want to be in an office either."

"Damn right," I said. "Too claustrophobic."

My computer was ready. I went to the file where I kept generic forms and motions and began to customize a pretrial motion to examine evidence.

"I'm working on your case right now, Patrick."

He looked at me in the mirror.

"What do you mean?"

"Well, I reviewed your file and there's something Mr. Vincent hadn't done that I think we need to do that may help."

"What's that?"

"Get an independent appraisal of the necklace you took. They list the value as twenty-five thousand and that bumps you up to a felony theft category. But it doesn't look like anybody ever challenged that."

"You mean like if the diamonds are bogus there's no felony?"

"It could work out like that. But I was thinking of something else, too."

"What?"

I pulled his file out of my bag so I could check a name.

"Let me ask you a few questions first, Patrick," I said. "What were you doing in that house where you took the necklace?"

He shrugged his shoulders.

"I was dating the old lady's youngest daughter. I met her on the beach and was sort of teaching her to surf. We went out a few times and hung out. One time there was a birthday party at the house and I was invited and the mother was given the necklace as a gift."

"That's when you learned its value."

"Yeah, the father said they were diamonds when he gave it to her. He was real proud of 'em."

"So then, the next time you were there at the house, you stole the necklace."

He didn't respond.

"It wasn't a question, Patrick. It's a fact. I'm your lawyer now and we need to discuss the facts of the case. Just don't ever lie to me or I won't be your lawyer anymore."

"Okay."

"So the next time you were in the house, you stole the necklace."

"Yeah."

"Tell me about it."

"We were there alone using the pool and I said I had to go to the

115

can, only I really just wanted to check the medicine cabinet for pills. I was hurting. There weren't any in the bathroom downstairs so I went upstairs and looked around. I looked in the old lady's jewelry box and saw the necklace. I just took it."

He shook his head and I knew why. He was thoroughly embarrassed and defeated by the actions his addiction had made him take. I had been there myself and knew that looking back from sobriety was almost as scary as looking forward.

"It's all right, Patrick. Thank you for being honest. What did the guy say when you pawned it?"

"He said he'd only give me four bills because the chain was gold but he didn't think the diamonds were legit. I told him he was full of shit but what could I do? I took the money and went down to TJ. I needed the tabs and so I took what he was giving. I was so messed up on the stuff, I didn't care."

"What's the name of the girl? It's not in the file."

"Mandolin, like the instrument. Her parents call her Mandy."

"Have you talked to her since you were arrested?"

"No, man. We're done."

Now the eyes in the mirror looked sad and humiliated.

"Stupid," Henson said. "The whole thing was stupid."

I thought about things for a moment and then reached into my jacket pocket and pulled out a Polaroid photograph. I handed it over the seat and tapped Patrick on the shoulder with it.

"Take a look at that."

He took the photo and held it on top of the steering wheel while he looked at it.

"What the hell happened to you?" he asked.

"I tripped over a curb and did a nice face plant in front of my house. Broke a tooth and my nose, opened up my forehead pretty good, too. They took that picture for me in the ER. To carry around as a reminder."

"Of what?"

"I had just gotten out of my car after driving my eleven-year-old daughter home to her mother. By then I was up to three hundred twenty milligrams of OxyContin a day. Crushing and snorting first thing in the morning, except for me, the mornings were the afternoon."

I let him register that for a few moments before continuing.

"So, Patrick, you think what you did was stupid? I was driving my little girl around on three hundred twenty migs of hillbilly heroin."

Now I shook my head.

"There's nothing you can do about the past, Patrick. Except keep it there."

He was staring directly at me in the mirror.

"I'm going to help you get through the legal stuff," I said. "It's up to you to do the rest. And the rest is the hard part. But you already know that."

He nodded.

"Anyway, I see a ray of light here, Patrick. Something Jerry Vincent didn't see."

"What is it?"

"The victim's husband gave her that necklace. His name is Roger Vogler and he's a big supporter of lots of elected people in the county."

"Yeah, he's big into politics. Mandolin told me that. They hold fund-raisers and stuff at the house."

"Well, if the diamonds on that necklace are phony, he's not going to want that coming up in court. Especially if his wife doesn't know."

"But how's he gonna stop it?"

"He's a contributor, Patrick. His contributions helped elect at least four members of the county board of supervisors. The county supervisors control the budget of the District Attorney's Office. The DA is prosecuting you. It's a food chain. If Dr. Vogler wants to send a message, believe me, it will be sent."

Henson nodded. He was beginning to see the light.

"The motion I'm going to file requests that we be allowed to independently examine and appraise the evidence, to wit, the diamond necklace. You never know, that word 'appraise' may stir things up. We'll just have to sit back and see what happens."

"Do we go to court to file it?"

"No. I'm going to write this thing up right now and send it to the court in an e-mail."

"That's cool!"

"The beauty of the Internet."

"Thanks, Mr. Haller."

"You're welcome, Patrick. Can I have my picture back now?"

He handed it over the seat and I took a look at it. I had a marble under my lip, and my nose was pointing in the wrong direction. There was also a bloody friction abrasion on my forehead. The eyes were the toughest part to study. Dazed and lost, staring unsteadily at the camera. This was me at my lowest point.

I put the photo back in my pocket for safekeeping.

We drove in silence for the next fifteen minutes while I finished the motion, went online and sent it. It was definitely a shot across the prosecution's bow and it felt good. The Lincoln lawyer was back on the beat. The Lone Ranger was riding again.

I made sure I looked up from the computer when we hit the tunnel that marks the end of the freeway and dumps out onto the Pacific Coast Highway. I cracked the window open. I always loved the feeling I got when I'd swing out of the tunnel and see and smell the ocean.

We followed the PCH as it took us north to Malibu. It was hard for me to go back to the computer when I had the blue Pacific right outside my office window. I finally gave up, lowered the window all the way and just rode.

Once we got past the mouth of Topanga Canyon I started seeing packs of surfers on the swells. I checked Patrick and saw him taking glances out toward the water.

"It said in the file you did your rehab at Crossroads in Antigua," I said.

"Yeah. The place Eric Clapton started."

"Nice?"

"As far as those places go, I suppose."

"True. Any waves there?"

"None to speak of. I didn't get much of a chance to use a board anyway. Did you do rehab?"

"Yeah, in Laurel Canyon."

"That place all the stars go to?"

"It was close to home."

"Yeah, well, I went the other way. I was as far from my friends and my home as possible. It worked."

"You thinking about going back into surfing?"

He glanced out the window before answering. A dozen surfers in wet suits were straddling their boards out there, waiting on the next set.

"I don't think so. At least not on a professional level. My shoulder's shot."

I was about to ask what he needed his shoulder for when he continued his answer.

"The paddling's one thing but the key thing is getting up. I lost my move when I fucked up my shoulder. Excuse the language."

"That's okay."

"Besides, I'm taking things one day at a time. They taught you that in Laurel Canyon, didn't they?"

"They did. But surfing's a one-day-at-a-time, one-wave-at-a-time sort of thing, isn't it?"

He nodded and I watched his eyes. They kept tripping to the mirror and looking back at me.

"What do you want to ask me, Patrick?"

"Um, yeah, I had a question. You know how Vincent kept my fish and put it on the wall?"

"Yeah."

"Well, I was, uh, wondering if he kept any of my boards somewhere."

I opened his file again and looked through it until I found the liquidator's report. It listed twelve surfboards and the prices obtained for them.

"You gave him twelve boards, right?"

"Yeah, all of them."

"Well, he gave them to his liquidator."

"What's that?"

"It's a guy he used when he took assets from clients — you know, jewelry, property, cars, mostly — and would turn them into cash to be applied toward his fee. According to the report here, the liquidator sold all twelve of them, took twenty percent and gave Vincent forty-eight hundred dollars."

Patrick nodded his head but didn't say anything. I watched him for a few moments and then looked back at the liquidator's inventory sheet. I remembered that Patrick had said in that first phone call that the two long boards were the most valuable. On the inventory, there were two boards described as ten feet long. Both were made by One World in Sarasota, Florida. One sold for $1,200 to a collector and the other for $400 on eBay, the online auction site. The disparity between the two sales made me think the eBay sale was bogus. The liquidator had probably sold the board to himself cheap. He would then turn around and sell it at a profit he'd keep for himself. Everybody's got an angle. Including me. I knew that if he hadn't resold the board yet, then I still had a shot at it.

"What if I could get you one of the long boards back?" I asked.

"That would be awesome! I just wish I had kept one, you know?"

"No promises. But I'll see what I can do."

I decided to pursue it later by putting my investigator on it. Cisco showing up and asking questions would probably make the liquidator more accommodating.

Patrick and I didn't speak for the rest of the ride. In another twenty minutes we pulled into the driveway of Walter Elliot's house. It was of Moorish design with white stone and dark brown shutters. The center facade rose into a tower silhouetted against the blue sky. A silver mid-level Mercedes was parked on the cobblestone pavers. We parked next to it.

"You want me to wait here?" Patrick asked.

"Yeah. I don't think I'll take too long."

"I know this house. It's all glass in the back. I tried to surf behind it a couple times but it closes out on the inside and the rip's really bad."

"Pop the trunk for me."

I got out and went to the back to retrieve my digital camera. I turned it on to make sure I had some battery power and took a quick shot of the front of the house. The camera was working and I was good to go.

I walked to the entrance and the front door opened before I could push the bell. Mrs. Albrecht stood there, looking as lovely as I had seen her the day before.

Eighteen

When Walter Elliot had told me he would have someone meet me at the house in Malibu, I hadn't expected it to be his executive assistant.

"Mrs. Albrecht, how are you today?"

"Very well. I just got here and thought maybe I had missed you."

"Nope. I just got here too."

"Come in, please."

The house had a two-story entry area below the tower. I looked up and saw a wrought-iron chandelier hanging in the atrium. There were cobwebs on it, and I wondered if they had formed because the house had gone unused since the murders or because the chandelier was too high up and too hard to get to with a duster.

"This way," Mrs. Albrecht said.

I followed her into the great room, which was larger than my entire home. It was a complete entertainment area with a glass wall on the western exposure that brought the Pacific right into the house.

"Beautiful," I said.

"It is indeed. Do you want to see the bedroom?"

Ignoring the question, I turned the camera on and took a few shots of the living room and its view.

"Do you know who has been in here since the Sheriff's Department relinquished control of it?" I asked.

Mrs. Albrecht thought for a moment before answering.

"Very few people. I do not believe that Mr. Elliot has been out here. But, of course, Mr. Vincent came out once and his investigator came out a couple of times, I believe. And the Sheriff's Department has come back twice since turning the property back over to Mr. Elliot. They had search warrants."

Copies of the search warrants were in the case file. Both times they were looking for only one thing — the murder weapon. The case against Elliot was all circumstantial, even with the gunshot residue on his hands. They needed the murder weapon to ice the case but they didn't have it. The notes in the file said that divers had searched the waters behind the house for two days after the murders but had also failed to come up with the gun.

"What about cleaners?" I asked. "Did someone come in and clean the place up?"

"No, no one like that. We were told by Mr. Vincent to leave things as they were in case he needed to use the place during the trial."

There was no mention in the case files of Vincent possibly using the house in any way during the trial. I wasn't sure what the thinking would have been there. My instinctive response upon seeing the place was that I wouldn't want a jury anywhere near it. The view and sheer opulence of the property would underline Elliot's wealth and serve to disconnect him from the jurors. They would understand that they weren't really a jury of his peers. They would know that he was from a completely different planet.

"Where's the master suite?" I asked.

"It comprises the entire top floor."

"Then, let's go up."

As we went up a winding white staircase with an ocean-blue banister, I asked Mrs. Albrecht what her first name was. I told her I felt uncomfortable being so formal with her, especially when her boss and I were on a first-name basis.

"My name is Nina. You can call me that if you want."

"Good. And you can call me Mickey."

The stairs led to a door that opened into a bedroom suite the size of some courtrooms I had been in. It was so big it had twin fireplaces on the north and south walls. There was a sitting area, a sleeping area and his-and-her bathrooms. Nina Albrecht pushed a button near the door, and the curtains covering the west view silently began to split and reveal a wall of glass that looked out over the sea.

The custom-made bed was double the size of a regular king. It had been stripped of the top mattress and all linens and pillows and I assumed these had been taken for forensic analysis. In two locations in the room, six-foot-square segments of carpet had been cut out, again, I believed, for the collection and analysis of blood evidence.

On the wall next to the door, there were blood-spatter marks that had been circled and marked with letter codes by investigators. There were no other signs of the violence that had occurred in the room.

I walked to the corner by the glass wall and looked back into the room. I raised the camera and took a few shots from different angles. Nina walked into the shot a couple times but it didn't matter. The photos weren't for court. I would use them to refresh my memory of the place while I was working out the trial strategy.

A murder scene is a map. If you know how to read it, you can sometimes find your way. The lay of the land, the repose of victims in death, the angle of views and light and blood. The spatial restrictions and geometric differentiations were all elements of the map. You can't always get all of that from a police photo. Sometimes you have to see it for yourself. This is why I had come to the house in Malibu. For the map.

For the geography of murder. When I understood it, I would be ready to go to trial.

From the corner, I looked at the square cut out of the white carpet near the bedroom door. This is where the male victim, Johan Rilz, had been shot down. My eyes traveled to the bed, where Mitzi Elliot had been shot, her naked body sprawled diagonally across it.

The investigative summary in the file suggested that the naked couple had heard an intruder in the house. Rilz went to the bedroom door and opened it, only to be immediately surprised by the killer. Rilz was shot down in the doorway and the killer stepped over his body and into the room.

Mitzi Elliot jumped up from the bed and stood frozen by its side, clutching a pillow in front of her naked body. The state believed that the elements of the crime suggested that she knew her killer. She might have pleaded for her life or might have known her death could not be stopped. She was shot twice through the pillow from a distance estimated at three feet and knocked back onto the bed. The pillow she had used as a shield fell to the floor. The killer then stepped forward to the bed and pressed the barrel of the gun against her forehead for the kill shot.

That was the official version anyway. Standing there in the corner of the room, I knew there were enough unfounded assumptions built into it that I would have no trouble slicing and dicing it at trial.

I looked at the glass doors that led out to a deck overlooking the Pacific. There had been nothing in the files about whether the curtain and doors had been open at the time of the murders. I was not sure it meant anything one way or the other but it was a detail I would've liked to know.

I walked over to the glass doors and found them locked. I had a hard time figuring out how to open them. Nina finally came over and helped me, holding her finger down on a safety lever while turning the bolt with her other hand. The doors opened outward and brought in the sounds of the crashing surf.

I immediately knew that if the doors had been open at the time of the murders, then the sound of the surf could have easily drowned out any noise an intruder might have made in the house. This would contradict the state's theory that Rilz was killed at the bedroom door because he had gone to the door after hearing an intruder. It would then raise a new question about what Rilz was doing naked at the door, but that didn't matter to the defense. I only needed to raise questions and point out discrepancies to plant the seed of doubt in a juror's mind. It took only one doubt in one juror's mind for me to be successful. It was the distort-or-destroy method of criminal defense.

I stepped out onto the deck. I didn't know if it was high or low tide but suspected it was somewhere in between. The water was close. The waves were coming in and washing right up to the piers on which the house was built.

There were six-foot swells but no surfers out there. I remembered what Patrick had said about attempting to surf in the cove.

I walked back inside, and as soon as I reentered the bedroom, I realized my phone was ringing but I had been unable to hear it because of the ocean noise. I checked to see who it was but it said PRIVATE CALLER on the screen. I knew that most people in law enforcement blocked their ID.

"Nina, I have to take this. Do you mind going out to my car and asking my driver to come in?"

"No problem."

"Thank you."

I took the call.

"Hello?"

"It's me. I'm just checking to see when you're coming by."

"Me" was my first ex-wife, Maggie McPherson. Under the recently revamped custody agreement, I got to be with my daughter on Wednesday nights and every other weekend only. It was a long way from the shared custody we'd once had. But I had blown that along with the second chance I'd had with Maggie.

"Probably around seven thirty. I have a meeting with a client this afternoon and it might run a little late."

There was silence and I sensed I had given the wrong answer.

"What, you've got a date?" I asked. "What time you want me there?"

"I'm supposed to leave at seven thirty."

"Then, I'll be there before that. Who's the lucky guy?"

"That wouldn't be any of your business. But speaking of lucky, I heard you got Jerry Vincent's whole practice."

Nina Albrecht and Patrick Henson entered the bedroom. I saw Patrick looking at the missing square in the carpet. I covered the phone and asked them to go back downstairs and wait for me. I then went back to the phone conversation. My ex-wife was a deputy district attorney assigned to the Van Nuys courthouse. This put her in a position to hear things about me.

"That's right," I said. "I'm his replacement, but I don't know how lucky that makes me."

"You should get a good ride on the Elliot case."

"I'm standing in the murder house right now. Nice view."

"Well, good luck in getting him off. If anyone can, it's certainly you."

She said it with a prosecutor's sneer.

"I guess I won't respond to that."

"I know how you would anyway. One other thing. You're not going to have company over tonight, are you?"

"What are you talking about?"

"I'm talking about two weeks ago. Hayley said a woman was there. I believe her name was Lanie? She felt very awkward about it."

"Don't worry, she won't be there tonight. She's just a friend and she used the guest room. But for the record, I can have anybody I want over at my house at any time because it's *my* house, and you are free to do the same at your house."

"And I'm also free to go to the judge and say you're exposing our daughter to people who are drug addicts."

I took a deep breath before responding as calmly as I could.

"How would you know who I am exposing Hayley to?"

"Because your daughter isn't stupid and her hearing is perfect. She told me a little bit of what was said and it was quite easy to figure out that your…friend is from rehab."

"And so that's a crime, consorting with people from rehab?"

"It's not a crime, Michael. I just don't think it is best for Hayley to be exposed to a parade of addicts when she stays with you."

"Now it's a parade. I guess the one addict you're most concerned with is me."

"Well, if the shoe fits…"

I almost lost it but once again calmed myself by gulping down some of the fresh sea air. When I spoke I was calm. I knew that showing anger would only hurt me in the long run when it came time to re-address the custody arrangement.

"Maggie, this is our daughter we're talking about here. Don't hurt her by trying to hurt me. She needs her father and I need my daughter."

"And that's my point. You are doing well. Hooking up with an addict is not a good idea."

I was squeezing my phone so hard I thought it might break. I could feel the scarlet burn of embarrassment on my cheeks and neck.

"I have to go."

My words came out strangled by my own failures.

"And so do I. I'll tell Hayley you'll be there by seven thirty."

She always did that, ended the call with inferences that I would disappoint my daughter if I was late or couldn't make a scheduled pickup. She hung up before I could respond.

The living room downstairs was empty but then I saw Patrick and Nina out on the lower deck. I stepped out and over to the railing where Patrick stood staring at the waves. I tried to put the upset from the conversation with my ex-wife out of my head.

"Patrick, you said you tried surfing here but the rip was too strong?"

"That's right."

"Are you talking about a riptide?"

"Yeah, it's tough out here. The shape of the cove creates it. The energy of the waves coming in on the north side is redirected under the surface and sort of ricochets south. It follows the contour of the cove and carries it all the way down and then out. I got caught in that pipeline a couple times, man. It took me all the way out past those rocks at the south end."

I studied the cove as he described what was happening beneath the surface. If he was right and there was a riptide on the day of the murders, then the sheriff's divers had probably searched in the wrong place for the murder weapon.

And now it was too late. If the killer had thrown the gun into the surf, it could have been carried in the underwater pipeline completely out of the cove and out to sea. I began to feel confident that the murder weapon would not be making a surprise appearance at trial.

As far as my client was concerned, that was a good thing.

I stared out at the waves and thought about how beneath the beautiful surface a hidden power never stopped moving.

Nineteen

The writers had taken the day off or moved their picket line to another protest location. At Archway Studios we made it through the security checkpoint without any of the delay of the day before. It helped that Nina Albrecht was in the car in front of us and had smoothed the way.

It was late and the studio was emptying out for the day. Patrick was able to get a parking spot right in front of Elliot's bungalow. Patrick was excited because he had never been inside the gates of a movie studio. I told him he was free to look around but to keep his phone handy because I was unsure how long the meeting with my client would last and I needed to stick to a schedule for picking up my daughter.

As I followed Nina in I asked her if there was a place for me to meet with Elliot other than his office. I said I had paperwork to spread out and that the table we had sat at the day before was too small. She said she would take me to the executive boardroom and I could set up there while she went to get her boss and bring him to the meeting. I said that would be fine. But the truth was I wasn't going to spread documents out. I just wanted to meet with Elliot in a neutral spot. If I was sitting across from him at his worktable, he would have command of the meeting. That was made clear during our first encounter. Elliot was a forceful personality. But I needed to be the one in charge from here on out.

It was a big room with twelve black leather chairs around the polished oval table. There was an overhead projector and a long box on the far wall containing the drop-down screen. The other walls were hung with framed posters of the movies that had been made on the lot. I assumed that these were the films that had made the studio money.

I took a seat and pulled the case files out of my bag. Twenty-five minutes later I was looking through the state's discovery documents when the door opened and Elliot finally walked in. I didn't bother to get up or extend my hand. I tried to look annoyed as I pointed him to a chair across the table from me.

Nina trailed him into the room to see what she could get us for refreshment.

"Nothing, Nina," I said before Elliot could respond. "We're going to be fine and we need to get started. We'll let you know if we need anything."

She seemed momentarily taken aback by the issuance of orders from someone other than Elliot. She looked to him for clarification and he simply nodded. She left, closing the double doors behind her. Elliot sat down in the chair I had pointed him to.

I looked across the table at my client for a long moment before speaking.

"I can't figure you out, Walter."

"What do you mean? What's to figure out?"

"Well, for starters, you spend a lot of time protesting your innocence. But I don't think you are taking this that seriously."

"You're wrong about that."

"Am I? You understand that if you lose this trial, you are going to prison? And there won't be any bail on a double-murder conviction while you appeal. You get a bad verdict and they'll cuff you in the court-room and take you away."

Elliot leaned a few inches toward me before responding again.

"I understand exactly the position I am in. So don't dare tell me I am not taking it seriously."

"Okay, then, when we set a meeting, let's be on time for it. There is a lot of ground to cover and not a lot of time to cover it. I know you have a studio to run but that is no longer the priority. For the next two weeks you have one priority. This case."

Now he looked at me for a long moment before responding. It may have been the first time in his life he had been chided for being late and then told what to do. Finally, he nodded.

"Fair enough," he said.

I nodded back. Our positions were now understood. We were in his boardroom and on his studio lot, but I was the alpha dog now. His future depended on me.

"Good," I said. "Now, the first thing I need to ask is whether we are speaking privately in here."

"Of course we are."

"Well, we weren't yesterday. It was pretty clear that Nina's got your office wired. That may be fine for your movie meetings but it's not fine when we're discussing your case. I'm your lawyer, and no one should hear our discussion. No one. Nina has no privilege. She could be sub-poenaed to testify against you. In fact, it won't surprise me if she ends up on the prosecution's witness list."

Elliot leaned back in his padded chair and raised his face toward the ceiling.

"Nina," he said. "Mute the feed. If I need anything I will call you on the line."

He looked at me and opened his hands. I nodded that I was satisfied.

"Thank you, Walter. Now let's get to work."

"I have a question first."

"Sure."

"Is this the meeting where I tell you I didn't do it and then you tell me that it doesn't matter to you whether I did it or not?"

I nodded.

"Whether you did it or not is irrelevant, Walter. It's what the state can prove beyond a —"

"No!"

He slammed an open palm down on the table. It sounded like a shot. I was startled but hoped I didn't show it.

"I am tired of that legal bullshit! That it doesn't matter whether I did it, only what can be proved. It does matter! Don't you see? It does matter. I need to be believed, goddamnit! I need *you* to believe me. I don't care what the evidence is against me. I did *NOT* do this. Do you understand me? Do you believe me? If my own lawyer doesn't believe me or care, then I don't have a chance."

I was sure Nina was going to come charging in to see if everything was all right. I leaned back in my padded chair and waited for her and to make sure Elliot was finished.

As expected, one of the doors opened and Nina was about to step in. But Elliot dismissed her with a wave of his hand and a harsh command not to bother us. The door closed again and he locked eyes with me. I held my hand up to stop him from speaking. It was my turn.

"Walter, there are two things I have to concern myself with," I said calmly. "Whether I understand the state's case and whether I can knock it down."

I tapped a finger on the discovery file as I spoke.

"At the moment I do understand the state's case. It's straightforward prosecution one-oh-one. The state believes that they have motive and opportunity in spades.

"Let's go with motive first. Your wife was having an affair and that made you angry. Not only that, but the prenuptial agreement she signed twelve years before had vested and the only way you could get rid of her without splitting everything up was to kill her. Next is opportunity. They have the time your car left through the gate at Archway that morning. They've made the run and timed it again and again and say you could've easily been at the Malibu house at the time of the killings. That is opportunity.

"And what the state is counting on is motive and opportunity being enough to sway the jury and win the day, while the actual evidence against you is quite thin and very circumstantial. So my job is to figure out a way of making the jury understand that there is a lot of smoke here but no real fire. If I do that, then you walk away."

"I still want to know if you believe I am innocent."

I smiled and shook my head.

"Walter, I'm telling you, it doesn't matter."

"It does to me. One way or the other, I need to know."

I relented and held my hands up in surrender.

"All right, then, I'll tell you what I think, Walter. I have studied the file forwards and backwards. I've read everything in here at least twice and most of it three times. I have now been out to the beach house where this unfortunate event happened and studied the geography of these murders. I have done all of that and I can see the very real possibility that you are innocent of these charges. Does that mean that I believe that you are an innocent man? No, Walter, it doesn't. I'm sorry but I have been doing this too long, and the reality is, I haven't seen too many innocent clients. So the best I can tell you is that I don't know. If that's not good enough for you, then I am sure you will have no trouble finding a lawyer who will tell you exactly what you want to hear, whether he believes it or not."

I rocked back in my chair while awaiting his response. He clasped his hands together on the table in front of him while he chewed on my words and then he finally nodded.

"Then, I guess that is the best I can ask for," he said.

I tried to let out my breath without his noticing. I still had the case. For the moment.

"But you know what I do believe, Walter?"

"What do you believe?"

"That you're holding out on me."

"Holding out? What are you talking about?"

"There's something I don't know about this case and you are holding back on it with me."

"I don't know what you are talking about."

"You are too confident, Walter. It's like you know you are going to walk."

"I *am* going to walk. I'm innocent."

"Being innocent is not enough. Innocent men sometimes get convicted and deep down everybody knows it. That's why I've never met a truly innocent man who wasn't scared. Scared that the system won't work right, that it's built to find guilty people guilty and not innocent people innocent. That's what you're missing, Walter. You're not scared."

"I don't know what you're talking about. Why should I be scared?"

I stared across the table at him, trying to read him. I knew my instincts were right. There was something I didn't know, something that I had missed in the files or that Vincent had carried in his head instead of his files. Whatever it was, Elliot wasn't sharing it with me yet.

For now that was okay. Sometimes you don't want to know what your client knows, because once the smoke comes out of the bottle, you can't put it back in.

"All right, Walter," I said. "To be continued. Meantime, let's go to work."

Without waiting for a reply I opened the defense file and looked at the notes I had written on the inside flap.

"I think we're set in terms of witnesses and strategy when it comes to the state's case. What I have not found in the file is a solid strategy for putting forth your defense."

"What do you mean?" Elliot asked. "Jerry told me we were ready."

"Maybe not, Walter. I know it's not something you want to see or hear but I found this in the file."

I slid a two-page document across the polished table to him. He glanced at it but didn't really look at it.

"What is it?"

"That is a motion for a continuance. Jerry drew it up but hadn't filed it. But it seems clear that he wanted to delay the trial. The coding on the motion indicates he printed it out Monday — just a few hours before he was killed."

Elliot shook his head and shoved the document back across the table.

"No, we talked about it and he agreed with me to move forward on schedule."

"That was Monday?"

"Yes, Monday. The last time I talked to him."

I nodded. That covered one of the questions I had. Vincent kept billing records in each of his files, and I had noted in the Elliot file that he had billed an hour on the day of his murder.

"Was that a conference at his office or yours?"

"It was a phone call. Monday afternoon. He'd left a message earlier and I called him back. Nina can get you the exact time if you need it."

"He has it down here at three. He talked to you about a delay?"

"That's right but I told him no delay."

Vincent had billed an hour. I wondered how long he and Elliot had sparred over the delay.

"Why did he want a continuance?" I asked.

"He just wanted more time to prepare and maybe pad his bill. I told him we were ready, like I'm telling you. We are ready!"

I sort of laughed and shook my head.

"The thing is, you're not the lawyer here, Walter. I am. And that's what I'm trying to tell you, I'm not seeing much here in terms of a defense strategy. I think that's why Jerry wanted to delay the trial. He didn't have a case."

"No, it's the prosecution that doesn't have the case."

I was growing tired of Elliot and his insistence on calling the legal shots.

"Let me explain how this works," I said wearily. "And forgive me if you know all of this, Walter. It's going to be a two-part trial, okay? The prosecutor goes first and he lays out his case. We get a chance to attack it as he goes. Then we get our shot and that's when we put up our evidence and alternate theories of the crime."

"Okay."

"And what I can tell from my study of the files is that Jerry Vincent was relying more on the prosecution's case than on a defense case. There are—"

"How so?"

"What I'm saying is that he's locked and loaded on the prosecution side. He has counter witnesses and cross-examination plans ready for everything the prosecution is going to put forward. But I'm missing something on the defense side of the equation. We've got no alibi, no alternate suspects, no alternate theories, nothing. At least nothing in the file. And that's what I mean when I say we have no case. Did he ever discuss with you how he planned to roll out the defense?"

"No. We were going to have that conversation but then he got killed. He told me that he was working all of that out. He said he had the magic bullet and the less I knew, the better. He was going to tell me when we got closer to trial but he never did. He never got the chance."

I knew the term. The "magic bullet" was your get-out-of-jail-and-go-home card. It was the witness or piece of evidence that you had in your back pocket that was going to either knock all the evidence down like dominoes or firmly and permanently fix reasonable doubt in the mind of every juror on the panel. If Vincent had a magic bullet, he hadn't noted it in the case file. And if he had a magic bullet, why was he talking about a delay on Monday?

"You have no idea what this magic bullet was?" I asked Elliot.

"Just what he told me, that he found something that was going to blow the state out of the water."

"That doesn't make sense if on Monday he was talking about delaying the trial."

Elliot shrugged.

"I told you, he just wanted more time to be prepared. Probably more time to charge me more money. But I told him, when we make a movie, we pick a date, and that movie comes out on that date no matter what. I told him we were going to trial without delay."

I nodded my head at Elliot's no-delay mantra. But my mind was on Vincent's missing laptop. Was the magic bullet in there? Had he saved his plan on the computer and not put it into the hard file? Was the magic bullet the reason for his murder? Had his discovery been so sensitive or dangerous that someone had killed him for it?

I decided to move on with Elliot while I had him in front of me.

"Well, Walter, I don't have the magic bullet. But if Jerry could find it, then so can I. I will."

I checked my watch and tried to give the outward appearance that I was not troubled by not knowing what was assuredly the key element in the case.

"Okay. Let's talk about an alternate theory."

"Meaning what?"

"Meaning that the state has its theory and we should have ours. The state's theory is that you were upset over your wife's infidelity and what it would cost you to divorce her. So you went out to Malibu and killed both your wife and her lover. You then got rid of the murder weapon in some way — either hid it or threw it into the ocean — and then called nine-one-one to report that you had discovered the murders. That theory gives them all they need. Motive and opportunity. But to back it up they have the GSR and almost nothing else."

"GSR?"

"Gunshot residue. Their evidentiary case—what little there is—firmly rests on it."

"That test was a false positive!" Elliot said forcefully. "I never shot any weapon. And Jerry told me he was bringing in the top expert in the country to knock it all down. A woman from John Jay in New York. She'll testify that the sheriff's lab procedures were sloppy and lax, prone to come up with the false positive."

I nodded. I liked the fervor of his denial. It could be useful if he testified.

"Yes, Dr. Arslanian—we still have her coming in," I said. "But she's no magic bullet, Walter. The prosecution will counter with their own expert saying exactly the opposite—that the lab is well run and that all procedures were followed. At best, the GSR will be a wash. The prosecution will still be leaning heavily on motive and opportunity."

"What motive? I loved her and I didn't even know about Rilz. I thought he was a faggot."

I held my hands up in a slow-it-down gesture.

"Look, do yourself a favor, Walter, and don't call him that. In court or anywhere else. If it is appropriate to reference his sexual orientation, you say you thought he was gay. Okay?"

"Okay."

"Now, the prosecution will simply say that you did know Johan Rilz was your wife's lover, and they'll trot out evidence and testimony that will indicate that a divorce forced by your wife's infidelity would cost you in excess of a hundred million dollars and possibly dilute your control of the studio. They plant all of that in the jury's minds and you start having a pretty good motivation for murder."

"And it's all bullshit."

"And I'll be able to potshot the hell out of it at trial. A lot of their positives can be turned into negatives. It will be a dance, Walter. We'll trade punches. We'll try to distort and destroy but ultimately they'll land more punches than we can block and that's why we're the underdog and why it's always good for the defense to float an alternate theory. We give the jury a plausible explanation for why these two people were killed. We throw suspicion away from you and at somebody else."

"Like the one-armed man in *The Fugitive*?"

I shook my head.

"Not exactly."

I remembered the movie and the television show before it. In both cases, there actually was a one-armed man. I was talking about a smoke screen, an alternate theory concocted by the defense because I wasn't buying into Elliot's "I-am-innocent rap"—at least not yet.

There was a buzzing sound and Elliot took a phone out of his pocket and looked at the screen.

"Walter, we have work here," I said.

He didn't take the call and reluctantly put the phone away. I continued.

"Okay, during the prosecution phase we are going to use cross-examination to make one thing crystal clear to the jury. That is, that once that GSR test came back positive on you, then—"

"False positive!"

"Whatever. The point is, once they had what they believed was a positive indication that you had very recently fired a weapon, all bets were off. A wide-open investigation became very tightly focused on one thing. You. It went from what they call a full-field investigation to a full investigation of you. So, what happened is that they left a lot of stones unturned. For example, Rilz had only been in this country four years. Not a single investigator went to Germany to check on his background and whether he had any enemies back there who wanted him dead.

That's just one thing. They didn't thoroughly background the guy in L.A. either. This was a man who was allowed entry into the homes and lives of some of the wealthiest women in this city. Excuse my bluntness, but was he banging other married clients, or just your wife? Were there other important and powerful men he could have angered, or just you?"

Elliot didn't respond to the crude questions. I had asked them that way on purpose, to see if it got a rise out of him or any reaction that contradicted his statements of loving his wife. But he showed no reaction either way.

"You see what I'm getting at, Walter? The focus, from almost the very start, was on you. When it's the defense's turn, we're going to put it on Rilz. And from that we'll grow doubts like stalks in a cornfield."

Elliot nodded thoughtfully as he looked down at his reflection in the polished tabletop.

"But this can't be the magic bullet Jerry told you about," I said. "And there are risks in going after Rilz."

Elliot raised his eyes to mine.

"Because the prosecutor knows this was a deficiency when the investigators brought in the case. He's had five months to anticipate that we might go this way, and if he is good, as I am sure he is, then he's been quietly getting ready for us to go in this direction."

"Wouldn't that come out in the discovery material?"

"Not always. There is an art to discovery. Most of the time it's what is not in the discovery file that is important and that you have to watch out for. Jeffrey Golantz is a seasoned pro. He knows just what he has to put in and what he can keep for himself."

"You know Golantz? You've gone to trial against him before?"

"I don't know him and have never gone up against him. It's his reputation I know. He's never lost at trial. He's something like twenty-seven and oh."

I checked my watch. The time had passed quickly and I needed to keep things moving if I was going to pick my daughter up on time.

"Okay," I said. "There are a couple other things we need to cover. Let's talk about whether you testify."

"That's not a question. That's a given. I want to clear my name. The jury will want me to say I did not do this."

"I knew you were going to say that and I appreciate the fervor I see in your denials. But your testimony has to be more than that. It has to offer an explanation and that's where we can get into trouble."

"I don't care."

"Did you kill your wife and her lover?"

"No!"

"Then why did you go out there to the house?"

"I was suspicious. If she was there with somebody, I was going to confront her and throw him out on his ass."

"You expect this jury to believe that a man who runs a billion-dollar movie studio took the afternoon off to drive out to Malibu to spy on his wife?"

"No, I'm no spy. I had suspicions and went out there to see for myself."

"And to confront her with a gun?"

Elliot opened his mouth to speak but then hesitated and didn't respond.

"You see, Walter?" I said. "You get up there and you open yourself up to anything—most of it not good."

He shook his head.

"I don't care. It's a given. Guilty guys don't testify. Everybody knows it. I'm testifying that I did not do this."

He poked a finger at me with each syllable of the last sentence. I still liked his forcefulness. He was believable. Maybe he could survive on the stand.

"Well, ultimately it is your decision," I said. "We'll get you prepared to testify but we won't make the decision until we get into the defense phase of the trial and we see where we stand."

"It's decided now. I'm testifying."

His face began to turn a deep shade of crimson. I had to tread lightly here. I didn't want him to testify but it was unethical for me to forbid it. It was a client decision, and if he ever claimed I took it away from him or refused to let him testify, I would have the bar swarming me like angry bees.

"Look, Walter," I said. "You're a powerful man. You run a studio and make movies and put millions of dollars on the line every day. I understand all of that. You are used to making decisions with nobody questioning them. But when we go into trial, I'm the boss. And while it will be you who makes this decision, I need to know that you are listening to me and considering my counsel. There's no use going further if you don't."

He rubbed his hand roughly across his face. This was hard for him.

"Okay. I understand. We make a final decision on this later."

He said it grudgingly. It was a concession he didn't want to make. No man wants to relinquish his power to another.

"Okay, Walter," I said. "I think that puts us on the same page."

I checked my watch again. There were a few more things on my list and I still had some time.

"Okay, let's move on," I said.

"Please."

"I want to add a couple people to the defense team. They will be ex—"

"No. I told you, the more lawyers a defendant has, the guiltier he looks. Look at Barry Bonds. Tell me people don't think he's guilty. He's got more lawyers than teammates."

"Walter, you didn't let me finish. These are not lawyers I'm talking about, and when we go to trial, I promise it is going to be just you and me sitting at the table."

"Then, who do you want to add?"

"A jury-selection consultant and somebody to work with you on image and testimony, all of that."

"No jury consultant. Makes it look like you're trying to rig things."

"Look, the person I want to hire will be sitting out in the gallery. No one will notice her. She plays poker for a living and just reads people's faces and looks for tells — little giveaways. That's it."

"No, I won't pay for that mumbo jumbo."

"Are you sure, Walter?"

I spent five minutes trying to convince him, telling him that picking the jury might be the most important part of the trial. I stressed that in circumstantial cases the priority had to be in picking jurors with open minds, ones who didn't believe that just because the police or prosecution say something, it's automatically true. I told him that I prided myself on my skills in picking a jury but that I could use the help of an expert who knew how to read faces and gestures. At the end of my plea Elliot simply shook his head.

"Mumbo jumbo. I will trust your skills."

I studied him for a moment and decided we'd talked enough for the day. I would bring up the rest with him the next time. I had come to realize that while he was paying lip service to the idea that I was the trial boss, there was no doubt that he was firmly in charge of things.

And I couldn't help but believe it might lead him straight to prison.

Twenty

By the time I dropped Patrick back at his car in downtown and headed to the Valley in heavy evening traffic, I knew I was going to be late and would tip off another confrontation with my ex-wife. I called to let her know but she didn't pick up and I left a message. When I finally got to her apartment complex in Sherman Oaks it was almost seven forty and I found mother and daughter out at the curb, waiting. Hayley had her head down and was looking at the sidewalk. I noticed she had begun to adopt this posture whenever her parents came into close proximity of one another. It was like she was just standing on the transporter circle and waiting to be beamed far away from us.

I popped the locks as I pulled to a stop, and Maggie helped Hayley into the back with her school backpack and her overnight bag.

"Thanks for being on time," she said in a flat voice.

"No problem," I said, just to see if it would put the flares in her eyes. "Must be a hot date if you're waiting out here for me."

"No, not really. Parent-teacher conference at the school."

That got through my defenses and hit me in the jaw.

"You should've told me. We could've gotten a babysitter and gone together."

"I'm not a baby," Hayley said from behind me.

"We tried that," Maggie said from my left. "Remember? You jumped on the teacher so badly about Hayley's math grade—the circumstance of which you knew nothing about—that they asked me to handle communications with the school."

The incident sounded only vaguely familiar. It had been safely locked away somewhere in my oxycodone-corrupted memory banks. But I felt the burn of embarrassment on my face and neck. I didn't have a comeback.

"I have to go," Maggie said quickly. "Hayley, I love you. Be good for your father and I'll see you tomorrow."

"Okay, Mom."

I stared out the window for a moment at my ex-wife before pulling away.

"Give 'em hell, Maggie McFierce," I said.

I pulled away from the curb and put my window up. My daughter asked me why her mother was nicknamed Maggie McFierce.

"Because when she goes into battle, she always knows she is going to win," I said.

"What battle?"

"Any battle."

We drove silently down Ventura Boulevard and stopped for dinner at DuPar's. It was my daughter's favorite place to eat dinner because I always let her order pancakes. Somehow, the kid thought ordering breakfast for dinner was crossing some line and it made her feel rebellious and brave.

I ordered a BLT with Thousand Island dressing on it and, considering my last cholesterol count, figured I was the one being rebellious and brave. We did her homework together, which was a breeze for her and taxing for me, then I asked her what she wanted to do. I was willing to do anything—a movie, the mall, whatever she wanted—but I was hoping she'd just want to go home to my place and hang out, maybe pull out some old family scrapbooks and look at the yellowed photos.

She hesitated in responding and I thought I knew why.

"There's nobody staying at my place if that's what you're worried about, Hay. The lady you met, Lanie? She doesn't visit me anymore."

"You mean like she's not your girlfriend anymore?"

"She never was my girlfriend. She was a friend. Remember when I stayed in the hospital last year? I met her there and we became friends. We try to watch out for each other, and every now and then she comes over when she doesn't want to stay home alone."

It was the shaded truth. Lanie Ross and I had met in rehab during group therapy. We continued the relationship after leaving the program but never consummated it as a romance, because we were emotionally incapable of it. The addiction had cauterized those nerve endings and they were slow to come back. We spent time with each other and were there for each other—a two-person support group. But once we were back in the real world, I began to recognize in Lanie a weakness. I instinctively knew she wasn't going to go the distance and I couldn't make the journey with her. There are three roads that can be taken in recovery. There is the clean path of sobriety and there is the road to relapse. The third way is the fast out. It is when the traveler realizes that relapse is just a slow suicide and there is no reason to wait. I didn't know which of those second two roads Lanie would go down but I couldn't follow either one. We finally went our separate ways, the day after Hayley had met her.

"You know, Hayley, you can always tell me if you don't like something or there's something I am doing that is bothering you."

"I know."

"Good."

We were silent for a few moments and I thought she wanted to say something else. I gave her the time to work up to it.

"Hey Dad?"

"What, baby?"

"If that lady wasn't your girlfriend, does that mean you and Mom might get back together?"

The question left me without words for a few moments. I could see the hope in Hayley's eyes and wanted her to see the same in mine.

"I don't know, Hay. I messed things up pretty good when we tried that last year."

Now the pain entered her eyes, like the shadows of clouds on the ocean.

"But I'm still working on it, baby," I said quickly. "We just have to take it one day at a time. I'm trying to show her that we should be a family again."

She didn't respond. She looked down at her plate.

"Okay, baby?"

"Okay."

"Did you decide what you want to do?"

"I think I just want to go home and watch TV."

"Good. That's what I want to do."

We packed up her schoolbooks and I put money down on the bill. On the drive over the hill, she said her mother had told her I had gotten an important new job. I was surprised but happy.

"Well, it's sort of a new job. I'm going back to work doing what I always did. But I have a lot of new cases and one big one. Did your mom tell you that?"

"She said you had a big case and everybody would be jealous but you would do real good."

"She said that?"

"Yeah."

I drove for a while, thinking about that and what it might mean.

Maybe I hadn't entirely blown things with Maggie. She still respected me on some level. Maybe that meant something.

"Um…"

I looked at my daughter in the rearview mirror. It was dark out now but I could see her eyes looking out the window and away from mine. Children are so easy to read sometimes. If only grown-ups were the same.

"What's up, Hay?"

"Um, I was just wondering, sort of, why you can't do what Mom does."

"What do you mean?"

"Like putting bad people in jail. She said your big case is with a man who killed two people. It's like you're always working for the bad guys."

I was quiet for a moment before finding my words.

"The man I am defending is accused of killing two people, Hayley. Nobody has proved he did anything wrong. Right now he's not guilty of anything."

She didn't respond and her skepticism was almost palpably emanating from the backseat. So much for the innocence of children.

"Hayley, what I do is just as important as what your mother does. When somebody is accused of a crime in our country, they are entitled to defend themselves. What if at school you were accused of cheating and you knew that you didn't cheat? Wouldn't you want to be able to explain and defend yourself?"

"I think so."

"I think so, too. It's like that with the courts. If you get accused of a crime, you can have a lawyer like me help you explain and defend yourself. The laws are very complicated and it's hard for someone to do it by themselves when they don't know all the rules of evidence and things like that. So I help them. It doesn't mean I agree with them or what they have done — if they have done it. But it's part of the system. An important part."

The explanation felt hollow to me as I said it. On an intellectual level I understood and believed the argument, every word of it. But on a father-daughter level I felt like one of my clients, squirming on the witness stand. How could I get her to believe it when I wasn't sure I believed it anymore myself?

"Have you helped any innocent people?" my daughter asked.

This time I didn't look in the mirror.

"A few, yes."

It was the best I could honestly say.

"Mom's made a lot of bad people go to jail."

I nodded.

"Yes, she has. I used to think we were a great balancing act. What she did and what I did. Now..."

There was no need to finish the thought. I turned the radio on and hit the preset button that tuned in the Disney music channel.

The last thing I thought about on the drive home was that maybe grown-ups were just as easy to read as their children.

Twenty-one

After dropping my daughter off at school Thursday morning I drove directly to Jerry Vincent's law offices. It was still early and traffic was light. When I got into the garage adjoining the legal center, I found that I almost had my pick of the place—most lawyers don't get into the office until closer to nine, when court starts. I had all of them beat by at least an hour. I drove up to the second level so I could park on the same floor as the office. Each level of the garage had its own entrance into the building.

I drove by the spot where Jerry Vincent had been parked when he was shot to death and parked farther up the ramp. As I walked toward the bridge that connected the garage to the Legal Center, I noticed a parked Subaru station wagon with surfboard racks on the roof. There was a sticker on the back window that showed the silhouette of a surfer riding the nose of a board. It said ONE WORLD on the sticker.

The back windows on the wagon were darkly tinted and I couldn't see in. I moved up to the front and looked into the car through the driver's side window. I could see that the backseat had been folded flat. Half the rear area was cluttered with open cardboard boxes full of clothes and personal belongings. The other half served as a bed for Patrick

Henson. I knew this because he was lying there asleep, his face turned from the light into the folds of a sleeping bag. And it was only then that I remembered something he had said during our first phone conversation when I had asked if he was interested in a job as my driver. He had told me he was living out of his car and sleeping in a lifeguard stand.

I raised my fist to knock on the window but then decided to let Patrick sleep. I wouldn't need him until later in the morning. There was no need to roust him. I crossed into the office complex, made a turn and headed down a hallway toward the door marked with Jerry Vincent's name. Standing in front of that door was Detective Bosch. He was listening to his music and waiting for me. He had his hands in his pockets and looked pensive, maybe even a little put out. I was pretty sure we had no appointment, so I didn't know what he was upset about. Maybe it was the music. He pulled out the earbuds as I approached and put them away.

"What, no coffee?" I said by way of a greeting.

"Not today. I could tell you didn't want it yesterday."

He stepped aside so I could use a key to open the door.

"Can I ask you something?" I said.

"If I said no, you'd ask anyway."

"You're probably right."

I opened the door.

"So then, just ask the question."

"All right. Well, you don't seem like an iPod sort of guy to me. Who were you listening to there?"

"Somebody I am sure you never heard of."

"I get it. It's Tony Robbins, the self-help guru?"

Bosch shook his head, not rising to take the bait.

"Frank Morgan," he said.

I nodded.

"The saxophone player? Yeah, I know Frank."

Bosch looked surprised as we entered the reception area.

"You know him," he said in a disbelieving tone.

"Yeah, I usually drop by and say hello when he plays at the Catalina or the Jazz Bakery. My father loved jazz and back in the fifties and sixties he was Frank's lawyer. Frank got into a lot of trouble before he got straight. Ended up playing in San Quentin with Art Pepper — you've heard of him, right? By the time I met Frank, he didn't need any help from a defense attorney. He was doing good."

It took Bosch a moment to recover from my surprise knowledge of Frank Morgan, the obscure heir to Charlie Parker who for two decades squandered the inheritance on heroin. We crossed the reception area and went into the main office.

"So how's the case going?" I asked.

"It's going," he said.

"I heard that before you came and saw me yesterday, you spent the night in Parker Center sweating a suspect. No arrest, though?"

I moved around behind Vincent's desk and sat down. I started pulling the files out of my bag. Bosch stayed standing.

"Who told you that?" Bosch asked.

There wasn't anything casual about the question. It was more of a demand. I acted nonchalant about it.

"I don't know," I said. "I must've heard it somewhere. Maybe a reporter. Who was the suspect?"

"That's none of your business."

"Then, what is my business with you, Detective? Why are you here?"

"I came to see if you had any more names for me."

"What happened to the names I gave you yesterday?"

"They've checked out."

"How could you check them all out already?"

He leaned down and put both hands on the desk.

"Because I'm not working this case alone, okay? I have help and we checked out every one of your names. Every one of them is in jail, dead or was not worried about Jerry Vincent anymore. We also checked out several of the people he put away as a prosecutor. It's a dead end."

I felt a real sense of disappointment and realized that maybe I had put too much hope in the possibility of one of those names from the past belonging to the killer, and his arrest being the end of any threat to me.

"What about Demarco, the gun dealer?"

"I took that one myself and it didn't take long to scratch him off the list. He's dead, Haller. Died two years ago in his cell up at Corcoran. Internal bleeding. When they opened him up they found a toothbrush shiv lodged in the anal cavity. It was never determined whether he'd put it up there for safekeeping himself or somebody else did it for him, but it was a good lesson for the rest of the inmates. They even put up a sign. Never put sharp objects up your ass."

I leaned back in my seat, as much repelled by the story as by the loss of a potential suspect. I recovered and tried to continue in nonchalant form.

"Well, what can I tell you, Detective? Demarco was my best shot. Those names were all I had. I told you I can't reveal anything about active cases, but here's the deal: There's nothing to reveal."

He shook his head in disbelief.

"I mean it, Detective. I've been through all of the active cases. There is nothing in any of them that constitutes a threat or reason for Vincent to feel threatened. There is nothing in any of them that connects to the FBI. There is nothing in any of them that indicates Jerry Vincent stumbled onto something that put him in harm's way. Besides, when you find out bad things about your clients, they're protected. So there's nothing there. I mean, he wasn't representing mobsters. He wasn't representing drug dealers. There wasn't anything in—"

"He represents murderers."

"Accused murderers. And at the time of his death he had only one murder case—Walter Elliot—and there isn't anything there. Believe me, I've looked."

I wasn't so sure I believed it as I said it but Bosch didn't seem to notice.

He finally sat down on the edge of the chair in front of the desk, and his face seemed to change. There was an almost desperate look to it.

"Jerry was divorced," I offered. "Did you check out the ex-wife?"

"They got divorced nine years ago. She's happily remarried and about to have her second kid. I don't think a woman seven months pregnant is going to come gunning for an ex-husband she hasn't talked to in nine years."

"Any other relatives?"

"A mother in Pittsburgh. The family angle is dry."

"Girlfriend?"

"He was banging his secretary but there was nothing serious there. And her alibi checks out. She was also banging his investigator. And they were together that night."

I felt my face turning red. That sordid scenario wasn't too far from my own current situation. At least Lorna, Cisco and I had been entangled at different times. I rubbed my face as if I were tired and hoped it would account for my new coloration.

"That's convenient," I said. "That they alibi each other."

Bosch shook his head.

"It checks out through witnesses. They were with friends at a screening at Archway. That big-shot client of yours got them the invitation."

I nodded and took an educated guess at something, then threw a zinger at Bosch.

"The guy you sweated in a room that first night was the investigator, Bruce Carlin."

"Who told you that?"

"You just did. You had a classic love triangle. It would've been the place to start."

"Smart lawyer. But like I said, it didn't pan out. We spent a night on it and in the morning we were still at square one. Tell me about the money."

He'd thrown a zinger right back at me.

"What money?"

"The money in the business accounts. I suppose you're going to tell me they are protected territory, too."

"Actually, I'd probably need to talk to the judge for an opinion on that, but I don't need to bother. My case manager is one of the best accounts people I've ever run across. She's been working with the books and she tells me they're clean. Every penny Jerry took in is accounted for."

Bosch didn't respond, so I continued.

"Let me tell you something, Detective. When lawyers get into trouble, most of the time it's because of the money. The books. It's the one place where there are no gray areas. It's the one place where the California bar loves to stick its nose in. I keep the cleanest books in the business because I don't ever want to give them a reason to come after me. So I would know and Lorna, my case manager, would know if there was something in these books that didn't add up. But there isn't. I think Jerry probably paid himself a little too quickly but there is nothing technically wrong with that."

I saw Bosch's eyes light on something I had said.

"What?"

"What's that mean, he 'paid himself too quickly'?"

"It means—let me just start at the start. The way it works is you take on a client and you receive an advance. That money goes into the client trust account. It's their money but you are holding it because you want to make sure you can get it when you earn it. You follow?"

"Yeah, you can't trust your clients because they're criminals. So you get the money up front and put it in a trust account. Then you pay yourself from it as you do the work."

"More or less. Anyway, it's in the trust and as you do the work, make appearances, prepare the case and so forth, you take your fees from the trust account. You move it into the operating account. Then, from the operating account you pay your own bills and salaries. Rent, secretary, investigator, car costs and so on and so forth. You also pay yourself."

"Okay, so how did Vincent pay himself too quickly?"

"Well, I am not exactly saying he did. It's a matter of custom and practice. But it looks from the books that he liked to keep a low balance in operating. He happened to have had a franchise client who paid a large advance up front and that money went through the trust and operating accounts pretty quickly. After costs, the rest went to Jerry Vincent in salary."

Bosch's body language indicated I was hitting on something that jibed with something else and was important to him. He had leaned slightly toward me and seemed to have tightened his shoulders and neck.

"Walter Elliot," he said. "Was he the franchise?"

"I can't give out that information but I think it's an easy guess to make."

Bosch nodded and I could see that he was working on something inside. I waited and he said nothing.

"How does this help you, Detective?" I finally asked.

"I can't give out that information but I think it's an easy guess to make."

I nodded. He'd nailed me back.

"Look, we both have rules we have to follow," I said. "We're flip sides of the same coin. I'm just doing my job. And if there is nothing else I can help you with, I'll get back to it."

Bosch stared at me and seemed to be deciding something.

"Who did Jerry Vincent bribe on the Elliot case?" he finally asked.

The question came out of left field. I wasn't expecting it but in the moments after he asked it, I realized that it was the question he had come to ask. Everything else up until this point had been window dressing.

"What, is that from the FBI?"

"I haven't talked to the FBI."

"Then, what are you talking about?"

"I'm talking about a payoff."

"To who?"

"That's what I'm asking you."

I shook my head and smiled.

"Look, I told you. The books are clean. There's—"

"If you were going to bribe someone with a hundred thousand dollars, would you put it in your books?"

I thought about Jerry Vincent and the time I turned down the subtle quid pro quo on the Barnett Woodson case. I turned him down and ended up hanging a not-guilty verdict on him. It changed Vincent's life and he was still thanking me for it from the grave. But maybe it didn't change his ways in the years that followed.

"I guess you're right," I said to Bosch. "I wouldn't do it that way. So what aren't you telling me?"

"This is in confidence, Counselor. But I need your help and I think you need to know this in order to help me."

"Okay."

"Then, say it."

"Say what?"

"That you will treat this information in confidence."

"I thought I did. I will. I'll keep it confidential."

"Not even your staff. Just you."

"Fine. Just me. Tell me."

"You have Vincent's work accounts. I have his private accounts. You said he paid himself the money from Elliot quickly. He—"

"I didn't say it was Elliot. You did."

"Whatever. The point is, that five months ago he accumulated a hundred grand in a personal investment account and a week later called his broker and told him he was cashing out."

"You mean he took a hundred thousand out in cash?"

"That's what I just said."

"What happened to it?"

"I don't know. But you can't just go into a broker's and pick up a hundred grand in cash. You have to order that kind of money. It took a couple days to put it together and then he went in to pick it up. His broker asked a lot of questions to make sure there wasn't a security issue. You know, like somebody being held hostage while he went and got the money. A ransom or something like that. Vincent said everything was fine, that he needed the money to buy a boat and that if he made the deal in cash, he would get the best deal and save a lot of money."

"So where's the boat?"

"There is no boat. The story was a lie."

"Are you sure?"

"We've checked all state transactions and asked questions all over Marina del Rey and San Pedro. We can't find any boat. We've searched his home twice and reviewed his credit-card purchases. No receipts or records of boat-related expenses. No photos, no keys, no fishing poles. No coast guard registration — required on a transaction that large. He didn't buy a boat."

"What about Mexico?"

Bosch shook his head.

"This guy hadn't left L.A. in nine months. He didn't go down to Mexico and he didn't go anywhere else. I'm telling you, he didn't buy a boat. We would've found it. He bought something else and your client Walter Elliot probably knows what it was."

I tracked his logic and could see it coming to the doorway of Walter Elliot. But I wasn't going to open it with Bosch looking over my shoulder.

"I think you've got it wrong, Detective."

"I don't think so, Counselor."

"Well, I can't help you. I have no idea about this and have seen no indication of it in any of the books or records I've got. If you can connect this alleged bribe to my client, then arrest him and charge him. Otherwise,

I'll tell you right now he's off limits. He's not talking to you about this or anything else."

Bosch shook his head.

"I wouldn't waste my time trying to talk to him. He used his lawyer as cover on this and I'll never be able to get past the attorney-client protection. But you should take it as a warning, Counselor."

"Yeah, how's that?"

"Simple. His lawyer got killed, not him. Think about it. And remember, that little trickle on the back of your neck and running down your spine? That's the feeling you get when you know you have to look over your shoulder. When you know you're in danger."

I smiled back at him.

"Oh, is that what that is? I thought it was the feeling I get when I know I'm being bullshitted."

"I'm only telling you the truth."

"You've been running a game on me for two days. Spinning bullshit about bribes and the FBI. You've been trying to manipulate me and it's been a waste of my time. You have to go now, Detective, because I have real work to do."

I stood up and extended a hand toward the door. Bosch stood up but didn't turn to go.

"Don't kid yourself, Haller. Don't make a mistake."

"Thanks for the advice."

Bosch finally turned and started to leave. But then he stopped and came back to the desk, pulling something from the inside pocket of his jacket as he approached.

It was a photograph. He put it down on the desk.

"You recognize that man?" Bosch asked.

I studied the photo. It was a grainy still taken off a video. It showed a man pushing out through the front door of an office building.

"This is the front entrance of the Legal Center, isn't it?"

"Do you recognize him?"

The shot was taken at a distance and blown up, spreading the pixels of the image and making it unclear. The man in the photograph looked to me to be of Latin origin. He had dark skin and hair and had a Poncho Villa mustache, like Cisco used to wear. He wore a panama hat and an open-collared shirt beneath what appeared to be a leather sport coat. As I looked more closely at the photograph, I realized why it was the frame they had chosen to take from the surveillance video. The man's jacket had pulled open as he'd pushed through the glass door. I could see what looked like the top of a pistol tucked into the belt line of his pants.

"Is that a gun? Is this the killer?"

"Look, can you answer one goddamn question without another question? Do you recognize this man? That's all I want to know."

"No, I don't, Detective. Happy?"

"That's another question."

"Sorry."

"You sure you haven't seen him before?"

"Not a hundred percent. But that's not a great photo you've got there. Where is it from?"

"A street camera on Broadway and Second. It sweeps the street and we got this guy for only a few seconds. This is the best we can do."

I knew that the city had been quietly installing street cameras on main arteries in the last few years. Streets like Hollywood Boulevard were completely visually wired. Broadway would have been a likely candidate. It was always crowded during the day with pedestrians and traffic. It was also the street used most often for protest marches organized by the underclasses.

"Well, then I guess it's better than having nothing. You think the hair and the mustache are a disguise?"

"Let me ask the questions. Could this guy be one of your new clients?"

"I don't know. I haven't met them all. Leave me the photo and I'll show it to Wren Williams. She'd know better than me if he's a client."

Bosch reached down and took the photo back.

"It's my only copy. When will she be in?"

"In about an hour."

"I'll come back later. Meantime, Counselor, watch yourself."

He pointed a finger at me like it was a gun, then turned and walked out of the room, closing the door behind him. I sat there thinking about what he had said and staring at the door, half expecting him to come back in and drop another ominous warning on me.

But when the door opened one minute later it was Lorna who entered.

"I just saw that detective in the hallway."

"Yeah, he was here."

"What did he want?"

"To scare me."

"And?"

"He did a pretty good job."

Twenty-two

Lorna wanted to convene another staff meeting and update me on things that had happened while I was out of the office visiting Malibu and Walter Elliot the day before. She even said I had a court hearing scheduled later on a mystery case that wasn't on the calendar we had worked up. But I needed some time to think about what Bosch had just revealed and what it meant.

"Where's Cisco?"

"He's coming. He left early to meet one of his sources before he came into the office."

"Did he have breakfast?"

"Not with me."

"Okay, wait till he gets in and then we'll go over to the Dining Car and have breakfast. We'll go over everything then."

"I already ate breakfast."

"Then, you can do all the talking while we do all the eating."

She put a phony frown on her face but went out into the reception office and left me alone. I got up from behind the desk and started to pace the office, hands in my pockets, trying to evaluate what the information from Bosch meant.

According to Bosch, Jerry Vincent had paid a sizable bribe to a person or persons unknown. The fact that the $100,000 came out of the Walter Elliot advance would indicate the bribe was somehow linked to the Elliot case, but this was by no means conclusive. Vincent could easily have used money from Elliot to pay a debt or a bribe relating to another case or something else entirely. It could have been a gambling debt he wanted to hide. The only fact was that Vincent had diverted the $100K from his account to an unknown destination and had wanted to hide the transaction.

Next to consider was the timing of the transaction and whether it was linked to Vincent's murder. Bosch said the money transfer had gone down five months ago. Vincent's murder was just three nights before and Elliot's trial was set to begin in a week. Again there was nothing definitive. The distance between the transaction and the murder seemed to me to strain any possibility of a link between the two.

But still, I could not push the two apart, and the reason for this was Walter Elliot himself. Through the filter of Bosch's information I now began to fill in some answers and to view my client—and myself—differently. I now saw Elliot's confidence in his innocence and eventual acquittal coming possibly from his belief that it had already been bought and paid for. I now saw his unwillingness to consider delaying the trial as a timing issue relating to the bribe. And I saw his willingness to quickly allow me to carry the torch for Vincent without checking a single reference as a move made so he could get to the trial without delay. It had nothing to do with any confidence in my skills and tenacity. I had not impressed him. I had simply been the one who showed up. I was simply a lawyer who would work in the scheme of things. In fact, I was perfect. I was pulled out of the lost-and-found bin. I had been on the shelf and was hungry and ready. I could be dusted off and suited up and sent in to replace Vincent, no questions asked.

The reality jolt this sent through me was as uncomfortable as the first night in rehab. But I also understood that this self-knowledge could give me an edge. I was in the middle of some sort of play but at least now I knew it was a play. That was an advantage. I could now make it my own play.

There was a reason for the hurry-up to trial and I now thought I knew what it was. The fix was in. Money had been paid for a specific fix, and that fix was tied to the trial remaining on schedule. The next question in this string was why. Why must the trial take place as scheduled? I didn't have an answer for that yet but I was going to get it.

I walked over to the windows and split the Venetian blinds with my hand. Out on the street I saw a van from Channel 5 parked with two wheels up on the curb. A camera crew and a reporter were on the sidewalk and they were getting ready to do a live shot, offering their viewers the latest on the Vincent case — the latest being the exact same report given the morning before: no arrests, no suspects, no news.

I left the window and stepped back into the middle of the room to continue my pacing. The next thing I needed to consider was the man in the photograph Bosch showed me. There was a contradiction at work here. The early indications of evidence were that Vincent had known the person who killed him and allowed him to get close. But the man in the photograph appeared to be in disguise. Would Jerry have lowered his window for the man in the photograph? The fact that Bosch had zeroed in on this man didn't make sense when applied to what was known about the crime scene.

The calls from the FBI to Vincent's cell phone were also part of the unknown equation. What did the bureau know and why had no agent come forward to Bosch? It might be that the agency was hiding its tracks. But I also knew that it might not want to come out of the shadows to reveal an ongoing investigation. If this was the case, I would need to step more carefully than I had been. If I ended up the least bit tainted in a federal corruption probe, I would never recover from it.

The last unknown to consider was the murder itself. Vincent had paid the bribe and was ready for trial as scheduled. Why had he become a liability? His murder certainly threatened the timetable and was an extreme response. Why was he killed?

There were too many questions and too many unknowns for now. I needed more information before I could draw any solid conclusions about how to proceed. But there was a basic conclusion I couldn't stop myself from reaching. It seemed uncomfortably clear that I was being mushroomed by my own client. Elliot was keeping me in the dark about the interior machinations of the case.

But that could work both ways. I decided that I would do exactly what Bosch had asked: keep the information the detective had given me confidential. I would not share it with my staff and certainly, at this point, I would not question Walter Elliot about his knowledge of these things. I would keep my head above the dark waters of the case and keep my eyes wide open.

I shifted focus from my thoughts to what was directly in front of me. I was looking at the gaping mouth of Patrick Henson's fish.

The door opened and Lorna reentered the office to find me standing there staring at the tarpon.

"What are you doing?" she asked.

"Thinking."

"Well, Cisco's here and we've got to go. You have a busy court schedule today and I don't want to make you late."

"Then, let's go. I'm starved."

I followed her out but not before glancing back at the big beautiful fish hanging on the wall. I thought I knew exactly how he felt.

Twenty-three

I had Patrick drive us over to the Pacific Dining Car, and Cisco and I ordered steak and eggs while Lorna had tea and honey. The Dining Car was a place where downtown power brokers liked to gather before a day of fighting it out in the glass towers nearby. The food was overpriced but good. It instilled confidence, made the downtown warrior feel like a heavy hitter.

As soon as the waiter took our order and left us, Lorna put her silverware to the side and opened a spiral-bound At-A-Glance calendar on the table.

"Eat fast," she said. "You have a busy day."

"Tell me."

"All right, the easy stuff first."

She flipped a couple of pages back and forth in the calendar, then proceeded.

"You have a ten a.m. in chambers with Judge Holder. She wants an updated client inventory."

"She told me I had a week," I protested. "Today's Thursday."

"Yeah, well, Michaela called and said the judge wants an interim update. I think she — the judge, that is — saw in the paper that you are continuing on as Elliot's lawyer. She's afraid you're spending all your time on Elliot and none on the other clients."

"That's not true. I filed a motion for Patrick yesterday and Tuesday I took the sentencing on Reese. I mean, I haven't even met all the clients yet."

"Don't worry, I have a hard-copy inventory back at the office for you to take with you. It shows who you've met, who you signed up and calendars on all of them. Just hit her with the paperwork and she won't be able to complain."

I smiled. Lorna was the best case manager in the business.

"Great. What else?"

"Then at eleven you have an in-chambers with Judge Stanton on Elliot."

"Status conference?"

"Yes. He wants to know if you are going to be able to go next Thursday."

"No, but Elliot won't have it any other way."

"Well, the judge will get to hear Elliot say that for himself. He's requiring the defendant's presence."

That was unusual. Most status conferences were routine and quick. The fact that Stanton wanted Elliot there bumped this one up into a more important realm.

I thought of something and pulled out my cell phone.

"Did you let Elliot know? He might—"

"Put it away. He knows and he'll be there. I talked to his assistant—Mrs. Albrecht—this morning and she knows he has to show and that the judge can revoke if he doesn't."

I nodded. It was a smart move. Threaten Elliot's freedom as a means of making sure he shows up.

"Good," I said. "That it?"

I wanted to get to Cisco to ask what else he had been able to find out about the Vincent investigation and whether his sources had mentioned anything about the man in the surveillance photo Bosch had shown me.

"Not by a long shot, my friend," Lorna responded. "Now we get to the mystery case."

"Let's hear it."

"We got a call yesterday afternoon from Judge Friedman's clerk, who called Vincent's office blind to see if there was anyone there taking over the cases. When the clerk was informed that you were taking over, she asked if you were aware of the hearing scheduled before Friedman today at two. I checked our new calendar and you didn't have a two o'clock on there for today. So there is the mystery. You have a hearing at two for a case we not only don't have on calendar but don't have a file for either."

"What's the client's name?"

"Eli Wyms."

It meant nothing to me.

"Did Wren know the name?"

Lorna shook her head in a dismissive way.

"Did you check the dead cases? Maybe it was just misfiled."

"No, we checked. There is no file anywhere in the office."

"And what's the hearing? Did you ask the clerk?"

Lorna nodded.

"Pretrial motions. Wyms is charged with attempted murder of a peace officer and several other weapons-related charges. He was arrested May second at a county park in Calabasas. He was arraigned, bound over and sent out to Camarillo for ninety days. He must've been found competent because the hearing today is to set a trial date and consider bail."

I nodded. From the shorthand, I could read between the lines. Wyms had gotten into some sort of confrontation involving weapons with the Sheriff's Department, which provided law enforcement services in the unincorporated area known as Calabasas. He was sent to the state's mental evaluation center in Camarillo, where the shrinks took three months deciding whether he was a crazy man or competent to stand trial on the charges against him. The docs determined he was competent, meaning he knew right from wrong when he tried to kill a peace officer, most likely the sheriff's deputy who confronted him.

It was a bare-bones sketch of the trouble Eli Wyms was in. There would be more detail in the file but we had no file.

"Is there any reference to Wyms in the trust account deposits?" I asked.

Lorna shook her head. I should've assumed she would be thorough and check the bank accounts in search of Eli Wyms.

"Okay, so it looks like maybe Jerry took him on pro bono."

Attorneys occasionally provide legal services free of charge — pro bono — to indigent or special clients. Sometimes this is an altruistic endeavor and sometimes it's because the client just won't pay up. Either way, the lack of an advance from Wyms was understandable. The missing file was another story.

"You know what I was thinking?" Lorna said.

"What?"

"That Jerry had the file with him — in his briefcase — when he left Monday night."

"And it got taken, along with his laptop and cell phone, by the killer."

She nodded and I nodded back.

It made sense. He was spending the evening preparing for the week and he had a hearing Thursday on Wyms. Maybe he had run out of gas and thrown the file in his briefcase to look at later. Or maybe he kept the file with him because it was important in a way I couldn't see yet. Maybe the killer wanted the Wyms file and not the laptop or the cell phone.

"Who's the prosecutor on the case?"

"Joanne Giorgetti, and I'm way ahead of you. I called her yesterday and explained our situation and asked if she wouldn't mind copying the discovery again for us. She said no problem. You can pick it up after your eleven with Judge Stanton and then have a couple hours to familiarize yourself with it before the hearing at two."

Joanne Giorgetti was a top-flight prosecutor who worked in the crimes-against-law-officers section of the DA's Office. She was also a longtime friend of my ex-wife's and was my daughter's basketball coach in the YMCA league. She had always been cordial and collegial with me, even after Maggie and I split up. It didn't surprise me that she would run off a copy of the discovery materials for me.

"You think of everything, Lorna," I said. "Why don't you just take over Vincent's practice and run with it? You don't need me."

She smiled at the compliment and I saw her eyes flick in the direction of Cisco. The read I got was that she wanted him to realize her value to the law firm of Michael Haller and Associates.

"I like working in the background," she said. "I'll leave center stage for you."

Our plates were served and I spread a liberal dose of Tabasco sauce on both my steak and the eggs. Sometimes hot sauce was the only way I knew I was still alive.

I was finally able to hear what Cisco had come up with on the Vincent investigation but he dug into his meal and I knew better than to try to keep him from his food. I decided to wait and asked Lorna how things were working out with Wren Williams. She answered in a low voice, as if Wren were sitting nearby in the restaurant and listening.

"She's not a lot of help, Mickey. She seems to have no idea of how the office worked or where Jerry put things. She'd be lucky to remember where she parked her car this morning. If you ask me, she was working there for some other reason."

I could have told her the reason—as it had been told to me by Bosch—but decided to keep it to myself. I didn't want to distract Lorna with gossip.

I looked over and saw Cisco mopping up the steak juice and hot sauce on his plate with a piece of toast. He was good to go.

"What do you have going today, Cisco?"

"I'm working on Rilz and his side of the equation."

"How's that going?"

"I think there'll be a couple things you can use. You want to hear about it?"

"Not yet. I'll ask when I need it."

I didn't want to be given any information about Rilz that I might have to turn over to the prosecution in discovery. At the moment, the less I knew, the better. Cisco understood this and nodded.

"I also have the Bruce Carlin debriefing this afternoon," Cisco added.

"He wants two hundred an hour," Lorna said. "Highway robbery, if you ask me."

I waved off her protest.

"Just pay it. It's a onetime expense and he probably has information we can use, and that might save Cisco some time."

"Don't worry, we're paying him. I'm just not happy about it. He's gouging us because he knows he can."

"Technically, he's gouging Elliot and I don't think he's going to care."

I turned back to my investigator.

"You have anything new on the Vincent case?"

Cisco updated me with what he had. It consisted mostly of forensic details, suggesting that the source he had inside the investigation came from that side of the equation. He said Vincent had been shot twice, both times in the area of the left temple. The spread on the entry wounds was less than an inch, and powder burns on the skin and hair indicated the weapon was nine to twelve inches away when fired. Cisco said this indicated that the killer had fired two quick shots and was fairly skilled. It was unlikely that an amateur would fire twice quickly and be able to cluster the impacts.

Additionally, Cisco said, the slugs never left the body and were recovered during the autopsy conducted late the day before.

"They were twenty-fives," he said.

I had handled countless cross-examinations of tool marks and ballistics experts. I knew my bullets and I knew a .25 caliber round came out of a small weapon but could do great damage, especially if fired into the cranial vault. The slugs would ricochet around inside. It would be like putting the victim's brain in a blender.

"They know the exact weapon yet?"

I knew that by studying the markings—lands and grooves—on the slugs they would be able to tell what kind of gun fired the rounds. Just as with the Malibu murders, in which the investigators knew what gun had been used, even though they didn't have it.

"Yeah. A twenty-five caliber Beretta Bobcat. Nice and small, you could almost hide it in your hand."

A completely different weapon than the one used to kill Mitzi Elliot and Johan Rilz.

"So what's all of this tell us?"

"It's a hitter's gun. You take it when you know it's going to be a head shot."

I nodded my agreement.

"So this was planned. The killer knew just what he was going to do. He waits in the garage, sees Jerry come out and comes right up to the car. The window goes down or it was already down, and the guy pops Jerry twice in the head, then reaches in for the briefcase that has the laptop, the cell phone, the portfolio and, we think, the Eli Wyms file."

"Exactly."

"Okay, what about the suspect?"

"The guy they sweated the first night?"

"No, that was Carlin. They cut him loose."

Cisco looked surprised.

"How'd you find out it was Carlin?"

"Bosch told me this morning."

"Are you saying they have another suspect?"

I nodded.

"He showed me a photo of a guy coming out of the building at the time of the shooting. He had a gun and was wearing an obvious disguise."

I saw Cisco's eyes flare. It was a point of professional pride that he provide me with information like that. He didn't like it happening the other way around.

"He didn't have a name, just the photo," I said. "He wanted to know if I had ever seen the guy before or if it was one of the clients."

Cisco's eyes darkened as he realized that his inside source was holding out on him. If I'd told him about the FBI calls, he probably would have picked the table up and thrown it through the window.

"I'll see what I can find out," he said quietly through a tight jaw.

I looked at Lorna.

"Bosch said he was coming back later to show the photo to Wren."

"I'll tell her."

"Make sure you look at it, too. I want everybody to be on alert for this guy."

"Okay, Mickey."

I nodded. We were finished. I put a credit card on the tab and pulled out my cell phone to call Patrick. Calling my driver reminded me of something.

"Cisco, there's one other thing I want you to try to do today."

Cisco looked at me, happy to move on from the idea that I had a better source on the investigation than he did.

"Go to Vincent's liquidator and see if he's sitting on one of Patrick's surfboards. If he is, I want it back for Patrick."

Cisco nodded.

"I can do that. No problem."

Twenty-four

Waylaid by the slow-moving elevators in the CCB, I was four minutes late when I walked into Judge Holder's courtroom and hustled through the clerk's corral toward the hallway leading to her chambers. I didn't see anyone and the door was closed. I knocked lightly and I heard the judge call for me to enter.

She was behind her desk and wearing her black robe. This told me she probably had a hearing in open court scheduled soon and my being late was not a good thing.

"Mr. Haller, our meeting was set for ten o'clock. I believe you were given proper notice of this."

"Yes, Your Honor, I know. I'm sorry. The elevators in this building are—"

"All lawyers take the same elevators and most seem to be on time for meetings with me."

"Yes, Your Honor."

"Did you bring your checkbook?"

"I think so, yes."

"Well, we can do this one of two ways," the judge said. "I can hold you in contempt of court, fine you and let you explain yourself to the California bar, or we can go informal and you take out your check-book and make a donation to the Make-A-Wish Foundation. It's one of my favorite charities. They do good things for sick children."

This was incredible. I was being fined for being four minutes late. The arrogance of some judges was amazing. I somehow was able to swallow my outrage and speak.

"I like the idea of helping out sick children, Your Honor," I said. "How much do I make it out for?"

"As much as you want to contribute. And I will even send it in for you."

She pointed to a stack of paperwork on the left side of her desk. I saw two other checks, most likely stroked out by two other poor bas-tards who had run afoul of the judge this week. I leaned down and rummaged through the front pocket of my backpack until I found my checkbook. I wrote a check for $250 to Make-A-Wish, tore it out and handed it across the desk. I watched the judge's eyes as she looked at the amount I was donating. She nodded approvingly and I knew I was all right.

"Thank you, Mr. Haller. They'll be sending you a receipt for your taxes in the mail. It will go to the address on the check."

"Like you said, they do good work."

"Yes, they do."

The judge put the check on top of the two others and then turned her attention back to me.

"Now, before we go over the cases, let me ask you a question," she said. "Do you know if the police are making any headway on the inves-tigation of Mr. Vincent's death?"

I hesitated a moment, wondering what I should be telling the chief judge of the superior court.

"I'm not really in the loop on that, Judge," I said. "But I was shown a photograph of a man I assume they're looking at as a suspect."

"Really? What kind of photo?"

"Like a surveillance shot from out on the street. A guy, and it looks like he has a gun. I think they matched it up timewise to the shooting in the garage."

"Did you recognize the man?"

I shook my head.

"No, the shot was too grainy. It looked like he might have had a disguise on anyway."

"When was this?"

"The night of the shooting."

"No, I mean, when was it that you were shown this photo?"

"Just this morning. Detective Bosch came to the office with it."

The judge nodded. We were quiet for a moment and then the judge got to the point of the meeting.

"Okay, Mr. Haller, why don't we talk about clients and cases now?"

"Yes, Your Honor."

I reached down and unzipped my bag, taking out the scorecard Lorna had prepared for me.

Judge Holder kept me at her desk for the next hour while I went over every case and client, detailing the status and conversations I'd had with each. By the time she finally let me go, I was late for my eleven o'clock hearing in Judge Stanton's chambers.

I left Holder's court and didn't bother with the elevators. I hit the exit stairs and charged up two flights to the floor where Stanton's courtroom was located. I was running eight minutes late and wondered if it was going to cost me another donation to another judge's favorite charity.

The courtroom was empty but Stanton's clerk was in her corral. She pointed with a pen to the open door to the hallway leading to the judge's chambers.

"They're waiting for you," she said.

I quickly moved by her and down the hall. The door to the chambers was open and I saw the judge sitting behind his desk. To his left rear side was a stenographer and across the desk from him were three chairs. Walter Elliot was sitting in the chair to the right, the middle chair was

empty and Jeffrey Golantz was in the third. I had never met the prosecutor before but he was recognizable because I had seen his face on TV
and in the newspapers. In the last few years, he had successfully handled a
series of high-profile cases and was making a name for himself. He was
the undefeated up-and-comer in the DA's Office.

I loved going up against undefeated prosecutors. Their confidence
often betrayed them.

"Sorry I'm late, Your Honor," I said as I slid into the empty seat.
"Judge Holder called me into a hearing and she ran long."

I hoped that mentioning the chief judge as the reason for my tardi-
ness would keep Stanton from further assaulting my checkbook and it
seemed to work.

"Let's go on the record now," he said.

The stenographer leaned forward and put her fingers on the keys of
her machine.

"In the matter of *California versus Walter Elliot,* we are in chambers today
for a status conference. Present is the defendant, along with Mr. Golantz for
the state and Mr. Haller, who is here in the late Mr. Vincent's stead."

The judge had to break there to give the stenographer the proper
spellings of all the names. He spoke in an authoritative voice that a
decade on the bench often gives a jurist. The judge was a handsome man
with a full head of bristly gray hair. He was in good shape, the black
robe doing little to disguise his well-developed shoulders and chest.

"So," he then said, "we're scheduled in this matter for voir dire next
Thursday—a week from today—and I notice, Mr. Haller, that I have
received no motion from you to continue the matter while you get up to
speed on the case."

"We don't want a delay," Elliot said.

I reached over and put my hand on my client's forearm and shook
my head.

"Mr. Elliot, in this session I want you to let your lawyer do the talking," the judge said.

"Sorry, Your Honor," I said. "But the message is the same whether from me or directly from Mr. Elliot. We want no delay. I have spent the week getting up to speed and I will be prepared to begin jury selection next Thursday."

The judge squinted his eyes at me.

"You sure about that, Mr. Haller?"

"Absolutely. Mr. Vincent was a good lawyer and he kept thorough records. I understand the strategy he built and will be ready to go on Thursday. The case has my full attention. That of my staff as well."

The judge leaned back in his high-backed chair and swiveled side to side as he thought. He finally looked at Elliot.

"Mr. Elliot, it turns out you do get to speak after all. I would like to hear directly from you that you are in full agreement with your new attorney here and that you understand the risk you run, bringing in a fresh lawyer so close to the start of trial. It's your freedom at stake here, sir. Let's hear what you have to say about it."

Elliot leaned forward and spoke in a defiant tone.

"Judge, first of all, I am in complete agreement. I want to get this thing to trial so I can blow the district attorney here right out of the water. I am an innocent man being persecuted and prosecuted for something I did not do. I don't want to spend a single extra day as the accused, sir. I loved my wife and I'll miss her forever. I didn't kill her and it pierces my heart when I hear the people on TV saying these vile things about me. What hurts the most is knowing that the real killer is out there someplace. The sooner Mr. Haller gets to prove my innocence to the world, the better."

It was O.J. 101 but the judge studied Elliot and nodded thoughtfully, then turned his attention to the prosecutor.

"Mr. Golantz? What is the state's view of this?"

The deputy district attorney cleared his throat. The word to describe him was telegenic. He was handsome and dark and his eyes seemed to carry the very wrath of justice in them.

"Your Honor, the state is prepared for trial and has no objection to proceeding on schedule. But I would ask that, if Mr. Elliot is so sure about proceeding without delay, he formally waive any appellate redress in this regard should things not go as he predicts in trial."

The judge swiveled his chair so that his focus could go back on me.

"What about that, Mr. Haller?"

"Your Honor, I don't think it's necessary for my client to waive any protections that might be afforded to—"

"I don't mind," Elliot said, cutting in on me. "I'll waive whatever you damn well please. I want to go to trial."

I looked sharply at him. He looked at me and shrugged.

"We're going to win this thing," he explained.

"You want to take a moment in the corridor, Mr. Haller?" the judge asked.

"Thank you, Judge."

I got up and signaled Elliot up.

"Come with me."

We walked out into the short hallway that led to the courtroom. I closed the door behind us. Elliot spoke before I could, underlining the problem.

"Look, I want this thing over and I—"

"Shut up!" I said in a forced whisper.

"What?"

"You heard me. Shut the fuck up. You understand? I am sure you are quite used to talking whenever you want and having everybody listen to every brilliant word you say. But you are not in Hollywood anymore, Walter. You aren't talking make-believe movies with this week's mogulito. You understand what I'm saying? This is real life. You don't speak unless you are spoken to. If you have something to say otherwise, then you whisper it into my ear and if I think it is worth repeating, then *I*—not you—will say it to the judge. You got it?"

It took Elliot a long time to answer. His face turned dark and I understood that I might be about to lose the franchise. But in the moment I didn't care. What I had said needed to be said. It was a welcome-to-my-world speech that was long overdue.

"Yes," he finally said, "I get it."

"Good, then remember it. Now, let's go back in there and see if we can avoid giving away your right to appeal if you happen to get convicted because I fucked up by being unprepared for trial."

"That won't happen. I have faith in you."

"I appreciate that, Walter. But the truth is, you have no basis for that faith. And whether you do or don't, it doesn't mean we have to give anything away. Let's go back in now, and let me do the talking. That's why I get the big bucks, right?"

I clapped him on the shoulder. We went in and sat back down. And Walter didn't say another word. I argued that he shouldn't have to give away his right to appellate review just because he wanted the speedy trial he was entitled to. But Judge Stanton sided with Golantz, ruling that if Elliot declined the offer to delay the trial, he couldn't come complaining after a conviction that his attorney hadn't had enough time to prepare. Faced with the ruling, Elliot stuck to his guns and declined the delay, as I knew he would. That was okay with me. Under the Byzantine rules of law, almost nothing was safe from appeal. I knew that if necessary, Elliot would still be able to appeal the ruling the judge had just made.

We moved on to what the judge called housekeeping after that. The first order of business was to have both sides sign off on a motion from Court TV to be allowed to broadcast segments of the trial live on its daily programming. Neither I nor Golantz objected. After all, it was free advertising—me for new clients, Golantz to further his political aspirations. And as far as Walter Elliot was concerned, he whispered to me that he wanted the cameras there to record his not-guilty verdict.

Next the judge outlined the schedule for submitting final discovery and witness lists. He gave us until Monday on the discovery materials and the witness lists were due the day after that.

"No exceptions, gentlemen," he said. "I look dimly on surprise additions after deadline."

This was not going to be a problem from the defense's side of the aisle. Vincent had already made two previous discovery filings and there was very little new since then for me to share with the prosecution. Cisco Wojciechowski was doing a good job of keeping me in the dark as to what he was finding out about Rilz. And what I didn't know I couldn't put in the discovery file.

When it comes to witnesses, my plan was to give Golantz the usual runaround. I would be submitting a list of potential witnesses, naming every law officer and forensic tech mentioned in the sheriff's reports. That was standard operating procedure. Golantz would have to puzzle over who I really would call to testify and who was important to the defense's case.

"All right, guys, I've probably got a courtroom full of lawyers out there waiting for me," Stanton finally said. "Are we clear on everything?"

Golantz and I nodded our heads. I couldn't help but wonder if either the judge or the prosecutor was the recipient of the bribe. Was I sitting with the man who would turn the case my client's way? If so, he had done nothing to give himself away. I finished the meeting thinking that Bosch had it all wrong. There was no bribe. There was a hundred-thousand-dollar boat somewhere in a harbor in San Diego or Cabo and it had Jerry Vincent's name on the title.

"Okay, then," the judge said. "We'll get this going next week. We can talk about ground rules Thursday morning. But I want to make it clear right now, I'm going to run this trial like a well-oiled machine. No surprises, no shenanigans, no funny stuff. Again, are we clear?"

Golantz and I both agreed once more that we were clear. But the judge swiveled his chair and looked directly at me. He squinted his eyes in suspicion.

"I'm going to hold you to that," he said.

It seemed to be a message intended only for me, a message that would never show on the stenographer's record.

How come, I wondered, it's always the defense attorney who gets the judicial squint?

Twenty-five

got to Joanne Giorgetti's office shortly before the noon break. I knew that getting there a minute after twelve would be too late. The DA's Offices literally empty during the lunch hour, the inhabitants seeking sunlight, fresh air and sustenance outside the CCB. I told the receptionist I had an appointment with Giorgetti and she made a call. Then she buzzed the door lock and told me to go back.

Giorgetti had a small, windowless office with most of the floor space taken up by cardboard file boxes. It was the same way in every prosecutor's office I had ever been in, big or small. She was at her desk but was hidden behind a wall of stacked motions and files. I carefully reached over the wall to shake her hand.

"How's it going, Joanne?"

"Not bad, Mickey. How about you?"

"I'm doing okay."

"You just got a lot of cases, I hear."

"Yeah, quite a few."

The conversation was stilted. I knew she and Maggie were tight, and there was no telling whether my ex-wife had opened up to her about my difficulties in the past year.

"So you're here for Wyms?"

"That's right. I didn't even know I had the case till this morning."

She handed me a file with an inch-thick stack of documents in it.

"What do you think happened to Jerry's file?" she asked.

"I think maybe the killer took it."

She made a cringing face.

"Weird. Why would the killer take this file?"

"Probably unintended. The file was in Jerry's briefcase along with his laptop, and the killer just took the whole thing."

"Hmmm."

"Well, is there anything unusual about this case? Anything that would have made Jerry a target?"

"I don't think so. Just your usual everyday crazy-with-a-gun sort of thing."

I nodded.

"Have you heard anything about a federal grand jury taking a look at the state courts?"

She knitted her eyebrows.

"Why would they be looking at this case?"

"I'm not saying they were. I've been out of the loop for a while. I was wondering what you've heard."

She shrugged.

"Just the usual rumors on the gossip circuit. Seems like there's always a federal investigation of something."

"Yeah."

I said nothing else, hoping she would fill me in on the rumor. But she didn't and it was time to move on.

"The hearing today is to set a trial date?" I asked.

"Yes, but I assume you'll want a continuance so you can get up to speed."

"Well, let me go look at the file during lunch and I'll let you know if that's what the plan is."

"Okay, Mickey. But just so you know. I won't oppose a continuance, considering what happened with Jerry."

"Thanks, CoJo."

She smiled as I used the name her young basketball players called her by at the Y.

"You seen Maggie lately?" she asked.

"Saw her last night when I went to pick up Hayley. She seems to be doing okay. Have you seen her?"

"Just at basketball practice. But she usually sits there with her nose in a file. We used to go out after with the girls to Hamburger Hamlet but Maggie's been too busy."

I nodded. She and Maggie had been foxhole buddies since day one, coming up through the ranks of the prosecutor's office. Competitors but not competitive with each other. But time goes by and distances work their way into any relationship.

"Well, I'll take this and look it all over," I said. "The hearing's with Friedman at two, right?"

"Yeah, two. I'll see you then."

"Thanks for doing this, Joanne."

"No problem."

I left the DA's Office and waited ten minutes to get on an elevator with the lunch crowd. The last one on, I rode down with my face two inches from the door. I hated the elevators more than anything else in the entire Criminal Courts Building.

"Hey, Haller."

It was a voice from behind me. I didn't recognize it but it was too crowded for me to turn around to see who it was.

"What?"

"Heard you scored all of Vincent's cases."

I wasn't going to discuss my business in a crowded elevator. I didn't respond. We finally hit bottom, and the doors spread open. I stepped out and looked back for the person who had spoken.

It was Dan Daly, another defense attorney who was part of a coterie of lawyers who took in Dodgers games occasionally and martinis routinely at Four Green Fields. I had missed the last season of booze and baseball.

"How ya doin', Dan?"

We shook hands, an indication of how long it had been since we'd seen each other.

"So, who'd you grease?"

He said it with a smile but I could tell there was something behind it. Maybe a dose of jealousy over my scoring the Elliot case. Every lawyer in town knew it was a franchise case. It could pay top dollar for years—first the trial and then the appeals that would come after a conviction.

"Nobody," I said. "Jerry put me in his will."

We started walking toward the exit doors. Daly's ponytail was longer and grayer. But what was most notable was that it was intricately braided. I hadn't seen that before.

"Then, lucky you," Daly said. "Let me know if you need a second chair on Elliot."

"He wants only one lawyer at the table, Dan. He said no dream team."

"Well, then keep me in mind as a writer in regard to the rest."

This meant he was available to write appeals on any convictions my new set of clients might incur. Daly had forged a solid reputation as an expert appeals man with a good batting average.

"I'll do that," I said. "I'm still reviewing everything."

"Good enough."

We came through the doors and I could see the Lincoln at the curb, waiting. Daly was going the other way. I told him I'd keep in touch.

"We miss you at the bar, Mick," he said over his shoulder.

"I'll drop by," I called back.

But I knew I wouldn't drop by, that I had to stay away from places like that.

I got in the back of the Lincoln—I tell my drivers never to get out and open the door for me—and told Patrick to take me over to Chinese

Friends on Broadway. I told him to drop me and go get lunch on his own. I needed to sit and read and didn't want any conversation.

I got to the restaurant between the first and second waves of patrons and waited no more than five minutes for a table. Wanting to get to work immediately, I ordered a plate of the fried pork chops right away. I knew they would be perfect. They were paper-thin and delicious and I'd be able to eat them with my fingers without taking my eyes off the Wyms documents.

I opened the file Joanne Giorgetti had given me. It contained copies only of what the prosecutor had turned over to Jerry Vincent under the rules of discovery — primarily sheriff's documents relating to the incident, arrest and follow-up investigation. Any notes, strategies or defense documents that Vincent had generated were lost with the original file.

The natural starting point was the arrest report, which included the initial and most basic summary of what had transpired. As is often the case, it started with 911 calls to the county communications-and-dispatch center. Multiple reports of gunfire came in from a neighborhood next to a park in Calabasas. The calls fell under Sheriff's Department jurisdiction because Calabasas was in an unincorporated area north of Malibu and near the western limits of the county.

The first deputy to respond was listed on the report as Todd Stallworth. He worked the night shift out of the Malibu substation and had been dispatched at 10:21 p.m. to the neighborhood off Las Virgenes Road. From there he was directed into the nearby Malibu Creek State Park, where the shots were being fired. Now hearing shots himself, Stallworth called for backup and drove into the park to investigate.

There were no lights in the rugged mountain park, as it was posted CLOSED AT SUNSET. As Stallworth entered on the main road, the headlights of his patrol car picked up a reflection, and the deputy saw a vehicle parked in a clearing ahead. He put on his spotlight and illuminated a pickup truck with its tailgate down. There was a pyramid of beer cans on the tailgate and what looked like a gun bag with several rifle barrels protruding from it.

Stallworth stopped his car eighty yards from the pickup and decided to wait until backup arrived. He was on the radio to the Malibu station, describing the pickup truck and saying that he was not close enough to read its license plate, when suddenly there was a gunshot and the searchlight located above the side-view mirror exploded with the bullet's impact. Stallworth killed the rest of the car's lights and bailed out, crawling into the cover of some bushes that lined the clearing. He used his handheld radio to call for additional backup and the special weapons and tactics team.

A three-hour standoff ensued, with the gunman hidden in the wooded terrain near the clearing. He fired his weapon repeatedly but apparently his aim was at the sky. No deputies were struck by bullets. No other vehicles were damaged. Finally, a deputy in black SWAT gear worked his way close enough to the pickup truck to read the license plate by using high-powered binoculars equipped with night-vision lenses. The plate number led to the name Eli Wyms, which in turn led to a cell-phone number. The shooter answered on the first ring and a SWAT team negotiator began a conversation.

The shooter was indeed Eli Wyms, a forty-four-year-old housepainter from Inglewood. He was characterized in the arrest report as drunk, angry and suicidal. Earlier in the day, he had been kicked out of his home by his wife, who informed him that she was in love with another man. Wyms had driven to the ocean and then north to Malibu and then over the mountains to Calabasas. He saw the park and thought it looked like a good place to stop the truck and sleep, but he drove on by and bought a case of beer at a gas station near the 101 Freeway. He then turned around and went back to the park.

Wyms told the negotiator that he started shooting because he heard noises in the dark and was afraid. He believed he was shooting at rabid coyotes that wanted to eat him. He said he could see their red eyes glowing in the dark. He said he shot out the spotlight on the first patrol car that arrived because he was afraid the light would give his position away to the animals. When asked about the shot from eighty yards, he said he had qualified as an expert marksman during the first war in Iraq.

The report estimated that Wyms fired at least twenty-seven times while deputies were on the scene and dozens of times before that. Investigators eventually collected a total of ninety-four spent bullet casings.

Wyms did not surrender that night until he ran out of beer. Shortly after crushing the last empty in his hand, he told the cell-phone negotiator that he would trade one rifle for a six-pack of beer. He was turned down. He then announced that he was sorry and ready for the incident and everything else to be over, that he was going to kill himself and literally go out with a bang. The negotiator tried to talk him out of it and kept the conversation going while a two-man SWAT unit moved through the heavy terrain toward his position in a dense stand of eucalyptus trees. But soon the negotiator heard snoring on the cell line. Wyms had passed out.

The SWAT team moved in and Wyms was captured without a shot being fired by law enforcement. Order was restored. Since Deputy Stallworth had taken the initial call and was the one fired upon, he was given the collar. The gunman was placed in Stallworth's squad car and transported to the Malibu substation and jailed.

Other documents in the file continued the Eli Wyms saga. At his arraignment the morning after his arrest, Wyms was declared indigent and assigned a public defender. The case moved slowly in the system, with Wyms being held in the Men's Central Jail. But then Vincent stepped in and offered his services pro bono. His first order of business was to ask for and receive a competency evaluation of his client. This had the effect of slowing the case down even further as Wyms was carted off to the state hospital in Camarillo for a ninety-day psych evaluation.

That evaluation period was over and the reports were now in. All of the doctors who examined, tested and talked to Wyms in Camarillo had agreed that he was competent and ready to stand trial.

In the hearing scheduled before Judge Mark Friedman at two, a trial date would be set and the case clock would begin to tick again. To me it was all a formality. One read of the case documents and I knew there would be no trial. What the day's hearing would do was set the time period I would have to negotiate a plea agreement for my client.

It was a cut-and-dried case. Wyms would enter a plea and probably face a year or two of incarceration and mental-health counseling. The only question I got from my survey of the file was why Vincent had taken the case in the first place. It didn't fall into line with the kinds of cases he usually handled, with paying or higher-profile clients. There didn't seem to be much of a challenge to the case either. It was routine and Wyms's crime wasn't even unusual. Was it simply a case Jerry took on to satisfy a need for pro bono work? It seemed to me if that was the case that Vincent could have found something more interesting, which would pay off in other ways, such as publicity. The Wyms case had initially drawn media attention because of the public spectacle in the park. But when it came to trial or disposition of the case, it would likely fly well below the media radar.

My next thought was to suspect that there was a connection to the Elliot case. Vincent had found some sort of link.

But on first read I couldn't nail it down. There were two general connections in that the Wyms incident had happened less than twelve hours before the beach house murders and both crimes had occurred in the Sheriff's Department's Malibu district. But those connections didn't hold up to further scrutiny. In terms of topography they weren't remotely connected. The murders were on the beach and the Wyms shooting spree took place far inland, in the county park on the other side of the mountains. As far as I could recall, none of the names in the Wyms file were mentioned in the Elliot materials I had reviewed. The Wyms incident happened on the night shift; the Elliot murders on the day shift.

I couldn't nail down any specific connection and in great frustration closed the file with the question unanswered. I checked my watch and saw I had to get back to the CCB if I wanted time to meet my client in lockup before the two o'clock hearing.

I called Patrick to come get me, paid for lunch and stepped out to the curb. I was on my cell, talking with Lorna, when the Lincoln pulled up and I jumped into the back.

"Has Cisco met with Carlin yet?" I asked her.

"No, that's at two."

"Have Cisco ask him about the Wyms case, too."

"Okay, what about it?"

"Ask him why Vincent even took it."

"You think they're connected? Elliot and Wyms?"

"I think it but I don't see it."

"Okay, I'll tell him."

"Anything else going on?"

"Not at the moment. You're getting a lot of calls from the media. Who's this guy Jack McEvoy?"

The name rang a bell but I couldn't place it.

"I don't know. Who is he?"

"He works at the *Times*. He called up all huffy about not hearing from you, saying you had an exclusive deal with him."

Now I remembered. The two-way street.

"Don't worry about him. I haven't heard from him either. What else?"

"Court TV wants to sit down and talk about Elliot. They're going to carry live coverage throughout the trial, making it their feature, and so they're hoping to get daily commentary from you at the end of court each day."

"What do you think, Lorna?"

"I think it's like free national advertising. You better do it. They told me they're giving the trial its own logo wrap at the bottom of the screen. 'Murder in Malibu,' they're calling it."

"Then, set it up. What else?"

"Well, while we're on the subject, I got a notice a week ago that your bus bench contract expires at the end of the month. I was just going to let it go because there was no money, but now you're back and you've got money. Should we renew?"

For the past six years I had advertised on bus benches strategically located in high-crime and -traffic locations around the city. Although I had dropped out for the past year, the benches still spawned a steady stream of calls, all of which Lorna deferred or referred.

"That's a two-year contract, right?"

"Yes."

I made a quick decision.

"Okay, renew it. Anything else?"

"That's it from here. Oh, wait. One other thing. The landlord for the building came in today. Called herself the leasing agent, which is just a fancy way of saying landlord. She wants to know if we're going to keep the office. Jerry's death is a lease breaker if we want it to be. I got the feeling there's a waiting list on the building and this is an opportunity to jack the rent up for the next lawyer who comes in here."

I looked out the window of the Lincoln as we cruised across the 101 overpass and back into the civic center area. I could see the newly built Catholic cathedral and past that, the waving steel skin of the Disney Concert Hall. It caught the sunlight and took on a warm orange glow.

"I don't know, Lorna, I like working from the backseat here. It's never boring. What do you think?"

"I'm not particularly fond of putting on makeup every morning."

Meaning she liked working out of her condo more than she liked getting ready and driving downtown to an office each day. As usual, we were on the same page.

"Something to think about," I said. "No makeup. No office overhead. No fighting for a spot in the parking garage."

She didn't respond. It was going to be my call. I looked ahead and saw we were a block from my drop-off point in front of the CCB.

"Let's talk about it later," I said. "I gotta jump out."

"Okay, Mickey. Be safe."

"You, too."

Twenty-six

Eli Wyms was still doped up from the three months he'd spent in Camarillo. He'd been sent back to county with a prescription for a drug therapy that wasn't going to help me defend him, let alone help him answer any questions about possible connections to the murders on the beach. It took me less than two minutes in courtside lockup to grasp the situation and to decide to submit a motion to Judge Friedman, requesting that all drug therapy be halted. I went back to the courtroom and found Joanne Giorgetti at her place at the prosecution table. The hearing was scheduled to start in five minutes.

She was writing something on the inside flap of a file when I walked up to the table. Without looking up she somehow knew it was me.

"You want a continuance, don't you?"

"And a cease-and-desist on the drugs. The guy's a zombie."

She stopped writing and looked up at me.

"Considering he was potshotting my deputies, I'm not sure I object to his being in that condition."

"But Joanne, I've got to be able to ask the guy basic questions in order to defend him."

"Really?"

She said it with a smile but the point was taken. I shrugged and crouched down so we were on an even eye line.

"You're right, I don't think we're talking about a trial here," I said. "I'd be happy to listen to any offers."

"Your client shot at an occupied sheriff's car. The state is interested in sending a message on this one. We don't like people doing that."

She folded her arms to signal the state's unwillingness to compromise on this. She was an attractive and athletically built woman. She drummed her fingers on one of her biceps and I couldn't help but notice the red fingernail polish. As long as I could remember dealing with Joanne Giorgetti, her nails were always painted bloodred. She did more than represent the state. She represented cops who had been shot at, assaulted, ambushed and spit on. And she wanted the blood of every miscreant who had the bad luck to be prosecuted by her.

"I would argue that my client, panicked as he was by the coyotes, was shooting at the light on the car, not into the car. Your own documents say he was an expert marksman in the U.S. Army. If he wanted to shoot the deputy, he could have. But he didn't."

"He was discharged from the army fifteen years ago, Mickey."

"Right, but some skills never go away. Like riding a bike."

"Well, that's an argument you could surely make to the jury."

My knees were about to give out. I reached over to one of the chairs at the defense table, wheeled it over and sat down.

"Sure, I can make that argument but it is probably in the state's best interest to bring this case to a close, get Mr. Wyms off the street and into some sort of therapy that will help prevent this from ever happening again. So what do you say? Should we go off into a corner someplace and work this out, or go at it in front of a jury?"

She thought for a moment before responding. It was the classic prosecutor's dilemma. It was a case she could easily win. She had to decide whether to pad her stats or do what might be the right thing.

"As long as I get to pick the corner."

"That's fine with me."

"Okay, I won't oppose a continuance if you make the motion."

"Sounds good, Joanne. What about the drug therapy?"

"I don't want this guy acting out again, even in Men's Central."

"Look, wait till they bring him out. You'll see, he's a zombie. You don't want this to go down and then have him challenge the deal because the state made him incompetent to make a decision. Let's get his head clear, do the deal and then you can have them pump him up with whatever you want."

She thought about it, saw the logic and finally nodded.

"But if he acts out in jail one time, I'm going to blame you and take it out on him."

I laughed. The idea of blaming me was absurd.

"Whatever."

I got up and started to push the chair back to the defense table. But then I turned back to the prosecutor.

"Joanne, let me ask you something else. Why did Jerry Vincent take on this case?"

She shrugged and shook her head.

"I don't know."

"Well, did it surprise you?"

"Sure. It was kind of strange, him showing up. I knew him from way back when, you know?"

Meaning when he was a prosecutor.

"Yeah, so what happened?"

"One day—a few months ago—I got notice of a competency motion on Wyms, and Jerry's name was on it. I called him up and said, 'What the hell,' you know? 'You don't even call to say, I'm taking over the case?' And he just said he wanted to get some pro bono in and asked the PD for a case. But I know Angel Romero, the PD who had the case originally. A couple months back, I ran into him on one of the floors and he asked me what was happening on Wyms. And in the course of the conversation, he told me that Jerry didn't just come in asking for a PB referral. He went to Wyms first in Men's Central, signed him up and then came in and told Angel to turn over the file."

"Why do you think he took the case?"

I've learned over the years that sometimes if you ask the same question more than once you get different responses.

"I don't know. I specifically asked him that and he didn't really answer. He changed the subject to something else and it was all kind of awkward. I remember thinking there was something else here, like maybe he had a connection to Wyms. But then when he sent him off to Camarillo, I knew he wasn't doing the guy any favors."

"What do you mean?"

"Look, you just spent a couple hours with the case and you know how it's going to go. This is a plea. Jail time, counseling and supervision. That's what it was before he was sent to Camarillo. So Wyms's time there wasn't really necessary. Jerry just prolonged the inevitable."

I nodded. She was right. Sending a client to the psych ward at Camarillo wasn't doing him any favors. The mystery case was getting more mysterious. Only, my client was in no condition to tell me why. His lawyer — Vincent — had kept him drugged up and locked away for three months.

"Okay, Joanne. Thanks. Let's — "

I was interrupted by the clerk, who called court into session, and I looked up to see Judge Friedman taking the bench.

Twenty-seven

Angel Romero was one of those human interest stories you read in the paper every now and then. The story about the gangbanger who grew up hard on the streets of East L.A. but fought his way through to an education and even law school, then turned around and gave back to the community. Angel's way to give back was to go into the Public Defenders Office and represent the underdogs of society. He was a lifer in the PD and had seen many young lawyers — myself included — come and go on their way to private practice and the supposed big bucks that came with it.

After the Wyms hearing — in which the judge granted the motion to continue in order to give Giorgetti and me time to work out a plea — I went down to the PD's office on the tenth floor and asked for Romero. I knew he was a working lawyer, not a supervisor, and that most likely meant he was in a courtroom somewhere in the building. The receptionist typed something into her computer and looked at the screen.

"Department one-twenty-four," she said.

"Thank you," I said.

Department 124 was Judge Champagne's courtroom on the thirteenth floor, the same floor I had just come from. But that was life in the CCB. It seemed to run in circles. I took the elevator back up and walked down the hall to 124, powering my phone down as I approached the double doors. Court was in session and Romero was in front of the judge, arguing a motion to reduce bail. I slid into the back row of the gallery and hoped for a quick ruling so I could get to Romero without a long wait.

My ears perked up when I heard Romero mention his client by name, calling him Mr. Scales. I slid further down the bench so I had a better visual angle on the defendant sitting next to Romero. He was a white guy in an orange jail jumpsuit. When I saw his profile, I knew it was Sam Scales, a con man and former client. The last I remembered of Scales, he had gone off to prison on a plea deal I'd obtained for him. That was three years ago. He obviously had gotten out and gotten right back into trouble — only this time he hadn't called me.

After Romero finished his bail argument, the prosecutor stood up and vigorously opposed bail, outlining in his argument the new charges against Scales. When I had represented him, he had been accused in a credit-card fraud in which he ripped off people donating to a tsunami relief organization. This time it was worse. He was once more charged with fraud but in this case the victims were the widows of military servicemen killed in Iraq. I shook my head and almost smiled. I was glad Sam hadn't called me. The public defender could have him.

Judge Champagne ruled quickly after the prosecutor finished. She called Scales a predator and a menace to society and kept his bail at a million dollars. She noted that if she'd been asked, she probably would have raised it. It was then that I remembered it had been Judge Champagne who had sentenced Scales in the earlier fraud. There was nothing worse for a defendant than coming back and facing the same judge for another crime. It was almost as if the judges took the failings of the justice system personally.

I slouched in my seat and used another observer in the gallery as a blind so that Scales couldn't see me when the court deputy stood him up, cuffed him and took him back into lockup. After he was gone, I straightened back up and was able to catch Romero's eye. I signaled him out into the hallway and he flashed five fingers at me. Five minutes. He still had some business to take care of in the court.

I went out into the hallway to wait for him and turned my phone back on. No messages. I was calling Lorna to check in when I heard Romero's voice behind me. He was four minutes early.

"Eenie, meenie, minie, moe, catch a killer by the toe. If his lawyer's Haller, let him go. Eenie, meenie, minie, moe. Hey bro."

He was smiling. I closed the phone and we bumped fists. I hadn't heard that homespun jingle since I was with the PD's Office. Romero had made it up after I had gotten the not-guilty verdict in the Barnett Woodson case back in 'ninety-two.

"What's up?" Romero asked.

"I'll tell you what's up. You're guzzling my clients, man. Sam Scales used to be mine."

I said it with a knowing smile and Romero smiled right back.

"You want him? You can have him. That's one dirty white boy. As soon as the media gets wind of this case, they're going to lynch his ass for what he's done."

"Taking war widows' money, huh?"

"Stealing government death benefits. I tell you, I've repped a lot of bad guys who did a lot of bad things, but I put Scales up there with the baby rapers, man. I can't stand the guy."

"Yeah, what are you doing with a white boy anyway? You work gang crimes."

Romero's face turned serious and he shook his head.

"Not anymore, man. They thought I was getting too close to the customers. You know, once a vato always a vato. So they took me off gangs. After nineteen years, I'm off gangs."

"Sorry to hear that, buddy."

Romero had grown up in Boyle Heights in a neighborhood ruled by a gang called Quatro Flats. He had the tattoos to prove it, if you could ever see his arms. It didn't matter how hot a day it was, he always wore long sleeves when he was working. And when he represented a banger accused of a crime, he did more than defend him in court. He worked to spring the man from the clutches of gang life. To pull him away from gang cases was an act of stupidity that could only happen in a bureaucracy like the justice system.

"What do you want with me, Mick? You didn't really come here to take Scales from me, right?"

"No, you get to keep Scales, Angel. I wanted to ask you about another client you had for a while earlier this year. Eli Wyms."

I was about to give the details of the case as a prompt but Romero immediately recognized the case and nodded.

"Yeah, Vincent took that one off me. You got it now with him being dead?"

"Yeah, I got all of Vincent's cases. I just found out about Wyms today."

"Well, good luck with them, bro. What do you need to know about Wyms? Vincent took it off me three months ago, at least."

I nodded.

"Yeah, I know. I got a handle on the case. What I'm curious about is Vincent taking it. According to Joanne Giorgetti, he went after it. Is that right?"

Romero checked the memory banks for a few moments before answering. He raised a hand and rubbed his chin as he did so. I could see faint scars across his knuckles from where he'd had tattoos removed.

"Yeah, he went down to the jail and talked Wyms into it. Got a signed discharge letter and brought it in. After that, the case was his. I gave him my file and I was done, man."

I moved in closer to him.

"Did he say why he wanted the case? I mean, he didn't know Wyms, did he?"

"I don't think so. He just wanted the case. He gave me the big wink, you know?"

"No, what do you mean? What's the 'big wink'?"

"I asked him why he was taking on a Southside homeboy who went up there in white-people country and shot the place up. Pro bono, no less. I thought he had some sort of racial angle on it or something. Something that would get him a little publicity. But he just sort of gave me the wink, like there was something else."

"Did you ask him what?"

Romero took an involuntary step back as I pressed his personal space.

"Yeah, man, I asked. But he wouldn't tell me. He just said that Wyms had fired the magic bullet. I didn't know what the hell he meant and I didn't have any more time to play games with him. I gave him the file and I went on to the next one."

There it was again. The magic bullet. I was getting close to something here and I could feel the blood in my veins start to move with high velocity.

"Is that it, Mick? I gotta get back inside."

My eyes focused on Romero and I realized he was looking at me strangely.

"Yeah, Angel, thanks. That's all. Go back in there and give 'em hell."

"Yeah, man, that's what I do."

Romero went back toward the door to Department 124 and I headed off quickly to the elevators. I knew what I would be doing for the rest of the day and into the night. Tracing a magic bullet.

Twenty-eight

entered the office and blew right by Lorna and Cisco, who were at the reception desk, looking at the computer. I spoke without stopping on my way to the inner sanctum.

"If you two have any updates for me or anything else I should know, then come in now. I'm about to go into lockdown."

"And hello to you, too," Lorna called after me.

But Lorna knew well what was about to happen. Lockdown was when I closed all the doors and windows, drew the curtains and killed the phones and went to work on a file and a case with total concentration and absorption. Lockdown for me was the ultimate DO NOT DISTURB sign hanging on the door. Lorna knew that once I was in lockdown mode, there was no getting me out until I had found what I was looking for.

I moved around Jerry Vincent's desk and dropped into the seat. I opened my bag on the floor and started pulling out the files. I viewed what I needed to do here as me against them. Somewhere in the files, I would find the key to Jerry Vincent's last secret. I would find the magic bullet.

Lorna and Cisco came into the office soon after I was settled.

"I didn't see Wren out there," I said before either could speak.

"And you never will again," Lorna said. "She quit."

"That was kind of abrupt."

"She went out to lunch and never came back."

"Did she call?"

"Yeah, she finally called. She said she got a better offer. She's going to be Bruce Carlin's secretary now."

I nodded. That seemed to make a certain amount of sense.

"Now, before you go into lockdown, we need to go over some things," Lorna said.

"That's what I said when I came in. What've you got?"

Lorna sat down in one of the chairs in front of the desk. Cisco stayed standing, more like pacing, behind her.

"All right," Lorna said. "Couple things while you were in court. First, you must've touched a nerve with that motion you filed on the evidence in Patrick's case."

"What happened?" I asked.

"The prosecutor's called three times today, wanting to talk about a dispo."

I smiled. The motion to examine the evidence had been a long shot but it looked like it might come through and I would be able to help Patrick.

"What's going on with that?" Lorna asked. "You didn't tell me you filed motions."

"From the car yesterday. And what's going on is that I think Dr. Vogler gave his wife phony diamonds for her birthday. Now, to make sure she never knows it, they're going to float a deal to Patrick if I withdraw my request to examine the evidence."

"Good. I think I like Patrick."

"I hope he gets the break. What's next?"

Lorna looked at the notes on her steno pad. I knew she didn't like to be rushed but I was rushing her.

"You're still getting a lot of calls from the local media. About Jerry Vincent or Walter Elliot or both. You want to go over them?"

"No. I don't have the time for any media calls."

"Well, that's what I've been telling them but it's not making them happy. Especially that guy from the *Times*. He's being an asshole."

"So what if they're not happy? I don't care."

"Well, you better be careful, Mickey. Hell hath no fury like the media scorned."

It was a good point. The media can love you one day and bury you the next. My father had spent twenty years as a media darling. But toward the end of his professional life, he had become a pariah because the reporters had grown weary of him getting guilty men off. He became the embodiment of a justice system that had different rules for well-heeled defendants with powerful attorneys.

"I'll try to be more accommodating," I said. "Just not now."

"Fine."

"Anything else to report?"

"I think that's—I told you about Wren, so that's all I have. You'll call the prosecutor on Patrick's case?"

"Yes, I will call him."

I looked over Lorna's shoulder at Cisco, who was still standing.

"Okay, Cisco, your turn. What've you got?"

"Still working on Elliot. Mostly in regard to Rilz and some hand-holding with our witnesses."

"I have a question about witnesses," Lorna interrupted. "Where do you want to put up Dr. Arslanian?"

Shamiram Arslanian was the gunshot residue authority Vincent had scheduled to bring in from New York as an expert witness to knock down the state's expert witness at trial. She was the best in the field and, with Walter Elliot's financial reserves, Vincent was going with the best money could buy. I wanted her close to the downtown CCB but the choice of hotels was limited.

"Try Checkers first," I said. "And get her a suite. If they're booked, then try the Standard and then the Kyoto Grand. But get a suite so we have room to work."

"Got it. And what about Muniz? You want him in close, too?"

Julio Muniz was a freelance videographer who lived in Topanga Canyon. Because of his home's proximity to Malibu he had been the first member of the media to respond to the crime scene after hearing the call out for homicide investigators on the sheriff's radio band. He had shot video of Walter Elliot with the sheriff's deputies outside the beach house. He was a valuable witness because his videotape and his own recollections could be used to confirm or contradict testimony offered by sheriff's deputies and investigators.

"I don't know," I said. "It can take anywhere from an hour to three hours to get from Topanga to downtown. I'd rather not risk it. Cisco, is he willing to come in and stay at a hotel?"

"Yeah, just as long as we're paying and he can order room service."

"Okay, then bring him in. Also, where's the video? There are only notes on it in the file. I don't want the first time I look at the video to be in court."

Cisco looked puzzled.

"I don't know. But if it's not around here, I can have Muniz dub off a copy."

"Well, I haven't seen it around here. So get me a copy. What else?"

"Couple other things. First, I got with my source on the Vincent thing and he didn't know anything about a suspect or this photo Bosch showed you this morning."

"Nothing?"

"Nada."

"What do you think? Does Bosch know your guy's the leak and is shutting him out?"

"I don't know. But everything I was telling him about this photo was news to him."

I took a few moments to consider what this meant.

"Did Bosch ever come back and show the photo to Wren?"

"No," Lorna said. "I was with her all morning. Bosch never came in then or after lunch."

I wasn't sure what any of this meant but I couldn't become bogged down with it. I had to get to the files.

"What was the second thing?" I asked Cisco.

"What?"

"You said you had a couple other things to tell me. What was the second thing?"

"Oh, yeah. I called Vincent's liquidator and you had that right. He's still got one of Patrick's long boards."

"What's he want for it?"

"Nothing."

I looked at Cisco and raised my eyebrows, asking where the catch was.

"Let's just say he'd like to do you the favor. He lost a good client in Vincent. I think he's hoping you'll use him for future liquidations. And I didn't dissuade him from the idea or tell him you usually don't barter property for services with your clients."

I understood. The surfboard would not come with any real strings attached.

"Thanks, Cisco. Did you take it with you?"

"No, he didn't have it at the office. But he made a call and somebody was supposed to bring it in to him this afternoon. I could go back and get it if you want."

"No, just get me an address and I'll have Patrick pick it up. What happened with Bruce Carlin? Didn't you debrief him today? Maybe he's got the Muniz tape."

I was anxious to hear about Bruce Carlin on several levels. Most important, I wanted to know if he had worked for Vincent on the Eli Wyms case. If so, he might be able to lead me to the magic bullet.

But Cisco didn't answer my question. Lorna turned and they looked at each other as if wondering which one of them should deliver the bad news.

"What's wrong?" I asked.

Lorna turned back to me.

"Carlin's fucking with us," she said.

I could see the angry set of her jaw. And I knew she reserved that kind of language for special occasions. Something had gone wrong with Carlin's debriefing and she was particularly upset.

"How so?"

"Well, he never showed up at two like he said he would. Instead, he called at two — right after Wren called and quit — and gave us the new parameters of his deal."

I shook my head in annoyance.

"His deal? How much does he want?"

"Well, I guess he realized that at two hundred dollars an hour he wouldn't make much, since he was probably going to bill only two or three hours tops. That's all Cisco would need with him. So he called up and said he wanted a flat fee or we could figure out things on our own."

"Like I said, how much?"

"Ten thousand dollars."

"You gotta be fucking kidding me."

"My words exactly."

I looked from her to Cisco.

"This is extortion. Isn't there a state agency that regulates you guys? Can't we come down on his shit somehow?"

Cisco shook his head.

"There are all kinds of regulatory agencies but this is a shady area."

"Yeah, I know it's shady. He's shady. I've thought that for years."

"What I mean is, he had no deal with Vincent. We can't find any contract. So he's not required to give us anything. We simply need to hire him and he's setting his price at ten grand. It's a bullshit rip-off but it's probably legal. I mean, you're the lawyer. You tell me."

I thought about it for a few moments and then tried to push it aside. I was still riding on the adrenaline charge I'd picked up in the courthouse. I didn't want it to dissipate with distractions.

"All right, I'll ask Elliot if he wants to pay it. Meantime, I'm going to hit all the files again tonight, and if I get lucky and crack through, then we won't need him. We say fuck you and are done with him."

"Asshole," Lorna muttered.

I was pretty sure that was directed at Bruce Carlin and not me.

"Okay, is that it?" I asked. "Anything else?"

I looked from one face to the other. Nobody had anything else to bring up.

"Okay, then, thank you both for all you've been putting up with and doing this week. Go out and have a good night."

Lorna looked at me curiously.

"You're sending us home?" she asked.

I checked my watch.

"Why not?" I said. "It's almost four thirty and I'm going to dive into the files and I don't want any distractions. You two go on home, have a good night and we'll start again tomorrow."

"You're going to work here alone tonight?" Cisco asked.

"Yeah, but don't worry. I'll lock the door and I won't let anybody in — even if I know him."

I smiled. Lorna and Cisco didn't. I pointed to the open door to the office. It had a slide bolt that could be used to lock it at the top of the doorframe. If necessary I would be able to secure both outside and inside perimeters. It gave new meaning to the idea of going into lockdown.

"Come on, I'll be fine. I've got work to do."

They slowly, reluctantly, started to make their way out of my office.

"Lorna," I called after them. "Patrick should be out there. Tell him to keep hanging. I might have something to tell him after I make that call."

Twenty-nine

I opened the Patrick Henson file on my desk and looked up the prosecutor's number. I wanted to get this out of the way before I went to work on the Elliot case.

The prosecutor was Dwight Posey, a guy I had dealt with before on cases and never liked. Some prosecutors deal with defense attorneys as though they are only one step removed from their clients. As pseudocriminals, not as educated and experienced professionals. Not as necessary cogs in the winding gears of the justice system. Most cops have this view and I can live with it. But it bothers me when fellow lawyers adopt the pose. Unfortunately, Dwight Posey was one of these, and if I could've gone through the rest of my life without ever having to talk to him, I would have been a happy man. But that was not going to be the case.

"So, Haller," he said after taking the call, "they've got you walking in a dead man's shoes, don't they?"

"What?"

"They gave you all of Jerry Vincent's cases, right? That's how you ended up with Henson."

"Yeah, something like that. Anyway, I'm returning your call, Dwight. Actually, your three calls. What's up? You get the motion I filed yesterday?"

I reminded myself that I had to step carefully here if I wanted to get everything I could out of the phone call. I couldn't let my distaste for the prosecutor affect the outcome for my client.

"Yes, I got the motion. It's sitting right here on my desk. That's why I've been calling."

He left it open for me to step in.

"And?"

"And, uh, well, we're not going to do that, Mick."

"Do what, Dwight?"

"Put our evidence out there for examination."

It was looking more and more like I had struck a major nerve with my motion.

"Well, Dwight, that's the beauty of the system, right? You don't get to make that decision. A judge does. That's why I didn't ask you. I put it in a motion and asked the judge."

Posey cleared his throat.

"No, actually, we do this time," he said. "We're going to drop the theft charge and just proceed with the drug charge. So you can withdraw your motion or we can inform the judge that the point is moot."

I smiled and nodded. I had him. I knew then that Patrick was going to walk.

"Only problem with that, Dwight, is that the drug charge came out of the theft investigation. You know that. When they popped my client, the warrant was for the theft. The drugs were found during the arrest. So you don't have one without the other."

I had the feeling that he knew everything I was saying and that the call was simply following a script. We were going where Posey wanted us to go and that was fine with me. This time I wanted to go there, too.

"Then, maybe we can just talk about a disposition on the matter," he said as if the idea had just occurred to him.

And there we were. We had come to the place Posey had wanted to get to from the moment he'd answered the call.

"I'm open to it, Dwight. You should know that my client voluntarily entered a rehab program after his arrest. He has completed the program, has full-time employment and has been clean for four months. He'll give his piss anytime, anywhere, to prove it."

"That is really good to hear," Posey said with false enthusiasm. "The DA's Office, as well as the courts, always look favorably upon voluntary rehabilitation."

Tell me something I don't know, I almost said.

"The kid is doing good. I can vouch for that. What do you want to do for him?"

I knew how the script would read now. Posey would turn it into a goodwill gesture from the prosecution. He would make it seem as though the D.A.'s Office were giving out the favor here, when the truth was that the prosecution was acting to insulate an important figure from political and personal embarrassment. That was fine with me. I didn't care about the political ends of the deal as long as my client got what I wanted him to get.

"Tell you what, Mick. Let's make it go away, and maybe Patrick can use this opportunity to move ahead with being a productive member of society."

"Sounds like a plan to me, Dwight. You're making my day. And his."

"Okay, then get me his rehab records and we'll put it into a package for the judge."

Posey was talking about making it a pretrial intervention case. Patrick would have to take biweekly drug tests and in six months the case would go away if he kept clean. He would still have an arrest on his record but no conviction. Unless...

"You willing to expunge his record?" I asked.

"Uh..., that's asking a lot, Mickey. He did, after all, break in and steal the diamonds."

"He didn't break in, Dwight. He was invited in. And the alleged diamonds are what this is all about, right? Whether or not he actually did steal any diamonds."

Posey must have realized he had misspoken by bringing up the diamonds. He folded his tent quickly.

"All right, fine. We'll put it into the package."

"You're a good man, Dwight."

"I try to be. You will withdraw your motion now?"

"First thing tomorrow. When do we go to court? I have a trial starting the end of next week."

"Then we'll go for Monday. I'll let you know."

I hung up the phone and called the reception desk on the intercom. Luckily, Lorna answered.

"I thought you were sent home," I said.

"We're about to go through the door. I'm going to leave my car here and go with Cisco."

"What, on his *donor*cycle?"

"Excuse me, *Dad,* but I don't think you have anything to say about that."

I groaned.

"But I do have a say over who works as my investigator. If I can keep you two apart, maybe I can keep you alive."

"Mickey, don't you dare!"

"Can you just tell Cisco I need that address for the liquidator?"

"I will. And I'll see you tomorrow."

"Hope so. Wear a helmet."

I hung up and Cisco came in, carrying a Post-it in one hand and a gun in a leather holster in the other. He walked around the desk, put the Post-it down in front of me, then opened a drawer and put the weapon in it.

"What are you doing?" I asked. "You can't give me a gun."

"It's totally legal and registered to me."

"That's great but you can't give it to me. That's il—"

"I'm not giving it to you. I'm just storing it here because I'm done work for the day. I'll get it in the morning, okay?"

"Whatever. I think you two are overreacting."

"Better than underreacting. See you tomorrow."

"Thank you. Will you send Patrick in before you go?"

"You got it. And by the way, I always make her wear a helmet."

I looked at him and nodded.

"That's good, Cisco."

He left the room, and Patrick soon came in.

"Patrick, Cisco talked to Vincent's liquidator and he still has one of your long boards. You can go by and pick it up. Just tell him you are picking it up for me and to call me if there is any problem."

"Oh man, thank you!"

"Yeah, well, I've got even better news than that on your case."

"What happened?"

I went over the phone call I'd just had with Dwight Posey. As I told Patrick that he would do no jail time if he stayed clean, I watched his eyes gain a little light. It was as if I could see the burden drop off his shoulders. He could look once again at the future.

"I have to call my mom," he said. "She's gonna be so happy."

"Yeah, well, I hope you are, too."

"I am, I am."

"Now, the way I figure it, you owe me a couple thousand for my work on this. That's about two and a half weeks of driving. If you want, you can stick with me until it's paid off. After that, we can talk about it and see where we're at."

"That sounds good. I like the job."

"Good, Patrick, then it's a deal."

Patrick smiled broadly and was turning to go.

"One other thing, Patrick."

He turned back to me.

"I saw you sleeping in your car in the garage this morning."

"Sorry. I'll find another spot."

He looked down at the floor.

"No, *I'm* sorry," I said. "I forgot that you told me when we talked on the phone the first time that you were living in your car and sleeping on a lifeguard stand. I just don't know how safe it is to be sleeping in the same garage where a guy got shot the other night."

"I'll find someplace else."

"Well, if you want, I can give you an advance on your pay. Would that help you maybe get a motel room or something?"

"Um, I guess."

I was glad to help him out but I knew that living out of a weekly motel was almost as depressing as living out of a car.

"I'll tell you what," I said. "If you want, you could stay with me for a couple weeks. Until you get some money in your pocket and maybe get a better plan going."

"At your place?"

"Yeah, you know, temporarily."

"With you?"

I realized my mistake.

"Nothing like that, Patrick. I've got a house and you'd have your own room. In fact, on Wednesday nights and every other weekend, it would be better if you stayed with a friend or in a motel. That's when I have my daughter."

He thought about it and nodded.

"Yeah, I could do that."

I reached across the desk and signaled him to give me back the Post-it with the liquidator's address on it. I wrote my own address on it while I spoke.

"Why don't you go pick up your board and then head over to my place at this second address. Fareholm is right off Laurel Canyon, one street before Mount Olympus. You go up the stairs to the front porch and there's a table and chairs out there and an ashtray. The extra key's under the ashtray. The guest bedroom is right next to the kitchen. Just make yourself at home."

"Thanks."

He took the Post-it back and looked at the address I'd written.

"I probably won't get there till late," I told him. "I've got a trial starting next week and a lot of work to do before then."

"Okay."

"Look, we're only talking about a few weeks. Till you get on your feet again. Meantime, maybe we can help each other out. You know, like if one of us starts to feel the pull, maybe the other one will be there to talk about it. Okay?"

"Okay."

We were quiet for a moment, probably both of us thinking about the deal. I didn't tell Patrick that he might end up helping me more than I would help him. In the past forty-eight hours, the pressure of the new caseload had begun to weigh on me. I could feel myself being pulled back, feel the desire to go to the cotton-wrapped world the pills could give me. The pills opened the space between where I was and the brick wall of reality. I was beginning to crave that distance.

Up front and deep down I knew I didn't want that again, and maybe Patrick could help me avoid it.

"Thanks, Mr. Haller."

I looked up at him from my thoughts.

"Call me Mickey," I said. "And I should be the one saying thanks."

"Why are you doing all of this for me?"

I looked at the big fish on the wall behind him for a moment, then back at him.

"I'm not sure, Patrick. But I'm hoping that if I help you, then I'll be helping myself."

Patrick nodded like he knew what I was talking about. That was strange because I wasn't sure myself what I had meant.

"Go get your board, Patrick," I said. "I'll see you at the house. And make sure you remember to call your mother."

Thirty

fter I was finally alone in the office, I started the process the way I always do, with clean pages and sharp points. From the supply closet I retrieved two fresh legal pads and four Black Warrior pencils. I sharpened their points and got down to work.

Vincent had broken the Elliot case into two files. One file contained the state's case, and the second, thinner file contained the defense case. The weight of the defense file was not of concern to me. The defense played by the same rules of discovery as the prosecution. Anything that went into the second file went to the prosecutor. A seasoned defense attorney knew to keep the file thin. Keep the rest in your head, or hidden on a microchip in your computer if it is safe. I had neither Vincent's head nor his laptop. But I was sure the secrets Jerry Vincent kept were hidden somewhere in the hard copy. The magic bullet was there. I just had to find it.

I began with the thicker file, the prosecution's case. I read straight through, every page and every word. I took notes on one legal pad and drew a time-and-action flowchart on the other. I studied the crime scene photographs with a magnifying glass I took from the desk drawer. I drew up a list of every single name I encountered in the file.

From there, I moved on to the defense file and again read every word on every page. The phone rang two different times but I didn't even look up to see what name was on the screen. I didn't care. I was in relentless pursuit and cared about only one thing. Finding the magic bullet.

When I was finished with the Elliot files, I opened the Wyms case and read every document and report it contained, a time-consuming process. Because Wyms was arrested following a public incident that had drawn several uniform and SWAT deputies, this file was thick with reports from the various units involved and personnel at the scene. It was stuffed with transcriptions of the conversations with Wyms, as well as weapons and ballistics reports, a lengthy evidence inventory, witness statements, dispatch records and patrol deployment reports.

There were a lot of names in the file and I checked every one of them against the list of names from the Elliot files. I also cross-referenced every address.

I had this client once. I don't even know her name because I was sure that the name she was under in the system was not her own. She was in on a first offense but she knew the system too well to be a virgin. In fact, she knew everything too well. Whatever her name was, she had some-how rigged the system and it had her down as someone she wasn't.

The charge was burglary of an occupied dwelling. But there was so much more than that behind the one charge. This woman liked to target hotel rooms where men with large amounts of money slept. She knew how to pick them, follow them, then finesse the door locks and the room safes while they slept. In one candid moment—probably the only one in our relationship—she told me of the white-hot adrenaline high she got every time the last digit fell into place and she heard the electronic gears of the hotel safe start to move and unlock. Opening the safe and finding what was inside was never as good as that magic moment when the gears began to grind and she felt the velocity of her blood moving in her veins. Nothing before or after was as good as that moment. The jobs weren't about the money. They were about the velocity of blood.

I nodded when she told me all of this. I had never broken into a hotel room while some guy was snoring on the bed. But I knew about the moment when the gears began to grind. I knew about the velocity.

I found what I was looking for an hour into my second run at the files. It had been there in front of me the whole time. First in Elliot's arrest report and then on the time-and-action chart I had drawn myself. I called the chart the Christmas tree. It always started basic and unadorned. Just the bare-bones facts of the case. Then, as I continued to study and make the case my own, I started hanging lights and ornaments on it. Details and witness statements, evidence and lab results. Soon the tree was lit up and bright. Everything about the case was there for me to see in the context of time and action.

I had paid particular attention to Walter Elliot as I had drawn the Christmas tree. He was the tree trunk and all branches came from him. I had his movements, statements and actions noted by time.

12:40 p.m. — WE arrives at beach house
12:50 p.m. — WE discovers bodies
 1:05 p.m. — WE calls 911
 1:24 p.m. — WE calls 911 again
 1:28 p.m. — Deputies arrive on scene
 1:30 p.m. — WE secured
 2:15 p.m. — Homicide arrives
 2:40 p.m. — WE taken to Malibu station
 4:55 p.m. — WE interviewed, advised
 5:40 p.m. — WE transported to Whittier
 7:00 p.m. — GSR testing
 8:00 p.m. — Second interview attempt, declined, arrested
 8:40 p.m. — WE transported to Men's Central

Some of the times I estimated but most came directly from the arrest report and other documents in the file. Law enforcement in this country is as much about the paperwork as anything else. I could always count on the prosecution file for reconstructing a time line.

On the second go-round I used both the pencil point and eraser and started adding decorations to the tree.

12:40 p.m. — WE arrives at beach house
        front door unlocked
12:50 p.m. — WE discovers bodies
        balcony door open
1:05 p.m. — WE calls 911 waits outside
1:24 p.m. — WE calls 911 again
        what's the holdup?
1:28 p.m. — Deputies arrive on scene
        Murray (4-alpha-1) and Harber (4-alpha-2)
1:30 p.m. — WE secured
        placed in patrol car
        Murray/Harber search house
2:15 p.m. — Homicide arrives
        first team: Kinder (#14492) and Ericsson (#21101)
        second team: Joshua (#22234) and Toles (#15154)
2:30 p.m. — WE taken inside house, describes discovery
2:40 p.m. — WE taken to Malibu station
        Joshua and Toles transport
4:55 p.m. — WE interviewed, advised
        Kinder takes lead in interview
5:40 p.m. — WE transported to Whittier
        Joshua/Toles
7:00 p.m. — GSR testing
        F.T. Anita Sherman
        Lab Transport, Sherman
8:00 p.m. — Second interview, Ericsson in lead, WE declines
        got smart
8:40 p.m. — WE transported to Men's Central
        Joshua/Toles

As I had constructed the Christmas tree, I kept a separate list on another page of every human being mentioned in the sheriff's reports. I knew this would become the witness list I would turn over to the prosecution the following week. As a rule I blanket the case, subpoenaing anybody mentioned in the investigative record just to be safe. You can always cut down a witness list at trial. Sometimes adding to it can be a problem.

From the witness list and the Christmas tree, I would be able to infer how the prosecution would roll out its case. I would also be able to determine which witnesses the prosecution team was avoiding and possibly why. It was while I was studying my work and thinking in these terms that I felt the gears begin to grind and the cold finger of revelation went down my spine. Everything became clear and bright and I found Jerry Vincent's magic bullet.

Walter Elliot had been taken from the crime scene to the Malibu station so that he would be out of the way and secured while the lead detectives continued their on-site investigation. One short interview was conducted at the station before Elliot ended it. He was then transported to sheriff's headquarters in Whittier, where a gunshot residue test was conducted and his hands tested positive for nitrates associated with gunpowder. Afterward, Kinder and Ericsson took another stab at interviewing their suspect but he wisely declined. He was then formally placed under arrest and booked into county jail.

It was standard procedure and the arrest report documented the chain of Elliot's custody. He was handled solely by the homicide detectives as he was moved from crime scene to substation to headquarters to jail. But it was how he was handled previous to their arrival that caught my eye. It was here that I saw something I had missed earlier. Something as simple as the designations of the uniform deputies who first responded to the call. According to the records, deputies Murray and Harber had the designations 4-alpha-1 and 4-alpha-2 after their names. And I had seen at least one of those designations in the Wyms file.

Jumping from case to case and from file to file, I found the Wyms arrest report and quickly scanned the narrative, not stopping until my eyes came to the first reference to the 4-alpha-1 designation.

Deputy Todd Stallworth had the designation written after his name. He was the deputy originally called to investigate the report of gunfire at Malibu Creek State Park. He was the deputy driving the car Wyms fired upon, and at the end of the standoff he was the deputy who formally placed Wyms under arrest and took him to jail.

I realized that 4-alpha-1 did not refer to a specific deputy but to a specific patrol zone or responsibility. The Malibu district covered the huge unincorporated areas of the west county, from the beaches of Malibu up over the mountains and into the communities of Thousand Oaks and Calabasas. I assumed that this was the fourth district and alpha was the specific designation for a patrol unit—a specific car. It seemed to be the only way to explain why deputies who worked different shifts would share the same designation on different arrest reports.

Adrenaline crashed into my veins and my blood took off running as everything came together. All in a moment I realized what Vincent had been up to and what he had been planning. I didn't need his laptop or his legal pads anymore. I didn't need his investigator. I knew exactly what the defense strategy was.

At least I thought I did.

I pulled my cell phone and called Cisco. I skipped the pleasantries.

"Cisco, it's me. Do you know any sheriff's deputies?"

"Uh, a few. Why?"

"Any of them work out of the Malibu station?"

"I know one guy who used to. He's in Lynwood now. Malibu was too boring."

"Can you call him tonight?"

"Tonight? Sure, I guess. What's up?"

"I need to know what the patrol designation four-alpha-one means. Can you get that?"

"Shouldn't be a problem. I'll call you back. But hold on a sec for Lorna. She wants to talk to you."

I waited while she was given the phone. I could hear TV noise in the background. I had interrupted a scene of domestic bliss.

"Mickey, are you still there at the office?"

"I'm here."

"It's eight-thirty. I think you should go home."

"I think I should, too. I'm going to wait to hear back from Cisco—he's checking something out for me—and then I think I'm going over to Dan Tana's to have steak and spaghetti."

She knew I went to Dan Tana's when I had something to celebrate. Usually a good verdict.

"You had steak for breakfast."

"Then I guess this will make it a perfect day."

"Things went well tonight?"

"I think so. Real well."

"You're going alone?"

She said it with sympathy in her voice, like now that she had hooked up with Cisco, she was starting to feel sorry for me, alone out there in the big bad world.

"Craig or Christian will keep me company."

Craig and Christian worked the door at Dan Tana's. They took care of me whether I came in alone or not.

"I'll see you tomorrow, Lorna."

"Okay, Mickey. Have fun."

"I already am."

I hung up and waited, pacing in the room and thinking it all through again. The dominoes went down one after the other. It felt good and it all fit. Vincent had not taken on the Wyms case out of any obligation to the law or the poor or the disenfranchised. He was using Wyms as camouflage. Rather than move the case toward the obvious plea agreement, he had stashed Wyms out at Camarillo for three months, thereby keeping the case alive and active. Meantime, he gathered information under the flag of the Wyms defense that he would use in the Elliot case, thereby hiding his moves and strategy from the prosecution.

Technically, he was probably acting within bounds, but ethically it was underhanded. Eli Wyms had spent ninety days in a state facility so Vincent could build a defense for Elliot. Elliot got the magic bullet while Wyms got the zombie cocktail.

The good thing was, I didn't have to worry about the sins of my predecessor. Wyms was out of Camarillo, and besides, they weren't my sins. I could just take the benefit of Vincent's discoveries and go to trial.

It didn't take too long before Cisco called back.

"I talked to my guy in Lynwood. Four-alpha is Malibu's lead car. The four is for the Malibu station and the alpha is for . . . alpha. Like the alpha dog. The leader of the pack. Hot shots — the priority calls — usually go to the alpha car. Four-alpha-one would be the driver, and if he's riding with a partner, then the partner would be four-alpha-two."

"So the alpha car covers the whole fourth district?"

"That's what he told me. Four-alpha is free to roam the district and scoop the cream off the top."

"What do you mean?"

"The best calls. The hot shots."

"Got it."

My theory was confirmed. A double murder and shots fired near a residential neighborhood would certainly be alpha-car calls. One designation but different deputies responding. Different deputies responding but one car. The dominoes clicked and fell.

"Does that help, Mick?"

"It does, Cisco. But it also means more work for you."

"On the Elliot case?"

"No, not Elliot. I want you to work on the Eli Wyms case. Find out everything you can about the night he was arrested. Get me details."

"That's what I'm here for."

Thirty-one

The night's discovery pushed the case off the paper and into my imagination. I was starting to get courtroom images in my head. Scenes of examinations and cross-examinations. I was laying out the suits I would wear to court and the postures I would take in front of the jury. The case was coming alive inside and this was always a good thing. It was a momentum thing. You time it right and you go into trial with the inescapable conviction that you will not lose. I didn't know what had happened to Jerry Vincent, how his actions might have brought about his demise, or whether his death was linked at all to the Elliot case, but I felt as though I had a bead on things. I had velocity and I was getting battle ready.

My plan was to sit in a corner booth at Dan Tana's and sketch out some of the key witness examinations, listing the baseline questions and probable answers for each. I was excited about getting to it, and Lorna need not have worried about me. I wouldn't be alone. I would have my case with me. Not Jerry Vincent's case. Mine.

After quickly repacking the files and adding fresh pencils and legal pads, I killed the lights and locked the office door. I headed down the hallway and then across the bridge to the parking garage. Just as I was entering the garage, I saw a man walking up the ramp from the first floor. He was fifty yards away and it was only a few moments and a few strides before I recognized him as the man in the photograph Bosch had shown me that morning.

My blood froze in my heart. The fight-or-flight instinct stabbed into my brain. The rest of the world didn't matter. There was just this moment and I had to make a choice. My brain assessed the situation faster than any computer IBM ever made. And the result of the computation was that I knew the man coming toward me was the killer and that he had a gun.

I swung around and started to run.

"Hey!" a voice called from behind me.

I kept running. I moved back across the bridge to the glass doors leading back into the building. One clear, single thought fired through every synapse in my brain. I had to get inside and get to Cisco's gun. I had to kill or be killed.

But it was after hours and the doors had locked behind me as I had left the building. I shot my hand into my pocket in search of the key, then jerked it out, bills, coins and wallet flying out with it.

As I jammed the key into the lock, I could hear running steps coming up quickly behind me. *The gun! Get the gun!*

I finally yanked the door open and bolted down the hallway toward the office. I glanced behind me and saw the man catch the door just before it closed and locked. He was still coming.

Key still in my hand, I reached the office door and fumbled the key while getting it into the lock. I could feel the killer closing in. Finally getting the door open, I entered, slammed it shut and threw the lock. I hit the light switch, then crossed the reception area and charged into Vincent's office.

The gun Cisco left for me was there in the drawer. I grabbed it, yanked it out of its holster and went back out to the reception area. Across the room I could see the killer's shape through the frosted glass.

He was trying to open the door. I raised the gun and pointed at the blurred image.

I hesitated and then raised the gun higher and fired two shots into the ceiling. The sound was deafening in the closed room.

"That's right!" I yelled. "Come on in!"

The image on the other side of the glass door disappeared. I heard footsteps moving away in the hallway and then the door to the bridge opening and closing. I stood stock-still and listened for any other sound. There was nothing.

Without taking my eyes off the door, I stepped over to the reception desk and picked up the phone. I called 911 and it was answered right away, but I got a recording that told me my call was important and that I needed to hold on for the next available emergency dispatcher.

I realized I was shaking, not with fear but with the overload of adrenaline. I put the gun on the desk, checked my pocket and found that I hadn't lost my cell phone. With the office phone in one hand, I used the other to open the cell and call Harry Bosch. He answered on the first ring.

"Bosch! That guy you showed me was just here!"

"Haller? What are you talking about? Who?"

"The guy in the photo you showed me today! The one with the gun!"

"All right, calm down. Where is he? Where are you?"

I realized that the stress of the moment had pulled my voice tight and sharp. Embarrassed, I took a deep breath and tried to calm myself before answering.

"I'm at the office. Vincent's office. I was leaving and I saw him in the garage. I ran back inside and he ran in after me. He tried to get into the office. I think he's gone but I'm not sure. I fired a couple of shots and then—"

"You have a gun?"

"Goddamn right I do."

"I suggest you put it away before somebody gets hurt."

"If that guy's still out there, he'll be the one getting hurt. Who the hell is he?"

There was a pause before he answered.

"I don't know yet. Look, I'm still downtown and was just heading home myself. I'm in the car. Sit tight and I'll be there in five minutes. Stay in the office and keep the door locked."

"Don't worry, I'm not moving."

"And don't shoot me when I get there."

"I won't."

I reached over and hung up the office phone. I didn't need 911 if Bosch was coming. I picked the gun back up.

"Hey, Haller?"

"What?"

"What did he want?"

"What?"

"The guy. What did he come there for?"

"That's a good goddamn question. But I don't have the answer."

"Look, stop fucking around and tell me!"

"I'm telling you! I don't know what he's after. Now quit talking and get over here!"

I involuntarily squeezed my hands into fists as I yelled and put an accidental shot into the floor. I jumped as though I had been shot at by someone else.

"Haller!" Bosch yelled. "What the hell was that?"

I pulled in a deep breath and took my time composing myself before answering.

"Haller? What's going on?"

"Get over here and you'll find out."

"Did you hit him? Did you put him down?"

Without answering I closed the phone.

Thirty-two

osch made it in six minutes but it felt like an hour. A dark image appeared on the other side of the glass and he knocked sharply.

"Haller, it's me, Bosch."

Carrying the gun at my side, I unlocked the door and let him in. He, too, had his gun out and at his side.

"Anything since we were on the phone?" he asked.

"Haven't seen or heard him. I guess I scared his ass away."

Bosch holstered his gun and threw me a look, as if to say my tough-guy pose was convincing no one except maybe myself.

"What was that last shot?"

"An accident."

I pointed toward the hole in the floor.

"Give me that gun before you get yourself killed."

I handed it over and he put it into the waistband of his pants.

"You don't own a gun — not legally. I checked."

"It's my investigator's. He leaves it here at night."

Bosch scanned the ceiling, until he saw the two holes I had put there. He then looked at me and shook his head.

He went over to the blinds and checked the street. Broadway was dead out there this time of night. A couple nearby buildings had been converted into residential lofts but Broadway still had a way to go before recapturing the nightlife it had had eighty years before.

"Okay, let's sit down," he said.

He turned from the window to see me standing behind him.

"In your office."

"Why?"

"Because we're going to talk about this."

I moved into the office and took a seat behind the desk. Bosch sat down across from me.

"First of all, here's your stuff. I found it out there on the bridge."

From the pocket of his jacket he pulled my wallet and loose bills. He put it all on the desk and then reached back in for the coins.

"Okay, now what?" I asked as I put my property back in my pocket.

"Now we talk," Bosch said. "First off, do you want to file a report on this?"

"Why bother? You know about it. It's your case. Why don't you know who this guy is?"

"We're working on it."

"That's not good enough, Bosch! He came after me! Why can't you ID him?"

Bosch shook his head.

"Because we think he's a hitter brought in from out of town. Maybe out of the country."

"That's fucking fantastic! Why did he come back here?"

"Obviously, because of you. Because of what you know."

"Me? I don't know anything."

"You've been in here for three days. You must know something that makes you a danger to him."

"I'm telling you, I've got nothing."

"Then, you have to ask yourself, why did that guy come back? What did he leave behind or forget the first time?"

I just stared at him. I actually wanted to help. I was tired of being under the gun—in more ways than one—and if I could've given Bosch just one answer, I would have.

I shook my head.

"I can't think of a single—"

"Come on, Haller!" Bosch barked at me. "Your life is threatened here! Don't you get it? What've you got?"

"I told you!"

"Who did Vincent bribe?"

"I don't know and I couldn't tell you if I did."

"What did the FBI want with him?"

"I don't know that, either!"

He started pointing at me.

"You fucking hypocrite. You're hiding behind the protections of the law, while the killer is out there waiting. Your ethics and rules won't stop a bullet, Haller. Tell me what you've got!"

"I told you! I don't have anything and don't point your fucking finger at me. This isn't my job. It's your job. And maybe if you would get it done, people around here would feel—"

"Excuse me?"

The voice came from behind Bosch. In one fluid move he turned and pivoted out of his chair, drawing his gun and aiming it at the door.

A man holding a trash bag stood there, his eyes going wide in fright.

Bosch immediately lowered his weapon, and the office cleaner looked like he might faint.

"Sorry," Bosch said.

"I come back later," the man said in a thick accent from Eastern Europe.

He turned and disappeared quickly through the door.

"Goddamn it!" Bosch cursed, clearly unhappy about pointing his gun at an innocent man.

"I doubt we'll ever get our trash cans emptied again," I said.

Bosch went over to the door and closed and bolted it. He came back to the desk and looked at me with angry eyes. He sat back down, took a deep breath and proceeded in a much calmer voice.

"I'm glad you can keep your sense of humor, Counselor. But enough with the fucking jokes."

"All right, no jokes."

Bosch looked like he was struggling internally with what to say or do next. His eyes swept the room and then held on me.

"All right, look, you're right. It is my job to catch this guy. But you had him right here. Right goddamn here! And so it stands to reason that he was here with a purpose. He came to either kill you, which seems unlikely, since he apparently doesn't even know you, or he came to get something from you. The question is, what is it? What is in this office or in one of your files that could lead to the identity of the killer?"

I tried to match him with an even-tempered voice of my own.

"All I can tell you is that I have had my case manager in here since Tuesday. I've had my investigator in here, and Jerry Vincent's own receptionist was in here up until lunchtime today, when she quit. And none of us, Detective, *none of us,* has been able to find the smoking gun you're so sure is here. You tell me that Vincent paid somebody a bribe. But I can find no indication in any file or from any client that that is true. I spent the last three hours in here looking at the Elliot file and I saw no indication — not one — that he paid anybody off or bribed somebody. In fact, I found out that he didn't *need* to bribe anybody. Vincent had a magic bullet and he had a shot at winning the case fair and square. So when I tell you I have nothing, I mean it. I'm not playing you. I'm not holding back. I have nothing to give you. Nothing."

"What about the FBI?"

"Same answer. Nothing."

Bosch didn't respond. I saw true disappointment cloud his face. I continued.

"If this mustache man is the killer, then, of course there is a reason that brought him back here. But I don't know it. Am I concerned about it? No, not concerned. I'm fucking scared shitless about it. I'm fucking scared shitless that this guy thinks I have something, because if I have it, I don't even know I have it, and that is not a good place to be."

Bosch abruptly stood up. He pulled Cisco's gun out of his waistband and put it down on the desk.

"Keep it loaded. And if I were you, I would stop working at night."

He turned and headed toward the door.

"That's it?" I called after him.

He spun in his tracks and came back to the desk.

"What else do you want from me?"

"All you want is information from me. Most of the time information I can't give. But you in turn give nothing back, and that's half the reason I'm in danger."

Bosch looked like he might be about to jump over the desk at me. But then I saw him calm himself once more. All except for the palpitation high on his cheek near his left temple. That didn't go away. That was his tell, and it was a tell that once again gave me a sense of familiarity.

"Fuck it," he finally said. "What do you want to know, Counselor? Go ahead. Ask me a question—any question—and I'll answer it."

"I want to know about the bribe. Where did the money go?"

Bosch shook his head and laughed in a false way.

"I give you a free shot and I say to myself that I'll answer your question, no matter what it is, and you go and ask me the question I don't have an answer to. You think if I knew where the money went and who got the bribe that I'd be here right now with you? Uh-uh, Haller, I'd be booking a killer."

"So you're sure one thing had to do with the other? That the bribe—if there was a bribe—is connected to the killing."

"I'm going with the percentages."

"But the bribe—if there was a bribe—went down five months ago. Why was Jerry killed now? Why's the FBI calling him now?"

"Good questions. Let me know if you come up with any answers. Meantime, anything else I can do for you, Counselor? I was heading home when you called."

"Yeah, there is."

He looked at me and waited.

"I was on my way out, too."

"What, you want me to hold your hand on the way to the garage? Fine, let's go."

I closed the office once again and we proceeded down the hall to the bridge to the garage. Bosch had stopped talking and the silence was nerve-racking. I finally broke it.

"I was going to go have a steak. You want to come? Maybe we'll solve the world's problems over some red meat."

"Where, Musso's?"

"I was thinking Dan Tana's."

Bosch nodded.

"If you can get us in."

"Don't worry. I know a guy."

Thirty-three

Bosch followed me but when I slowed on Santa Monica Boulevard to pull into the valet stop in front of the restaurant, he kept going. I saw him drive by and turn right on Doheny.

I went in by myself and Craig sat me in one of the cherished corner booths. It was a busy night but things were tapering off. I saw the actor James Woods finishing dinner in a booth with a movie producer named Mace Neufeld. They were regulars and Mace gave me a nod. He had once tried to option one of my cases for a film but it didn't work out. I saw Corbin Bernsen in another booth, the actor who had given the best approximation of an attorney I had ever seen on television. And then in another booth, the man himself, Dan Tana, was having a late dinner with his wife. I dropped my eyes to the checkered tablecloth. Enough who's who. I had to prepare for Bosch. During the drive, I had thought long and hard about what had just happened back at the office and now I only wanted to think about how best to confront Bosch about it. It was like preparing for the cross-examination of a hostile witness.

Ten minutes after I was seated, Bosch finally appeared in the doorway and Craig led him to me.

"Get lost?" I asked as he squeezed into the booth.

"I couldn't find a parking space."

"I guess they don't pay you enough for valet."

"No, valet's a beautiful thing. But I can't give my city car to a valet. Against the rules."

I nodded, guessing that it was probably because he packed a shotgun in the trunk.

I decided to wait until after we ordered to make a play with Bosch. I asked if he wanted to look at the menu and he said he was ready to order. When the waiter came, we both ordered the Steak Helen with spaghetti and red sauce on the side. Bosch ordered a beer and I asked for a bottle of flat water.

"So," I said, "where's your partner been lately?"

"He's working on other aspects of the investigation."

"Well, I guess it's good to hear there are other aspects to it."

Bosch studied me for a long moment before replying.

"Is that supposed to be a crack?"

"Just an observation. Doesn't seem from my end to be much happening."

"Maybe that's because your source dried up and blew away."

"My source? I don't have any source."

"Not anymore. I figured out who was feeding your guy and that ended today. I just hope you weren't paying him for the information because IAD will take him down for that."

"I know you won't believe me, but I have no idea who or what you are talking about. I get information from my investigator. I don't ask him how he gets it."

Bosch nodded.

"That's the best way to do it, right? Insulate yourself and then you don't get any blowback in your face. In the meantime, if a police captain loses his job and pension, those are the breaks."

I hadn't realized Cisco's source was so highly placed.

The waiter brought our drinks and a basket of bread. I drank some of the water as I contemplated what to say next. I put the glass down and looked at Bosch. He raised his eyebrows like he was expecting something.

"How'd you know when I was leaving the office tonight?"

Bosch looked puzzled.

"What do you mean?"

"I figure it was the lights. You were out there on Broadway, and when I killed the lights, you sent your guy into the garage."

"I don't know what you are talking about."

"Sure you do. The photo of the guy with the gun coming out of the building. It was a phony. You set it up—choreographed it—and used it to smoke out your leak, then you tried to scam me with it."

Bosch shook his head and looked out of the booth as if he were looking for someone to help him interpret what I was saying. It was a bad act.

"You set up the phony picture and then you showed it to me because you knew it would come back around through my investigator to your leak. You'd know that whoever asked you about the photo was the leak."

"I can't discuss any aspect of the investigation with you."

"And then you used it to try to play me. To see if I was hiding something and to scare it out of me."

"I told you, I can't—"

"Well, you don't have to, Bosch. I know it's what you did. You know what your mistakes were? First of all, not coming back like you said you would to show the photo to Vincent's secretary. If the guy in the picture was legit, you would've shown it to her because she knows the clients better than me. Your second mistake was the gun in the waistband of your hit man. Vincent was shot with a twenty-five—too small for a waistband. I missed that when you showed me the photo, but I've got it now."

Bosch looked toward the bar in the middle of the restaurant. The overhead TV was showing sports highlights. I leaned across the table closer to him.

"So who's the guy in the photo? Your partner with a stick-on mustache? Some clown from vice? Don't you have better things to do than to be running a game on me?"

Bosch leaned back and continued to look around the place, his eyes moving everywhere but to me. He was contemplating something and I gave him all the time he needed. Finally, he looked at me.

"Okay, you got me. It was a scam. I guess that makes you one smart lawyer, Haller. Just like the old man. I wonder why you're wasting it defending scumbags. Shouldn't you be out there suing doctors or defending big tobacco or something noble like that?"

I smiled.

"Is that how you like to play it? You get caught being underhanded, so you respond by accusing the other guy of being underhanded?"

Bosch laughed, his face colored red as he turned away from me. It was a gesture that struck me as familiar, and his mention of my father brought him to mind. I had a vague memory of my father laughing uneasily and looking away as he leaned back at the dinner table. My mother had accused him of something I was too young to understand.

Bosch put both arms on the table and leaned toward me.

"You've heard of the first forty-eight, right?"

"What are you talking about?"

"The first forty-eight. The chances of clearing a homicide diminish by almost half each day if you don't solve it in the first forty-eight hours."

He looked at his watch before continuing.

"I'm coming up on seventy-two hours and I've got nothing," he said. "Not a suspect, not a viable lead, nothing. And I was hoping that tonight I might be able to scare something out of you. Something that would point me in the right direction."

I sat there, staring at him, digesting what he had said. Finally, I found my voice.

"You actually thought I knew who killed Jerry and wasn't telling?"

"It was a possibility I had to consider."

"Fuck you, Bosch."

Just then the waiter came with our steaks and spaghetti. As the plates were put down, Bosch looked at me with a knowing smile on his face. The waiter asked what else he could get for us and I waved him away without breaking eye contact.

"You're an arrogant son of a bitch," I said. "You can just sit there with a smile on your face after accusing me of hiding evidence or knowledge in a murder. A murder of a guy I knew."

Bosch looked down at his steak, picked up his knife and fork and cut into it. I noticed he was left-handed. He put a chunk of meat into his mouth and stared at me while he ate it. He rested his fists on either side of his plate, fork and knife in his grips, as if guarding the food from poachers. A lot of my clients who had spent time in prison ate the same way.

"Why don't you take it easy there, Counselor," he said. "You have to understand something. I'm not used to being on the same side of the line as the defense lawyer, okay? It has been my experience that defense attorneys have tried to portray me as stupid, corrupt, bigoted, you name it. So with that in mind, yes, I tried to run a game on you in hopes that it would help me solve a murder. I apologize all to hell and back. If you want, I will have them wrap up my steak and I'll take it to go."

I shook my head. Bosch had a talent for trying to make me feel guilty for his transgressions.

"Maybe now you should be the one who takes it easy," I said. "All I'm saying is that from the start, I have acted openly and honestly with you. I have stretched the ethical bounds of my profession. And I have told you what I could tell you, when I could tell you. I didn't deserve to have the shit scared out of me tonight. And you're damn lucky I didn't put a bullet in your man's chest when he was at the office door. He made a beautiful target."

"You weren't supposed to have a gun. I checked."

Bosch started eating again, keeping his head down as he worked on the steak. He took several bites and then moved to the side plate of spaghetti. He wasn't a twirler. He chopped at the pasta with his fork before putting a bite into his mouth. He spoke after he swallowed his food.

"So now that we have that out of the way, will you help me?"

I blew out my breath in a laugh.

"Are you kidding? Have you heard a single thing I've said here?"

"Yeah, I heard it all. And no, I'm not kidding. When all is said and done, I still have a dead lawyer—your colleague—on my hands and I could still use your help."

I started cutting my first piece of steak. I decided he could wait for me to eat, like I had waited for him.

Dan Tana's was considered by many to serve the best steak in the city. Count me as one of the many. I was not disappointed. I took my time, savoring the first bite, then put my fork down.

"What kind of help?"

"We draw out the killer."

"Great. How dangerous will it be?"

"Depends on a lot of things. But I'm not going to lie to you. It could get dangerous. I need you to shake some things up, make whoever's out there think there's a loose end, that you might be dangerous to them. Then we see what happens."

"But you'll be there. I'll be covered."

"Every step of the way."

"How do we shake things up?"

"I was thinking a newspaper story. I assume you've been getting calls from the reporters. We pick one and give them the story, an exclusive, and we plant something in there that gets the killer thinking."

I thought about this and remembered what Lorna had warned about playing fair with the media.

"There's a guy at the *Times*," I said. "I kind of made a deal with him to get him off my back. I told him that when I was ready to talk, I would talk to him."

"That's a perfect setup. We'll use him."

I didn't say anything.

"So, are you in?"

I picked up my fork and knife and remained silent while I cut into the steak again. Blood ran onto the plate. I thought about my daughter getting to the point of asking me the same questions her mother asked and that I could never answer. *It's like you're always working for the bad guys.* It wasn't as simple as that but knowing this didn't take away the sting or the look I remembered seeing in her eyes.

I put the knife and fork down without taking a bite. I suddenly was no longer hungry.

"Yeah," I said. "I'm in."

PART THREE

— To Speak the Truth

Thirty-four

Everybody lies.

Cops lie. Lawyers lie. Clients lie. Even jurors lie.

There is a school of belief in criminal law that says every trial is won or lost in the choosing of the jury. I've never been ready to go all the way to that level but I do know that there is probably no phase in a murder trial more important than the selection of the twelve citizens who will decide your client's fate. It is also the most complex and fleeting part of the trial, reliant on the whims of fate and luck and being able to ask the right question of the right person at the right time.

And yet we begin each trial with it.

Jury selection in the case of *California v. Elliot* began on schedule in Judge James P. Stanton's courtroom at ten a.m. Thursday. The courtroom was packed, half filled with the venire — the eighty potential jurors called randomly from the jury pool on the fifth floor of the CCB — and half filled with media, courthouse professionals, well-wishers and just plain gawkers who had been able to squeeze in.

I sat at the defense table alone with my client — fulfilling his wish for a legal team of just one. Spread in front of me was an open but empty manila file, a Post-it pad and three different markers, red, blue and black.

Back at the office, I had prepared the file by using a ruler to draw a grid across it. There were twelve blocks, each the size of a Post-it. Each block was for one of the twelve jurors who would be chosen to sit in judgment of Walter Elliot. Some lawyers use computers to track potential jurors. They even have software that can take information revealed during the selection process, filter it through a sociopolitical pattern–recognition program and spit out instant recommendations on whether to keep or reject a juror. I had been using the old-school grid system since I had been a baby lawyer in the Public Defender's Office. It had always worked well for me and I wasn't changing now. I didn't want to use a computer's instincts when it came to picking a jury. I wanted to use my own. A computer can't hear how someone gives an answer. It can't see someone's eyes when they lie.

The way it works is that the judge has a computer-generated list from which he calls the first twelve citizens from the venire, and they take seats in the jury box. At that point each is a member of the jury. But they get to keep their seats only if they survive voir dire — the questioning of their background and views and understanding of the law. There is a process. The judge asks them a series of basic questions and then the lawyers get the chance to follow up with a more narrow focus.

Jurors can be removed from the box in one of two ways. They can be rejected for cause if they show through their answers or demeanor or even their life's circumstances that they cannot be fair judges of credibility or hear the case with an open mind. There is no limit to the number of challenges for cause at the disposal of the attorneys. Oftentimes the judge will make a dismissal for cause before the prosecutor or defense attorney even raises an objection. I have always believed that the quickest way off a jury panel is to announce that you are convinced that all cops lie or all cops are always right. Either way, a closed mind is a challenge for cause.

The second method of removal is the preemptory challenge, of which each attorney is given a limited supply, depending on the type of case and charges. Because this trial involved charges of murder, both the prosecution and defense would have up to twenty preemptory challenges each. It is in the judicious and tactful use of these preemptories that strategy and instinct come into play. A skilled attorney can use his challenges to help sculpt the jury into a tool of the prosecution or defense. A preemptory challenge lets the attorney strike a juror for no reason other than his instinctual dislike of the individual. An exception to this would be the obvious use of preemptories to create a bias on the jury. A prosecutor who continually removed black jurors, or a defense attorney who did the same with white jurors, would quickly run afoul of the opposition as well as the judge.

The rules of voir dire are designed to remove bias and deception from the jury. The term itself comes from the French phrase "to speak the truth." But this of course is contradictory to each side's cause. The bottom line in any trial is that I want a biased jury. I want them biased against the state and the police. I want them predisposed to be on my side. The truth is that a fair-minded person is the last person I want on my jury. I want somebody who is already on my side or can easily be pushed there. I want twelve lemmings in the box. Jurors who will follow my lead and act as agents for the defense.

And, of course, the man sitting four feet from me in the courtroom wanted to achieve a diametrically opposite result out of jury selection. The prosecutor wanted his own lemmings and would use his challenges to sculpt the jury his way, and at my expense.

By ten fifteen the efficient Judge Stanton had looked at the printout from the computer that randomly selected the first twelve candidates and had welcomed them to the jury box by calling out code numbers issued to them in the jury-pool room on the fifth floor. There were six men and six women. We had three postal workers, two engineers, a housewife from Pomona, an out-of-work screenwriter, two high school teachers and three retirees.

We knew where they were from and what they did. But we didn't know their names. It was an anonymous jury. During all pretrial conferences the judge had been adamant about protecting the jurors from public attention and scrutiny. He had ordered that the Court TV camera be mounted on the wall over the jury box so that the jurors would not be seen in its view of the courtroom. He had also ruled that the identities of all prospective jurors be withheld from even the lawyers and that each be referred to during voir dire by their seat number.

The process began with the judge asking each prospective juror questions about what they did for a living and the area of Los Angeles County they lived in. He then moved on to basic questions about whether they had been victims of crime, had relatives in prison or were related to any police officers or prosecutors. He asked what their knowledge of the law and court procedures was. He asked who had prior jury experience. The judge excused three for cause: a postal employee whose brother was a police officer; a retiree whose son had been the victim of a drug-related murder; and the screenwriter because although she had never worked for Archway Studios, the judge felt she might harbor ill will toward Elliot because of the contentious relationship between screenwriters and studio management in general.

A fourth prospective juror — one of the engineers — was dismissed when the judge agreed with his plea for a hardship dismissal. He was a self-employed consultant and two weeks spent in a trial were two weeks with no income other than the five bucks a day he made as a juror.

The four were quickly replaced with four more random selections from the venire. And so it went. By noon I had used two of my preemptories on the remaining postal workers and would have used a third to strike the second engineer from the panel but decided to take the lunch hour to think about it before making my next move. Meanwhile, Golantz was holding fast with a full arsenal of challenges. His strategy was obviously to let me use my strikes up and then he would come in with the final shaping of the jury.

Elliot had adopted the pose of CEO of the defense. I did the work in front of the jury but he insisted that he be allowed to sign off on each of my preemptory challenges. It took extra time because I needed to explain to him why I wanted to dump a juror and he would always offer his opinion. But each time, he ultimately nodded his approval like the man in charge, and the juror was struck. It was an annoying process but one I could put up with, just as long as Elliot went along with what I wanted to do.

Shortly after noon, the judge broke for lunch. Even though the day was devoted to jury selection, technically it was the first day of my first trial in over a year. Lorna Taylor had come to court to watch and show her support. The plan was to go to lunch together and then she would go back to the office and start packing it up.

As we entered the hallway outside the courtroom, I asked Elliot if he wanted to join us but he said he had to make a quick run to the studio to check on things. I told him not to be late coming back. The judge had given us a very generous ninety minutes for the lunch break and he would not look kindly on any late returns.

Lorna and I hung back and let the prospective jurors crowd onto the elevators. I didn't want to ride down with them. Inevitably when you do that, one of them opens their mouth and asks something that is improper and you then have to go through the motions of reporting it to the judge.

When one of the elevators opened, I saw the reporter Jack McEvoy push his way out past the jurors, scan the hallway and zero in on me.

"Great," I said. "Here comes trouble."

McEvoy came directly toward me.

"What do you want?" I said.

"To explain."

"What, you mean explain why you're a liar?"

"No, look, when I told you it was going to run Sunday, I meant it. That's what I was told."

247

"And here it is Thursday and no story in the paper, and when I've tried to call you about it, you don't call me back. I've got other reporters interested, McEvoy. I don't need the *Times*."

"Look, I understand. But what happened was that they decided to hold it so it would run closer to the trial."

"The trial started two hours ago."

The reporter shook his head.

"You know, the real trial. Testimony and evidence. They're running it out front this coming Sunday."

"The front page on Sunday. Is that a promise?"

"Monday at the latest."

"Oh, now it's Monday."

"Look, it's the news business. Things change. It's supposed to run out front on Sunday but if something big happens in the world, they might kick it over till Monday. It's either-or."

"Whatever. I'll believe it when I see it."

I saw that the area around the elevators was clear. Lorna and I could go down now and not encounter any prospective jurors. I took Lorna by the arm and started leading her that way. I pushed past the reporter.

"So we're okay?" McEvoy said. "You'll hold off?"

"Hold off on what?"

"Talking to anyone else. On giving away the exclusive."

"Whatever."

I left him hanging and headed toward the elevators. When we got out of the building, we walked a block over to City Hall and I had Patrick pick us up there. I didn't want any prospective jurors who might be hanging around the courthouse to see me getting into the back of a chauffeured Lincoln. It might not sit well with them. Among my pretrial instructions to Elliot had been a directive for him to eschew the studio limo and drive himself to court every day. You never know who might see what outside the courtroom and what the effect might be.

I told Patrick to take us over to the French Garden on Seventh Street. I then called Harry Bosch's cell phone and he answered right away.

"I just talked to the reporter," I said.

"And?"

"And it's finally running Sunday or Monday. On the front page, he says, so be ready."

"Finally."

"Yeah. You going to be ready?"

"Don't worry about it. I'm ready."

"I have to worry. It's my — Hello?"

He was gone already. I closed the phone.

"What was that?" Lorna asked.

"Nothing."

I realized that I had to change the subject.

"Listen, when you go back to the office today, I want you to call Julie Favreau and see if she can come to court tomorrow."

"I thought Elliot didn't want a jury consultant."

"He doesn't have to know we're using her."

"Then, how will you pay her?"

"Take it out of general operating. I don't care. I'll pay her out of my own pocket if I have to. But I'm going to need her and I don't care what Elliot thinks. I already burned through two strikes and have a feeling that by tomorrow I'm going to have to make whatever I have left count. I'll want her help on the final chart. Just tell her the bailiff will have her name and will make sure she gets a seat. Tell her to sit in the gallery and not to approach me when I'm with my client. Tell her she can text me on the cell when she has something important."

"Okay, I'll call her. Are you doing all right, Mick?"

I must've been talking too fast or sweating too much. Lorna had picked up on my agitation. I was feeling a little shaky and I didn't know if it was because of the reporter's bullshit or Bosch's hanging up or the growing realization that what I had been working toward for a year would soon be upon me. Testimony and evidence.

"I'm fine," I said sharply. "I'm just hungry. You know how I get when I'm hungry."

"Sure," she said. "I understand."

The truth was, I wasn't hungry. I didn't even feel like eating. I was feeling the weight on me. The burden of a man's future.

And it wasn't my client's future I was thinking of.

Thirty-five

By three o'clock on the second day of jury selection, Golantz and I had traded preemptory and cause challenges for more than ten hours of court time. It had been a battle. We had quietly savaged each other, identifying each other's must-have jurors and striking them without care or conscience. We had gone through almost the entire venire, and my jury seating chart was covered in some spots with as many as five layers of Post-its. I had two preemptory challenges left. Golantz, at first judicious with his challenges, had caught up and then passed me and was down to his final preemptory. It was zero hour. The jury box was about to be complete.

In its current composition, the panel now included an attorney, a computer programmer, two new postal service employees and three new retirees, as well as a male nurse, a tree trimmer and an artist.

From the original twelve seated the morning before, there were still two prospective jurors remaining. The engineer in seat seven and one of the retirees, in seat twelve, had somehow gone the distance. Both were white males and both, in my estimation, leaning toward the state. Neither was overtly on the prosecution's side, but on my chart I had written notes about each in blue ink — my code for a juror who I perceived as being cold to the defense. But their leanings were so slight that I had still not used a precious challenge on either.

I knew I could take them both out in my final flourish and use of preemptory strikes, but that was the risk of voir dire. You strike one juror because of blue ink and the replacement might end up being neon blue and a greater risk to your client than the original was. It was what made jury selection such an unpredictable proposition.

The latest addition to the box was the artist who took the opening in seat number eleven after Golantz had used his nineteenth preemptory to remove a city sanitation worker who I'd had down as a red juror. Under the general questioning of Judge Stanton, the artist revealed that she lived in Malibu and worked in a studio off the Pacific Coast Highway. Her medium was acrylic paint and she had studied at the Art Institute of Philadelphia before coming to California for the light. She said she didn't own a television and didn't regularly read any newspapers. She said she knew nothing about the murders that had taken place six months earlier in the beach house not far from where she lived and worked.

Almost from the start I had taken notes about her in red and grew happier and happier with her on my jury as the questions progressed. I knew that Golantz had made a tactical error. He had eliminated the sanitation worker with one challenge and had ended up with a juror seemingly even more detrimental to his cause. He would now have to live with the mistake or use his final challenge to remove the artist and run the same risk all over again.

When the judge finished his general inquiries, it was the lawyers' turn. Golantz went first and asked a series of questions he hoped would draw out a bias so that the artist could be removed for cause instead of through the use of his last preemptory. But the woman held her own, appearing very honest and open-minded.

Four questions into the prosecutor's effort, I felt a vibration in my pocket and reached in for my cell. I held it down below the defense table between my legs and at an angle where it could not be seen by the judge. Julie Favreau had been texting me all day.

Favreau: She's a keeper.

I sent her one back immediately.

Haller: I know. What about 7, 8 and 10? Which one next?

Favreau, my secret jury consultant, had been in the fourth row of the gallery during both the morning and afternoon sessions. I had also met her for lunch while Walter Elliot had once again gone back to the studio to check on things, and I had allowed her to study my chart so that she could make up her own. She was a quick study and knew exactly where I was with my codes and challenges.

I got a response to my text message almost immediately. That was one thing I liked about Favreau. She didn't overthink things. She made quick, instinctive decisions based solely on visual tells in relation to verbal answers.

Favreau: Don't like 8. Haven't heard enough from 10. Kick 7 if you have to.

Juror eight was the tree trimmer. I had him in blue because of some of the answers he gave when questioned about the police. I also thought he was too eager to be on the jury. This was always a flag in a murder case. It signaled to me that the potential juror had strong feelings about law and order and wasn't hesitant about the idea of sitting in judgment of another person. The truth was, I was suspicious of anybody who liked to sit in judgment of another. Anybody who relished the idea of being a juror was blue ink all the way.

Judge Stanton was allowing us a lot of leeway. When it came time to question a prospective juror, the attorneys were allowed to trade their time to question anyone else on the panel. He was also allowing the liberal use of back strikes, meaning it was acceptable to use a preemptory challenge to strike out anybody on the panel, even if they had already been questioned and accepted.

When it was my turn to question the artist, I walked to the lectern and told the judge I accepted her on the jury at this time without further questioning. I asked to be allowed instead to make further inquiries of juror number eight, and the judge allowed me to proceed.

"Juror number eight, I just want to clarify a couple of your views on things. First, let me ask you, at the end of this trial, after you've heard all the testimony, if you think my client might be guilty, would you vote to convict him?"

The tree trimmer thought for a moment before answering.

"No, because that wouldn't be beyond a reasonable doubt."

I nodded, letting him know that he had given the right answer.

"So you don't equate 'might've' with 'beyond a reasonable doubt'?"

"No, sir. Not at all."

"Good. Do you believe that people get arrested in church for singing too loud?"

A puzzled look spread across the tree trimmer's face, and there was a murmur of laughter in the gallery behind me.

"I don't understand."

"There's a saying that people don't get arrested in church for singing too loud. In other words, where there's smoke there's fire. People don't get arrested without good reason. The police usually have it right and arrest the right people. Do you believe that?"

"I believe that everybody makes mistakes from time to time—including the police—and you have to look at each case individually."

"But do you believe that the police *usually* have it right?"

He was cornered. Any answer would raise a flag for one side or the other.

"I think they probably do—they're the professionals—but I would look at every case individually and not think that just because the police usually get things right, they automatically got the right man in this case."

That was a good answer. From a tree trimmer, no less. Again I gave him the nod. His answers were right but there was something almost practiced about his delivery. It was smarmy, holier-than-thou. The tree trimmer wanted very badly to be on the jury and that didn't sit well with me.

"What kind of car do you drive, sir?"

The unexpected question was always good for a reaction. Juror number eight leaned back in his seat and gave me a look like he thought I was trying to trick him in some way.

"My car?"

"Yes, what do you drive to work?"

"I have a pickup. I keep my equipment and stuff in it. It's a Ford one-fifty."

"Do you have any bumper stickers on the back?"

"Yeah…a few."

"What do they say?"

He had to think a long moment to remember his own bumper stickers.

"Uh, I got the NRA sticker on there, and then I got another that says, If you can read this, then back off. Something like that. Maybe it doesn't say it that nice."

There was laughter from his fellow members of the venire, and number eight smiled proudly.

"How long have you been a member of the National Rifle Association?" I asked. "On the juror information sheet you didn't list that."

"Well, I'm not really. Not a member, I mean. I just have the sticker on there."

Deception. He was either lying about being a member and leaving it off his info sheet, or he wasn't a member and was using his bumper sticker to hold himself out as something he was not, or as part of an organization he believed in but didn't want to officially join. Either way it was deceptive and it confirmed everything I was feeling. Favreau was right. He had to go. I told the judge I was finished my questioning and sat back down.

When the judge asked if the prosecution and defense accepted the panel as composed, Golantz attempted to challenge the artist for cause. I opposed this and the judge sided with me. Golantz had no choice but to use his last preemptory to remove her. I then used my second-to-last challenge to remove the tree trimmer. The man looked angry as he made the long walk out of the courtroom.

Two more names were called from the venire and a real-estate agent and one more retiree took seats eight and eleven in the box. Their answers to the questions from the judge put them right down the middle of the road. I coded them black and heard nothing that raised a flag. Halfway through the judge's voir dire I got another text from Favreau.

Favreau: Both of them +/– if you ask me. Both lemmings.

In general, having lemmings on the panel was good. Jurors with no indication of forceful personality and with middle-of-the-road convictions could oftentimes be manipulated during deliberations. They look for someone to follow. The more lemmings you have, the more important it is to have a juror with a strong personality and one who you believe is predisposed to be for the defense. You want somebody in the deliberations room who will pull the lemmings with him.

Golantz, in my view, had made a basic tactical error. He had exhausted his preemptory challenges before the defense and, far worse, had left an attorney on the panel. Juror three had made it through and my gut instinct was that Golantz had been saving his last preemptory for him. But the artist got that and now Golantz was stuck with a lawyer on the panel.

Juror number three didn't practice criminal law but he'd had to study it to get his ticket and from time to time must have flirted with the idea of practicing it. They didn't make movies and TV shows about real-estate lawyers. Criminal law had the pull and juror three would not be immune to this. In my view, that made him an excellent juror for the defense. He was lit up all red on my chart and was my number-one choice for the panel. He would go into the trial and the deliberations that come after it knowing the law and the absolute underdog status of the defense. It not only made him sympathetic to my side but it made him the obvious candidate as foreman — the juror elected by the panel to make communications with the judge and to speak for the entire panel. When the jury got back in there to begin deliberations, the person they would all turn to first would be the lawyer. If he was red, then he was going to pull and push many of his fellow jurors toward a not-guilty. And at minimum, his ego as an attorney would insist that his verdict was correct, and he would hold out for it. He alone could be the one who hung the jury and kept my client from a conviction.

It was a lot to bank on, considering juror number three had answered questions from the judge and the lawyers for less than thirty minutes. But that was what jury selection came down to. Quick, instinctual decisions based on experience and observation.

The bottom line was that I was going to let the two lemmings ride on the panel. I had one preemptory left and I was going to use it on juror seven or juror ten. The engineer or the retiree.

I asked the judge for a few moments to confer with my client. I then turned to Elliot and slid my chart over in front of him.

"This is it, Walter. We're down to our last bullet. What do you think? I think we need to get rid of seven and ten but we can get rid of only one."

Elliot had been very involved. Since the first twelve were seated the morning before, he had expressed strong and intuitive opinions about each juror I wanted to strike. But he had never picked a jury before. I had. I put up with his comments but ultimately made my own choices.

This last choice, however, was a toss-up. Either of the jurors could be damaging to the defense. Either could turn out to be a lemming. It was a tough call and I was tempted to let my client's instincts be the deciding factor.

Elliot tapped a finger on the block for juror ten on my grid. The retired technical writer for a toy manufacturer.

"Him," he said. "Get rid of him."

"You sure?"

"Absolutely."

I looked at the grid. There was a lot of blue on block ten, but there was an equal amount on block seven. The engineer.

I had a hunch that the technical writer was like the tree trimmer. He wanted badly to be on the jury but probably for a wholly different set of reasons. I thought maybe his plan was to use his experience as research for a book or maybe a movie script. He had spent his career writing instruction manuals for toys. In retirement, he had acknowledged during voir dire, he was trying to write fiction. There would be nothing like a front-row seat on a murder trial to help stimulate the imagination and creative process. That was fine for him but not for Elliot. I didn't want anybody who relished the idea of sitting in judgment—for any reason—on my jury.

Juror seven was blue for another reason. He was listed as an aerospace engineer. The industry he worked in had a large presence in Southern California and consequently I had questioned several engineers during voir dire over the years. In general, engineers were conservative politically and religiously, two very blue attributes, and they worked for companies that relied on huge government contracts and grants. A vote for the defense was a vote against the government, and that was a hard leap for them to make.

Last, and perhaps most important, engineers exist in a world of logic and absolutes. These are things you often cannot apply to a crime or crime scene or even to the criminal justice system as a whole.

"I don't know," I said. "I think the engineer should go."

"No, I like him. I've liked him since the beginning. He's given me good eye contact. I want him to stay."

I turned from Elliot and looked over at the box. My eyes traveled from juror seven to juror ten and then back again. I was hoping for some sign, some tell that would reveal the right choice.

"Mr. Haller," Judge Stanton said. "Do you wish to use your last challenge or accept the jury as it is now composed? I remind you, it is getting late in the day and we still have to choose our alternate jurors."

My phone was buzzing while the judge addressed me.

"Uh, one more moment, Your Honor."

I turned back toward Elliot and leaned into him as if to whisper something. But what I really was doing was pulling my phone.

"Are you sure, Walter?" I whispered. "The guy's an engineer. That could be trouble for us."

"Look, I make my living reading people and rolling the dice," Elliot whispered back. "I want that man on my jury."

I nodded and looked down between my legs where I was holding the phone. It was a text from Favreau.

Favreau: Kick 10. I see deception. 7 fits prosecution profile but I see good eye contact and open face. He's interested in your story. He likes your client.

Eye contact. That settled it. I slipped the phone back into my pocket and stood up. Elliot grabbed me by the sleeve of my jacket. I bent down to hear his urgent whisper.

"What are you doing?"

I shook off his grasp because I didn't like his public display of attempting control over me. I straightened back up and looked up at the judge.

"Your Honor, the defense would like to thank and excuse juror ten at this time."

While the judge dismissed the technical writer and called a new candidate to the tenth chair in the box, I sat down and turned to Elliot.

"Walter, don't ever grab me like that in front of the jury. It makes you look like an asshole and I'm already going to have a tough enough time convincing them you're not a killer."

I turned so that my back was to him as I watched the latest and most likely the last juror take the open seat in the box.

PART FOUR

— Fillet of Soul

Walking in a
Dead Man's Shoes

Attorney Takes Over for Murdered Colleague
First Case; The Trial of the Decade

BY JACK McEVOY, *Times Staff Writer*

It wasn't the 31 cases dropped in his lap that were the difficulty. It was the big one with the big client and highest stakes attached to it. Defense Attorney Michael Haller stepped into the shoes of the murdered Jerry Vincent two weeks ago and now finds himself at the center of this year's so-called Trial of the Decade.

Today testimony is scheduled to begin in the trial of Walter Elliot, the 54-year-old chairman of Archway Studios, charged with murdering his wife and her alleged lover six months ago in Malibu. Haller stepped into the case after

263

Vincent, 45, was found shot to death in his car in downtown Los Angeles.

Vincent had made legal provisions that allowed Haller to step into his practice in the event of his death. Haller, who had been at the end of a year-long sabbatical from practicing law, went to sleep one night with zero cases and woke up the next day with 31 new clients to handle.

"I was excited about coming back to work but I wasn't expecting anything like this," said Haller, the 42-year-old son of the late Michael Haller Sr., one of Los Angeles's storied defense attorneys in the 50's and 60's. "Jerry Vincent was a friend and colleague and, of course, I would gladly go back to having no cases if he could be alive today."

The investigation of Vincent's murder is ongoing. There have been no arrests, and detectives say there are no suspects. He was shot twice in the head while sitting in his car in the garage next to the building where he kept his office, in the 200 block of Broadway.

Following Vincent's death, the fallen attorney's entire law practice was turned over to Haller. His job was to cooperate with investigators within the bounds of attorney-client protections, inventory the cases and make contact with all active clients. There was an immediate surprise. One of Vincent's clients was due in court the day after the murder.

"My staff and I were just beginning to put all the cases together when we saw that Jerry—and now, of course, I—had a sentencing with a client," Haller said. "I had to drop all of that, race over to the Criminal Courts Building, and be there for the client."

That was one down and 30 other active cases to go. Every client on that list had to be quickly contacted, informed of

Vincent's death, and given the option of hiring a new lawyer or continuing with Haller handling the case.

A handful of clients decided to seek other representation but the vast majority of cases remain with Haller. By far the biggest of these is the "Murder in Malibu" case. It has drawn wide public attention. Portions of the trial are scheduled to be broadcast live nationally on Court TV. Dominick Dunne, the premier chronicler of courts and crime for *Vanity Fair,* is among members of the media who have requested seats in the courtroom.

The case came to Haller with one big condition. Elliot would agree to keep Haller as his attorney only if Haller agreed not to delay the trial.

"Walter is innocent and has insisted on his innocence since day one," Haller told the *Times* in his first interview since taking on the case. "There were early delays in the case and he has waited six months for his day in court and the opportunity to clear his name. He wasn't interested in another delay in justice and I agreed with him. If you're innocent, why wait? We've been working almost around the clock to be ready and I think we are."

It wasn't easy to be ready. Whoever killed Vincent also stole his briefcase from his car. It contained Vincent's laptop computer and his calendar.

"It was not too difficult to rebuild the calendar but the laptop was a big loss," Haller said. "It was really the central storage point for case information and strategy. The hard files we found in the office were incomplete. We needed the laptop and at first I thought we were dead in the water."

But then Haller found something the killer had not taken. Vincent backed his computer up on a digital flash drive attached to his key chain. Wading through the megabytes of data, Haller began to find bits and pieces of strategy for the Elliot trial. Jury selection took place last week and when the testimony begins today, he said he will be fully prepared.

"I don't think Mr. Elliot is going to have any drop-off in his defense whatsoever," Haller said. "We're locked and loaded and ready to go."

Elliot did not return calls for comment for this story and has avoided speaking to the media, except for one press conference after his arrest, in which he vehemently denied involvement in the murders and mourned the loss of his wife.

Prosecutors and investigators with the Los Angeles County Sheriff's Department said Elliot killed his wife, Mitzi, 39, and Johan Rilz, 35, in a fit of rage after finding them together at a weekend home owned by the Elliots on the beach in Malibu. Elliot called deputies to the scene and was arrested following the crime scene investigation. Though the murder weapon has never been found, forensic tests determined that Elliot had recently fired a weapon. Investigators said he also gave inconsistent statements while initially interviewed at the crime scene and afterwards. Other evidence against the movie mogul is expected to be revealed at trial.

Elliot remains free on $20 million bail, the highest amount ever ordered for a suspect in a crime in Los Angeles County history.

Legal experts and courthouse observers say it is expected that the defense will attack the handling of evidence in the investigation and the testing procedures that determined that Elliot had fired a gun.

Deputy Dist. Atty. Jeffrey Golantz, who is prosecuting the case, declined comment for this story. Golantz has never lost a case as a prosecutor and this will be his eleventh murder case.

Thirty-six

The jury came out in a single-file line like the Lakers taking the basketball court. They weren't all wearing the same uniform but the same feeling of anticipation was in the air. The game was about to begin. They split into two lines and moved down the two rows of the jury box. They carried steno pads and pens. They took the same seats they were in on Friday when the jury was completed and sworn in.

It was almost ten a.m. Monday and a later-than-expected start. But earlier, Judge Stanton had had the lawyers and the defendant back in chambers for almost forty minutes while he went over last-minute ground rules and took the time to give me the squint and express his displeasure over the story published on the front page of the morning's *Los Angeles Times*. His chief concern was that the story was weighted heavily on the defense side and cast me as a sympathetic underdog. Though on Friday afternoon he had admonished the new jury not to read or watch any news reports on the case or trial, the judge was concerned that the story might have slipped through.

In my own defense, I told the judge that I had given the interview ten days earlier for a story I had been told would run at least a week before the trial started. Golantz smirked and said my explanation suggested I was trying to affect jury selection by giving the interview earlier but was now tainting the trial instead. I countered by pointing out that the story clearly stated that the prosecution had been contacted but refused to comment. If the story was one-sided, that was why.

Stanton grumpily seemed to accept my story but cautioned us about talking to the media. I knew then that I had to cancel my agreement to give commentary to Court TV at the end of each day's trial session. The publicity would've been nice but I didn't want to be on the wrong side of the judge.

We moved on to other things. Stanton was very interested in budgeting time for the trial. Like any judge, he had to keep things moving. He had a backlog of cases, and a long trial only backed things up further. He wanted to know how much time each side expected to take putting forth his case. Golantz said he would take a minimum of a week and I said I needed the same, though realistically I knew I would probably take much less time. Most of the defense case would be made, or at least set up, during the prosecution phase.

Stanton frowned at the time estimates and suggested that both the prosecution and defense think hard about streamlining. He said he wanted to get the case to the jury while their attention was still high.

I studied the jurors as they took their seats and looked for indications of biases or anything else. I was still happy with the jury, especially with juror three, the lawyer. A few others were questionable but I had decided over the weekend that I would make my case to the lawyer and hope that he would pull and push the others along with him when he voted for acquittal.

The jurors all kept their eyes to themselves or looked up at the judge, the alpha dog of the courtroom. As far as I could tell, no juror even glanced at the prosecution or defense table.

I turned and looked back at the gallery. The courtroom once again was packed with members of the media and the public, as well as those with a blood link to the case.

Directly behind the prosecution's table sat Mitzi Elliot's mother, who had flown in from New York. Next to her sat Johan Rilz's father and two brothers, who had traveled all the way from Berlin. I noticed that Golantz had positioned the grieving mother on the end of the aisle, where she and her constant flow of tears would be fully visible to the jury.

The defense had five seats on reserve in the first row behind me. Sitting there were Lorna, Cisco, Patrick and Julie Favreau — the last on hand because I had hired her to ride through the trial and observe the jury for me. I couldn't watch the jurors at all times, and sometimes they revealed themselves when they thought none of the lawyers were watching.

The empty fifth seat had been reserved for my daughter. My hope had been that over the weekend I would convince my ex-wife to allow me to take Hayley out of school for the day so she could go with me to court. She had never seen me at work before and I thought opening statements would be the perfect time. I felt very confident in my case. I felt bulletproof and I wanted my daughter to see her father this way. The plan was for her to sit with Lorna, whom she knew and liked, and watch me operate in front of the jury. In my argument I had even employed the Margaret Mead line about taking her out of school so that she could get an education. But it was a case I ultimately couldn't win. My ex-wife refused to allow it. My daughter went to school and the reserved seat went unused.

Walter Elliot had no one in the gallery. He had no children and no relatives he was close to. Nina Albrecht had asked me if she would be allowed to sit in the gallery to show her support, but because she was listed on both the prosecution and defense witness lists, she was excluded from watching the trial until her testimony was completed. Otherwise, my client had no one. And this was by design. He had plenty of associates, well-wishers and hangers-on who wanted to be there for him. He even had A-list movie actors willing to sit behind him and show their support. But I told him that if he had a Hollywood entourage or his corporate lawyers in the seats behind him, he would be broadcasting the wrong message and image to the jury. It is all about the jury, I told him. Every move that is made—from the choice of tie you wear to the witnesses you put on the stand—is made in deference to the jury. Our anonymous jury.

After the jurors were seated and comfortable, Judge Stanton went on the record and began the proceedings by asking if any jurors had seen the story in the morning's *Times*. None raised their hands and Stanton responded with another reminder about not reading or watching reports on the trial in the media.

He then told jurors that the trial would begin with opening statements from the opposing attorneys.

"Ladies and gentlemen, remember," he said, "these are statements. They are not evidence. It's up to each side to present the evidence that backs the statements up. And you will be the ones at the end of the trial who decide if they have done that."

With that, he gestured to Golantz and said the prosecution would go first. As outlined in a pretrial conference, each side would have an hour for its opening statement. I didn't know about Golantz but I wouldn't take close to that.

Handsome and impressive-looking in a black suit, white shirt and maroon tie, Golantz stood up and addressed the jury from the prosecution table. For the trial he had a second chair, an attractive young lawyer named Denise Dabney. She sat next to him and kept her eyes on the jury the whole time he spoke. It was a way of double-teaming, two pairs of eyes constantly sweeping across the faces of the jurors, doubly conveying the seriousness and gravity of the task at hand.

After introducing himself and his second, Golantz got down to it.

"Ladies and gentleman of the jury, we are here today because of unchecked greed and anger. Plain and simple. The defendant, Walter Elliot, is a man of great power, money and standing in our community. But that was not enough for him. He did not want to divide his money and power. He did not want to turn the cheek on betrayal. Instead, he lashed out in the most extreme way possible. He took not just one life, but two. In a moment of high anger and humiliation, he raised a gun and killed both his wife, Mitzi Elliot, and Johan Rilz. He believed his money and power would place him above the law and save him from punishment for these heinous crimes. But that will not be the case. The state will prove to you beyond any reasonable doubt that Walter Elliot pulled the trigger and is responsible for the deaths of two innocent human beings."

I was turned in my seat, half to obscure the jury's view of my client and half to keep a view of Golantz and the gallery rows behind him. Before his first paragraph was completed, the tears were flowing from Mitzi Elliot's mother, and that was something I would need to bring up with the judge out of earshot of the jury. The theatrics were prejudicial and I would ask the judge to move the victim's mother to a seat that was less of a focal point for the jury.

I looked past the crying woman and saw hard grimaces on the faces of the men from Germany. I was very interested in them and how they would appear to the jury. I wanted to see how they handled emotion and the surroundings of an American courtroom. I wanted to see how threatening they could be made to look. The grimmer and more menacing they looked, the better the defense strategy would work when I focused on Johan Rilz. Looking at them now, I knew I was off to a good start. They looked angry and mean.

Golantz laid his case out to the jurors, telling them what he would be presenting in testimony and evidence and what he believed it meant. There were no surprises. At one point I got a one-line text from Favreau, which I read below the table.

Favreau: They are eating this up. You better be good.

Right, I thought. Tell me something I don't know.
There was an unfair advantage to the prosecution built into every

trial. The state has the power and the might on its side. It comes with an assumption of honesty and integrity and fairness. An assumption in every juror's and onlooker's mind that we wouldn't be here if smoke didn't lead to a fire.

It is that assumption that every defense has to overcome. The person on trial is supposed to be presumed innocent. But anybody who has ever stepped foot into a courtroom as a lawyer or defendant knows that presumed innocence is just one of the idealistic notions they teach in law school. There was no doubt in my mind or anybody else's that I started this trial with a defendant who was presumed guilty. I had to find a way to either prove him innocent or prove the state guilty of malfeasance, ineptitude or corruption in its preparation of the case.

Golantz lasted his entire allotted hour, seemingly leaving no secrets about his case hidden. He showed typical prosecutorial arrogance; put it all out there and dare the defense to try to contradict it. The prosecution was always the six-hundred-pound gorilla, so big and strong it didn't have to worry about finesse. When it painted its picture, it used a six-inch brush and hung it on the wall with a sledgehammer and spike.

The judge had told us in the pretrial session that we would be required to remain at our tables or to use the lectern placed between them while addressing witnesses during testimony. But opening statements and closing arguments were an exception to this rule. During these bookend moments of the trial, we would be free to use the space in front of the jury box—a spot the veterans of the defense bar called the "proving grounds" because it was the only time during a trial when the lawyers spoke directly to the jury and either made their case or didn't.

Golantz finally moved from the prosecution table to the proving grounds when it was time for his big finish. He stood directly in front of the midpoint of the box and held his hands wide, like a preacher in front of his flock.

"I'm out of time here, folks," he said. "So in closing, I urge you to take great care as you listen to the evidence and the testimony. Common sense will lead you. I urge you not to get confused or sidetracked by the roadblocks to justice the defense will put before you. Keep your eyes on the prize. Remember, two people had their lives stolen from them. Their future was ripped away. That is why we are here today. For them. Thank you very much."

The old keep-your-eyes-on-the-prize opener. That one had been kicking around the courthouse since I was a public defender. Nevertheless, it was a solid beginning from Golantz. He wouldn't win any orator-of-the-year trophies but he had made his points. He'd also addressed the jurors as "folks" at least four times by my count, and that was a word I would never use with a jury.

Favreau had texted me twice more during the last half hour of his delivery with reports of declining jury interest. They might have been eating it up at the start but now they were apparently full. Sometimes you can go on too long. Golantz had trudged through a full fifteen rounds like a heavyweight boxer. I was going to be a welterweight. I was interested in quick jabs. I was going to get in and get out, make a few points, plant a few seeds and raise a few questions. I was going to make them like me. That was the main thing. If they liked me, they would like my case.

Once the judge gave me the nod, I stood up and immediately moved into the proving grounds. I wanted nothing between me and the jury. I was also aware that this put me right in front and in focus of the Court TV camera mounted on the wall above the jury box.

I faced the jury without physical gesture except for a slight nod of my head.

"Ladies and gentlemen, I know the judge already introduced me but I would like to introduce myself and my client. I am Michael Haller, the attorney representing Walter Elliot, whom you see here sitting at the table by himself."

I pointed to Elliot and by prior design he nodded somberly, not offering any form of a smile that would appear as falsely ingratiating as calling the jurors folks.

"Now, I am not going to take a lot of time here, because I want to get to the testimony and the evidence — what little there is of it — and get this show on the road. Enough talk. It's time to put up or shut up. Mr. Golantz wove a big and complicated picture for you. It took him a whole hour just to get it out. But I am here to tell you that this case is not that complicated. What the prosecution's case amounts to is a labyrinth of smoke and mirrors. And when we blow away the smoke and get through the labyrinth, you will understand that. You will find that there is no fire, that there is no case against Walter Elliot. That there is more than reasonable doubt here, that there is outrage that this case was ever brought against Walter Elliot in the first place."

Again I turned and pointed to my client. He sat with his eyes cast downward on the pad of paper he was now writing notes on — again, by prior design, depicting my client as busy, actively involved in his own defense, chin up and not worried about the terrible things the prosecutor had just said about him. He had right on his side, and right was might.

I turned back to the jury and continued.

"I counted six times that Mr. Golantz mentioned the word 'gun' in his speech. Six times he said Walter took a gun and blew away the woman he loved and a second, innocent bystander. Six times. But what he didn't tell you six times is that there is no gun. He has no gun. The Sheriff's Department has no gun. They have no gun and have no link between Walter and a gun because he has never owned or had such a weapon.

"Mr. Golantz told you that he will introduce indisputable evidence that Walter fired a gun, but let me tell you to hold on to your hats. Keep that promise in your back pocket and let's see at the end of this trial whether that so-called evidence is indisputable. Let's just see if it is even left standing."

As I spoke, my eyes washed back and forth across the jurors like the spotlights sweeping the sky over Hollywood at night. I remained in constant but calm motion. I felt a certain rhythm in my thoughts and cadence, and I instinctively knew I was holding the jury. Each one of them was riding with me.

"I know that in our society we want our law enforcement officers to be professional and thorough and the best they can possibly be. We see crime on the news and in the streets and we know that these men and women are the thin line between order and disorder. I mean, I want that as much as you do. I've been the victim of a violent crime myself. I know what that is like. And we want our cops to step in and save the day. After all, that's what they are there for."

I stopped and swept the whole jury box, holding every set of eyes for a brief moment before continuing.

"But that's not what happened here. The evidence — and I'm talking about the state's own evidence and testimony — will show that from the start the investigators focused on one suspect, Walter Elliot. The evidence will show that once Walter became that focus, then all other bets were off. All other avenues of investigation were halted or never even pursued. They had a suspect and what they believed was a motive, and they never looked back. They never looked anywhere else either."

For the first time I moved from my position. I stepped forward to the railing in front of juror number one. I slowly walked along the front of the box, hand sliding along the railing.

"Ladies and gentlemen, this case is about tunnel vision. The focus on one suspect and the complete lack of focus on anything else. And I will promise you that when you come out of the prosecution's tunnel, you're going to be looking at one another and squinting your eyes against the bright light. And you're going to be wondering where the hell their case is. Thank you very much."

My hand trailed off the railing and I headed back to my seat. Before I sat down, the judge recessed court for lunch.

Thirty-seven

Once more my client eschewed lunch with me so he could get back to the studio and make his business-as-usual appearance in the executive offices. I was beginning to think he viewed the trial as an annoying inconvenience in his schedule. He was either more confident than I was in the defense's case, or the trial simply wasn't a priority.

Whatever the reason, that left me with my entourage from the first row. We went over to Traxx in Union Station because I felt it was far enough away from the courthouse to avoid our ending up in the same place as one of the jurors. Patrick drove and I had him valet the Lincoln and join us so that he would feel like part of the team.

They gave us a table in a quiet enclosure next to a window that looked out on the train station's huge and wonderful waiting room. Lorna had made the seating arrangements and I ended up next to Julie Favreau. Ever since Lorna had hooked up with Cisco, she had decided that I needed to be with someone and had endeavored to be something of a matchmaker. This effort coming from an ex-wife—an ex-wife I still cared for on many levels—was decidedly uncomfortable and it felt clumsy when Lorna overtly pointed me to the chair next to my jury consultant. I was in the middle of day one of a trial and the possibility of romance was the last thing I was thinking about. Besides that, I was incapable of a relationship. My addiction had left me with an emotional distance from people and things that I was only now beginning to close. As such, I had made it my priority to reconnect with my daughter. After that, I would worry about finding a woman to spend time with.

Romance aside, Julie Favreau was wonderful to work with. She was an attractive, diminutive woman with delicate facial features and raven hair that fell around her face in curls. A spray of youthful freckles across her nose made her look younger than she was. I knew she was thirty-three years old. She had once told me her story. She'd come to Los Angeles by way of London to act in film and had studied with a teacher who believed that internal thoughts of character could be shown externally through facial tells, tics and body movements. It was her job as an actor to bring these giveaways to the surface without making them obvious. Her student exercises became observation, identification and interpretation of these tells in others. Her assignments took her anywhere from the poker rooms in the south county, where she learned to read the faces of people trying not to give anything away, to the courtrooms of the CCB, where there were always lots of faces and giveaways to read.

After seeing her in the gallery for three days straight of a trial in which I was defending an accused serial rapist, I approached her and asked who she was. Expecting to find out she was a previously unknown victim of the man at the defense table, I was surprised to hear her story and to learn she was simply there to practice reading faces. I took her to lunch, got her number and the next time I picked a jury, I hired her to help me. She had been dead-on in her observations and I had used her several times since.

"So," I said as I spread a black napkin on my lap. "How is my jury doing?"

I thought it was obvious that the question was directed at Julie but Patrick spoke up first.

"I think they want to throw the book at your guy," he said. "I think they think he's a stuck-up rich guy who thinks he can get away with murder."

I nodded. His take probably wasn't too far off.

"Well, thanks for the encouraging word," I said. "I'll make sure I tell Walter to not be so stuck-up and rich from now on."

Patrick looked down at the table and seemed embarrassed.

"I was just saying, is all."

"No, Patrick, I appreciate it. Any and all opinions are welcome and they all matter. But some things you can't change. My client is rich beyond anything any of us can imagine and that gives him a certain style and image. An off-putting countenance that I'm not sure I can do anything about. Julie, what do you think of the jury so far?"

Before she could answer, the waiter came and took our drink orders. I stuck with water and lime, while the others ordered iced tea and Lorna asked for a glass of Mad Housewife Chardonnay. I gave her a look and she immediately protested.

"What? I'm not working. I'm just watching. Plus, I'm celebrating. You're in trial again and we're back in business."

I grudgingly nodded.

"Speaking of which, I need you to go to the bank."

I pulled an envelope out of my jacket pocket and handed it across the table to her. She smiled because she knew what was in it: a check from Elliot for $150,000, the remainder of the agreed-upon fee for my services.

Lorna put the envelope away and I turned my attention back to Julie.

"So what are you seeing?"

"I think it's a good jury," she said. "Overall, I see a lot of open faces. They are willing to listen to your case. At least right now. We all know they are predisposed to believe the prosecution, but they haven't shut the door on anything."

"You see any change from what we talked about Friday? I still present to number three?"

"Who is number three?" Lorna asked before Julie could answer.

"Golantz's slip-up. Three's a lawyer, and the prosecution should've never left him in the box."

"I still think he's a good one to present to," Julie said. "But there are others. I like eleven and twelve, too. Both retirees and sitting right next to each other. I have a feeling that they're going to bond and almost work as a team when it gets to deliberations. You win one over and you win them both."

I loved her English accent. It wasn't upper-crust at all. It had a street-smarts tone to it that gave what she said validity. She had not been very successful as an actress so far, and she had once told me that she got a lot of audition calls for period pieces requiring a dainty English accent that she hadn't quite mastered. Her income was primarily earned in the poker rooms, where she now played for keeps, and from jury reading for me and the small group of lawyers I had introduced her to.

"What about juror seven?" I asked. "During selection he was all eyes. Now he won't look at me."

Julie nodded.

"You noticed that. Eye contact has completely dropped off the chart. Like something changed between Friday and today. I would have to say at this point that that's a sign he's in the prosecution's camp. While you're presenting to number three, you can bet Mr. Undefeated's going to number seven."

"So much for listening to my client," I said under my breath.

We ordered lunch and told the waiter to hurry the order because we needed to get back to court. While we waited I checked with Cisco on our witnesses and he said we were good to go in that department. I then asked him to hang around after court and see if he could follow the Germans out of the courthouse and stay with them until they reached their hotel. I wanted to know where they were staying. It was just a precaution.

Before the trial was over, they were not going to be very happy with me. It was good strategy to know where your enemies were.

I was halfway through my grilled-chicken salad when I glanced through the window into the waiting room. It was a grand mixture of architectural designs but primarily it had an art deco vibe to it. There were rows and rows of big leather chairs for travelers to wait in and huge chandeliers hanging above. I saw people sleeping in chairs and others sitting with their suitcases and belongings gathered close around them.

And then I saw Bosch. He was sitting alone in the third row from my window. He had his earbuds in. Our eyes held for a moment and then he looked away. I put my fork down and reached into my pocket for my cash. I had no idea how much Mad Housewife cost per glass but Lorna was into her second round. I put five twenties down on the table and told the others to finish eating while I stepped out to make a phone call.

I left the restaurant and called Bosch's cell. He pulled his plugs and answered it as I was approaching the third row of seats.

"What?" he said by way of a greeting.

"Frank Morgan again?"

"Actually, Ron Carter. Why are you calling me?"

"What did you think of the story?"

I sat in the open seat across from him, gave him a glance but acted like I was talking to someone far away from me.

"This is kind of stupid," Bosch said.

"Well, I didn't know whether you wanted to stay undercover or —"

"Just hang up."

We closed our phones and looked at each other.

"Well?" I asked. "Are we in play?"

"We won't know until we know."

"What's that mean?"

"The story is out there. I think it did what we wanted it to do. Now we wait and see. If something happens, then, yes, we're in play. We won't know we're in play until we're in play."

I nodded, even though what he had said made no sense to me.

"Who's the woman in black?" he asked. "You didn't tell me you had a girlfriend. We should probably put coverage on her, too."

"She's my jury reader, that's all."

"Oh, she helps you pick out the cop haters and antiestablishment types?"

"Something like that. Is it just you here? Are you watching me by yourself?"

"You know, I had a girlfriend once. She always asked questions in bunches. Never one at a time."

"Did you ever answer any of her questions? Or did you just cleverly deflect them like you are doing now?"

"I'm not alone, Counselor. Don't worry. You have people around you that you'll never see. I've got people on your office whether you are there or not."

And cameras. They had been installed ten days earlier, when we had thought that the *Times* story was imminent.

"Yeah, good, but we won't be there for long."

"I noticed. Where are you moving to?"

"Nowhere. I work out of my car."

"Sounds like fun."

I studied him a moment. He had been sarcastic in his tone as usual. He was an annoying guy but somehow he had gotten me to entrust my safety to him.

"Well, I've got to get to court. Is there something I should be doing? Any particular way you want me to act or place you want me to go?"

"Just do what you always do. But there is one thing. Keeping an eye on you in motion takes a lot of people. So, at the end of the day, when you are home for the night, call me and tell me so I can release some people."

"Okay. But you'll still have somebody watching, right?"

"Don't worry. You'll be covered twenty-four-seven. Oh, and one other thing."

"What?"

"Don't ever approach me again like this."

I nodded. I was being dismissed.

"Got it."

I stood up and looked toward the restaurant. I could see Lorna counting the twenties I had left and putting them down on the check. It looked like she was using them all. Patrick had left the table and gone to get the car from the valet.

"See ya, Detective," I said without looking at him.

He didn't respond. I walked away and caught up with my party as they were coming out of the restaurant.

"Was that Detective Bosch you were with?" Lorna asked.

"Yeah, I saw him out there."

"What was he doing?"

"He said he likes to come over here for lunch, sit in those big, comfortable chairs and just think."

"That's a coincidence that we were here too."

Julie Favreau shook her head.

"There are no coincidences," she said.

Thirty-eight

After lunch Golantz began to present his case. He went with what I called the "square one" presentation. He started at the very beginning—the 911 call that brought the double murder to public light—and proceeded in linear fashion from there. The first witness was an emergency operator with the county's communications center. She was used to introduce the tape recordings of Walter Elliot's calls for help. I had sought in a pretrial motion to thwart the playing of the two tapes, arguing that printed transcripts would be clearer and more useful to the jurors but the judge had ruled in the prosecution's favor. He ordered Golantz to provide transcripts so jurors could read along with the audio when the tapes were played in court.

I had tried to halt the playing of the tapes because I knew they were prejudicial to my client. Elliot had calmly spoken to the dispatcher in the first call, reporting that his wife and another person had been murdered. In that calm demeanor was room for an interpretation of calculated coldness that I didn't want the jury to make. The second tape was worse from a defense standpoint. Elliot sounded annoyed and also indicated he knew and disliked the man who had been killed with his wife.

Tape 1 — 13:05 — 05/02/07

Dispatcher: Nine-one-one. Do you have an emergency?

Walter Elliot: I...well, they look dead. I don't think anybody can help them.

Dispatcher: Excuse me, sir. Who am I talking to?

Walter Elliot: This is Walter Elliot. This is my house.

Dispatcher: Yes, sir. And you say somebody is dead?

Walter Elliot: I found my wife. She's shot. And there's a man here. He's shot, too.

Dispatcher: Hold on a moment, sir. Let me type this in and get help going to you.

— break —

Dispatcher: Okay, Mr. Elliot, I have paramedics and deputies on their way.

Walter Elliot: It's too late for them. The paramedics, I mean.

Dispatcher: I have to send them, sir. You said they are shot? Are you in danger?

Walter Elliot: I don't know. I just got here. I didn't do this thing. Are you recording this?

Dispatcher: Yes, sir. Everything is recorded. Are you in the house right now?

Walter Elliot: I'm in the bedroom. I didn't do it.

Dispatcher: Is there anybody else in the house besides you and the two people who are shot?

Walter Elliot: I don't think so.

Dispatcher: Okay, I want you to step outside so the deputies will see you when they pull up. Stand out where they can see you.

Walter Elliot: Okay, I'm going out.

— end —

The second tape involved a different dispatcher but I allowed Golantz to play it. I had lost the big argument about whether the tapes could be played at all. I saw no sense in wasting the court's time by making the prosecutor bring in the second dispatcher to establish and introduce the second tape.

This one was made from Elliot's cell phone. He was outside, and the slight sound of the ocean's waves could be heard in the background.

Tape 2 — 13:24 — 05/02/07

Dispatcher: Nine-one-one, what is your emergency?

Walter Elliot: Yeah, I called before. Where is everybody?

Dispatcher: You called nine-one-one?

Walter Elliot: Yeah, my wife's shot. So's the German. Where is everybody?

Dispatcher: Is this the call in Malibu on Crescent Cove Road?

Walter Elliot: Yeah, that's me. I called at least fifteen minutes ago and nobody's here.

Dispatcher: Sir, my screen shows our alpha unit has an ETA of less than one minute. Hang up the phone and stand out front so they will see you when they arrive. Will you do that, sir?

Walter Elliot: I'm already standing out here.

Dispatcher: Then wait right there, sir.

Walter Elliot: If you say so. Good-bye.

— end —

Elliot not only sounded annoyed in the second call by the delay but said the word "German" with almost a sneer in his voice. Whether or not guilt could be extrapolated from his verbal tones didn't matter. The tapes helped set the prosecution's theme of Walter Elliot's being arrogant and believing he was above the law. It was a good start for Golantz.

I passed on questioning the dispatcher because I knew there was nothing to be gained for the defense. Next up for the prosecution was sheriff's deputy Brendan Murray, who was driving the alpha car that first responded to the 911 call. In a half hour of testimony, in minute detail Golantz led the deputy through his arrival and discovery of the bodies. He paid special attention to Murray's recollections of Elliot's behavior, demeanor and statements. According to Murray, the defendant showed no emotions when leading them up the stairs to the bedroom where his wife lay shot to death and naked on the bed. He calmly stepped over the legs of the dead man in the doorway and pointed to the body on the bed.

"He said, 'That's my wife. I'm pretty sure she's dead,'" Murray testified.

According to Murray, Elliot also said at least three times that he had not killed the two people in the bedroom.

"Well, was that unusual?" Golantz asked.

"Well, we're not trained to get involved in murder investigations," Murray said. "We're not supposed to. So I never asked Mr. Elliot if he did it. He just kept telling us he didn't."

I had no questions for Murray either. He was on my witness list and I would be able to recall him during the defense phase if I needed to. But I wanted to wait for the prosecution's next witness, Christopher Harber, who was Murray's partner and a rookie in the Sheriff's Department. I thought that if either of the deputies was to make a mistake that might help the defense, it would be the rookie.

Harber's testimony was shorter than Murray's and he was used primarily to confirm his partner's testimony. He heard the same things Murray heard. He saw the same things as well.

"Just a few questions, Your Honor," I said when Stanton inquired about cross-examination.

While Golantz had been conducting his direct examination from the lectern, I remained at the defense table for the cross. This was a ploy. I wanted the jury, the witness and the prosecutor to think I was just going through the motions and asking a few questions on cross. The truth was I was about to plant what would be a key point in the defense's case.

"Now, Deputy Harber, you are a rookie, correct?"

"That is correct."

"Have you ever testified in court before?"

"Not in a murder case."

"Well, don't be nervous. Despite what Mr. Golantz may have told you, I don't bite."

There was a polite murmur of laughter in the courtroom. Harber's face turned a little pink. He was a big man with sandy hair cut military-short, the way they like it in the Sheriff's Department.

"Now, when you and your partner arrived at the Elliot house, you said you saw my client standing out front in the turnaround. Is that correct?"

"That is correct."

"Okay, what was he doing?"

"Just standing there. He had been told to wait there for us."

"Okay, now, what did you know about the situation when the alpha car pulled in there?"

"We only knew what dispatch had told us. That a man named Walter Elliot had called from the house and said that two people were dead inside. They had been shot."

"Had you ever had a call like that before?"

"No."

"Were you scared, nervous, jacked-up, what?"

"I would say that the adrenaline was flowing, but we were pretty calm."

"Did you draw your weapon when you got out of your car?"

"Yes, I did."

"Did you point it at Mr. Elliot?"

"No, I carried it at my side."

"Did your partner draw his weapon?"

"I believe so."

"Did he point it at Mr. Elliot?"

Harber hesitated. I always liked it when witnesses for the prosecution hesitated.

"I don't recall. I wasn't really looking at him. I was looking at the defendant."

I nodded like that made sense to me.

"You had to be safe, correct? You didn't know this guy. You just knew that there supposedly were two dead people inside."

"That's right."

"So it would be correct to say you approached Mr. Elliot cautiously?"

"That's right."

"When did you put your weapon away?"

"That was after we had searched and secured the premises."

"You mean after you went inside and confirmed the deaths and that there was no one else inside?"

"Correct."

"Okay, so when you were doing this, Mr. Elliot was with you the whole time?"

"Yes, we needed to keep him with us so he could show us where the bodies were."

"Now was he under arrest?"

"No, he was not. He volunteered to show us."

"But you handcuffed him, didn't you?"

Harber's second hesitation followed the question. He was in uncharted water and probably remembering the lines he'd rehearsed with Golantz or his young second chair.

"He had voluntarily agreed to be handcuffed. We explained to him that we were not arresting him but that we had a volatile situation inside the house and that it would be best for his safety and ours if we could handcuff him until we secured the premises."

"And he agreed."

"Yes, he agreed."

In my peripheral vision I saw Elliot shake his head. I hoped the jury saw it too.

"Were his hands cuffed behind his back or in the front?"

"In the back, according to procedure. We are not allowed to handcuff a subject in the front."

"A subject? What does that mean?"

"A subject can be anybody involved in an investigation."

"Someone who is arrested?"

"Including that, yes. But Mr. Elliot was not under arrest."

"I know you are new on the job, but how often have you handcuffed someone who was not under arrest?"

"It's happened on occasion. But I don't recall the number of times."

I nodded but I hoped it was clear that I wasn't nodding because I believed him.

"Now, your partner testified and you have testified that Mr. Elliot on three occasions told you both that he was not responsible for the killings in that house. Right?"

"Right."

"You heard those statements?"

"Yes, I did."

"Was that when you were outside or inside or where?"

"That was inside, when we were up in the bedroom."

"So that means that he made these supposedly uninvited protestations of his innocence while he was handcuffed with his arms behind his back and you and your partner had your weapons drawn and ready, is that correct?"

The third hesitation.

"Yes, I believe that would be so."

"And you are saying he was not under arrest at this time?"

"He was not under arrest."

"Okay, so what happened after Mr. Elliot led you inside and up to the bodies and you and your partner determined that there was no one else in the house?"

"We took Mr. Elliot back outside, we sealed the house and we called detective services for a homicide call-out."

"Was that all according to sheriff's procedure, too?"

"Yes, it was."

"Good. Now, Deputy Harber, did you take the handcuffs off of Mr. Elliot then, since he was not under arrest?"

"No, sir, we didn't. We placed Mr. Elliot in the back of the car, and it is against procedure to place a subject in a sheriff's car without handcuffs."

"Again, there's that word 'subject.' Are you sure Mr. Elliot wasn't under arrest?"

"I am sure. We did not arrest him."

"Okay, how long was he in the backseat of that car?"

"Approximately one half hour while we waited for the homicide team."

"And what happened when the team arrived?"

"When the investigators arrived, they looked in the house first. Then they came out and took custody of Mr. Elliot. I mean, took him out of the car."

There was a slip I dove into.

"He was in custody at that time?"

"No, I made a mistake there. He voluntarily agreed to wait in the car and then they arrived and took him out."

"You are saying he voluntarily agreed to be handcuffed in the back of a patrol car?"

"Yes."

"If he had wanted to, could he have opened the door and gotten out?"

"I don't think so. The back doors have security locks. You can't open them from inside."

"But he was in there voluntarily."

"Yes, he was."

Even Harber didn't look like he believed what he was saying. His face had turned a deeper shade of pink.

"Deputy Harber, when did the handcuffs finally come off of Mr. Elliot?"

"When the detectives removed him from the car, they took the cuffs off and gave them back to my partner."

"Okay."

I nodded like I was finished and flipped up a few pages on my pad to check for questions I missed. I kept my eyes down on the pad when I spoke.

"Oh, Deputy? One last thing. The first call to nine-one-one went out at one-oh-five according to the dispatch log. Mr. Elliot had to call again nineteen minutes later to make sure he hadn't been forgotten about, and then you and your partner finally arrived four minutes after that. A total of twenty-three minutes to respond."

I now looked up at Harber.

"Deputy, why did it take so long to respond to what must've been a priority call?"

"The Malibu district is our largest geographically. We had to come all the way over the mountain from another call."

"Wasn't there another patrol car that was closer and also available?"

"My partner and I were in the alpha car. It's a rover. We handle the priority calls and we accepted this one when it came in from dispatch."

"Okay, Deputy, I have nothing further."

On redirect Golantz followed the misdirection I'd set up. He asked

Harber several questions that revolved around whether Elliot had been under arrest or not. The prosecutor sought to diffuse this idea, as it would play into the defense's tunnel-vision theory. That was what I wanted him to think I was doing and it had worked. Golantz spent another fifteen minutes eliciting testimony from Harber that underlined that the man he and his partner had handcuffed outside the scene of a double murder was not under arrest. It defied common sense but the prosecution was sticking with it.

When the prosecutor was finished, the judge adjourned for the afternoon break. As soon as the jury had cleared the courtroom, I heard a whispered voice call my name. I turned around and saw Lorna, who pointed her finger toward the back of the courtroom. I turned further to look back, and there were my daughter and her mother, squeezed into the back row of the gallery. My daughter surreptitiously waved to me and I smiled back.

Thirty-nine

met them in the hallway outside the courtroom, away from the clot of reporters who surrounded the other principals of the trial as they exited. Hayley hugged me and I was overwhelmed that she had come. I saw an empty wooden bench and we sat down.

"How long were you guys in there?" I asked. "I didn't see you."

"Unfortunately, not that long," Maggie said. "Her last period today was PE, so I decided to take the afternoon off, pull her out early and come on down. We saw most of your cross with the deputy."

I looked from Maggie to our daughter, who was sitting between us. She had her mother's looks; dark hair and eyes, skin that held a tan long into the winter.

"What did you think, Hay?"

"Um, I thought it was really interesting. You asked him a lot of questions. He looked like he was getting mad."

"Don't worry, he'll get over it."

I looked over her head and winked at my ex-wife.

"Mickey?"

I turned around and saw it was McEvoy from the *Times*. He had come over, his pad and pen ready.

293

"Not now," I said.

"I just had a quick —"

"And I just said, not now. Leave me alone."

McEvoy turned and walked back to one of the groups circling Golantz.

"Who was that?" Hayley asked.

"A newspaper reporter. I'll talk to him later."

"Mom said there was a big story about you today."

"It wasn't really about me. It was about the case. That's why I was hoping you could come see some of it."

I looked at my ex-wife again and nodded my thanks. She had put aside any anger she had toward me and placed our daughter first. No matter what else, I could always count on her for that.

"Do you go back in there?" Hayley asked.

"Yes, this is just a little break so people can get something to drink or use the bathroom. We have one more session and then we'll go home and start it all over tomorrow."

She nodded and looked down the hall toward the courtroom door. I followed her eyes and saw that people were starting to go back in.

"Um, Daddy? Did that man in there kill somebody?"

I looked at Maggie and she shrugged as if to say, *I didn't tell her to ask the question.*

"Well, honey, we don't know. He is accused of that, yes. And a lot of people think he did. But nothing has been proven yet and we're going to use this trial to decide that. That's what the trial is for. Remember how I explained that to you?"

"I remember."

"Mick, is this your family?"

I looked over my shoulder and froze when I looked into the eyes of Walter Elliot. He was smiling warmly, expecting an introduction. Little did he know who Maggie McFierce was.

"Uh, hi, Walter. This is my daughter, Hayley, and this is her mom, Maggie McPherson."

"Hi," Hayley said shyly.

Maggie nodded and looked uncomfortable.

Walter made the mistake of thrusting his hand out to Maggie. If she could have acted more stiffly, I couldn't imagine it. She shook his hand once and then quickly pulled away from his grasp. When his hand moved toward Hayley, Maggie literally jumped up, put her arms on our daughter's shoulders and pulled her from the bench.

"Hayley, let's go into the restroom real quick before court starts again."

She hustled Hayley off toward the restroom. Walter watched them go and then looked at me, his hand still held out and empty. I stood up.

"Sorry, Walter, my ex-wife's a prosecutor. She works for the DA."

His eyebrows climbed his forehead.

"Then, I guess I understand why she's an ex-wife."

I nodded just to make him feel better. I told him to go on back into the courtroom and that I would be along shortly.

I walked toward the restrooms and met Maggie and Hayley as they were coming out.

"I think we're going to head home," Maggie said.

"Really?"

"She's got a lot of homework and I think she's seen enough for today."

I could've argued that last point but I let it go.

"Okay," I said. "Hayley, thanks for coming. It means a lot to me."

"Okay."

I bent down and kissed her on the top of her head, then pulled her in close for a hug. It was only at times like this with my daughter that the distance I had opened in my life came closed. I felt connected to something that mattered. I looked up at Maggie.

"Thanks for bringing her."

She nodded.

"For what it's worth, you're doing good in there."

"It's worth a lot. Thank you."

She shrugged and let a small smile slip out. And that was nice, too.

I watched them walk toward the elevator alcove, knowing they weren't going home to my house and wondering how it was that I had messed up my life so badly.

"Hayley!" I called after them.

My daughter looked back at me.

"See you Wednesday. Pancakes!"

She was smiling as they joined the crowd waiting for an elevator. I noticed that my former wife was smiling, too. I pointed at her as I walked back toward the courtroom.

"And you can come, too."

She nodded.

"We'll see," she said.

An elevator opened and they moved toward it. "We'll see." Those two words seemed to cover it all for me.

Forty

In any murder trial, the main witness for the prosecution is always the lead investigator. Because there are no living victims to tell the jury what happened to them, it falls upon the lead to tell the tale of the investigation as well as to speak for the dead. The lead investigator brings the hammer. He puts everything together for the jury, makes it clear and makes it sympathetic. The lead's job is to sell the case to the jury and, like any exchange or transaction, it is often just as much about the salesman as it is about the goods being sold. The best homicide men are the best salesmen. I've seen men as hard as Harry Bosch on the stand shed a tear when they've described the last moments a murder victim spent on earth.

Golantz called the case's lead investigator to the stand after the afternoon break. It was a stroke of genius and master planning. John Kinder would hold center stage until court was adjourned for the day, and the jurors would go home with his words to consider over dinner and then into the night. And there was nothing I could do about it but watch.

Kinder was a large, affable black man who spoke with a fatherly baritone. He wore reading glasses slipped down to the end of his nose when referring to the thick binder he'd carried with him to the stand.

Between questions he would look over the rims at Golantz or the jury. His eyes seemed comfortable, kind, alert and wise. He was the one witness I didn't have a comeback for.

With Golantz's precise questioning and a series of blow-ups of crime scene photos—which I had been unsuccessful in keeping out on the grounds they were prejudicial—Kinder led the jury on a tour of the murder scene and what the evidence told the investigative team. It was purely clinical and methodical but it was supremely interesting. With his deep, authoritative voice, Kinder came off as something akin to a professor, teaching Homicide 101 to every person in the courtroom.

I objected here and there when I could in an effort to break the Golantz/Kinder rhythm, but there was little I could do but nut it out and wait. At one point I got a text on my phone from the gallery and it didn't help ease my concerns.

Favreau: They love this guy! Isn't there anything you can do?

Without turning to glance back at Favreau I simply shook my head while looking down at the phone's screen under the defense table.

I then glanced at my client and it appeared that he was barely paying attention to Kinder's testimony. He was writing notes on a legal pad but they weren't about the trial or the case. I saw a lot of numbers and the heading FOREIGN DISTRIBUTION underlined on the page. I leaned over and whispered to him.

"This guy's killing us up there," I said. "Just in case you're wondering."

A humorless smile bent his lips and Elliot whispered back.

"I think we're doing fine. You've had a good day."

I shook my head and turned back to watch the testimony. I had a client who wasn't concerned by the reality of his situation. He was well aware of my trial strategy and that I had the magic bullet in my gun. But nothing is a sure thing when you go to trial. That's why ninety percent of all cases are settled by disposition before trial. Nobody wants to roll the dice. The stakes are too high. And a murder trial is the biggest gamble of them all.

But from day one, Walter Elliot didn't seem to get this. He just went about the business of making movies and working out foreign distribution and seemingly believed that there was no question that he would walk at the end of the trial. I felt my case was bulletproof but not even I had that kind of confidence.

After the basics of the crime scene investigation were thoroughly covered with Kinder, Golantz moved the testimony toward Elliot and the investigator's interaction with him.

"Now, you have testified that the defendant remained in Deputy Murray's patrol car while you initially surveyed the crime scene and sort of got the lay of the land, correct?"

"Yes, that is correct."

"When did you first speak with Walter Elliot?"

Kinder referred to a document in the binder open on the shelf at the front of the witness stand.

"At approximately two thirty, I came out of the house after completing my initial survey of the crime scene and I asked the deputies to take Mr. Elliot out of the car."

"And then what did you do?"

"I told one of deputies to take the handcuffs off him because I didn't think that was necessary any longer. There were several deputies and investigators on the scene by this point and the premises were very secure."

"Well, was Mr. Elliot under arrest at that point?"

"No, he wasn't and I explained that to him. I told him that the guys—the deputies—had been taking every precaution until they knew what they had. Mr. Elliot said he understood this. I asked if he wanted to continue to cooperate and show the members of my team around inside and he said, yes, he would do it."

"So you took him back inside the house?"

"Yes. We had him put on booties first so as not to contaminate anything and then we went back inside. I had Mr. Elliot retrace the exact steps he said he had taken when he came in and found the bodies."

I made a note about the booties being a bit late, since Elliot had already shown the first deputies around inside. I'd potshot Kinder with that on cross.

"Was there anything unusual about the steps he said he had taken or anything inconsistent in what he told you?"

I objected to the question, saying that it was too vague. The judge agreed. Score one inconsequential point for the defense. Golantz simply rephrased and got more specific.

"Where did Mr. Elliot lead you in the house, Detective Kinder?"

"He walked us in and we went straight up the stairs to the bedroom. He told us this was what he had done when he entered. He said he then found the bodies and called nine-one-one from the phone next to the bed. He said the dispatcher told him to leave the house and go out front to wait and that's what he did. I asked him specifically if he had been anywhere else in the house and he said no."

"Did that seem unusual or inconsistent to you?"

"Well, first of all, I thought it was odd if true that he'd gone inside and directly up to the bedroom without initially looking around the first level of the house. It also didn't jibe with what he told us when we got back outside the house. He pointed at his wife's car, which was parked in the circle out front, and said that was how he knew she had somebody with her in the house. I asked him what he meant and he said that she parked out front so that Johan Rilz, the other victim, could use the one space available in the garage. They had stored a bunch of furniture and stuff in there and that left only one space. He said the German had hidden his Porsche in there and his wife had to park outside."

"And what was the significance of that to you?"

"Well, to me it showed deception. He'd told us that he hadn't been anywhere in the house but the bedroom upstairs. But it was pretty clear to me he had looked in the garage and seen the second victim's Porsche."

Golantz nodded emphatically from the lectern, driving home the point about Elliot being deceptive. I knew I would be able to handle this point on cross but I wouldn't get the chance until the next day, after it had percolated in the brains of the jury for almost twenty-four hours.

"What happened after that?" Golantz asked.

"Well, there was still a lot of work to do inside the house. So I had a couple members of my team take Mr. Elliot to the Malibu substation so he could wait there and be comfortable."

"Was he arrested at this time?"

"No, once again I explained to him that we needed to talk to him and if he was still willing to be cooperative, we were going to take him to an interview room at the station, and I said that I would get there as soon as possible. Once again he agreed."

"Who transported him?"

"Investigators Joshua and Toles took him in their car."

"Why didn't they go ahead and interview him once they got to the Malibu station?"

"Because I wanted to know more about him and the crime scene before we talked to him. Sometimes you get only one chance, even with a cooperating witness."

"You used the word 'witness.' Wasn't Mr. Elliot a suspect at this time?"

It was a cat-and-mouse game with the truth. It didn't matter how Kinder answered, everybody in the courtroom knew that they had drawn a bead on Elliot.

"Well, to some extent anybody and everybody is a suspect," Kinder answered. "You go into a situation like that and you suspect everybody. But at that point, I didn't know a lot about the victims, I didn't know a lot about Mr. Elliot and I didn't know exactly what we had. So at that time, I was viewing him more as a very important witness. He found the bodies and he knew the victims. He could help us."

"Okay, so you stashed him at the Malibu station while you went to work at the crime scene. What were you doing?"

"My job was to oversee the documentation of the crime scene and the gathering of any evidence in that house. We were also working the phones and the computers and confirming the identities and back-grounding the parties involved."

"What did you learn?"

"We learned that neither of the Elliots had a criminal record or had any guns legally registered to them. We learned that the other victim, Johan Rilz, was a German national and appeared to have no criminal record or own any weapons. We learned that Mr. Elliot was the head of a studio and very successful in the movie business, things like that."

"At some point did a member of your team draw up search warrants in the case?"

"Yes, we did. Proceeding with an abundance of caution, we drew up and had a judge sign off on a series of search warrants so we had the authority to continue the investigation and take it wherever it led."

"Is it unusual to take such steps?"

"Perhaps. The courts have granted law enforcement wide leeway in the gathering of evidence. But we determined that because of the parties involved in this case, we would go the extra mile. We went for the search warrants even though we might not need them."

"What specifically were the search warrants for?"

"We had warrants for the Elliot house and for the three cars, Mr. Elliot's, his wife's and the Porsche in the garage. We also had a search warrant granting us permission to conduct tests on Mr. Elliot and his clothing to determine if he had discharged a gun in recent hours."

The prosecutor continued to lead Kinder through the investigation up until he cleared the crime scene and interviewed Elliot at the Malibu station. This set up the introduction of a videotape of the first sit-down interview with Elliot. This was a tape I had viewed several times during preparation for trial. I knew it was unremarkable in terms of the content of what Elliot told Kinder and his partner, Roland Ericsson. What was important to the prosecution about the tape was Elliot's demeanor. He didn't look like somebody who had just discovered the naked body of his dead wife with a bullet hole in the center of her face and two more in her chest. He appeared as calm as a summer sunset, and that made him look like an ice-cold killer.

A video screen was set up in front of the jury box and Golantz played the tape, often stopping it to ask Kinder a question and then starting it again. The taped interview lasted ten minutes and was nonconfrontational. It was simply an exercise in which the investigators locked in Elliot's story. There were no hard questions. Elliot was asked broadly about what he did and when. It ended with Kinder presenting a search warrant to Elliot that the investigator explained granted the Sheriff's Department access to test his hands, arms and clothing for gunshot residue.

Elliot smiled slightly as he replied.

"Have at it, gentlemen," he said. "Do what you have to do."

Golantz checked the clock on the back wall of the courtroom and then used a remote to freeze the image of Elliot's half smile on the video screen. That was the image he wanted the jurors to take with them. He wanted them to think about that catch-me-if-you-can smile as they drove home in five o'clock traffic.

"Your Honor," he said. "I think now would be a good time to break for the day. I will be moving with Deputy Kinder in a new direction after this and maybe we should start that tomorrow morning."

The judge agreed, adjourning court for the day after once more admonishing the jurors to avoid all media reports on the trial.

I stood at the defense table and watched the jurors file into the deliberation room. I was pretty sure that the prosecution had won the first day, but that was to be expected. We still had our shots coming. I looked over at my client.

"Walter, what do you have going tonight?" I asked.

"A small dinner party with friends. They've invited Dominick Dunne. Then I am going to watch the first cut of a film my studio is producing with Johnny Depp playing a detective."

"Well, call your friends and call Johnny and cancel it all. You're having dinner with me. We're going to work."

"I don't understand."

"Yes, you do. You've been ducking me since the trial began. That was okay because I didn't want to know what I didn't need to know. Now it's different. We're in trial, we're past discovery, and I need to know. Everything, Walter. So, we're going to talk tonight, or you're going to have to hire another lawyer in the morning."

I saw his face grow tight with checked anger. In that moment, I knew he could be a killer, or at least someone who could order it done.

"You wouldn't dare," he said.

"Try me."

We stared at each other for a moment and I saw something about his face relax.

"Make your calls," I finally said. "We'll take my car."

Forty-one

Since I had insisted on the meeting, Elliot insisted on the place. With a thirty-second phone call he got us a private booth at the Water Grill over by the Biltmore and had a martini waiting on the table for him when we got there. As we sat down, I asked for a bottle of flat water and some sliced lemons.

I sat across from my client and watched him study the fresh fish menu. For the longest time I had wanted to be in the dark about Walter Elliot. Usually the less you know about your client, the better able you are to provide a defense. But we were past that time now.

"You called it a dinner meeting," Elliot said without taking his eyes from the menu. "Aren't you going to look?"

"I'm having what you're having, Walter."

He put the menu to the side and looked at me.

"Fillet of sole."

"Sounds good."

He signaled a waiter who had been standing nearby but too intimidated to approach the table. Elliot ordered for us both, adding a bottle of Chardonnay to come with the fish, and told the waiter not to forget about my flat water and lemon. He then clasped his hands on the table and looked expectantly at me.

"I could be dining with Dominick Dunne," he said. "This better be good."

"Walter, this *is* going to be good. This is going to be where you stop hiding from me. This is where you tell me the whole story. The true story. You see, if I know what you know, then I'm not going to get sand-bagged by the prosecution. I am going to know what moves Golantz is going to make before he makes them."

Elliot nodded as though he agreed it was time to deliver the goods.

"I did not kill my wife or her Nazi friend," he said. "I have told you that from day one."

I shook my head.

"That's not good enough. I said I want the story. I want to know what really happened, Walter. I want to know what's going on or I'm going to be moving on."

"Don't be ridiculous. No judge is going to let you walk away in the middle of a trial."

"You want to bet your freedom on that, Walter? If I want off this case, I will find a way off it."

He hesitated and studied me before answering.

"You should be careful what you ask for. Guilty knowledge could be a dangerous thing."

"I'll risk it."

"But I'm not sure I can."

I leaned across the table to him.

"What does that mean, Walter? What is going on? I'm your lawyer. You can tell me what you've done and it stays with me."

Before he could speak, the waiter brought a bottle of European water to the table and a side plate of sliced lemons. Enough for every-body in the restaurant. Elliot waited until he had filled my glass and moved away and out of earshot before responding.

"What is going on is that you have been hired to present my defense to the jury. In my estimation you have done an excellent job so far and your preparations for the defense phase are on the highest level. All of this in two weeks. Astonishing!"

"Drop the bullshit!"

I said it too loud. Elliot looked outside the booth and stared down a woman at a nearby table who had heard the expletive.

"You'll have to keep your voice down," he said. "The bond of attorney-client confidentiality ends at this table."

I looked at him. He was smiling but I also knew he was reminding me of what I had already assured him of, that what was said here stayed here. Was it a signal that he was willing to finally talk? I played the only ace I had.

"Tell me about the bribe Jerry Vincent paid," I said.

At first I detected a momentary shock in his eyes. Then came a knowing look as the wheels turned inside and he put something together. Then I thought I saw a quick flash of regret. I wished Julie Favreau had been sitting next to me. She could have read him better than I could.

"That is a very dangerous piece of information to be in possession of," he said. "How did you get it?"

I obviously couldn't tell my client I got it from a police detective I was now cooperating with.

"I guess you could say it came with the case, Walter. I have all of Vincent's records, including his financials. It wasn't hard to figure out that he funneled a hundred thousand of your advance to an unknown party. Is the bribe what got him killed?"

Elliot raised his martini glass with two fingers clenching the delicate stem and drank what was left in it. He then nodded to someone unseen over my shoulder. He wanted another. Then he looked at me.

"I think it is safe to say a confluence of events led to Jerry Vincent's death."

"Walter, I'm not fucking around with you. I need to know—not only to defend you, but to protect myself."

He put his empty glass to the side of the table and someone whisked it away within two seconds. He nodded as if in agreement with me and then he spoke.

"I think you may have found the reason for his death," he said. "It was in the file. You even mentioned it to me."

"I don't understand. What did I mention?"

Elliot responded in an impatient tone.

"He planned to delay the trial. You found the motion. He was killed before he could file it."

I tried to put it together but I didn't have enough of the parts.

"I don't understand, Walter. He wanted to delay the trial and that got him killed? Why?"

Elliot leaned across the table toward me. He spoke in a tone just above a whisper.

"Okay, you asked for it and I'll tell you. But don't blame me when you wish you didn't know what you know. Yes, there was a bribe. He paid it and everything was fine. The trial was scheduled and all we had to do was be ready to go. We had to stay on schedule. No delays, no continuances. But then he changed his mind and wanted to delay."

"Why?"

"I don't know. I think he actually thought he could win the case without the fix."

It appeared that Elliot didn't know about the FBI's phone calls and apparent interest in Vincent. If he did know, now would have been the time to mention it. The FBI's focus on Vincent would have been as good a reason as any to delay a trial involving a bribery scheme.

"So delaying the trial got him killed?"

"That's my guess, yes."

"Did you kill him, Walter?"

"I don't kill people."

"You had him killed."

Elliot shook his head wearily.

"I don't *have* people killed either."

A waiter moved up to the booth with a tray and a stand and we both leaned back to let him work. He deboned our fish, plated them and put them down on the table along with two small serving pitchers with beurre blanc sauce in them. He then placed Elliot's fresh martini down along with two wineglasses. He uncorked the bottle Elliot had ordered and asked if he wanted to taste the wine yet. Elliot shook his head and told the waiter to go away.

"Okay," I said when we were left alone. "Let's go back to the bribe. Who was bribed?"

Elliot took down half his new martini in one gulp.

"That should be obvious when you think about it."

"Then I'm stupid. Help me out."

"A trial that cannot be delayed. Why?"

My eyes stayed on him but I was no longer looking at him. I went inside to work the riddle until it came to me. I ticked off the possibilities — judge, prosecutor, cops, witnesses, jury...I realized that there was only one place where a bribe and an unmovable trial intersected. There was only one aspect that would change if the trial were delayed and rescheduled. The judge, prosecutor and all the witnesses would remain the same no matter when it was scheduled. But the jury pool changes week to week.

"There's a sleeper on the jury," I said. "You got to somebody."

Elliot didn't react. He let me run with it and I did. My mind swept along the faces in the jury box. Two rows of six. I stopped on juror number seven.

"Number seven. You wanted him in the box. You knew. He's the sleeper. Who is he?"

Elliot nodded slightly and gave me that half smile. He took his first bite of fish before answering my question as calmly as if we were talking about the Lakers' chances at the playoffs and not the rigging of a murder trial.

"I have no idea who he is and don't really care to know. But he's ours. We were told that number seven would be ours. And he's no sleeper. He's a persuader. When it gets to deliberations, he will go in there and turn the tide for the defense. With the case Vincent built and you're delivering, it probably won't take more than a little push. I'm banking on us getting our verdict. But at minimum he will hold out for acquittal and we'll have a hung jury. If that happens, we just start all over and do it again. They will never convict me, Mickey. Never."

I pushed my plate aside. I couldn't eat.

"Walter, no more riddles. Tell me how this went down. Tell me from the start."

"From the start?"

"From the start."

Elliot chuckled at the thought of it and poured himself a glass of wine without first tasting from the bottle. A waiter swooped in to take over the operation but Elliot waved him away with the bottle.

"This is a long story, Mickey. Would you like a glass of wine to go with it?"

He held the mouth of the bottle poised over my empty glass. I was tempted but I shook my head.

"No, Walter, I don't drink."

"I'm not sure I can trust someone who doesn't take a drink from time to time."

"I'm your lawyer. You can trust me."

"I trusted the last one, too, and look what happened to him."

"Don't threaten me, Walter. Just tell me the story."

He drank heavily from his wineglass and then put it down too hard on the table. He looked around to see if anyone in the restaurant had noticed and I got the sense that it was all an act. He was really checking to see if we were being watched. I scanned the angles I had without being obvious. I didn't see Bosch or anyone else I pegged as a cop in the restaurant.

Elliot began his story.

"When you come to Hollywood, it doesn't matter who you are or where you come from as long as you've got one thing in your pocket."

"Money."

"That's right. I came here twenty-five years ago and I had money. I put it in a couple of movies first and then into a half-assed studio nobody gave two shits about. And I built that place into a contender. Another five years and it will no longer be the Big Four they talk about. It will be the Big Five. Archway will be right up there with Paramount and Warner's and the rest."

I wasn't anticipating going back twenty-five years when I told him to start the story from the beginning.

"Okay, Walter, I get all of that about your success. What are you saying?"

"I'm saying it wasn't my money. When I came here, it wasn't my money."

"I thought the story was that you came from a family that owned a phosphate mine or shipping operation in Florida."

He nodded emphatically.

"All true, but it depends on your definition of family."

It slowly came to me.

"Are you talking about the mob, Walter?"

"I am talking about an organization in Florida with a tremendous cash flow that needed legitimate businesses to move it through and legitimate front men to operate those businesses. I was an accountant. I was one of those men."

It was easy to put together. Florida twenty-five years ago. The heyday of the uninhibited flow of cocaine and money.

"I was sent west," Elliot said. "I had a story and I had suitcases full of money. And I loved movies. I knew how to pick 'em and put 'em together. I took Archway and turned it into a billion-dollar enterprise. And then my wife..."

A sad look of regret crossed his face.

"What, Walter?"

He shook his head.

"On the morning after our twelfth anniversary — after the prenuptial agreement was vested — she told me she was leaving. She was going to get a divorce."

I nodded. I understood. With the prenup vested, Mitzi Elliot would be entitled to half of Walter Elliot's holdings in Archway Studios. Only he was just a front. His holdings actually belonged to the organization and it wasn't the type of organization that would allow half of its investment to walk out the door in a skirt.

"I tried to change her mind," Elliot said. "She wouldn't listen. She was in love with that Nazi bastard and thought he could protect her."

"The organization had her killed."

It sounded so strange to say those words out loud. It made me look around and sweep my eyes across the restaurant.

"I wasn't supposed to be there that day," Elliot said. "I was told to stay away, to make sure I had a rock-solid alibi."

"Why'd you go, then?"

His eyes held on mine before he answered.

"I still loved her in some way. Somehow I still did and I wanted her. I wanted to fight for her. I went out there to try to stop it, maybe be the hero, save the day and win her back. I don't know. I didn't have a plan. I just didn't want it to happen. So I went out there... but I was too late. They were both dead when I got there. Terrible..."

Elliot was staring at the memory, perhaps the scene in the bedroom in Malibu. I dropped my eyes down to the white tablecloth in front of me. A defense attorney never expects his client to tell him the whole truth. Parts of the truth, yes. But never the cold, hard and complete truth. I had to think that there were things Elliot had left out. But what he had told me was enough for now. It was time to talk about the bribe.

"And then came Jerry Vincent," I prompted.

His eyes came back into focus and he looked at me.

"Yes."

"Tell me about the bribe."

"I don't have a lot to tell. My corporate attorney hooked me up with Jerry and he was fine. We worked out the fee arrangement and then he came to me—this was early on, at least five months ago—and he said he had been approached by someone who could salt the jury. You know, put someone on the jury who would be for us. No matter what happened he would be a holdout for acquittal but he would also work for the defense on the inside—during deliberations. He would be a talker, a skilled persuader—a con man. The catch was that once it was in play, the trial would have to stay on schedule so that this person would end up on my jury."

"And you and Jerry took the offer."

"We took it. This was five months ago. At the time, I didn't have much of a defense. I didn't kill my wife but it seemed the odds were stacked against me. We had no magic bullet...and I was scared. I was innocent but could see that I was going to be convicted. So we took the offer."

"How much?"

"A hundred thousand up front. Like you found out, Jerry paid it through his fees. He inflated his fee and I paid him and then he paid for the juror. Then it was going to be another hundred for a hung jury and two-fifty for an acquittal. Jerry told me that these people had done it before."

"You mean fixed a jury?"

"Yes, that's what he said."

I thought maybe the FBI had gotten wind of the earlier fixes and that was why they had come to Vincent.

"Were they Jerry's trials that were fixed before?" I asked.

"He didn't say and I didn't ask."

"Did he ever say anything about the FBI sniffing around your case?"

Elliot leaned back, as if I had just said something repulsive.

"No. Is that what's going on?"

He looked very concerned.

"I don't know, Walter. I'm just asking questions here. But Jerry told you he was going to delay the trial, right?"

Elliot nodded.

"Yes. That Monday. He said we didn't need the fix. He had the magic bullet and he was going to win the trial without the sleeper on the jury."

"And that got him killed."

"It had to be. I don't think these kinds of people just let you change your mind and pull out of something like this."

"What kind of people? The organization?"

"I don't know. Just these kinds of people. Whoever does this sort of thing."

"Did you tell anyone that Jerry was going to delay the case?"

"No."

"You sure?"

"Of course I'm sure."

"Then, who did Jerry tell?"

"I wouldn't know."

"Well, who did Jerry make the deal with? Who did he bribe?"

"I don't know that either. He wouldn't tell me. Said it would be better if I didn't know names. Same thing I'm telling you."

It was a little late for that. I had to end this and get away by myself to think. I glanced at my untouched plate of fish and wondered if I should take it to go for Patrick or if someone back in the kitchen would eat it.

"You know," Elliot said, "not to put any more pressure on you, but if I get convicted, I'm dead."

I looked at him.

"The organization?"

He nodded.

"A guy gets busted and he becomes a liability. Normally, they wipe him out before he even gets to court. They don't take the chance that he'll try to cut a deal. But I still have control of their money, you see. They wipe me out and they lose it all. Archway, the real estate, everything. So they're hanging back and watching. If I get off, then we go back to normal and everything's good. If I get convicted, I'm too much of a liability and I won't last two nights in prison. They'll get to me in there."

It's always good to know exactly what the stakes are but I probably could have gone without the reminder.

"We're dealing with a higher authority here," Elliot continued. "It goes way beyond things like attorney-client confidentiality. That's small change, Mick. The things I've told you tonight can go no further than this table. Not into court or anywhere else. What I've told you here could get you killed in a heartbeat. Just like Jerry. Remember that."

Elliot had spoken matter-of-factly and concluded the statement by calmly draining the wine from his glass. But the threat was implicit in every word he had said. I would have no trouble remembering it.

Elliot waved down a waiter and asked for the check.

Forty-two

I was thankful that my client liked his martinis before dinner and his Chardonnay with it. I wasn't sure I would have gotten what I got from Elliot without the alcohol smoothing the way and loosening his tongue. But afterward I didn't want him running the risk of getting pulled over on a DUI in the middle of a murder trial. I insisted that he not drive home. But Elliot insisted he wasn't going to leave his $400,000 Maybach overnight in a downtown garage. So I had Patrick take us to the car and then I drove Elliot home while Patrick followed.

"This car cost four hundred grand?" I asked him. "I'm scared to drive it."

"A little less, actually."

"Yeah, well, do you have anything else to drive? When I told you not to take the limo, I didn't expect you'd be tooling up to your murder trial in one of these. Think about the impressions you are putting out there, Walter. This doesn't look good. Remember what you told me the first day we met? About having to win outside of the courtroom too? A car like this doesn't help you with that."

"My other car is a Carrera GT."

"Great. What's that worth?"

"More than this one."

"Tell you what, why don't you borrow one of my Lincolns. I even have one that has a plate that says NOT GUILTY. You can drive that."

"That's okay. I have access to a nice modest Mercedes. Is that all right?"

"Perfect. Walter, despite everything you told me tonight, I'm going to do my best for you. I think we have a good shot at this."

"Then, you believe I'm innocent."

I hesitated.

"I believe you didn't shoot your wife and Rilz. I'm not sure that makes you innocent, but put it this way: I don't think you're guilty of the charges you're facing. And that's all I need."

He nodded.

"Maybe that's the best I can ask for. Thank you, Mickey."

After that we didn't talk much as I concentrated on not wrecking the car, which was worth more than most people's houses.

Elliot lived in Beverly Hills in a gated estate in the flats south of Sunset. He pushed a button on the car's ceiling that opened the steel entry gate and we slipped through, Patrick coming in right behind me in the Lincoln. We got out and I gave Elliot his keys. He asked if I wanted to come in for another drink and I reminded him that I didn't drink. He stuck out his hand and I shook it and it felt awkward, as if we were sealing some sort of deal on what had been revealed earlier. I said good night and got into the back of my Lincoln.

The internal gears were working all the way back to my house. Patrick had been a quick study of my nuances and seemed to know that it was not the time to interrupt with small talk. He let me work.

I sat leaning against the door, my eyes gazing out the window but not seeing the neon world go by. I was thinking about Jerry Vincent and the deal he had made with a party unknown. It wasn't hard to figure out how it was done. The question of who did it was another matter.

I knew that the jury system relied on random selection on multiple levels. This helped ensure the integrity and cross-social composition of juries. The initial pool of hundreds of citizens summoned to jury duty each week was drawn randomly from voter registrations as well as property and public utility records. Jurors culled from this larger group for the jury selection process in a specific trial were again chosen randomly—this time by a courthouse computer. The list of those prospective jurors was given to the judge presiding over the trial, and the first twelve names or code numbers on the list were called to take the seats in the box for the initial round of voir dire. Again, the order of names or numbers on the list was determined by computer-generated random selection.

Elliot told me that after a trial date had been set in his case, Jerry Vincent was approached by an unknown party and told that a sleeper could be placed on the jury. The catch was that there could be no delays. If the trial moved, the sleeper couldn't move with it. All of this told me that this unknown party had full access to all levels of the random processes of the jury system: the initial summons to show for jury duty at a specific courthouse on a specific week; the random selection of the venire for the trial; and the random selection of the first twelve jurors to go into the box.

Once the sleeper was in the box, it was up to him to stay there. The defense would know not to oust him with a preemptory strike, and by appearing to be pro-prosecution he would avoid being challenged by the prosecution. It was simple enough, as long as the trial's date didn't change.

Stepping it out this way gave me a better understanding of the manipulation involved and who might have engineered it. It also gave me a better understanding of the ethical predicament I was in. Elliot had admitted several crimes to me over dinner. But I was his lawyer and these admissions would remain confidential under the bonds of the attorney-client relationship. The exception to this rule was if I were endangered by my knowledge or had knowledge of a crime that was planned but had not yet occurred. I knew that someone had been bribed by Vincent. That crime had already occurred. But the crime of jury tampering had not yet occurred. That crime wouldn't take place until deliberations began, so I was duty-bound to report it. Elliot apparently didn't know of this exception to the rules of client confidentiality or was convinced that the threat of my meeting the same end as Jerry Vincent would keep me in check.

I thought about all of this and realized there was one more exception to consider. I would not have to report the intended jury tampering if I were to stop the crime from happening.

I straightened up and looked around. We were on Sunset coming into West Hollywood. I looked ahead and saw a familiar sign.

"Patrick, pull over up here in front of Book Soup. I want to run in for a minute."

Patrick pulled the Lincoln to the curb in front of the bookstore. I told him to wait in front and I jumped out. I went in the store's front door and back into the stacks. Although I loved the store, I wasn't there to shop. I needed to make a phone call and I didn't want Patrick to hear it.

The mystery aisle was too crowded with customers. I went further back and found an empty alcove where big coffee-table books were stacked heavily on the shelves and tables. I pulled my phone and called my investigator.

"Cisco, it's me. Where are you?"

"At home. What's up?"

"Lorna there?"

"No, she went to a movie with her sister. She should be back in —"

"That's all right. I wanted to talk to you. I want you to do something and you may not want to do it. If you don't, I understand. Either way, I don't want you to talk about it with anybody. Including Lorna."

There was a hesitation before he answered.

"Who do I kill?"

We both started to laugh and it relieved some of the tension that had been building through the night.

"We can talk about that later but this might be just as dicey. I want you to shadow somebody for me and find out everything you can about him. The catch is, if you get caught, we'll both probably get our tickets pulled."

"Who is it?"

"Juror number seven."

Forty-three

As soon as I got back in the Lincoln, I started to regret what I was doing. I was walking a fine gray line that could lead me into big trouble. On the one hand, it is perfectly reasonable for an attorney to investigate a report of jury misconduct and tampering. But on the other hand, that investigation could be viewed as tampering in itself. Judge Stanton had taken steps to ensure the anonymity of the jury. I had just asked my investigator to subvert that. If it blew up in our faces, Stanton would be more than upset and would do more than give me the squint. This wasn't a Make-A-Wish infraction. Stanton would complain to the bar, the chief judge and all the way up the line to the Supreme Court if he could get them to listen. He would see to it that the Elliot trial was my last.

Patrick drove up Fareholm and pulled the car into the garage below my house. We walked out and then up the stairs to the front deck. It was almost ten o'clock and I was beat after a fourteen-hour day. But my adrenaline kicked in when I saw a man sitting in one of the deck chairs, his face in silhouette with the lights of the city behind him. I put my arm out to stop Patrick from advancing, the way a parent would stop a child from stepping blindly into the street.

"Hello, Counselor."

Bosch. I recognized the voice and the greeting. I relaxed and let Patrick continue. We stepped up onto the porch and I unlocked the door to let Patrick go in. I then closed the door and turned to Bosch.

"Nice view," he said. "Defending scumbags got you this place?"

I was too tired to do the dance with him.

"What are you doing here, Detective?"

"I figured you might be heading home after the bookstore," he said. "So I just went on ahead and waited for you up here."

"Well, I'm done for the night. You can give your team the word, if there really is a team."

"What makes you think there's not?"

"I don't know. I just haven't seen anybody. I hope you weren't bullshitting me, Bosch. I've got my ass way out in the wind on this."

"After court you had dinner with your client at Water Grill. You both had the fillet of sole and both of you raised your voices at times. Your client drank liberally, which resulted in you driving him home in his car. On your way back from there you stopped into Book Soup and made a phone call you obviously didn't want your driver to hear."

I was impressed.

"Okay, then, never mind that. I get it. They're out there. What do you want, Bosch? What's going on?"

Bosch stood up and approached me.

"I was going to ask you the same thing," he said. "What was Walter Elliot so hot and bothered about tonight at dinner? And who'd you call in the back of the bookstore?"

"First of all, Elliot's my client and I'm not telling you what we talked about. I'm not crossing that line with you. And as far as the call in the bookstore goes, I was ordering pizza because, as you and your colleagues might have noticed, I didn't eat my dinner tonight. Stick around if you want a slice."

Bosch looked at me with that half smile of his, the knowing look with his flat dead eyes.

"So that's how you want to play it, Counselor?"

"For now."

We didn't speak for a long moment. We just sort of stood there, waiting for the next clever line. It didn't come and I decided I really was tired and hungry.

"Good night, Detective Bosch."

I went in and closed the door, leaving Bosch out there on the deck.

Forty-four

My turn at Detective Kinder did not come until late on Tuesday, after the prosecutor had spent several more hours drawing the details of the investigation out on direct examination. This worked in my favor. I thought the jury — and Julie Favreau confirmed this by text message — was getting bored by the minutiae of the testimony and would welcome a new line of questions.

The direct testimony primarily regarded the investigative efforts that took place after Walter Elliot's arrest. Kinder described at length his delving into the defendant's marriage, the discovery of a recently vested prenuptial agreement, and the efforts Elliot made in the weeks before the murders to determine how much money and control of Archway Studios he would lose in a divorce. With a time chart he was also able to establish through Elliot's statements and documented movements that the defendant had no credible alibi for the estimated time of the murders.

Golantz also took the time to question Kinder about all the dead ends and offshoots of the investigation that proved to be ancillary. Kinder described the many unfounded leads that were called in and dutifully checked out, the investigation of Johan Rilz in an effort to determine if he had been the main target of the killer, and the comparison of the double murder to other cases that were similar and unsolved.

In all, Golantz and Kinder appeared to have done a thorough job of nailing my client to the murders in Malibu, and by midafternoon the young prosecutor was satisfied enough to say, "No more questions, Your Honor."

It was now finally my turn and I had decided to go after Kinder in a cross-examination that would stay tightly focused on just three areas of his direct testimony, and then surprise him with an unexpected punch to the gut. I moved to the lectern to conduct the questioning.

"Detective Kinder, I know we will be hearing from the medical examiner later in the trial, but you testified that you were informed after the autopsy that the time of death of Mrs. Elliot and Mr. Rilz was estimated to be between eleven a.m. and noon on the day of the murders."

"That is correct."

"Was it closer to eleven or closer to noon?"

"It's impossible to tell for sure. That is just the time frame in which it happened."

"Okay, and once you had that frame, you then proceeded to make sure that the man you had already arrested had no alibi, correct?"

"I would not put it that way, no."

"Then, how would you put it?"

"I would say that it was my obligation to continue to investigate the case and prepare it for trial. Part of that due diligence would be to keep an open mind to the possibility that the suspect had an alibi for the murders. In carrying out that obligation, I determined according to multiple interviews as well as records kept at the gate at Archway Studios that Mr. Elliot left the studio, driving by himself, at ten forty that morning. This gave him plenty of time to—"

"Thank you, Detective. You've answered the question."

"I haven't finished my answer."

Golantz stood and asked the judge if the witness could finish his answer, and Stanton allowed it. Kinder continued in his Homicide 101 tone.

"As I was saying, this gave Mr. Elliot plenty of time to get to the Malibu house within the parameters of the estimated time of death."

"Did you say plenty of time to get there?"

"Enough time."

"Earlier you described making the drive yourself several times. When was that?"

"The first time was exactly one week after the murders. I left the gatehouse at Archway at ten forty in the morning and drove to the Malibu house. I arrived at eleven forty-two, well within the murder window."

"How did you know that you were taking the same route that Mr. Elliot would have taken?"

"I didn't. So I just took what I considered the most obvious and quickest route that somebody would take. Most people don't take the long cut. They take the short cut—the shortest amount of time to their destination. From Archway I took Melrose to La Brea and then La Brea down to the ten. At that point I headed west to the Pacific Coast Highway."

"How did you know that the traffic you encountered would be the same that Mr. Elliot encountered?"

"I didn't."

"Traffic in Los Angeles can be a very unpredictable thing, can it not?"

"Yes."

"Is that why you drove the route several times?"

"One reason, yes."

"Okay, Detective Kinder, you testified that you drove the route a total of five times and got to the Malibu house each time before your so-called murder window closed, right?"

"Correct."

"In regard to these five driving tests, what was the earliest time you got to the house in Malibu?"

Kinder looked at his notes.

"That would have been the first time, when I got there at eleven forty-two."

"And what was the worst time?"

"The worst?"

"What was the longest drive time you recorded during your five trips?"

Kinder checked his notes again.

"The latest I got there was eleven fifty-one."

"Okay, so your best time was still in the last third of the window the medical examiner set for the time of these murders, and your worst time would have left Mr. Elliot less than ten minutes to sneak into his house and murder two people. Correct?"

"Yes, but it could have been done."

"Could have? You don't sound very confident, Detective."

"I am very confident that the defendant had the time to commit these murders."

"But only if the murders took place at least forty-two minutes after the killing window opened, correct?"

"If you want to look at it that way."

"It's not how I am looking at it, Detective. I'm working with what the medical examiner has given us. So, in summary for the jury, you are saying that Mr. Elliot left his studio at ten forty and got all the way out to Malibu, snuck into his house, surprised his wife and her lover in the upstairs bedroom and killed them both, all before that window slammed shut at noon. Do I have all of that right?"

"Essentially. Yes."

I shook my head as if it was a lot to swallow.

"Okay, Detective, let's move on. Please tell the jury how many times you began the driving route to Malibu but broke it off when you knew that you weren't going to make it before that window closed at noon."

"That never happened."

But there had been a slight hesitation in Kinder's response. I was sure the jury picked up on it.

"Yes or no, Detective, if I were to produce records and even video that showed you started at the Archway gate at ten forty in the morning seven times and not five, then those records would be false?"

Kinder's eyes flicked to Golantz and then back to me.

"What you're suggesting happened didn't happen," he said.

"And you're not answering the question, Detective. Once again, yes or no: If I introduced records that showed you conducted your driving study at least seven times but have only testified to five times, would those records be false?"

"No, but I didn't—"

"Thank you, Detective. I only asked for a yes or no response."

Golantz stood and asked the judge to allow the witness to fully answer the question but Stanton told him he could take it up on redirect. But now I hesitated. Knowing that Golantz would go after Kinder's explanation on redirect, I had the opportunity to get it now and possibly still control it and turn the admission to my advantage. It was a gamble because at the moment, I felt I had dinged him pretty good, and if I went with him until court adjourned for the day, then the jurors would go home with police suspicion percolating in their brains. That was never a bad thing.

I decided to risk it and try to control it.

"Detective, tell us how many of these test drives you broke off before reaching the house in Malibu."

"There were two."

"Which ones?"

"The second time and the last time—the seventh."

I nodded.

"And you stopped these because you knew you would never make it to the house in Malibu within the murder window, correct?"

"No, that's very incorrect."

"Then, what was the reason you stopped the test drives?"

"One time, I was called back to the office to conduct an interview of somebody waiting there, and the other time, I was listening to the radio and I heard a deputy call for backup. I diverted to back him up."

"Why didn't you document these in your report on your driving time investigation?"

"I didn't think they were germane, because they were incomplete tests."

"So these incompletes were not documented anywhere in that thick file of yours?"

"No, they were not."

"And so we have only your word about what caused you to stop them before reaching the Elliot house in Malibu, correct?"

"That would be correct."

I nodded and decided I had flogged him enough on this front. I knew Golantz could rehabilitate Kinder on redirect, maybe even come up with documentation of the calls that pulled Kinder off the Malibu route. But I hoped that I had raised at least a question of trust in the minds of the jurors. I took my small victory and moved on.

I next hammered Kinder on the fact that there was no murder weapon recovered and that his six-month investigation of Walter Elliot had never linked him to a gun of any sort. I hit this from several angles so that Kinder had to repeatedly acknowledge that a key part of the investigation and prosecution was never located, even though if Elliot was the killer, he'd had little time to hide the weapon.

Finally, in frustration, Kinder said, "Well, it's a big ocean out there, Mr. Haller."

It was an opening I was waiting for.

"A big ocean, Detective? Are you suggesting that Mr. Elliot had a boat and dumped the gun out in the middle of the Pacific?"

"No, nothing like that."

"Then, like what?"

"I am just saying the gun could have ended up in the water and the currents took it away before our divers got out there."

"It *could have* ended up out there? You want to take Mr. Elliot's life and livelihood away from him on a *'could have,'* Detective Kinder?"

"No, that's not what I am saying."

"What you are saying is that you don't have a gun, you can't connect a gun to Mr. Elliot, but you have never wavered in believing he is your man, correct?"

"We had a gunshot residue examination that came back positive. In my mind that connected Mr. Elliot to a gun."

"What gun was that?"

"We don't have it."

"Uh-huh, and can you sit there and say to a scientific certainty that Mr. Elliot fired a gun on the day his wife and Johan Rilz were murdered?"

"Well, not to a scientific certainty, but the test—"

"Thank you, Detective Kinder. I think that answers the question. Let's move on."

I flipped the page on my notepad and studied the next set of questions I had written the night before.

"Detective Kinder, in the course of your investigation, did you determine when Johan Rilz and Mitzi Elliot became acquainted?"

"I determined that she hired him for his interior decorating services in the fall of two thousand five. If she was acquainted with him before that, I do not know."

"And when did they become lovers?"

"That was impossible for us to determine. I do know that Mr. Rilz's appointment book showed regular appointments with Mrs. Elliot at one home or the other. The frequency increased about six months before her death."

"Was he paid for each one of those appointments?"

"Mr. Rilz kept very incomplete books. It was hard to determine if he was paid for specific appointments. But in general, the payments to Mr. Rilz from Mrs. Elliot increased when the frequency of the appointments increased."

I nodded like this answer fit with a larger picture I was seeing.

"Okay, and you have also testified that you learned that the murders occurred just thirty-two days after the prenuptial agreement between Walter and Mitzi Elliot vested, thereby giving Mrs. Elliot a full shot at the couple's financial holdings in the event of a divorce."

"That's right."

"And that is your motive for these killings."

"In part, yes. I call it an aggravating factor."

"Do you see any inconsistency in your theory of the crime, Detective Kinder?"

"No, I do not."

"Was it not obvious to you from the financial records and the appointment frequency that there was some sort of romantic or at least a sexual relationship going on between Mr. Rilz and Mrs. Elliot?"

"I wouldn't say it was obvious."

"You wouldn't?"

I said it with surprise. I had him in a little corner. If he said the affair was obvious, he would be giving me the answer he knew I wanted. If he said it was not obvious, then he came off as a fool because everyone else in the courtroom thought it was obvious.

"In retrospect it might look obvious but at the time I think it was hidden."

"Then how did Walter Elliot find out about it?"

"I don't know."

"Doesn't the fact that you were unable to find a murder weapon indicate that Walter Elliot planned these murders?"

"Not necessarily."

"Then it's easy to hide a weapon from the entire Sheriff's Department?"

"No, but like I told you, it could have simply been thrown into the ocean off the back deck and the currents took over from there. That wouldn't take a lot of planning."

Kinder knew what I wanted and where I was trying to go. I couldn't get him there so I decided to use a shove.

"Detective, didn't it ever occur to you that if Walter Elliot knew about his wife's affair, it would have made better sense just to divorce her before the prenuptial agreement vested?"

"There was no indication of when he learned of the affair. And your question does not take into account things like emotions and rage. It was possible that the money had nothing to do with it as a motivating factor. It could have just been betrayal and rage, pure and simple."

I hadn't gotten what I wanted. I was annoyed with myself and chalked it up to rust. I was prepared for the cross but it was the first time I had gone head-to-head with a seasoned and cagey witness in a year. I decided to back off here and to hit Kinder with the punch he wouldn't see coming.

Forty-five

asked the judge for a moment and then went to the defense table. I bent down to my client's ear.

"Just nod like I am telling you something really important," I whispered.

Elliot did as instructed and then I picked up a file and went back to the lectern. I opened the file and then looked at the witness stand.

"Detective Kinder, at what point in your investigation did you determine that Johan Rilz was the primary target of this double murder?"

Kinder opened his mouth to respond immediately, then closed it and sat back and thought for a moment. It was just the kind of body language I was hoping the jury would pick up on.

"At no point did I ever determine that," Kinder finally responded.

"At no point was Johan Rilz front and center in your investigation?"

"Well, he was the victim of a homicide. That made him front and center the whole time in my book."

Kinder seemed pretty proud of that answer but I didn't give him much time to savor it.

"Then his being front and center explains why you went to Germany to investigate his background, correct?"

"I did not go to Germany."

"What about France? His passport indicates he lived there before coming to the United States."

"I didn't go there."

"Then, who on your team did?"

"No one. We didn't believe it was necessary."

"Why wasn't it necessary?"

"We had asked Interpol for a background check on Johan Rilz and it came back clean."

"What is Interpol?"

"It stands for International Criminal Police Organization. It's an organization that links the police in more than a hundred countries and facilitates cross-border cooperation. It has several offices throughout Europe and enjoys total access and cooperation from its host countries."

"That's nice but it means you didn't go directly to the police in Berlin, where Rilz was from?"

"No, we did not."

"Did you directly check with police in Paris, where Rilz lived five years ago?"

"No, we relied on our Interpol contacts for background on Mr. Rilz."

"The Interpol background pretty much was a check of a criminal arrest record, correct?"

"That was included, yes."

"What else was included?"

"I'm not sure what else. I don't work for Interpol."

"If Mr. Rilz had worked for the police in Paris as a confidential informant on a drug case, would Interpol have given you this information?"

Kinder's eyes widened for a split second before he answered. It was clear he wasn't expecting the question, but I couldn't get a read on whether he knew where I was heading or if it was all new to him.

"I don't know whether they would have given us that information or not."

"Law enforcement agencies usually don't give out the names of their confidential informants willy-nilly, do they?"

"No, they don't."

"Why is that?"

"Because it might put the informants in danger."

"So being an informant in a criminal case can be dangerous?"

"On occasion, yes."

"Detective, have you ever investigated the murder of a confidential informant?"

Golantz stood up before Kinder could answer and asked the judge for a sidebar conference. The judge signaled us up. I grabbed the file off the lectern and followed Golantz up. The court reporter moved next to the bench with her steno machine. The judge rolled his chair over and we huddled.

"Mr. Golantz?" the judge prompted.

"Judge, I would like to know where this is going, because I'm feeling like I'm being sandbagged here. There has been nothing in any of the defense's discovery that even hints at what Mr. Haller is asking the witness about."

The judge swiveled in his chair and looked at me.

"Mr. Haller?"

"Judge, if anybody is being sandbagged, it's my client. This was a sloppy investigation that—"

"Save it for the jury, Mr. Haller. Whaddaya got?"

I opened the file and put a computer printout down in front of the judge, which positioned it upside down to Golantz.

"What I've got is a story that ran in *Le Parisien* four and a half years ago. It names Johan Rilz as a witness for the prosecution in a major drug case. He was used by the Direction de la Police Judiciaire to make buys and get inside knowledge of the drug ring. He was a CI, Your Honor, and these guys over here never even looked at him. It was tunnel vision from the—"

"Mr. Haller, again, save your argument for the jury. This printout is in French. Do you have the translation?"

"Sorry, Your Honor."

I took the second of three sheets out of the file and put it down on top of the first, again in the direction of the judge. Golantz was twisting his head awkwardly as he tried to read it.

"How do we know this is the same Johan Rilz?" Golantz said. "It's a common name over there."

"Maybe in Germany, but not in France."

"So how do we know it's him?" the judge asked this time. "This is a translated newspaper article. This isn't any kind of official document."

I pulled the last sheet from the file and put it down.

"This is a photocopy of a page from Rilz's passport. I got it from the state's own discovery. It shows that Rilz left France for the United States in March, two thousand three. One month after this story was published. Plus, you've got the age. The article has his age right and it says he was making drug buys for the cops out of his business as an interior decorator. It obviously is him, Your Honor. He betrayed a lot of people over there and put them in jail, then he comes here and starts over."

Golantz started shaking his head in a desperate sort of way.

"It's still no good," he said. "This is a violation of the rules of discovery and is inadmissible. You can't sit on this and then sucker punch the state with it."

The judge swiveled his view to me and this time gave me the squint as well.

"Your Honor, if anybody sat on anything, it was the state. This is stuff the prosecution should've come up with and given to me. In fact, I think the witness did know about this and *he* sat on it."

"That is a serious accusation, Mr. Haller," the judge intoned. "Do you have evidence of that?"

"Judge, the reason I know about this at all is by accident. On Sunday I was reviewing my investigator's prep work and noticed that he had run all the names associated with this case through the LexisNexis search engine. He had used the computer and account I inherited with Jerry Vincent's law practice. I checked the account and noticed that the default setting was for English-language search only. Having looked at the photocopy of Rilz's passport in the discovery file and knowing of his background in Europe, I did the search again, this time including French and German languages. I came up with this French newspaper article in about two minutes, and I find it hard to believe that I found something that easily that the entire Sheriff's Department, the prosecution and Interpol didn't know about. So Judge, I don't know if that is evidence of anything but the defense is certainly feeling like the party that's been damaged here."

I couldn't believe it. The judge swiveled to Golantz and gave him the squint. The first time ever. I shifted to my right so that a good part of the jury had an angle on it.

"What about that, Mr. Golantz?" the judge asked.

"It's absurd, Your Honor. We have sat on nothing, and anything that we have found has gone into the discovery file. And I would like to ask why Mr. Haller didn't alert us to this yesterday when he just admitted that he made this discovery Sunday and the printout is dated then as well."

I stared deadpan at Golantz when I answered.

"If I had known you were fluent in French I would have given it to you, Jeff, and maybe you could've helped out. But I'm not fluent and I didn't know what it said and I had to get it translated. I was handed that translation about ten minutes before I started my cross."

"All right," the judge said, breaking up the stare-down. "This is still a printout of a newspaper article. What are you going to do about verifying the information it contains, Mr. Haller?"

"Well, as soon as we break, I'm going to put my investigator on it and see if we can contact somebody in the Police Judiciaire. We're going to be doing the job the Sheriff's Department should have done six months ago."

"We're obviously going to verify it as well," Golantz added.

"Rilz's father and two brothers are sitting in the gallery. Maybe you can start with them."

The judge held up a hand in a calming gesture like he was a parent quelling an argument between two brothers.

"Okay," he said. "I am going to stop this line of cross-examination. Mr. Haller, I will allow you to lay the foundation for it during the presentation of the defense. You can call the witness back then, and if you can verify the report and the identity, then I will give you wide latitude in pursuing it."

"Your Honor, that puts the defense at a disadvantage," I protested.

"How so?"

"Because now that the state's been made aware of this information, it can take steps to hinder my verification of it."

"That's absurd," Golantz said.

But the judge nodded.

"I understand your concern and I am putting Mr. Golantz on notice that if I find any indication of that, then I will become...shall we say, very agitated. I think we are done here, gentlemen."

The judge rolled back into position and the lawyers returned to theirs. On my way back, I checked the clock on the back wall of the courtroom. It was ten minutes until five. I figured if I could stall for a few more minutes, the judge would recess for the day and the jurors would have the French connection to mull over for the night.

I stood at the lectern and asked the judge for a few moments. I then acted like I was studying my notepad, trying to decide if there was anything else I wanted to ask Kinder about.

"Mr. Haller, how are we doing?" the judge finally prompted.

"We're doing fine, Judge. And I look forward to exploring Mr. Rilz's activities in France more thoroughly during the defense phase of the trial. Until then, I have no further questions for Detective Kinder."

I returned to the defense table and sat down. The judge then announced that court was recessed for the day.

I watched the jury file out of the courtroom and picked up no read from any of them. I then glanced behind Golantz to the gallery. All three of the Rilz men were staring at me with hardened, dead eyes.

Forty-six

C isco called me at home at ten o'clock. He said he was nearby in Hollywood and that he could come right over. He said he already had some news about juror number seven.

After hanging up I told Patrick that I was going out on the deck to meet privately with Cisco. I put on a sweater because there was a chill in the air outside, grabbed the file I'd used in court earlier and went out to wait for my investigator.

The Sunset Strip glowed like a blast furnace fire over the shoulder of the hills. I'd bought the house in a flush year because of the deck and the view it offered of the city. It never ceased to entrance me, day or night. It never ceased to charge me and tell me the truth. That truth being that anything was possible, that anything could happen, good or bad.

"Hey, boss."

I jumped and turned. Cisco had climbed the stairs and come up behind me without my even hearing him. He must've come up the hill on Fairfax and then killed the engine and freewheeled down to my house. He knew I'd be upset if his pipes woke up everybody in the neighborhood.

"Don't scare me like that, man."

"What are you so jumpy about?"

"I just don't like people sneaking up on me. Sit down out here."

I pointed him to the small table and chairs positioned under the roof's eave and in front of the living room window. It was uncomfortable outdoor furniture I almost never used. I liked to contemplate the city from the deck and draw the charge. The only way to do that was standing.

The file I'd brought out was on the table. Cisco pulled out a chair and was about to sit down when he stopped and used a hand to sweep the smog dust and crud off the seat.

"Man, don't you ever spray this stuff off?"

"You're wearing jeans and a T-shirt, Cisco. Just sit down."

He did and I did and I saw him look through the translucent window shade into the living room. The television was on and Patrick was in there watching the extreme-sports channel on cable. People were doing flips on snowmobiles.

"Is that a sport?" Cisco asked.

"To Patrick, I guess."

"How's it working out with him?"

"It's working. He's only staying a couple weeks. Tell me about number seven?"

"Down to business. Okay."

He reached behind him and pulled a small journal out of his back pocket.

"You got any light out here?"

I got up, went to the front door and reached in to turn on the deck light. I glanced at the TV and saw the medical staff attending to a snowmobile driver who apparently had failed to complete his flip and had three hundred pounds of sled land on him.

I closed the door and sat back down across from Cisco. He was studying something in his journal.

"Okay," he said. "Juror number seven. I haven't had much time on this but I've got a few things I wanted to get right to you. His name is David McSweeney and I think almost everything he put on his J-sheet is false."

The J-sheet was the single-page form each juror fills out as part of the voir dire process. The sheets carry the prospective juror's name, profession and area of residence by zip code as well as a checklist of basic questions designed to help attorneys form opinions about whether they want the individual on their jury. In this case the name would've been excised but all the other information was on the sheet I had given Cisco to start with.

"Give me some examples."

"Well, according to the zip on the sheet, he lives down in Palos Verdes. Not true. I followed him from the courthouse directly to an apartment off of Beverly over there behind CBS."

Cisco pointed south in the general direction of Beverly Boulevard and Fairfax Avenue, where the CBS television studio was located.

"I had a friend run the plate on the pickup he drove home from court and it came back to David McSweeney on Beverly, same address I saw him go into. I then had my guy run his DL and shoot me over the photo. I looked at it on my phone and McSweeney is our guy."

The information was intriguing but I was more concerned with how Cisco was conducting his investigation of juror number seven. We had already blown up one source on the Vincent investigation.

"Cisco, man, your prints are going to be all over this. I told you I can't have any blowback on this."

"Chill, man. There's no fingerprints. My guy isn't going to go volunteering that he did a search for me. It's illegal for a cop to do an outside search. He'd lose his job. And if somebody comes looking, we still don't need to worry, because he doesn't use his terminal or user ID when he does these for me. He cadged an old lieutenant's password. So there are no prints, okay? No trails. We're safe on this."

I reluctantly nodded. Cops stealing from cops. Why didn't that surprise me?

"All right," I said. "What else?"

"Well, for one thing, he's got an arrest record and he checked the box on the sheet that said he'd never been popped before."

"What was the arrest for?"

"Two arrests. ADW in 'ninety-seven and conspiracy to commit fraud in 'ninety-nine. No convictions but that is all I know for right now. When the court opens I can get more if you want."

I wanted to know more, especially about how arrests for fraud and assault with a deadly weapon could result in no convictions, but if Cisco pulled records on the case, then he'd have to show ID and that would leave a trail.

"Not if you have to sign out the files. Let it go for now. You got anything else?"

"Yeah, I'm telling you, I think it's all phony. On the sheet he says he's an engineer with Lockheed. As far as I can tell, that's not true. I called Lockheed and they don't have a David McSweeney in the phone directory. So unless the guy's got a job with no phone, then..."

He raised his hands palm up, as if to say there was no explanation but deception.

"I've only had t'night on this, but everything's coming up phony and that probably includes the guy's name."

"What do you mean?"

"Well, we don't officially know his name, do we? It was blacked out on the J-sheet."

"Right."

"So I followed juror number seven and IDed him as David McSweeney, but who's to say that's the same name that was blacked out on the sheet. Know what I mean?"

I thought for a moment and then nodded.

"You're saying that McSweeney could've hijacked a legitimate juror's name and maybe even his jury summons and is masquerading as that person in the courthouse."

"Exactly. When you get a summons and show up at the juror check-in window, all they do is check your DL against the list. These are minimum-wage court clerks, Mick. It would not be difficult to get a dummy DL by one of them, and we both know how easy it is to get a dummy."

I nodded. Most people want to get out of jury duty. This was a scheme to get into it. Civic duty taken to extreme.

Cisco said, "If you can somehow get me the name the court has for number seven, I would check it, and I'm betting I find out there *is* a guy at Lockheed with that name."

I shook my head.

"There's no way I can get it without leaving a trail."

Cisco shrugged.

"So what's going on with this, Mick? Don't tell me that fucking prosecutor put a sleeper on the jury."

I thought a moment about telling him but decided against it.

"At the moment it's better if I don't tell you."

"Down periscope."

It meant that we were taking the submarine — compartmentalizing so if one of us sprang a leak it wouldn't sink the whole sub.

"It's best this way. Did you see this guy with anybody? Any KAs of interest?"

"I followed him over to the Grove tonight and he met somebody for a coffee in Marmalade, one of the restaurants they've got over there. It was a woman. It looked like a casual thing, like they sort of ran into each other unplanned and sat down together to catch up. Other than that, I've got no known associates so far. I've really only been with the guy since five, when the judge cut the jury loose."

I nodded. He had gotten me a lot in a short amount of time. More than I'd anticipated.

"How close did you get to him and the woman?"

"Not close. You told me to take all precautions."

"So you can't describe her?"

"I just said I didn't get close, Mick. I can describe her. I even got a picture of her on my camera."

He had to stand up to get his big hand into one of the front pockets of his jeans. He pulled out a small, black, non-attention-getting camera and sat back down. He turned it on and looked at the screen on the back. He clicked some buttons on the top and then handed it across the table to me.

"They start there and you can scroll through till you get to the woman."

I manipulated the camera and scrolled through a series of digital photos showing juror number seven at various times during the evening. The last three shots were of him sitting with a woman in Marmalade. She had jet-black hair that hung loose and shadowed her face. The photos also weren't very crisp because they had been taken from long distance and without a flash.

I didn't recognize the woman. I handed the camera back to Cisco.

"Okay, Cisco, you did good. You can drop it now."

"Just drop it?"

"Yeah, and go back to this."

I slid the file across the table to him. He nodded and smiled slyly as he took it.

"So what did you tell the judge up there at the sidebar?"

I had forgotten he had been in the courtroom, waiting to start his tail of juror seven.

"I told him I realized that you had done the original background search on the English-language default so I redid it to include French and German. I even printed the story out again Sunday so I would have a fresh date on it."

"Nice. But I look like a fuckup."

"I had to come up with something. If I'd told him you came across it a week ago and I'd been sitting on it since, we wouldn't be having this conversation. I'd probably be in lockup for contempt. Besides, the judge thinks Golantz is the fuckup for not finding it before the defense."

That seemed to placate Cisco. He held up the file.

"So then, what do you want me to do with it?" he asked.

"Where's the translator you used on the printout?"

"Probably in her dorm over in Westwood. She's an exchange student I came up with on the Net."

"Well, call her up and pick her up because you're going to need her tonight."

"I have a feeling Lorna isn't going to like this. Me and a twenty-year-old French girl."

"Lorna doesn't speak French, so she will understand. They're what, nine hours ahead over there in Paris?"

"Yeah, nine or ten. I forget."

"Okay, then I want you to get with the translator and at midnight start working the phones. Call all the gendarmes, or whatever they call themselves, who worked that drug case and get one of them on a plane over here. At least three of them are named in that article. You can start there."

"Just like that? You think one of those guys is going to just jump on a plane for us?"

"They'll probably be stabbing one another in the back, trying to get the ticket. Tell them we'll fly first class and put whoever comes out in the hotel where Mickey Rourke stays."

"Yeah, what hotel's that?"

"I don't know but I hear he's big over there. They think he's like a genius or something. Anyway, look, what I'm saying is, just tell them whatever they want to hear. Spend whatever needs to be spent. If two want to come, then bring over two and we vet them and put the best one on the stand. Just get somebody over here. It's Los Angeles, Cisco. Every cop in the world wants to see this place and then go back home and tell everybody what and who he saw."

"Okay, I'll get somebody on a plane. But what if he can't leave right away?"

"Then get him going as soon as possible and let me know. I can stretch things in court. The judge wants to hurry everything along but I can slow it down if I need to. Probably next Tuesday or Wednesday is as far as I can go. Get somebody here by then."

"You want me to call you tonight when I have it set up?"

"No, I need my beauty rest. I'm not used to being on my toes in court all day and I'm wiped out. I'm going to bed. Just call me in the morning."

"Okay, Mick."

He stood up and so did I. He slapped me on the shoulder with the file and then tucked it into the waistband at the back of his jeans. He descended the steps and I walked to the edge of the deck to look down on him as he mounted his horse by the curb, dropped it into neutral and silently started to glide down Fareholm toward Laurel Canyon Boulevard.

I then looked up and out at the city and thought about the moves I was making, my personal situation and my professional deceit in front of the judge in court. I didn't ponder it all too long and I didn't feel guilty about any of it. I was defending a man I believed was innocent of the murders he was charged with but complicit in the reason they had occurred. I had a sleeper on the jury whose placement was directly related to the murder of my predecessor. And I had a detective watching over me whom I was holding back on and couldn't be sure was considering my safety ahead of his own desire to break open the case.

I had all of that and I didn't feel guilty or fearful about anything. I felt like a guy flipping a three-hundred-pound sled in midair. It might not be a sport but it was dangerous as hell and it did what I hadn't been able to do in more than a year's time. It shook off the rust and put the charge back in my blood.

It gave it a fierce momentum.

I heard the sound of the pipes on Cisco's panhead finally fire up. He had made it all the way down to Laurel Canyon before kicking over the engine. The throttle roared deeply as he headed into the night.

PART FIVE

— Take the Nickel

Forty-seven

On Monday morning I had my Corneliani suit on. I was sitting next to my client in the courtroom and was ready to begin to present his defense. Jeffrey Golantz, the prosecutor, sat at his table, ready to thwart my efforts. And the gallery behind us was maxed out once again. But the bench in front of us was empty. The judge was sequestered in his chambers and running almost an hour behind his own nine-o'clock start time. Something was wrong or something had come up, but we had not yet been informed. We had seen sheriff's deputies escort a man I didn't recognize into chambers and then out again but there had been no word on what was going on.

"Hey, Jeff, what do you think?" I finally asked across the aisle.

Golantz looked over at me. He was wearing his nice black suit, but he had been wearing it every other day to court and it wasn't as impressive anymore. He shrugged.

"No idea," he said.

"Maybe he's back there reconsidering my request for a directed verdict."

I smiled. Golantz didn't.

"I'm sure he is," he said with his best prosecutorial sarcasm.

The prosecution's case had strung out through the entire previous week. I had helped with a couple of protracted cross-examinations but for the most part it had been Golantz engaging in overkill. He kept the medical examiner who had conducted the autopsies on Mitzi Elliot and Johan Rilz on the witness stand for nearly an entire day, describing in excruciating detail how and when the victims died. He kept Walter Elliot's accountant on the stand for half a day, explaining the finances of the Elliot marriage and how much Walter stood to lose in a divorce. And he kept the sheriff's forensic tech on for nearly as long, explaining his finding of high levels of gunshot residue on the defendant's hands and clothes.

In between these anchor witnesses he conducted shorter examinations of lesser witnesses and then finally finished his case Friday afternoon with a tearjerker. He put Mitzi Elliot's lifelong best friend on the stand. She testified about Mitzi confiding in her the plans to divorce her husband as soon as the prenuptial agreement vested. She told of the fight between husband and wife when the plan was revealed and of seeing bruises on Mitzi Elliot's arms the next day. She never stopped crying during her hour on the stand and continually veered into hearsay testimony that I objected to.

As is routine, I asked the judge as soon as the prosecution rested for a directed verdict of acquittal. I argued that the state had not come close to establishing a prima facie case against Elliot. But as is also routine, the judge flatly denied my motion and said the trial would move to the defense phase promptly at nine a.m. the following Monday. I spent the weekend strategizing and preparing my two anchor witnesses: Dr. Shamiram Arslanian, my GSR expert, and a jet-lagged French police captain named Malcolm Pepin. It was now Monday morning and I was locked and loaded and ready to go. But there was no judge on the bench to let me.

"What's going on?" Elliot whispered to me.

I shrugged.

"Your guess is as good as mine. Most times when the judge doesn't come out, it has nothing to do with the case at hand. Usually, it's about the next trial on his calendar."

Elliot wasn't appeased. A deep furrow had settled into the center of his brow. He knew something was up. I turned and looked back into the gallery. Julie Favreau was sitting three rows back with Lorna. I gave them a wink and Lorna sent back a thumbs-up. I swept the rest of the gallery and noticed that behind the prosecution table, there was a gap in the shoulder-to-shoulder spectators. No Germans. I was about to ask Golantz where Rilz's family members were, when a uniformed sheriff's deputy walked up to the rail behind the prosecutor.

"Excuse me."

Golantz turned and the deputy beckoned him with a document he was holding.

"Are you the prosecutor?" the deputy said. "Who do I talk to about this?"

Golantz got up and walked over to the rail. He took a quick look at the document and handed it back.

"It's a defense subpoena. Are you Deputy Stallworth?"

"That's right."

"Then you're in the right spot."

"No, I'm not. I didn't have anything to do with this case."

Golantz took the subpoena back and studied it. I could see the wheels begin turning, but it was going to be too late when he figured things out.

"You weren't on the scene at the house? What about the perimeter or traffic control?"

"I was home asleep, man. I work midnight shift."

"Hold it a second."

Golantz went back to his desk and opened a file. I saw him check the final witness list I had submitted two weeks before.

"What is this, Haller?"

"What's what? He's on there."

"This is bullshit."

"No, it's not. He's been on there for two weeks."

I got up and went to the rail. I held out my hand.

"Deputy Stallworth, I'm Michael Haller."

Stallworth refused to shake my hand. Embarrassed in front of the whole gallery, I pressed on.

"I'm the one who summoned you. If you wait out in the hall, I'll try to get you in and out as soon as court starts. There's some sort of delay with the judge. But sit tight and I'll get to you."

"No, this is wrong. I didn't have anything to do with this case. I just got off duty and I'm going home."

"Deputy Stallworth, there is no mistake here and even if there were, you can't walk out on a subpoena. Only the judge can release you at my request. You go home and you're going to make him mad. I don't think you want him mad at you."

The deputy huffed like he was being put out in a big way. He looked over at Golantz for help but the prosecutor was holding a cell phone to his ear and whispering into it. I had a feeling it was an emergency call.

"Look," I said to Stallworth, "just go out into the hall and I'll—"

I heard my name along with the prosecutor's called from the front of the courtroom. I turned and saw the clerk signaling us to the door that led to the judge's chambers. Finally, something was happening. Golantz ended his call and got up. I turned from Stallworth and followed Golantz toward the judge's chambers.

The judge was sitting behind his desk in his black robe. He appeared ready to go as well, but something was holding him back.

"Gentlemen, sit down," he said.

"Judge, did you want the defendant in here?" I asked.

"No, I don't think that's necessary. Just have a seat and I'll tell you what's going on."

Golantz and I sat side by side in front of the judge. I could tell that Golantz was silently steaming over the Stallworth subpoena and what it might mean. Stanton leaned forward and clasped his hands together on top of a folded piece of paper on the desk in front of him.

"We have an unusual situation involving juror misconduct," he said. "It is still…developing and I apologize for keeping you out there in the dark."

He stopped there and we both looked at him, wondering if we were supposed to leave now and go back to the courtroom, or if we could ask questions. But Stanton continued after a moment.

"My office received a letter Thursday addressed personally to me. Unfortunately, I didn't get a chance to open it until after court on Friday — kind of an end-of-the-week catch-up session after everybody was sent home. The letter said — well, here is the letter. I've already handled it but don't either of you touch it."

He unfolded the piece of paper he'd weighted with his hands and allowed us to read it. I stood up so I could lean over the desk. Golantz was tall enough — even sitting down — that he didn't have to.

Judge Stanton, you should know that juror number seven is not who you think he is and not who he says he is. Check Lockheed and check his prints. He's got an arrest record.

The letter looked like it had come out of a laser printer. There were no other markings on the page other than the two creases from where it had been folded.

I sat back down.

"Did you keep the envelope it came in?" I asked.

"Yes," Stanton said. "No return address and the postmark is Hollywood. I'm going to have the sheriff's lab take a look at the note and the envelope."

"Judge, I hope you haven't spoken to this juror," Golantz said. "We should be present and part of any questioning. This could just be a ploy by someone to get that juror off the panel."

I expected Golantz to rush to the juror's defense. As far as he was concerned, number seven was a blue juror.

I rushed to my own defense.

"He's talking about this being a ploy by the defense and I object to the accusation."

The judge quickly held his hands up in a calming gesture.

"Just hold your horses, both of you. I didn't talk to number seven yet. I spent the weekend thinking about how to proceed with it when I came to court today. I conferred with a few other judges on the matter and I was fully prepared to bring it up with counsel present this morning. The only problem is, juror number seven didn't show up today. He's not here."

That brought a pause to both Golantz and me.

"He's not here?" Golantz said. "Did you send deputies to—?"

"Yes, I sent court deputies to his home, and his wife told them that he was at work but she didn't know anything about court or a trial or anything like that. They went over to Lockheed and found the man and brought him here a few minutes ago. It wasn't him. He was not juror number seven."

"Judge, you're losing me," I said. "I thought you said they found him at work."

The judge nodded.

"I know. I did. This is beginning to sound like Laurel and Hardy and that 'Who's on first?' thing."

"Abbott and Costello," I said.

"What?"

"Abbott and Costello. They did the 'Who's on first?' thing."

"Whichever. The point is, juror number seven was not juror number seven."

"I'm still not following you, Judge," I said.

"We had number seven down in the computer as Rodney L. Banglund, engineer from Lockheed, resident of Palos Verdes. But the man who has been sitting for two weeks in seat number seven is not Rodney Banglund. We don't know who he was and now he's missing."

"He took Banglund's place but Banglund didn't know about it," Golantz said.

"Apparently," the judge said. "Banglund—the real one—is being interviewed about it now, but when he was in here he didn't seem to know anything about this. He said he never got a jury summons in the first place."

"So his summons was sort of hijacked and used by this unknown person?" I said.

The judge nodded.

"So it appears. The question is why, and the sheriff's department will hopefully get that answered."

"What does this do to the trial?" I asked. "Do we have a mistrial?"

"I don't think so. I think we bring the jury out, we explain that number seven's been excused for reasons they don't need to know about, we drop in the first alternate and go from there. Meantime, the sheriff's department quietly makes damn sure everybody else in that box is exactly who they are supposed to be. Mr. Golantz?"

Golantz nodded thoughtfully before speaking.

"This is all rather shocking," he said. "But I think the state would be prepared to continue—as long as we find out that this whole thing stops at juror number seven."

"Mr. Haller?"

I nodded my approval. The session had gone as I had hoped.

"I've got witnesses from as far as Paris in town and ready to go. I don't want a mistrial. My client doesn't want a mistrial."

The judge sealed the deal with a nod.

"Okay, go on back out there and we'll get this thing going in ten minutes."

On the way down the hall to the courtroom Golantz whispered a threat to me.

"He's not the only one who's going to investigate this, Haller."

"Yeah, what's that supposed to mean?"

"It means when we find this bastard we're also going to find out what he was doing on the jury. And if there is any tie to the defense, then I'm go—"

I pushed by him toward the door to the courtroom. I didn't need to listen to the rest.

"Good for you, Jeff," I said as I entered the courtroom.

I didn't see Stallworth and hoped the deputy had gone out into the hallway as I had instructed and was waiting. Elliot was all over me when I got to the defense table.

"What happened? What's going on?"

I used my hand to signal him to keep his voice down. I then whispered to him.

"Juror number seven didn't show up today and the judge looked into it and found out he was a phony."

Elliot stiffened and looked like somebody had just pressed a letter opener two inches into his back.

"My God, what does this mean?"

"For us, nothing. The trial continues with an alternate juror in his place. But there will be an investigation of who number seven was, and hopefully, Walter, it doesn't come to your door."

"I don't see how it could. But we can't go on now. You have to stop this. Get a mistrial."

I looked at the pleading look on my client's face and realized he'd never had any faith in his own defense. He had been counting solely on the sleeping juror.

"The judge said no on a mistrial. We go with what we've got."

Elliot rubbed a shaking hand over his mouth.

"Don't worry, Walter. You're in good hands. We're going to win this thing fair and square."

Just then the clerk called the courtroom to order and the judge bounded up the steps to the bench.

"Okay, back on the record with *California versus Elliot*," he said. "Let's bring in our jury."

Forty-eight

The first witness for the defense was Julio Muniz, the freelance videographer from Topanga Canyon who got the jump on the rest of the local media and arrived ahead of the pack at the Elliot house on the day of the murders. I quickly established through my questions how Muniz made his living. He worked for no network or local news channel. He listened to police scanners in his home and car and picked up addresses for crime scenes and active police situations. He responded to these scenes with his video camera and took film he then sold to the local news broadcasts that had not responded. In regard to the Elliot case, it began for him when he heard a call-out for a homicide team on his scanner and went to the address with his camera.

"Mr. Muniz, what did you do when you arrived there?" I asked.

"Well, I got my camera out and started shooting. I noticed that they had somebody in the back of the patrol car and I thought that was probably a suspect. So I shot him and then I shot the deputies stringing crime scene tape across the front of the property, things like that."

I then introduced the digital videocassette Muniz used that day as the first defense exhibit and rolled the video screen and player in front of the jury. I put in the cassette and hit "play." It had been previously

357

spooled to begin at the point that Muniz began shooting outside the Elliot house. As the video played, I watched the jurors paying close attention to it. I was already familiar with the video, having watched it several times. It showed Walter Elliot sitting in the back passenger seat of the patrol car. Because the video had been shot at an angle above the car, the 4A designation painted on its roof was clearly visible.

The video jumped from the car to scenes of the deputies cordoning off the house and then jumped back again to the patrol car. This time it showed Elliot being removed from the car by detectives Kinder and Ericsson. They uncuffed him and led him into the house.

Using a remote, I stopped the video and rewound it back to a point where Muniz had come in close on Elliot in the backseat of the patrol car. I started the video forward again and then froze the image so the jury could see Elliot leaning forward because his hands were cuffed behind his back.

"Okay, Mr. Muniz, let me draw your attention to the roof of the patrol car. What do you see painted there?"

"I see the car's designation painted there. It is four-A, or four alpha, as they say on the sheriff's radio."

"Okay, and did you recognize that designation? Had you seen it before?"

"Well, I listen to the scanner a lot and so I am familiar with the four-alpha designation. And I had actually seen the four-alpha car earlier that day."

"And what were the circumstances of that?"

"I had been listening to the scanner and I heard about a hostage situation in Malibu Creek State Park. I went out to shoot that, too."

"What time was this?"

"About two a.m."

"So, about ten hours before you were videoing the activities at the Elliot house you went out to shoot video at this hostage situation, correct?"

"That's correct."

"And the four-alpha car was involved also in this earlier incident?"

"Yes, when the suspect was finally captured, he was transported in four-alpha. The same car."

"About what time did that occur?"

"That wasn't until almost five in the morning. It was a long night."

"Did you shoot video of this?"

"Yes, I did. That footage comes earlier on the same tape."

He pointed to the frozen image on the screen.

"Then, let's see," I said.

I hit the "rewind" button on the remote. Golantz immediately stood, objected and asked for a sidebar. The judge waved us up and I brought along the witness list I had submitted to the court two weeks earlier.

"Your Honor," Golantz said angrily. "The defense is once again sandbagging. There has been no indication in discovery or otherwise of Mr. Haller's intent to explore some other crime with this witness. I object to this being introduced."

I calmly slid the witness list in front of the judge. Under the rules of discovery, I had to list each witness I intended to call and give a brief summary of what their testimony was expected to include. Julio Muniz was on my list. The summary was brief but all-inclusive.

"It clearly says he would testify about video he shot on May second, the day of the murders," I said. "The video he shot at the park was shot on the day of the murders, May two. It's been on there for two weeks, Judge. If anybody is sandbagging, then it's Mr. Golantz sandbagging himself. He could have talked to this witness and checked out his videos. He apparently didn't."

The judge studied the witness list for a moment and nodded.

"Objection overruled," he said. "You may proceed, Mr. Haller."

I went back and rewound the video and started to play it. The jury continued to pay maximum interest. It was a night shoot and the images were more grainy and the scenes seemed to jump around more than in the first sequence.

Finally, it came to footage showing a man with his hands cuffed behind his back being placed in a patrol car. A deputy closed the door and slapped the roof twice. The car drove off and came directly by the camera. As it was going by I froze the image.

The screen showed a grainy shot of the patrol car. The light of the camera illuminated the man sitting in the backseat as well as the roof of the car.

"Mr. Muniz, what's the designation on the roof of that car?"

"Again it's four-A or four-alpha."

"And the man being transported, where is he sitting?"

"In the rear right passenger seat."

"Is he handcuffed?"

"Well, he was when they put him in the car. I shot it."

"His hands were cuffed behind his back, correct?"

"Correct."

"Now, is he in the same position and seat in the patrol car that Mr. Elliot was in when you videotaped him about eight hours later?"

"Yes, he is. Exact same position."

"Thank you, Mr. Muniz. No further questions."

Golantz passed on cross-examination. There was nothing about the direct that could be attacked and the video didn't lie. Muniz stepped down. I told the judge I wanted to leave the video screen in place for my next witness and I called Deputy Todd Stallworth to the stand.

Stallworth looked angrier as he came into the courtroom. This was good. He also looked beat and his uniform looked like it had wilted on his body. One of the sleeves of his shirt had a black scuff mark on it, presumably from some struggle during the night.

I quickly established Stallworth's identity and that he was driving the alpha car in the Malibu district during the first shift on the day of the murders in the Elliot house. Before I could ask another question, Golantz once more objected and asked for another sidebar. When we got there, he raised his hands palms up in a *What's this?* gesture. His style was getting old with me.

"Judge, I object to this witness. The defense hid him on the witness list among the many deputies who were on the scene and have no bearing on the case."

Once again I had the witness list ready. This time I slapped it down in front of the judge with frustration, then ran my finger down the column of names until I reached Todd Stallworth. It was there in the middle of a list of five other deputies, all of whom had been on the scene at the Elliot house.

"Judge, if I was hiding Stallworth, I was hiding him in plain sight. He's clearly listed there under law enforcement personnel. The explanation is the same as before. It says he'll testify about his activities on May 2. That's all I put down because I never talked to him. I'm hearing what he has to say for the first time right now."

Golantz shook his head and tried to maintain his composure.

"Judge, from the start of this trial, the defense has relied on trickery and deception to—"

"Mr. Golantz," the judge interrupted, "don't say something you can't back up and that will get you in trouble. This witness, just like the first one Mr. Haller called, has been on this list for two weeks. Right there in black-and-white. You had every opportunity to find out what these people were going to say. If you didn't take that opportunity, then that was your decision. But this is not trickery or deception. You better watch yourself."

Golantz stood with his head bowed for a moment before speaking.

"Your Honor, the state requests a brief recess," he finally said in a quiet voice.

"How brief?"

"Until one o'clock."

"I wouldn't call two hours brief, Mr. Golantz."

"Your Honor," I cut in. "I object to any recess. He just wants to grab my witness and turn his testimony."

"Now *that* I object to," Golantz said.

"Look, no recess, no delay and no more bickering," the judge said. "We've already lost most of the morning. Objection overruled. Step back."

We returned to our places and I played a thirty-second cut of the video showing the handcuffed man being placed in the back of the 4-alpha car at Malibu Creek State Park. I froze the image in the same spot as before, just as the car was speeding by the camera. I left it on the screen as I continued my direct examination.

"Deputy Stallworth, is that you driving that car?"

"Yes, it is."

"Who is the man in the backseat?"

"His name is Eli Wyms."

"I noticed that he was handcuffed before being placed in the car. Is that because he was under arrest?"

"Yes, he was."

"What was he arrested for?"

"For trying to kill me, for one. He was also charged with unlawful discharge of a weapon."

"How many counts of unlawful discharge of a weapon?"

"I can't recall the exact number."

"How about ninety-four?"

"That sounds about right. It was a lot. He shot the place up out there."

Stallworth was tired and subdued but unhesitant in his answers. He had no idea how they fit into the Elliot case and didn't seem to care about trying to protect the prosecution with short, nonresponsive answers. He was probably mad at Golantz for not getting him out of testifying.

"So you arrested him and took him to the nearby Malibu station?"

"No, I transported him all the way to the county jail in downtown, where he could be placed on the psych level."

"How long did that take? The drive, I mean."

"About an hour."

"And then you drove back to Malibu?"

"No, first I had four-alpha repaired. Wyms had fired a shot that took out the side lamp. While I was downtown, I went to the motor pool and had it replaced. That took up the rest of my shift."

"So when did the car return to Malibu?"

"At shift change. I turned it over to the day-watch guys."

I looked down at my notes.

"That would have been deputies…Murray and Harber?"

"That's right."

Stallworth yawned and there was murmured laughter in the courtroom.

"I know we have you past your bedtime, Deputy. I won't take too much longer. When you turn the car over from shift to shift, do you clean it out or disinfect the car in any way?"

"You're supposed to. Realistically, unless you've got puke in the backseat, nobody does that. The cars get taken out of rotation once or twice a week and the motor guys clean them up."

"Did Eli Wyms puke in your car?"

"No, I would've known."

More murmured laughter. I looked down from the lectern at Golantz and he wasn't smiling at all.

"Okay, Deputy Stallworth, let me see if I got this right. Eli Wyms was arrested for shooting at you and firing at least ninety-three other shots that morning. He was arrested, his hands were cuffed behind his back and he was transported by you downtown. Do I have all of that right?"

"Sounds right to me."

"In the video, Mr. Wyms can be seen in the rear passenger side seat. Did he stay there for the whole hour-long ride downtown?"

"Yes, he did. I had him belted in."

"Is it standard procedure to place someone who is in custody on the passenger side?"

"Yes, it is. You don't want him behind you when you're driving."

"Deputy, I also noticed on the tape that you did not place Mr. Wyms's hands in plastic bags or anything of that nature before placing him in your patrol car. Why is that?"

"Didn't think it was necessary."

"Why?"

"Because it was not going to be an issue. The evidence was overwhelming that he had fired the weapons in his possession. We weren't worried about gunshot residue."

"Thank you, Deputy Stallworth. I hope you can go get some sleep now."

I sat down and left the witness for Golantz. He slowly got up and took the lectern. He knew exactly where I was going now but there was little he was going to be able to do to stop me. But I had to give him credit. He found a small crack in my direct and tried his best to exploit it.

"Deputy Stallworth, approximately how long did you wait for your car to be repaired at the downtown motor hub?"

"About two hours. They only have a couple guys work midnight watch and they were juggling jobs down there."

"Did you stay with the car for those two hours?"

"No, I grabbed a desk in the office and wrote up the arrest report on Wyms."

"And you testified earlier that no matter what the procedure is supposed to be, you generally rely on the motor pool to keep the fleet cars clean, is that correct?"

"Yes, correct."

"Do you make a formal request or do people working in the motor hub just take it upon themselves to clean and maintain the car?"

"I've never made a formal request. It just gets done, I guess."

"Now, during those two hours that you were away from the car and writing the report, do you know if the employees in the motor hub cleaned or disinfected the car?"

"No, I do not."

"They could have and you wouldn't necessarily know about it, right?"

"Right."

"Thank you, Deputy."

I hesitated but got up for redirect.

"Deputy Stallworth, you said it took them two hours to repair the car because they were short-handed and busy, correct?"

"Correct."

He said it in a boy-am-I-getting-tired-of-this tone.

"So it is unlikely that these guys would have taken the time to clean your car if you didn't ask, right?"

"I don't know. You'd have to ask them."

"Did you specifically ask them to clean the car?"

"Nope."

"Thank you, Deputy."

I sat down and Golantz passed on another round.

It was now almost noon. The judge adjourned for lunch but gave the jury and lawyers only a forty-five-minute break as he sought to make up for time lost during the morning. That was fine with me. My star witness was next and the sooner I got her on the stand, the closer my client was going to be to a verdict of acquittal.

Forty-nine

D r. Shamiram Arslanian was a surprise witness. Not in terms of her presence at the trial — she had been on the witness list longer than I had been on the case. But in terms of her physical appearance and personality. Her name and pedigree in forensics conjured an image of a woman deep, dark and scientific. A white lab coat and hair ironed back in a knot. But she was none of that. She was a vivacious, blue-eyed blonde with a cheerful disposition and easy smile. She wasn't just photogenic. She was telegenic. She was articulate and confident but never came close to being arrogant. The one-word description for her was the one-word description every lawyer wants for every one of his witnesses: likable. And it was rare to get that in a witness delivering your forensic case.

I had spent most of the weekend with Shami, as she preferred to be called. We had gone over the gunshot residue evidence in the Elliot case and the testimony she would give for the defense, as well as the cross-examination she could expect to receive from Golantz. This had been delayed until so late in the game to avoid discovery issues. What my expert didn't know she couldn't reveal to the prosecutor. So she was kept in the dark about the magic bullet until the last possible moment.

There was no doubt that she was a celebrity gun for hire. She had once hosted a show about her own exploits on Court TV. She was asked twice for her autograph when I took her to dinner at the Palm and was on a first-name basis with a couple of TV execs who visited the table. She charged a celebrity-level fee as well. For four days in Los Angeles to study, prepare and testify she would receive a flat rate of $10,000 plus expenses. Nice work if you could get it, and she could. She was known to study the many requests for her time and to choose only those in which she steadfastly believed there had been a grievous error committed or a miscarriage of justice. It also didn't hurt if you had a case that was getting the attention of the national media.

I knew after spending the first ten minutes with her that she was going to be worth every penny Elliot would pay her. She would be double trouble for the prosecution. Her personality was going to win over the jury, and her facts were going to seal the deal. So much of trial work comes down to who is testifying, not what the testimony actually reveals. It's about selling your case to the jury, and Shami could sell burnt matches. The state's forensic witness was a lab geek with the personality of a test tube. My witness had hosted a television show called *Chemically Dependent*.

I heard the low hum of recognition in the courtroom as my big-haired witness made her entrance from the back, holding all eyes as she walked up the center aisle, through the gate and across the proving grounds to the witness stand. She wore a navy blue suit that fit her curves snugly and accentuated the cascade of blonde curls over her shoulders. Even Judge Stanton seemed infatuated. He asked the courtroom deputy to get her a glass of water before she had even taken the oath. He hadn't asked the state's forensic geek if he had wanted jack shit.

After she gave her name and spelled it and took the oath to tell nothing but the truth, I got up with my legal pad and went to the lectern.

"Good afternoon, Dr. Arslanian. How are you?"

"I'm doin' just fine. Thanks for asking."

There was a slight trace of a southern accent in her voice.

"Before we go over your curriculum vitae, I want to get something out of the way up front. You are a paid consultant to the defense, is that correct?"

"Yes, that is correct. I'm paid to be here, not paid to testify to anything other than my own opinion — whether it's in line with the defense or not. That's my deal and I never change it."

"Okay, tell us where you are from, Doctor."

"I live in Ossining, New York, right now. I was born and raised in Florida and spent a lot of years in the Boston area, going to different schools here and there."

"Shamiram Arslanian. That doesn't sound like a Florida name."

She smiled brilliantly.

"My father is one hundred percent Armenian. So I guess that makes me half Armenian and half Floridian. My father said I was Armageddian when I was a girl."

Many in the courtroom chuckled politely.

"What is your background in forensic sciences?" I asked.

"Well, I've got two related degrees. I got my master's at MIT — the Massachusetts Institute of Technology — and that is in chemical engineering. I then got a PhD in criminology and that was awarded to me from John Jay College in New York."

"When you say 'awarded,' does that mean it's an honorary degree?"

"Hell, no," she said forcefully. "I worked my butt off two years to get that sucker."

This time laughter broke out across the courtroom and I noticed that even the judge smiled before politely tapping his gavel one time for order.

"I saw on your résumé that you have two undergraduate degrees as well. Is that true?"

"I've got two of everything, it seems. Two kids. Two cars. I've even got two cats at home, named Wilbur and Orville."

I glanced over at the prosecution table and saw that Golantz and his second were staring straight forward and had not so much as cracked a smile. I then checked the jury and saw all twenty-four eyes holding on my witness with rapt attention. She had them eating out of her hand and she hadn't even started yet.

"What are your undergraduate degrees?"

"I got one from Harvard in engineering and one from the Berklee College of Music. I went to both schools at the same time."

"You have a music degree?" I said with feigned surprise.

"I like to sing."

More laughter. The hits kept coming. One surprise after another. Shami Arslanian was the perfect witness.

Golantz finally stood and addressed the judge.

"Your Honor, the state would ask that the witness provide testimony regarding forensics and not music or pet names or things not germane to the serious nature of this trial."

The judge grudgingly asked me to keep my examination on point. Golantz sat down. He had won the point but lost the position. Everybody in the room now viewed him as a spoilsport, stealing what little levity there was in such a serious matter.

I asked a few more questions, which revealed that Dr. Arslanian currently worked as a teacher and researcher at John Jay. I covered her history and limited availability as an expert witness and finally brought her testimony to her study of the gunshot residue found on Walter Elliot's body and clothing on the day of the murders in Malibu. She testified that she reviewed the procedures and results of the sheriff's lab and conducted her own evaluations and modeling. She said she also reviewed all videotapes submitted to her by the defense in conjunction with her studies.

"Now, Dr. Arslanian, the state's forensic witness testified earlier in this trial that the tabs wiped on Mr. Elliot's hands and sleeves and jacket tested positive for elevated levels of certain elements associated with gunshot residue. Do you agree with that conclusion?"

"Yes, I do," my witness said.

A low vibration of surprise rolled through the room.

"You are saying that your studies concluded that the defendant had gunshot residue on his hands and clothes?"

"That is correct. Elevated levels of barium, antimony and lead. In combination, these are indications of gunshot residue."

"What does 'elevated levels' mean?"

"It just means that some of these materials you would find on a person's body whether they had fired or handled a weapon or not. Just from everyday life."

"So it is elevated levels of all three materials that are required for a positive result in gunshot residue testing, correct?"

"Yes, that and concentration patterns."

"Can you explain what you mean by 'concentration patterns'?"

"Sure. When a gun discharges — in this case we think we're talking about a handgun — there is an explosion in the chamber that gives the bullet its energy and velocity. That explosion sends gases out the barrel with the bullet as well as out any little crack and opening in the gun. The breech — that is, the part at the rear of the gun's barrel — comes open after a shot has been fired. The escaping gases propel these microscopic elements we're talking about backward onto the shooter."

"And that's what happened in this case, correct?"

"No, not correct. Based on the totality of my investigation I cannot say that."

I raised my eyebrows in feigned surprise.

"But Doctor, you just said you agreed with the state's conclusion that there was gunshot residue on the defendant's hands and sleeves."

"I do agree with the state's conclusion that there was GSR on the defendant. But that wasn't the question you asked."

I took a moment as if to retrace my question.

"Dr. Arslanian, are you saying that there could be an alternate explanation for the gunshot residue on Mr. Elliot?"

"Yes, I am."

We were there. We had finally arrived at the crux of the defense's case. It was time to shoot the magic bullet.

"Did your study of the materials provided to you over the weekend by the defense lead you to an alternate explanation for the gunshot residue on Walter Elliot's hands and clothing?"

"Yes, they did."

"And what is that explanation?"

"It is very highly likely, in my opinion, that the residue on Mr. Elliot's hands and clothes was transferred there."

"Transferred? Are you suggesting someone intentionally planted GSR on him?"

"No, I am not. I am suggesting that it occurred inadvertently by happenstance or mistake. Gunshot residue is basically microscopic dust. It moves. It can be transferred by contact."

"What does 'transferred by contact' mean?"

"It means the material we are talking about lights on a surface after it is discharged from the firearm. If that surface comes into contact with another, some of the material will transfer. It will rub off, is what'm saying. This is why there are law enforcement protocols for safeguarding against this. The victims and suspects in gun crimes often have their clothes removed for preservation and study. Some agencies put evidence bags over people's hands to preserve and guard against transference."

"Can this material be transferred more than once?"

"Yes, it can, with depreciating levels. This is a solid material. It's not a gas. It doesn't dissipate like a gas. It is microscopic but solid and it has to be someplace at the end of the day. I have conducted numerous studies of this and found that transference can repeat and repeat."

"But in the case of repeated transference, wouldn't the amount of material depreciate with each transfer until negligible?"

"That's right. Each new surface will hold less than the prior surface. So it's all a matter of how much you start with. The more you start with, the greater the amount that can be transferred."

I nodded and took a small break by flipping up pages on my pad as if I were looking for something. I wanted there to be a clear line between the discussion of theory and the specific case at hand.

"Okay, Doctor," I finally said. "With these theories in mind, can you tell us what happened in the Elliot case?"

"I can tell you *and* show you," Dr. Arslanian said. "When Mr. Elliot was handcuffed and placed in the back of the four-alpha patrol car, he was literally placed in a hotbed of gunshot residue. That is where and when the transference took place."

"How so?"

"His hands, arms and clothing were placed in direct contact with gunshot residue from another case. Transfer to him would have been inevitable."

Golantz quickly objected, saying I had not laid the groundwork for such an answer. I told the judge I intended to do that right now and asked permission to set the video equipment up in front of the jury again.

Dr. Arslanian had taken the video shot by my first witness, Julio Muniz, and edited it into one demonstration video. I introduced it as a defense exhibit over Golantz's failed objection. Using it as a visual aid, I carefully walked my witness through the defense's theory of transference. It was a demonstration that took nearly an hour and was one of the most thorough presentations of alternate theory I had ever been involved in.

We started with Eli Wyms's arrest and his placement in the backseat of the alpha car. We then cut to Elliot being placed in the same patrol car less than ten hours later. The same car and the same seat. Both men's hands cuffed behind their backs. She was stunningly authoritative in her conclusion.

"A man who had fired weapons at least ninety-four times was placed in that seat," she said. "Ninety-four times! He would have literally been reeking of gunshot residue."

"And is it your expert opinion that gunshot residue would have transferred from Eli Wyms to that car seat?" I asked.

"Most definitely."

"And is it your expert opinion that the gunshot residue on that seat could then have been transferred to the next person who sat there?"

"Yes, it is."

"And is it your expert opinion that this was the origin of the gunshot residue on Walter Elliot's hands and clothes?"

"Again, with his hands behind his back like that, he came in direct contact with a transfer surface. Yes, in my expert opinion, I do believe that this is how he got the gunshot residue on his hands and clothes."

I paused again to drive home the expert's conclusions. If I knew anything about reasonable doubt, I knew I had just embedded it in every juror's consciousness. Whether they would later vote their conscience was another matter.

Fifty

t was now time to bring in the big prop to drive Dr. Arslanian's testimony home.

"Doctor, did you draw any other conclusions from your analysis of the GSR evidence that supported the theory of transference you have outlined here?"

"Yes, I did."

"And what was that?"

"Can I use my mannequin to demonstrate?"

I asked the judge for permission to allow the witness to use a mannequin for demonstration purposes and he granted it without objection from Golantz. I then stepped through the clerk's corral to the hallway leading to the judge's chambers. I had left Dr. Arslanian's mannequin here until it had been ruled admissible. I wheeled it out to the center of the proving grounds in front of the jury — and the Court TV camera. I signaled to Dr. Arslanian to come down from the witness stand to make her demonstration.

The mannequin was a full-body model with fully manipulating limbs, hands and even fingers. It was made of white plastic and had several smudges of gray on its face and hands from experiments and demonstrations conducted over the years. It was dressed in blue jeans and a dark blue collared shirt beneath a windbreaker with a design on the back commemorating a University of Florida national football championship earlier in the year. The mannequin was suspended two inches off the ground on a metal brace and wheeled platform.

I realized I had forgotten something and went over to my rolling bag. I quickly pulled out the wooden dummy gun and collapsing pointer. I handed them both to Dr. Arslanian and then went back to the lectern.

"Okay, what do we have here, Doctor?"

"This is Manny, my demonstration mannequin. Manny, this is the jury."

There was a bit of laughter and one juror, the lawyer, even nodded his hello to the dummy.

"Manny's a Florida Gator fan?"

"Uh, he is today."

Sometimes the messenger can obscure the message. With some witnesses you want that because their testimony isn't all that helpful. But that was not the case with Dr. Arslanian. I knew I had been walking a tightrope with her: too cute and entertaining on one side; solid scientific evidence on the other. The proper balance would make her and her information leave the strongest impression on the jury. I knew it was now time to get back to serious testimony.

"Why do we need Manny here, Doctor?"

"Because an analysis of the SEMS tabs collected by the sheriff's forensic expert can show us why the gunshot residue on Mr. Elliot did not come from his firing of a weapon."

"I know the state's expert explained these procedures to us last week but I would like you to refresh us. What is a SEMS tab?"

"The GSR test is conducted with round tabs or disks that have a peel-off sticky side. The tabs are patted on the area to be tested and they collect all the microscopic material on the surface. The tab then goes into a scanning electron microscope, or SEMS, as we call it. Through the microscope, we see or don't see the three elements we have been talking about here. Barium, antimony and lead."

"Okay, then, do you have a demonstration for us?"

"Yes, I do."

"Please explain it to the jury."

Dr. Arslanian extended her pointer and faced the jury. Her demonstration had been carefully planned and rehearsed, right down to my always referring to her as 'doctor' and her always referring to the state's forensic man as 'mister.'

"Mr. Guilfoyle, the Sheriff's Department forensic expert, took eight different samples from Mr. Elliot's body and clothes. Each tab was coded so that the location it sampled would be known and charted."

She used the pointer on the mannequin as she discussed the locations of the samples. The mannequin stood with its arms down at its sides.

"Tab A was the top of the right hand. Tab B was the top of the left hand. Tab C was the right sleeve of Mr. Elliot's windbreaker and D was the left sleeve. Then we have tabs E and F being the right- and left-front panels of the jacket, and G and H being the chest and torso portions of the shirt Mr. Elliot wore beneath the open jacket."

"Are these the clothes he was wearing that day?"

"No, they are not. These are exact duplicates of what he was wearing, right down to the size and manufacturer."

"Okay, what did you learn from your analysis of the eight tabs?"

"I've prepared a chart for the jurors so they can follow along."

I presented the chart as a defense exhibit. Golantz had been given a copy of it that morning. He now stood and objected, saying his late receipt of the chart violated the rules of discovery. I told the judge the chart had only been composed the night before after my meetings with Dr. Arslanian on Saturday and Sunday. The judge agreed with the prosecutor, saying that the direction of my examination of the witness was obvious and well prepared and that I therefore should have drawn the chart sooner. The objection was sustained, and Dr. Arslanian now had to wing it on her own. It had been a gamble but I didn't regret the move. I would rather have my witness talking to the jurors without a net than have had Golantz in possession of my strategy in advance of its implementation.

"Okay, Doctor, you can still refer to your notes and the chart. The jurors just need to follow along. What did you learn from your analysis of the eight SEMS tabs?"

"I learned that the levels of gunshot residue on the different tabs greatly differed."

"How so?"

"Well, tabs A and B, which came from Mr. Elliot's hands, were where the highest levels of GSR were found. From there we get a steep drop-off in the GSR levels: tabs C, D, E and F with much lower levels, and no GSR reading at all on tabs G and H."

Again she used the pointer to illustrate.

"What did that tell you, Doctor?"

"That the GSR on Mr. Elliot's hands and clothes did not come from firing a weapon."

"Can you illustrate why?"

"First, comparable readings coming from both hands indicate that the weapon was fired in a two-handed grip."

She went to the mannequin and raised its arms, forming a V by pulling the hands together out front. She bent the hands and fingers around the wooden gun.

"But a two-handed grip would also have to result in higher levels of GSR on the sleeves of the jacket in particular and the rest of the clothes as well."

"But the tabs processed by the sheriff's department don't show that, am I right?"

"You're right. They show the opposite. While a drop-off from the readings on the hands is expected, it is not expected to be of this rate."

"So in your expert opinion, what does it mean?"

"A compound-transfer exposure. The first exposure occurred when he was placed with his hands and arms behind his back in the four-alpha car. After that, the material was on his hands and arms, and some of it was then transferred for a second time onto the front panels of his jacket during normal hand and arm movement. This would have occurred continuously until the clothing was collected from him."

"What about the zero reading on the tabs from the shirt beneath the jacket?"

"We discount that because the jacket could have been zipped closed during the commission of the shooting."

"In your expert opinion, Doctor, is there any way that Mr. Elliot could have gotten this pattern of GSR on his hands and clothing by discharging a firearm?"

"No, there is not."

"Thank you, Doctor Arslanian. No further questions."

I returned to my seat and leaned over to whisper into Walter Elliot's ear.

"If we didn't just give them reasonable doubt, then I don't know what it is."

Elliot nodded and whispered back to me.

"The best ten thousand dollars I've ever spent."

I didn't think I had done so badly myself but I let it go. Golantz asked the judge for the midafternoon break before cross-examination of the witness began and the judge agreed. I noticed what I believed to be a higher energy in the verbal buzz of the courtroom after the adjournment. Shami Arslanian had definitely given the defense momentum.

In fifteen minutes I would see what Golantz had in his arsenal for impeaching my witness's credibility and testimony but I couldn't imagine he had much. If he had something, he wouldn't have asked for the break. He would have gotten up and charged right after her.

After the jury and the judge had vacated the courtroom and the observers were pushing out into the hallway, I sauntered over to the prosecutor's table. Golantz was writing out questions on a legal pad. He didn't look up at me.

"What?" he said.

"The answer's no."

"To what question?"

"The one you were going to ask about my client taking a plea agreement. We're not interested."

Golantz smirked.

"You're funny, Haller. So what, you've got an impressive witness. The trial's a long way from over."

"And I've got a French police captain who's going to testify tomorrow that Rilz ratted out seven of the most dangerous, vindictive men he's ever investigated. Two of them happened to get out of prison last year and they disappeared. Nobody knows where they are. Maybe they were in Malibu last spring."

Golantz put his pen down and finally looked up at me.

"Yeah, I talked to your Inspector Clouseau yesterday. It's pretty clear he's saying whatever you want him to say, as long as you fly him first class. At the end of the depo, he pulled out one of those star maps and asked me if I could show him where Angelina Jolie lives. He's one serious witness you came up with."

I had told Captain Pepin to cool it with the star map stuff. He apparently hadn't listened. I needed to change the subject.

"So, where are the Germans?" I asked.

Golantz checked behind him as if to make sure Johan Rilz's family members weren't there.

"I told them that they had to be prepared for your strategy of building a defense by shitting all over the memory of their son and brother," he said. "I told them you were going to take Johan's problems in France five years ago and use them to try to get his killer off. I told them that you were going to depict him as a German gigolo who seduced rich clients, men and women, all over Malibu and the west side. You know what the father said to me?"

"No, but you'll tell me."

"He said that they'd had enough of American justice and were going back home."

I tried to retort with a clever and cynical comeback line. But I came up empty.

"Don't worry," Golantz said. "Up or down, I'll call them and tell them the verdict."

"Good."

I left him there and went out into the hallway to look for my client. I saw him in the center of a ring of reporters. Feeling cocky after the success of Dr. Arslanian's testimony, he was now working the big jury — public opinion.

"All this time they've concentrated on coming after me, the real killer's been out there running around free!"

A nice concise sound bite. He was good. I was about to push through the crowd to grab him, when Dennis Wojciechowski intercepted me first.

"Come with me," he said.

We walked down the hallway away from the crowd.

"What's up, Cisco? I was wondering where you've been."

"I've been busy. I got the report from Florida. Do you want to hear it?"

I had told him what Elliot had told me about fronting for the so-called organization. Elliot's story had seemed sincere enough but in the light of day I reminded myself of a simple truism — everybody lies — and told Cisco to see what he could do about confirming it.

"Give it to me," I said.

"I used a PI in Fort Lauderdale who I've worked with before. Tampa's on the other side of the state but I wanted to go with a guy I knew and trusted."

"I understand. What did he come up with?"

"Elliot's grandfather founded a phosphate-shipping operation seventy-eight years ago. He worked it, then Elliot's father worked it and then Elliot himself worked it. Only he didn't like getting his hands dirty in the phosphate business and he sold it a year after his father died of a heart attack. It was a privately owned company, so the record of the sale is not public. Newspaper articles at the time put the sale at about thirty-two million."

"What about organized crime?"

"My guy couldn't find a whiff of it. Looked to him like it was a good, clean operation—legally, that is. Elliot told you he was a front and he was sent out here to invest their money. He didn't say anything about him selling his own company and bringing the money out here. The man's lying to you."

I nodded.

"Okay, Cisco, thanks."

"You need me in court? I've got a few things I'm still working on. I heard juror number seven went missing this morning."

"Yeah, he's in the wind. And I don't need you in court."

"Okay, man, I'll talk to you."

He headed off toward the elevators and I was left to stare at my client holding forth with the reporters. A slow burn started in me and it gained heat as I waded into the crowd to get to him.

"Okay, that's all, people," I said. "No further comment. No further comment."

I grabbed Elliot by the arm, pulled him out of the crowd and walked him down the hall. I shooed a couple of trailing reporters away until we were finally far enough from all other ears and could speak privately.

"Walter, what were you doing?"

He was smiling gleefully. He made a fist and pumped it into the air.

"Sticking it up their asses. The prosecutor and the sheriffs, all of them."

"Yeah, well, you better wait on that. We've still got a ways to go. We may have won the day but we haven't won the war yet."

"Oh, come on. It's in the bag, Mick. She was fucking outstanding in there. I mean, I want to marry her!"

"Yeah, that's nice but let's see how she does on cross before you buy the ring, okay?"

Another reporter came up and I told her to take a hike, then turned back to my client.

"Listen, Walter, we need to talk."

"Okay, talk."

"I had a private investigator check your story out in Florida and I just found out it was bullshit. You lied to me, Walter, and I told you never to lie to me."

Elliot shook his head and looked annoyed with me for taking the wind out of his sails. To him, being caught in the lie was a minor inconvenience, an annoyance that I would even bring it up.

"Why did you lie to me, Walter? Why'd you spin that story?"

He shrugged and looked away from me when he spoke.

"The story? I read it in a script once. I turned the project down, actually. But I remembered the story."

"But why? I'm your lawyer. You can tell me anything. I asked you to tell me the truth and you lied to me. Why?"

He finally looked me in the eyes.

"I knew I had to light a fire under you."

"What fire? What are you talking about?"

"Come on, Mickey. Let's not get—"

He was turning to go back to the courtroom but I grabbed him roughly by the arm.

"No, I want to hear. What fire did you light?"

"Everybody's going back in. The break is over and we should be in there."

I gripped him even harder.

"What fire, Walter?"

"You're hurting my arm."

I relaxed my grip but didn't let go. And I didn't take my eyes off his.

"What fire?"

He looked away from me and put an "aw, shucks" grin on his face. I finally let go of his arm.

"Look," he said. "From the start I needed you to believe I didn't do it. It was the only way for me to know you would bring your best game. That you would be goddamn relentless."

I stared at him and saw the smile become a look of pride.

"I told you I could read people, Mick. I knew you needed something to believe in. I knew if I was a little bit guilty but not guilty of the big crime, then it would give you what you needed. It would give you your fire back."

They say the best actors in Hollywood are on the wrong side of the camera. At that moment I knew that was true. I knew that Elliot had killed his wife and her lover and was even proud of it. I found my voice and spoke.

"Where'd you get the gun?"

"Oh, I'd had it. Bought it under the table at a flea market back in the seventies. I was a big Dirty Harry fan and I wanted a forty-four mag. I kept it out at the beach house for protection. You know, a lot of drifters down on the beach."

"What really happened in that house, Walter?"

He nodded like it was his plan all along to take this moment to tell me.

"What happened was I went out there to confront her and whoever she was fucking every Monday like clockwork. But when I got there, I realized it was Rilz. She'd passed him off in front of me as a faggot, had him to dinners and parties and premieres with us, and they probably laughed all about it later. Laughed about me, Mick.

"It got me mad. Enraged, actually. I got the gun out of the cabinet, put on rubber gloves from under the sink and I went upstairs. You should have seen the look on their faces when they saw that big gun."

I stared at him for a long moment. I'd had clients confess to me before. But usually they were crying, wringing their hands, battling the demons their crimes had created inside. But not Walter Elliot. He was cold to the bone.

"How'd you get rid of the gun?"

"I hadn't gone out there alone. I had somebody with me and they took the gun, the gloves and my first set of clothes, then walked down the beach, got back up to the PCH and caught a cab. Meantime, I washed up and changed, then I dialed nine-one-one."

"Who was it that helped you?"

"You don't need to know that."

I nodded. Not because I agreed with him. I nodded because I already knew. I had a flash vision of Nina Albrecht easily unlocking the door to the deck when I couldn't figure it out. It showed a familiarity with her boss's bedroom that had struck me the moment I saw it.

I looked away from my client and down at the floor. It had been scuffed by a million people who had trod a million miles for justice.

"I never counted on the transference, Mick. When they said they wanted to do the test, I was all for it. I thought I was clean and they would see that and it would be the end of it. No gun, no residue, no case."

He shook his head at such a close call.

"Thank God for lawyers like you."

I jerked my eyes up to his.

"Did you kill Jerry Vincent?"

Elliot looked me in the eye and shook his head.

"No, I didn't. But it was a lucky break because I ended up with a better lawyer."

I didn't know how to respond. I looked down the hall to the court-room door. The deputy was there. He waved to me and signaled me into the courtroom. The break was over and the judge was ready to start. I nodded and held up one finger. Wait. I knew the judge wouldn't take the bench until he was told the lawyers were in place.

"Go back in," I said to Elliot. "I have to use the restroom."

Elliot calmly walked toward the waiting deputy. I quickly stepped into the nearby restroom and went to one of the sinks. I splashed cold water on my face, spotting my best suit and shirt but not caring at all.

Fifty-one

That night I sent Patrick to the movies because I wanted the house to myself. I wanted no television or conversation. I wanted no interruption and no one watching me. I called Bosch and told him I was in for the night. It was not so that I could prepare for what likely would be the last day of the trial. I was more than ready for that. I had the French police captain primed and ready to deliver another dose of reasonable doubt to the jury.

And it was not because I now knew that my client was guilty. I could count the truly innocent clients I'd had over the years on one hand. Guilty people were my specialty. But I was feeling bruised because I had been used so well. And because I had forgotten the basic rule: Everybody lies.

And I was feeling bruised because I knew that I, too, was guilty. I could not stop thinking about Rilz's father and brothers, about what they had told Golantz about their decision to go home. They were not waiting to see the verdict if it first meant seeing their dead loved one dragged through the sewers of the American justice system. I had spent the good part of twenty years defending guilty and sometimes evil men. I had always been able to accept that and deal with it. But I didn't feel very good about myself or the work that I would perform the next day.

It was in these moments that I felt the strongest desire to return to old ways. To find that distance again. To take the pill for the physical pain that I knew would numb me to the internal pain. It was in these moments that I realized that I had my own jury to face and that the coming verdict was guilty, that there would be no more cases after this one.

I went outside to the deck, hoping the city could pull me out of the abyss into which I had fallen. The night was cool and crisp and clear. Los Angeles spread out in front of me in a carpet of lights, each one a verdict on a dream somewhere. Some people lived the dream and some didn't. Some people cashed in their dreams a dime on the dollar and some kept them close and as sacred as the night. I wasn't sure if I even had a dream left. I felt like I only had sins to confess.

After a while a memory washed over me and somehow I smiled. It was one of my last clear memories of my father, the greatest lawyer of his time. An antique glass ball — an heirloom from Mexico passed down through my mother's family — had been found broken beneath the Christmas tree. My mother brought me to the living room to view the damage and to give me the chance to confess my guilt. By then my father was sick and wasn't going to get better. He had moved his work — what was left of it — home to the study next to the living room. I didn't see him through the open door but from that room I heard his voice in a sing-song nursery rhyme.

In a pickle, take the nickel . . .

I knew what it meant. Even at five years old I was my father's son in blood and the law. I refused to answer my mother's questions. I refused to incriminate myself.

Now I laughed out loud as I looked at the city of dreams. I leaned down, elbows on the railing, and bowed my head.

"I can't do this anymore," I whispered to myself.

The song of the Lone Ranger suddenly burst from the open door behind me. I stepped back inside and looked at the cell phone left on the table with my keys. The screen said PRIVATE NUMBER. I hesitated, knowing exactly how long the song would play before the call went to message.

At the last moment I took the call.

"Is this Michael Haller, the lawyer?"

"Yes, who is this?"

"This is Los Angeles police officer Randall Morris. Do you know an individual named Elaine Ross, sir?"

I felt a fist grip my guts.

"Lanie? Yes. What happened? What's wrong?"

"Uh, sir, I have Miss Ross up here on Mulholland Drive and she shouldn't be driving. In fact, she sort of passed out after she handed me your card."

I closed my eyes for a moment. The call seemed to confirm my fears about Lanie Ross. She had fallen back. An arrest would put her back into the system and probably cost her another stay in jail and rehab.

"Which jail are you taking her to?" I asked.

"I gotta be honest, Mr. Haller. I'm code seven in twenty minutes. If I take her down to book her, I'm looking at two more hours and I'm tapped on my overtime allowance this month. I was going to say, if you can come get her or send somebody for her, I'm willing to give her the break. You know what I mean?"

"Yes, I do. Thank you, Officer Morris. I'll come get her if you give me the address."

"You know where the overlook is above Fryman Canyon?"

"Yes, I do."

"We're right here. Make it quick."

"I'll be there in less than fifteen minutes."

Fryman Canyon was only a few blocks from the converted garage guesthouse where a friend allowed Lanie to live rent free. I could get her home, walk back to the park and retrieve her car afterward. It would take me less than an hour and it would keep Lanie out of jail and her car out of the tow lot.

I left the house and drove Laurel Canyon up the hill to Mulholland. When I reached the top, I took a left and headed west. I lowered the windows and let the cool air in as I felt the first pulls of fatigue from the day grab me. I followed the serpentine road for half a mile, slowing once when my headlights washed across a scruffy coyote standing vigil on the side of the road.

My cell phone buzzed as I had been expecting it to.

"What took you so long to call, Bosch?" I said by way of a greeting.

"I've been calling but there's no cell coverage in the canyon," Bosch said. "Is this some kind of test? Where the hell are you going? You called and said you were done for the night."

"I got a call. A . . . client of mine got busted on a deuce up here. The cop's giving her a break if I drive her home."

"From where?"

"The Fryman Canyon overlook. I'm almost there."

"Who was the cop?"

"Randall Morris. He didn't say whether he was Hollywood or North Hollywood."

Mulholland was a boundary between the two police divisions. Morris could work out of either one.

"Okay, pull over until I can check it out."

"Pull over? Where?"

Mulholland was a winding two-lane road with no pull-over spots except for the overlooks. If you pulled over anywhere else, you would get plowed into by the next car to come around the bend.

"Then, slow down."

"I'm already here."

The Fryman Canyon overlook was on the Valley side. I took a right to turn in and drove right by the sign that said that the parking area was closed after sunset.

I didn't see Lanie's car or a police cruiser. The parking area was empty. I checked my watch. It had been only twelve minutes since I had told Officer Morris that I would be there in less than fifteen.

"Damn!"

"What?" Bosch asked.

I hit the heel of my palm on the steering wheel. Morris hadn't waited. He'd gone ahead and taken Lanie to jail.

"What?" Bosch repeated.

"She's not here," I said. "And neither is the cop. He took her to jail."

I would now have to figure out which station Lanie had been transported to and probably spend the rest of the night arranging bail and getting her home. I'd be wrecked in court the next day.

I put the car in park and got out and looked around. The lights of the Valley spread out below the precipice for miles and miles.

"Bosch, I gotta go. I have to try to find —"

I saw movement in my peripheral vision to the left. I turned and saw a crouching figure coming out of the tall brush next to the parking clearing. At first I thought coyote but then I saw that it was a man. He was dressed in black and a ski mask was pulled down over his face. As he straightened from the crouch, I saw that he was raising a gun at me.

"Wait a minute," I said. "What is —"

"Drop the fucking phone!"

I dropped the phone and raised my hands.

"Okay, okay, what is this? Are you with Bosch?"

The man moved quickly toward me and shoved me backwards. I stumbled to the ground and then felt him grab the back of my jacket's collar.

"Get up!"

"What is — ?"

"Get up! Now!"

He started pulling me up.

"Okay, okay. I'm getting up."

The moment I was on my feet I was shoved forward and crossed through the lights at the front of my car.

"Where are we going? What is — ?"

I was shoved again.

"Who are you? Why are you — ?"

"You ask too many questions, lawyer."

He grabbed the back of my collar and shoved me toward the precipice. I knew it was almost a sheer drop-off at the edge. I was going to end up in somebody's backyard hot tub — after a three-hundred-foot high dive.

I tried to dig my heels in and slow my forward momentum but that resulted in an even harder shove. I had velocity now and the man in the mask was going to run me off the edge into the blackness of the abyss.

"You can't — "

Suddenly there was a shot. Not from behind me. But from the right and from a distance. Almost simultaneously, there was a metal snapping sound from behind me and the man in the mask yelped and fell into the brush to the left.

Then came voices and shouting.

"Drop your weapon! Drop your weapon!"

"Get on the ground! Get down on the ground!"

I dove facedown to the dirt at the edge of the precipice and put my hands over my head for protection. I heard more yelling and the sound of running. I heard engines roaring and vehicles crunching across the gravel. When I opened my eyes, I saw blue lights flashing in repeated patterns off the dirt and brush. Blue lights meant cops. It meant I was safe.

"Counselor," a voice said from above me. "You can get up now."

I craned my neck to look up. It was Bosch, his shadowed face silhouetted by the stars above him.

"You cut that one pretty close," he said.

Fifty-two

The man in the black mask groaned in pain as they cuffed his hands behind his back.

"My hand! Jesus, you assholes, my hand is broken!"

I climbed to my feet and saw several men in black windbreakers moving about like ants on a hill. Some of the plastic raid jackets said LAPD on them but most had FBI printed across the back. Soon a helicopter came overhead and lit the entire parking clearing with a spotlight.

Bosch stepped over to the FBI agents huddling over the man in the mask.

"Was he hit?" he asked.

"There is no wound," an agent said. "The round must have hit the gun, but that still hurts like a son of a bitch."

"Where is the gun?"

"We're still looking," the agent said.

"It may have gone over the side," another agent said.

"If we don't find it tonight, we find it in daylight," said a third.

They pulled the man up into a standing position. Two of the FBI agents stood on either side of him, holding him at the elbows.

"Let's see who we've got," Bosch said.

The ski mask was unceremoniously yanked off and a flashlight was aimed point-blank at the man's face. Bosch turned and looked back at me.

"Juror number seven," I said.

"What are you talking about?"

"Juror number seven from the trial. He didn't show up today and the Sheriff's Department was looking for him."

Bosch turned back to the man I knew was named David McSweeney.

"Hold him right there."

He then turned and signaled to me to follow him. He walked out of the circle of activity and into the parking clearing near my car. He stopped and turned back to me. But I got my question in first.

"What just happened?"

"What just happened was we just saved your life. He was going to push you over the side."

"I know that, but what *happened?* Where did you and everybody else come from? You said you would let people go at night after I was tucked in. Where did all of these cops come from? And what's the FBI doing here?"

"Things were different tonight. Things happened."

"What things happened? What changed?"

"We can go over that later. Let's talk about what we've got here first."

"I don't know what we've got here."

"Tell me about juror number seven. Why didn't he show up today?"

"Well, you should probably ask him that. All I can tell you is that this morning the judge called us into chambers and said he got an anonymous letter saying number seven was a phony and he lied about having a record. The judge planned to question him but he didn't show up. The sheriffs were sent to his house and his job and they brought back a guy who wasn't juror number seven."

Bosch raised his hand like a traffic cop.

"Hold on, hold on. You're not making sense. I know you just had a scare but — "

He stopped when one of the men in an LAPD jacket came over to address him.

"You want us to call paramedics? He says he thinks his hand is broken."

"No, just hold him there. We'll have him checked after we book him."

"You sure?"

"Fuck him."

The man nodded and went back to the spot where they were holding McSweeney.

"Yeah, fuck him," I said.

"Why did he want to kill you?" Bosch asked.

I raised my empty hands.

"I don't know. Maybe because of the story we planted. Wasn't that the plan, to draw him out?"

"I think you're holding out on me, Haller."

"Look, I've told you what I could tell you all along. You're the one holding out and playing games. What's the FBI doing here?"

"They've been in it from the start."

"Right, and you just forgot to tell me."

"I told you what you needed to know."

"Well, I need to know it all now or my cooperation with you ends now. That includes being any sort of witness against that man over there."

I waited a moment and he said nothing. I turned to walk toward my car and Bosch put his hand on my arm. He smiled in frustration and shook his head.

"Come on, man, cool your jets. Don't be throwing empty threats around."

"You think it's an empty threat? Why don't we see how empty it is when I start stringing out the federal grand jury subpoena I know is going to come out of this. I can argue client confidentiality all the way to the Supreme Court—I bet that will only take about two years—and your newfound pals over in the bureau are going to wish you had just come clean with me when you had the chance."

Bosch thought a moment and pulled me by the arm.

"All right, tough guy, come over here."

We walked to a spot in the parking area even further from the law enforcement ant hill. Bosch started to talk.

"The bureau contacted me a few days after the Vincent murder and said that he had been a person of interest to them. That's all. A person of interest. He was one of the lawyers whose names came up in their look at the state courts. Nothing specific, just based on rumors, things he had supposedly told clients he could get done, connections he claimed to have, that sort of thing. They'd drawn up a list of lawyers they heard might be bent and Vincent was on it. They invited him in as a cooperating witness and he declined. They were increasing the pressure on him when he got hit."

"So they tell you all of this and you join forces. Isn't that wonderful? Thanks for telling me."

"Like I said, you didn't need to know."

A man in an FBI jacket crossed the parking area behind Bosch, and his face was momentarily lit from above. He looked familiar to me but I couldn't place him. But then I imagined a mustache on him.

"Hey, there's the asshole you sent after me the other night," I said loud enough for the passing agent to hear. "He's lucky I didn't put a bullet in his face at the door."

Bosch put his hands on my chest and pushed me back a few steps.

"Calm down, Counselor. If it weren't for the bureau, I wouldn't have had the manpower to keep the watch on you. And right now you could be lying down there at the bottom of the mountain."

I pushed his hands off me but settled down. My anger dissipated as I accepted the reality of what Bosch had just said. And the reality that I had been used as a pawn from the beginning. By my client and now by Bosch and the FBI. Bosch took the moment to signal over another agent, who was standing nearby watching.

"This is Agent Armstead. He's been running the bureau's side of things and he's got some questions for you."

"Why not?" I said. "Nobody answers mine. I might as well answer yours."

Armstead was a young, clean-cut agent with a precision military haircut.

"Mr. Haller, we'll get to your questions as soon as we can," he said. "Right now we have a fluid situation here and your cooperation will be greatly appreciated. Is juror number seven the man Vincent paid the bribe to?"

I looked at Bosch with a "who is this guy?" expression.

"Man, how would I know that? I wasn't part of this thing. You want an answer to that, go ask him."

"Don't worry. We will be asking him a lot of questions. What were you doing up here, Mr. Haller?"

"I told you people. I told Bosch. I got a call from somebody who said he was a cop. He said he had a woman I know personally up here and she was under the influence and that I could come up and drive her home and save her the trouble of getting booked on a deuce."

"We checked that name you gave me on the phone," Bosch said. "There is one Randall Morris in the department. He's on gang detail in South Bureau."

I nodded.

"Yeah, well, I think it's pretty clear now that it was a fake call. But he knew my friend's name and he had my cell. It seemed convincing at the time, all right?"

"How did he get the woman's name?" Armstead asked.

"Good question. I had a relationship with her—a platonic relationship—but I haven't talked to her in almost a month."

"Then, how would he know about her?"

"Man, you're asking me shit I don't know. Go ask McSweeney."

I immediately realized I had slipped up. I wouldn't know that name unless I had been investigating juror number seven.

Bosch looked at me curiously. I didn't know if he realized the jury was supposed to be anonymous, even to the lawyers on the case. Before he could come up with a question, I was saved by someone yelling from the brush where I had almost been pushed over the side.

"I've got the gun!"

Bosch pointed a finger at my chest.

"Stay right here."

I watched Bosch and Armstead trot over and join a few of the others as they studied the found weapon under a flashlight beam. Bosch didn't touch the weapon but bent down into the light to examine it closely.

The *William Tell* Overture started to play behind me. I turned around and saw my phone lying on the gravel, its tiny square screen glowing like a beacon. I went over and picked it up. It was Cisco and I took the call.

"Cisco, I gotta call you back."

"Make it quick. I've got some good shit for you. You're going to want to know this."

I closed the phone and watched as Bosch finished his study of the weapon and then stepped over to McSweeney. He leaned close to him and whispered something into his ear. He didn't wait for a response. He just turned and walked back toward me. I could tell even in the dim moonlight that he was excited. Armstead was following behind him.

"The gun's a Beretta Bobcat, like we were looking for on Vincent," he said. "If the ballistics match, then we've got that guy locked in a box. I'll make sure you get a commendation from City Hall."

"Good. I'll frame it."

"Put this together for me, Haller, and you can start with him being the one who killed Vincent. Why did he want to kill you, too?"

"I don't know."

"The bribe," Armstead asked. "Is he the one who got the money?"

"Same answer I gave you five minutes ago. I don't know. But it makes sense, doesn't it?"

"How did he know your friend's name on the phone?"

"I don't know that either."

"Then, what good are you?" Bosch asked.

It was a good question and the immediate answer didn't sit well with me.

"Look, Detective, I —"

"Don't bother, man. Why don't you just get in your car and get the fuck out of here? We'll take it from here."

He turned and started walking away and Armstead followed. I hesitated and then called out to Bosch. I waved him back. He said something to the FBI agent and came back to me alone.

"No bullshit," he said impatiently. "I don't have the time."

"Okay, this is the thing," I said. "I think he was going to make it look like I jumped."

Bosch considered this and then shook his head.

"Suicide? Who would believe that? You've got the case of the decade, man. You're hot. You're on TV. And you've got a kid to worry about. Suicide wouldn't sell."

I nodded.

"Yes, it would."

He looked at me and said nothing, waiting for me to explain.

"I'm a recovering addict, Bosch. You know anything about that?"

"Why don't you tell me?"

"The story would go that I couldn't take the pressure of the big case and all the attention, and I either had or was about to relapse. So

I jumped instead of going back to that. It's not an uncommon thing, Bosch. They call it the fast out. And it makes me think that..."

"What?"

I pointed across the clearing toward juror number seven.

"That he and whoever he was doing this for knew a lot about me. They did a deep background. They came up with my addiction and rehab and Lanie's name. Then they came up with a solid plan for getting rid of me because they couldn't just shoot down another lawyer without bringing down massive scrutiny on what it is they've got going. If I went down as a suicide, there'd be a lot less pressure."

"Yeah, but why did they need to get rid of you?"

"I guess they think I know too much."

"Do you?"

Before I could answer, McSweeney started yelling from the other side of the clearing.

"Hey! Over there with the lawyer. I want to make a deal. I can give you some big people, man! I want to make a deal!"

Bosch waited to see if there was more but that was it.

"My tip?" I said. "Go over there and strike while the iron's hot. Before he remembers he's entitled to a lawyer."

Bosch nodded.

"Thanks, Coach," he said. "But I think I know what I'm doing."

He started to head across the clearing.

"Hey, Bosch, wait," I called. "You owe me something before you go over there."

Bosch stopped and signaled to Armstead to go to McSweeney. He then came back to me.

"What do I owe you?"

"One answer. Tonight I called you and told you I was in for the night. You were supposed to cut the surveillance down to one car. But this is the whole enchilada up here. What changed your mind?"

"You haven't heard, have you?"

"Heard what?"

"You get to sleep late tomorrow, Counselor. There's no trial anymore."

"Why not?"

"Because your client's dead. Somebody—probably our friend over there who wants to make a deal—took Elliot and his girlfriend out tonight when they came home from dinner. His electric gate wouldn't open and when he got out to push it open, somebody came up and put a bullet in the back of his head. Then he hit the woman in the car."

I took a half step back in shock. I knew the gate Bosch was talking about. I had been to Elliot's mansion in Beverly Hills just the other night. And as far as the girlfriend went, I also thought I knew who that would be. I'd had Nina Albrecht figured for that position ever since Elliot told me he'd had help on the day of the murders in Malibu.

Bosch didn't let the stunned look on my face keep him from continuing.

"I got tipped from a friend in the medical examiner's office and figured that somebody might be out there cleaning the slate tonight. I figured I ought to call the team back and see what happens at your place. Lucky for you I did."

I stared right through Bosch when I answered.

"Yeah," I said. "Lucky for me."

Fifty-three

There was no longer a trial but I went to court on Tuesday morning to see the case through to its official end. I took my place next to the empty seat Walter Elliot had occupied for the past two weeks. The news photographers who had been allowed access to the courtroom seemed to like that empty chair. They took a lot of photos of it.

Jeffrey Golantz sat across the aisle. He was the luckiest prosecutor on earth. He had left court one day, thinking he was facing a career-hobbling loss, and came back the next day with his perfect record intact. His upward trajectory in the DA's office and city politics was safe for now. He had nothing to say to me as we sat and waited for the judge.

But there was a lot of talk in the gallery. People were buzzing with news of the murders of Walter Elliot and Nina Albrecht. No one made mention of the attempt on my life and the events at the Fryman Canyon overlook. For the moment, that was all secret. Once McSweeney told Bosch and Armstead that he wanted to deal, the investigators had asked me to keep quiet so they could move slowly and carefully with their cooperating suspect. I was happy to cooperate with that myself. To a point.

Judge Stanton took the bench promptly at nine. His eyes were puffy and he looked like he'd had very little sleep. I wondered if he knew as many details of what had transpired the night before as I did.

The jury was brought in and I studied their faces. If any of them knew what had happened, they weren't showing it. I noticed several of them check out the empty seat beside me as they took their own.

"Ladies and gentlemen, good morning," the judge said. "At this time I am going to discharge you from service in this trial. As I am sure you can see, Mr. Elliot is not in his seat at the defense table. This is because the defendant in this trial was the victim of a homicide last night."

Half of the jurors' mouths dropped open in unison. The others expressed their surprise with their eyes. A low murmur of excited voices went through the courtroom and then a slow and deliberate clapping began from behind the prosecution table. I turned to see Mitzi Elliot's mother applauding the news of Elliot's demise.

The judge brought his gavel down harshly just as Golantz jumped from his seat and rushed to her, grabbing her hands gently and stopping her from continuing. I saw tears rolling down her cheeks.

"There will be no demonstrations from the gallery," the judge said harshly. "I don't care who you are or what connection you might have to the case, everyone in here will show respect to the court or I will have you removed."

Golantz returned to his seat but the tears continued to flow from the mother of one of the victims.

"I know that to all of you, this is rather shocking news," Stanton told the jurors. "Be assured that the authorities are investigating the matter thoroughly and hopefully will soon bring the individual or individuals responsible to justice. I am sure you will learn all about it when you read the paper or watch the news, as you are now free to do. As far as today goes, I want to thank you for your service. I know you all were very attentive to the presentation of the prosecution and defense cases and I hope your time here was a positive experience. You are free now to go back to the deliberation room to gather your things and go home. You are excused."

We stood one last time for the jury and I watched them file through the doorway to the deliberation room. After they were gone, the judge thanked Golantz and me for our professional demeanor during trial, thanked his staff and quickly adjourned court. I hadn't bothered to unpack any files from my bag, so I stood motionless for the longest time after the judge left the courtroom. My reverie wasn't broken until Golantz approached me with his hand out. Without thinking I reached out and shook it.

"No hard feelings on anything, Mickey. You're a damn good lawyer."

Was, I thought.

"Yeah," I said. "No hard feelings."

"You going to hang around and talk to jurors, see which way they were leaning?" he asked.

I shook my head.

"No, I'm not interested."

"Me neither. Take care of yourself."

He clapped me on the shoulder and pushed out through the gate. I was sure there would be a throng of media out in the hall waiting and he'd tell them that in some strange way he felt that justice had been served. Live by the gun, die by the gun. Or words to that effect.

I'd leave the media for him. Instead, I gave him a good lead and then followed him out. The reporters were already surrounding him and I was able to hug the wall and escape notice. All except for Jack McEvoy from the *Times.* He spotted me and started trailing. He caught me as I got to the stairwell entrance.

"Hey, Mick!"

I glanced at him but didn't stop walking. I knew from experience not to. If one member of the media downed you, the rest of the pride would catch up and pile on. I didn't want to be devoured. I hit the stairwell door and started down.

"No comment."

He stayed with me, stride for stride.

"I'm not writing about the trial. I'm covering the new murders. I thought maybe you and I could have the same deal again. You know, trade informa—"

"No deal, Jack. And no comment. Catch you later."

I put my hand out and stopped him on the first landing. I left him there, went down two more landings and then out into the hallway. I walked down to Judge Holder's courtroom and entered.

Michaela Gill was in the clerk's pod and I asked if I could see the judge for a few minutes.

"But I don't have you down for an appointment," she said.

"I know that, Michaela, but I think the judge will want to see me. Is she back there? Can you tell her I only want ten minutes? Tell her it's about the Vincent files."

The clerk picked up the phone, punched a button and gave the judge my request. Then she hung up and told me I could go right back to her chambers.

"Thank you."

The judge was behind her desk with her half-glasses on, a pen poised in her hand as if I had interrupted her in the middle of signing an order.

"Well, Mr. Haller," she said. "It's certainly been an eventful day. Have a seat."

I sat in the familiar chair in front of her.

"Thank you for seeing me, Judge."

"What can I do for you?"

She asked the question without looking at me. She started scribbling signatures on a series of documents.

"I just wanted you to know I will be resigning as counsel on the rest of the Vincent cases."

She put the pen down and looked over her glasses at me.

"What?"

"I'm resigning. I came back too soon or probably should never have come back at all. But I'm finished."

"That's absurd. Your defense of Mr. Elliot has been the talk of this courthouse. I watched parts of it on television. You clearly were schooling Mr. Golantz and I don't think there were many observers who would have bet against an acquittal."

I waved the compliments away.

"Anyway, Judge, it doesn't matter. It's not really why I'm here."

She took her glasses off and put them down on the desk. She looked hesitant but then asked the next question.

"Then, why are you here?"

"Because, Judge, I wanted you to know that I know. And soon enough everybody else will as well."

"I am sure I don't know what you are talking about. What do you know, Mr. Haller?"

"I know that you are for sale and that you tried to have me killed."

She barked out a laugh but there was no mirth in her eyes, only daggers.

"Is this some kind of joke?"

"No, it's no joke."

"Then, Mr. Haller, I suggest you calm down and compose yourself. If you go around this courthouse making these kinds of outlandish accusations, then there will be consequences for you. Severe consequences. Maybe you are right. You are feeling the stress of coming back too soon from rehab."

I smiled and I could tell by her face that she immediately realized her mistake.

"Slipped up there, didn't you, Judge? How'd you know I was in rehab? Better yet, how did juror number seven know how to lure me away from home last night? The answer is, you had me backgrounded. You set me up and sent McSweeney out to kill me."

"I don't know what you are talking about and I don't know this man you say tried to kill you."

"Well, I think he knows you, and the last time I saw him he was about to start playing *Let's Make a Deal* with the federal government."

It hit her like a punch in the gut. I knew revealing it to her wasn't going to endear me to Bosch or Armstead, but I didn't care. Neither of them was the guy who had been used like a pawn and had nearly taken the high dive off Mulholland. I was that guy and that entitled me to confront the person I knew was behind it.

"I put it together without having to make a deal with anybody," I said. "My investigator traced McSweeney. Nine years ago he was arrested for an ADW and who was his attorney? Mitch Lester, your husband. The next year he was popped again for fraud and once again it was Mitch Lester on the case. There's the connection. It makes a nice little triangle, doesn't it? You have access to and control of the jury pool and the selection process. You can get into the computers and it was you who planted the sleeper on my jury. Jerry Vincent paid you but then he changed his mind after the FBI came sniffing around. You couldn't run the risk that Jerry might get jammed up with the FBI and try to deal a judge to them. So you sent McSweeney.

"Then, when it all turned to shit yesterday, you decided to clean house. You sent McSweeney—juror number seven—after Elliot and Albrecht, and then me. How am I doing, *Judge?* I miss anything so far?"

I said the word "judge" like it had the same meaning as garbage. She stood up.

"This is insane. You have no evidence connecting me to anyone but my husband. And making the leap from one of his clients to me is completely absurd."

"You're right, Judge. I don't have evidence but we're not in court here. This is just you and me. I just have my gut instincts and they tell me that this all comes back to you."

"I want you to leave now."

"But the feds on the other hand? They have McSweeney."

I could see it strike fear in her eyes.

"Guess you haven't heard from him, have you? Yeah, I don't think they're letting him make any calls while they debrief him. You better hope he doesn't have any of that evidence. Because if he puts you in that triangle, then you'll be trading your black robe for an orange jumpsuit."

"Get out or I will call courthouse security and have you arrested!"

She pointed toward the door. I calmly and slowly stood up.

"Sure, I'll go. And you know something? I may never practice law again in this courthouse. But I promise you that I'll come back to watch you prosecuted. You and your husband. Count on it."

The judge stared at me, her arm still extended toward the door, and I saw the anger in her eyes slowly change to fear. Her arm drooped a little and then she let it drop all the way. I left her standing there.

I took the stairs all the way down because I didn't want to get on a crowded elevator. Eleven flights down. At the bottom I pushed through the glass doors and left the courthouse. I pulled my phone and called Patrick and told him to pull the car around. Then I called Bosch.

"I decided to light a fire under you and the bureau," I told him.

"What do you mean? What did you do?"

"I didn't want to wait around while the bureau took its usual year and a half to make a case. Sometimes justice can't wait, Detective."

"What did you do, Haller?"

"I just had a conversation with Judge Holder — yes, I figured it out without McSweeney's help. I told her the feds had McSweeney and he was cooperating. If I were you and the bureau, I'd hurry the fuck up with your case and in the meantime keep tabs on her. She doesn't seem like a runner to me, but you never know. Have a good day."

I closed the phone before he could protest my actions. I didn't care. He had used me the whole time. It felt good to turn the tables on him, make him and the FBI do the dancing at the end of the string.

PART SIX

— The Last Verdict

Fifty-four

osch knocked on my door early Thursday morning. I hadn't combed my hair yet but I was dressed. He, on the other hand, looked like he had pulled an all-nighter.

"I wake you?" he asked.

I shook my head.

"I have to get my kid ready for school."

"That's right. Wednesday nights and every other weekend."

"What's up, Detective?"

"I've got a couple of questions and I thought you might be interested in knowing where things stand on everything."

"Sure. Let's sit out here. I don't want her hearing this."

I patted down my hair as I walked toward the table.

"I don't want to sit," Bosch said. "I don't have a lot of time."

He turned to the railing and leaned his elbows down on it. I changed directions and did the same thing right next to him.

"I don't like to sit when I'm out here either."

"I have the same sort of view at my place," he said. "Only it's on the other side."

"I guess that makes us flip sides of the same mountain."

He turned his eyes from the view to me for a moment.

"Something like that," he said.

"So, what's happening? I thought you'd be too angry with me to ever tell me what was going on."

"Truth is, I think the bureau moves too slowly myself. They didn't like what you did very much but I didn't mind. It got things rolling."

Bosch straightened up and leaned back on the railing, the view of the city behind him.

"So then, what's happening?" I asked.

"The grand jury came back with indictments last night. Holder, Lester, Carlin, McSweeney, and a woman who's a supervisor in the jury office and was the one who gave them access to the computers. We're taking them all down simultaneously this morning. So keep it under your hat until we have everybody hooked up."

It was nice that he trusted me enough to tell me before the arrests. I thought it might be even nicer to go down to the CCB and watch them take Holder out of there in handcuffs.

"Is it solid?" I asked. "Holder *is* a judge, you know. You better have it nailed down."

"It's solid. McSweeney gave it all up. We've got phone records, money transfers. He even taped her husband during some of the conversations."

I nodded. It sounded like the typical federal package. One reason I never took on federal cases when I was practicing was that when the Big G made a case, it usually stayed made. Victories for the defense were rare. Most times you just got flattened like roadkill.

"I didn't know Carlin was hooked up in this," I said.

"He's right at the center. He goes way back with the judge and she used him to approach Vincent in the first place. Vincent used him to deliver the money. Then when Vincent started getting cold feet because the FBI was sniffing around, Carlin got wind of it and told the judge.

She thought the best thing to do was get rid of the weak link. She and her husband sent McSweeney to take care of Vincent."

"Got wind of it how? Wren Williams?"

"Yeah, we think. He got close to her to keep tabs on Vincent. We don't think she knew what was going on. She's not smart enough."

I nodded and thought about how all the pieces fit together.

"What about McSweeney? He just did what he was told? The judge tells him to hit a guy and he just does it?"

"First of all, McSweeney was a con man before he was a killer. So I don't for a minute think we're getting the whole truth out of him. But he says the judge can be very persuasive. The way she explained it to him, either Vincent went down or they all went down. There was no choice. Besides, she also promised to increase his cut after he went through with the trial and tipped the case."

I nodded.

"So what are the indictments?"

"Conspiracy to commit murder, corruption. This is only the first wave. There will be more down the road. This wasn't the first time. McSweeney told us he'd been on four juries in the last seven years. Two acquittals and two hangers. Three different courthouses."

I whistled as I thought of some of the big cases that had ended in shocking acquittals or hung juries in recent years.

"Robert Blake?"

Bosch smiled and shook his head.

"I wish," he said. "O.J., too. But they weren't in business back then for that one. We just lost those cases on our own."

"Doesn't matter. This is going to be huge."

"Biggest one I've ever had."

He folded his arms and glanced over his shoulder at the view.

"You've got the Sunset Strip and I've got Universal," he said.

I heard the door open and looked back to see Hayley peeking out.

"Dad?"

"What's up, Hay?"

"Is everything all right?"

"Everything's fine. Hayley, this is Detective Bosch. He's a policeman."

"Hello, Hayley," Bosch said.

I think it was the only time I had ever seen him put a real smile on his face.

"Hi," my daughter said.

"Hayley, did you eat your cereal?" I asked.

"Yes."

"Okay, then you can watch TV until it's time to go."

She disappeared inside and closed the door. I checked my watch. She still had ten minutes before we had to leave.

"She's a cute kid," Bosch said.

I nodded.

"I gotta ask you a question," he said. "You started this whole thing tumbling, didn't you? You sent that anonymous letter to the judge."

I thought for a moment before answering.

"If I say yes, am I going to become a witness?"

I had not been called to the federal grand jury after all. With McSweeney giving everything up, they apparently didn't need me. And I didn't want to change that now.

"No, it's just for me," Bosch said. "I just want to know if you did the right thing."

I considered not telling him but ultimately I wanted him to know.

"Yeah, that was me. I wanted to get McSweeney off the jury and then win the case fair and square. I didn't expect Judge Stanton to take the letter and consult other judges about it."

"He called up the chief judge and asked her advice."

I nodded.

"It's gotta be what happened," I said. "He calls her, not knowing she was behind the whole thing. She then tipped McSweeney and told him not to show up for court, then used him to try to clean up the mess."

Bosch nodded as though I was confirming things he already knew.

"And you were part of the mess. She must've figured you sent the letter to Judge Stanton. You knew too much and had to go—just like Vincent. It wasn't about the story we planted. It was about you tipping Judge Stanton."

I shook my head. My own actions had almost brought about my own demise in the form of a high dive off Mulholland.

"I guess I was pretty stupid."

"I don't know about that. You're still standing. After today none of them will be."

"There's that. What kind of deal did McSweeney cut?"

"No death penalty and consideration. If everybody goes down, then he'll probably get fifteen. In the federal system that means he'll still do thirteen."

"Who's his lawyer?"

"He's got two. Dan Daly and Roger Mills."

I nodded. He was in good hands. I thought about what Walter Elliot had told me, that the guiltier you were, the more lawyers you needed.

"Pretty good deal for three murders," I said.

"One murder," Bosch corrected.

"What do you mean? Vincent, Elliot and Albrecht."

"He didn't kill Elliot and Albrecht. Those two didn't match up."

"What are you talking about? He killed them and then he tried to kill me."

Bosch shook his head.

"He did try to kill you but he didn't kill Elliot and Albrecht. It was a different weapon. On top of that, it didn't make sense. Why would he ambush them and then try to make you look like a suicide? It doesn't connect. McSweeney is clean on Elliot and Albrecht."

I was stunned silent for a long moment. For the last three days I had believed that the man who killed Elliot and Albrecht was the same man who had tried to kill me and that he was safely locked in the hands of the authorities. Now Bosch was telling me there was a second killer somewhere out there.

"Does Beverly Hills have any ideas?" I finally asked.

"Oh, yeah, they're pretty sure they know who did it. But they'll never make a case."

The hits kept coming. One surprise after another.

"Who?"

"The family."

"You mean like the Family, with a capital *F*? Organized crime?"

Bosch smiled and shook his head.

"The family of Johan Rilz. They took care of it."

"How do they know that?"

"Lands and grooves. The bullets they dug out of the two victims were nine-millimeter Parabellums. Brass jacket and casing and manufactured in Germany. BHPD took the bullet profile and matched them to a C-ninety-six Mauser, also manufactured in Germany."

He paused to see if I had any questions. When I didn't, he continued.

"Over at BHPD they're thinking it's almost like somebody was sending a message."

"A message from Germany."

"You got it."

I thought of Golantz telling the Rilz family how I was going to drag Johan through the mud for a week. They had left rather than witness that. And Elliot was killed before it could happen.

"Parabellum," I said. "You know your Latin, Detective?"

"Didn't go to law school. What's it mean?"

"Prepare for war. It's part of a saying. 'If you want peace, prepare for war.' What will happen with the investigation now?"

Bosch shrugged.

"I know a couple of Beverly Hills detectives who'll get a nice trip to

Germany out of it. They fly their people business class with the seats that fold down into beds. They'll go through the motions and the due diligence. But if the hit was done right, nothing will ever happen."

"How'd they get the gun over here?"

"It could be done. Through Canada or Der FedEx if it absolutely, positively has to be there on time."

I didn't smile. I was thinking about Elliot and the equilibrium of justice. Somehow Bosch seemed to know what I was thinking.

"Remember what you said to me when you told me you had told Judge Holder you knew she was behind all of this?"

I shrugged.

"What did I say?"

"You said sometimes justice can't wait."

"And?"

"And you were right. Sometimes it doesn't wait. In that trial, you had the momentum and Elliot looked like he was going to walk. So somebody decided not to wait for justice and he delivered his own verdict. Back when I was riding patrol, you know what we called a killing that came down to simple street justice?"

"What?"

"The brass verdict."

I nodded. I understood. We were both silent for a long moment.

"Anyway, that's all I know," Bosch finally said. "I gotta go and get ready to put people in jail. It's going to be a good day."

Bosch pushed his weight off the railing, ready to go.

"It's funny you coming here today," I said. "Last night I decided I was going to ask you something the next time I saw you."

"Yeah, what's that?"

I thought about it for a moment and then nodded. It was the right thing to do.

"Flip sides of the same mountain.... Do you know you look a lot like your father?"

He said nothing. He just stared at me for a moment, then nodded once and turned to the railing. He cast his gaze out at the city.

"When did you put that together?" he asked.

"Technically last night, when I was looking at old photos and scrapbooks with my daughter. But I think on some level I've known it for a long time. We were looking at photos of my father. They kept reminding me of somebody and then I realized it was you. Once I saw it, it seemed obvious. I just didn't see it at first."

I walked to the railing and looked out at the city with him.

"Most of what I know about him came from books," I said. "A lot of different cases, a lot of different women. But there are a few memories that aren't in books and are just mine. I remember coming into the office he had set up at home when he started to get sick. There was a painting framed on the wall—a print actually, but back then I thought it was a real painting. *The Garden of Earthly Delights.* Weird, scary stuff for a little kid . . .

"The memory I have is of him holding me on his lap and making me look at the painting and telling me that it wasn't scary. That it was beautiful. He tried to teach me to say the painter's name. Hieronymus Bosch. Rhymes with 'anonymous,' he told me. Only back then, I don't think I could say 'anonymous' either."

I wasn't seeing the city out there. I was seeing the memory. I was quiet for a while after that. It was my half brother's turn. Eventually, he leaned his elbows down on the railing and spoke.

"I remember that house," he said. "I visited him once. Introduced myself. He was on the bed. He was dying."

"What did you say to him?"

"I just told him I'd made it through. That's all. There wasn't really anything else to say."

Like right now, I thought. What was there to say? Somehow, my thoughts jumped to my own shattered family. I had little contact with the siblings I knew I had, let alone Bosch. And then there was my daughter, whom I saw only eight days a month. It seemed like the most important things in life were the easiest to break apart.

"You've known all these years," I finally said. "Why didn't you ever make contact? I have another half brother and three half sisters. They're yours, too, you know."

Bosch didn't say anything at first, then he gave an answer I guessed he had been telling himself for a few decades.

"I don't know. I guess I didn't want to rock anybody's boat. Most of the time people don't like surprises. Not like this."

For a moment I wondered what my life would've been like if I had known about Bosch. Maybe I would've been a cop instead of a lawyer. Who knows?

"I'm quitting, you know."

I wasn't sure why I had said it.

"Quitting what?"

"My job. The law. You could say the brass verdict was my last verdict."

"I quit once. It didn't take. I came back."

"We'll see."

Bosch glanced at me and then put his eyes back out on the city. It was a beautiful day with low-flying clouds and a cold-air front that had compressed the smog layer to a thin amber band on the horizon. The sun had just crested the mountains to the east and was throwing light out on the Pacific. We could see all the way out to Catalina.

"I came to the hospital that time you got shot," he said. "I wasn't sure why. I saw it on the news and they said it was a gut shot and I knew those could go either way. I thought maybe if they needed blood or something, I could...I figured we matched, you know? Anyway, there were all these reporters and cameras. I ended up leaving."

I smiled and then I started to laugh. I couldn't help it.

"What's so funny?"

"You, a cop, volunteering to give blood to a defense attorney. I don't think they would've let you back into the clubhouse if they knew about that."

Now Bosch smiled and nodded.

"I guess I didn't think about that."

And just like that, both our smiles disappeared and the awkwardness of being strangers returned. Eventually Bosch checked his watch.

"The warrant teams are meeting in twenty minutes. I gotta roll."

"Okay."

"I'll see you around, Counselor."

"I'll see you around, Detective."

He went down the steps and I stayed where I was. I heard his car start up, then pull away and go down the hill.

Fifty-five

stayed out on the deck after that and looked out at the city as the light
moved across it. Many different thoughts filtered through my head
and flew off into the sky like the clouds up there, remotely beautiful and untouchable. Distant. I was left feeling that I would never see
Bosch again. That he would have his side of the mountain and I would
have mine and that's all there would be.

After a while I heard the door open and steps on the deck. I felt my
daughter's presence by my side and I put my hand on her shoulder.

"What are you doing, Dad?"

"Just looking."

"Are you all right?"

"I'm fine."

"What did that policeman want?"

"Just to talk. He's a friend of mine."

We were both silent for a moment before she moved on.

"I wish Mom had stayed with us last night," she said.

I looked down at her and squeezed the back of her neck.

"One thing at a time, Hay," I said. "We got her to have pancakes
with us last night, didn't we?"

She thought about it and gave me the nod. She agreed. Pancakes were a start.

"I'm going to be late if we don't go," she said. "One more time and I'll get a conduct slip."

I nodded.

"Too bad. The sun's just about to hit the ocean."

"Come on, Dad. That happens every day."

I nodded.

"Somewhere, at least."

I went in for the keys, then locked up and we went down the steps to the garage. By the time I backed the Lincoln out and had it pointed down the hill, I could see the sun was spinning gold on the Pacific.

Acknowledgments

In no particular order, the author wishes to thank the following individuals for contributions to the research and writing of this story that ranged from small to incredibly selfless and gigantic:

Daniel Daly, Roger Mills, Dennis Wojciechowski, Asya Muchnick, Bill Massey, S. John Drexel, Dennis McMillan, Pamela Marshall, Linda Connelly, Jane Davis, Shannon Byrne, Michael Pietsch, John Wilkinson, David Ogden, John Houghton, Michael Krikorian, Michael Roche, Greg Stout, Judith Champagne, Rick Jackson, David Lambkin, Tim Marcia, Juan Rodriguez, and Philip Spitzer.

This is a work of fiction. Any errors in the law, evidence and courtroom tactics are wholly those of the author.

About the Author

Michael Connelly is the author of the bestselling Harry Bosch series of novels as well as the #1 *New York Times* bestseller *The Lincoln Lawyer*, featuring Mickey Haller. He is a former newspaper reporter who has won numerous awards for his journalism and his novels. He spends his time in California and Florida.